MESSIAHS

THE KING & SLATER SERIES BOOK SEVEN

MATT ROGERS

Copyright © 2020 by Matt Rogers
All rights reserved.

Cover design by Onur Aksoy.
www.onegraphica.com

Join the Reader's Group and get a free 200-page book by Matt Rogers!

Sign up for a free copy of '**BLOOD MONEY**'.

Meet Ruby Nazarian, a government operative for a clandestine initiative known only as Lynx. She's in Monaco to infiltrate the entourage of Aaron Wayne, a real estate tycoon on the precipice of dipping his hands into blood money. She charms her way aboard the magnate's superyacht, but everyone seems suspicious of her, and as the party ebbs onward she prepares for war…

Maybe she's paranoid.

Maybe not.

Just click here.

Follow me on Facebook!
https://www.facebook.com/mattrogersbooks

Expect regular updates, cover reveals, giveaways, and more. I love interacting with fans. Feel free to send me a private message with any questions or comments. Looking forward to having you!

BOOKS BY MATT ROGERS

THE JASON KING SERIES

Isolated (Book 1)

Imprisoned (Book 2)

Reloaded (Book 3)

Betrayed (Book 4)

Corrupted (Book 5)

Hunted (Book 6)

THE JASON KING FILES

Cartel (Book 1)

Warrior (Book 2)

Savages (Book 3)

THE WILL SLATER SERIES

Wolf (Book 1)

Lion (Book 2)

Bear (Book 3)

Lynx (Book 4)

Bull (Book 5)

Hawk (Book 6)

THE KING & SLATER SERIES

Weapons (Book 1)

Contracts (Book 2)

Ciphers (Book 3)

Outlaws (Book 4)

Ghosts (Book 5)

Sharks (Book 6)

Messiahs (Book 7)

LYNX SHORTS

Blood Money (Book 1)

BLACK FORCE SHORTS

The Victor (Book 1)

The Chimera (Book 2)

The Tribe (Book 3)

The Hidden (Book 4)

The Coast (Book 5)

The Storm (Book 6)

The Wicked (Book 7)

The King (Book 8)

The Joker (Book 9)

The Ruins (Book 10)

"The inclination to aggression is an original, self-subsisting, instinctual disposition in man."

— Sigmund Freud

PROLOGUE

Water ran down the man's bald head.

Water taken from the rapids of a nearby river in the Thunder Basin National Grassland, untrammelled by human interference. Water from the earth itself, in beautiful northeast Wyoming, some of the most quiet and serene land in the United States.

A modern frontier, home to those savouring solitude.

You can lose yourself in the grasslands, in the prairie, simply because you don't wish to be disturbed.

Or you can find the barren stretches deliberately, because you don't want anyone to see what you're doing.

Maeve Riordan hovered over the bald man, her shoulders back to accentuate her posture. He knelt with his head bowed, as if unworthy of catching a glimpse of her.

She reached down with a perfectly manicured finger, touched it to the base of his jaw, and tilted his head upward.

He stared up at her with unrestrained amazement.

Her voice trance-like, she said, 'Are you ready to join the cause?'

He nodded, tears in his eyes.

She bathed him in a smile, offering warmth he'd longed for, warmth that had always eluded him, leaving an acid heart in its absence.

'Then you are home,' she said, monotonic. 'Mother Libertas welcomes you.'

The tears flowed freely, mixing with the river water, further wetting his face.

She said, 'Are you ready to recite the creed?'

He nodded against her finger. 'There's nothing I want more.'

'First...'

She reached into a small pocket of the farm dress that flowed down below her knees and withdrew a glass vial, no bigger than her index finger. Within was a cloudy substance, maybe a dozen millilitres in total, golden in colour. Like sweet nectar or honey. Artificially tinged, but he didn't need to know that. Neatly imprinted in the glass of the vial was the word: BODHI.

She unscrewed the tiny cap and handed it to the man as delicately as she could.

'What is this?' he said.

'It will set you free.'

Her words were verbal nectar to complement the physical substance, and he drank it down without hesitation. Maeve's husband's complex food engineering process made the stuff taste like the sweetest candy, with no hint of the bitter pharmacological concoction constituting the bulk of the vial. He'd honed and refined the blend over the years until it was indescribably good, like an orgasm to the dopamine receptors.

It would hit the new disciple like nothing he'd ever felt before.

But the barrage of drugs took time to bind to receptors,

so she lowered the bald man's head back to the floor and whispered soothing reassurances in his ear, coaxing him back into a meditative state. She waited twenty long minutes, then brought the same finger back to his jaw. His eyes flew open. They were swelling with ... *something.*

Soon the compound would have him in its seductive grasp.

She said, 'It's time for the creed.'

Squeezing his eyes shut again, he shivered in anticipation.

Maeve whispered, 'Mother, lift me from despondency.'

He echoed her words. *'Mother, lift me from despondency.'*

'Mother, free me from complacency.'

'Mother, free me from complacency.'

'Mother, bloom my power.'

'Mother, bloom my power.'

'Mother, bloom my spirit.'

'Mother, bloom my spirit.'

'Mother, give me strength.'

'Mother, give me strength.'

'Mother, be with me.'

'Mother, be with me.'

'Mother, awaken.'

The man's voice rose. *'Mother, awaken.'*

'Mother, awaken!'

'Mother, awaken!'

'MOTHER, AWAKEN!'

His echo of the last command was a scream to match hers. *'MOTHER, AWAKEN!'*

She gripped him by the throat, applying just enough pressure to send the blood rushing to his face, took a knee in front of him, and stared deep into his eyes. She didn't look away. She didn't waver. To do so would ruin the illusion.

She bared her brilliant white teeth. 'Do you see, my child? Do you see?'

The Bodhi hit him in all its glory.

He cried irrepressible tears of joy, laughing and moaning until the whites in his unblinking eyes turned bloodshot.

She said, 'Answer me.'

'Yes,' he sobbed. 'Yes, I see.'

'Come with me.'

She took him by the hand, helped him to his feet, and led him out of the small antechamber. They moved through the long shadow down a corridor, then Maeve opened a door insulated with soundproofing material. It was deliberate foresight. Disciples-to-be completed their initiation in the sacristy of the church in perceived silence, and when the Bodhi peaked in their brain they were introduced to the sensory assault of the main space. Having never heard a peep beforehand, they became convinced that the procession had descended from the heavens.

Maeve led the bald man up onto the altar, so he could see the transept and the nave.

A sea of disciples, maybe two hundred strong, filled the pews.

The chant was deafening, every syllable synchronised, the power of their collective voices appearing to shake the room.

'*MOTHER, AWAKEN!*'
'*MOTHER, AWAKEN!*'
'*MOTHER, AWAKEN!*'

The bald man cried more tears than he ever thought he could.

Maeve gripped his throat again and pulled him close so she could speak into his ear. 'Join them.'

A wide-eyed woman in the front row beckoned. The bald man descended the steps at the front of the altar and walked up to her. He took her hand and lifted his free hand to the sky. He joined the chant, screaming his lungs out.

The faint aroma of body odour seeped through the hall — no one but Maeve noticed. In the grip of ecstasy, ordinary cleanliness falls aside, and she didn't blame her disciples for their neglect. What they lacked in presentability they more than made up for in raw untamed passion for the cause.

And that, she knew, was all that was vital.

A soft hand pressed down on her shoulder. If it was anyone else it would have been punishable by immediate self-flagellation, but she knew the touch of her husband without having to turn. It didn't surprise her that he was there, watching from the shadows of the perimeter, refusing to join the chanting. His role in the organisation mirrored what the KGB achieved so effectively in Soviet Russia.

What's the use of all that devotion if dissidents have the ability to tear belief apart at the seams?

Dane Riordan leant in close so she could hear him above the furore and said, 'A word.'

She followed him back into the sacristy, sealing them off from bass-rich bellows of, '*MOTHER, AWAKEN!*'

Before they made it to her office, she turned in the middle of the corridor.

'What?' she said. 'Is this important?'

'I chased up the family situation of the newbie, as you asked.'

'And?'

'Parents won't miss him. The father's a copper miner and the mother's an opiate addict. Neither have the energy to worry about anything other than their job and their next hit respectively. It's backbreaking work in the mines, and it's backbreaking work selling yourself for another pain pill.'

'This is all wonderful,' Maeve said, accentuating the sarcasm, 'but why's it made it to my ears?'

'Because that was only context leading up to the sister. She's worried sick.'

'Where is she now?'

'Her name's Karlie. She's twenty-four, a janitor in—'

'Where is she now?' Maeve said, colder.

Superfluous details had no purpose.

Dane smirked. 'Taking no shit today, huh? She's at the motel in Gillette.'

'Which one?'

'Ours.'

'Coincidence?'

'Yes. She's not a major problem. She's just nosy. Quizzing locals for information, putting out feelers. She won't find anything, and she'll go south back to Laramie eventually.'

'If we let her off the hook she might make too much noise. Better if our business model isn't even discussed in quiet whispers. And if there's a chain of noisemakers, then there's a pattern.'

Dane said, 'I really think—'

She seared him with her gaze. 'You're getting soft on me? After all we've built?'

'No.'

'Get it done. Give Wyatt what he needs.'

'Okay.'

'Anything else?'

His eyes said *I'd like you to reconsider* but his lips remained sealed.

Finally he said, 'I'll give the orders.'

'Good. Send two of our most ardent fanatics. Be sure they make it quick.'

Dane nodded and bled away, heading for the quiet of the office.

Maeve returned to her disciples.

BRANDON SAID, 'ROOM 46, RIGHT?'

From the driver's seat of the old Ford pickup he looked at the motel across the street. It was a single-storey number, built half a century ago, maintained by the owner with scrupulous care over the majority of his adult life. Wyatt Nelson ran a one-man operation, handling all the administration and room service himself, figuring if he had the time to take care of everything it'd only be lazy to hire help. It was dark in Gillette, the sun disappearing hours previously, and only two windows blazed in the motel's facade.

The "Vacancy" sign burned bright neon in the night.

In the passenger seat, Addison said, 'Yup. 46.'

They glanced at each other.

Brandon was four years her junior — nineteen to her twenty-three — but she'd always treated him like the big brother. He had initiative and she had impulse; he had foresight and forward thinking and she had an unending desire for instant gratification. He'd taken care of her when their parents hadn't, and six months ago when he'd spoken of a revolutionary movement hidden in the grasslands southeast of Gillette, she'd taken it at face value. Now she wasn't so sure, but it was far too late for doubt.

Brandon was all-in, and she pretended she was, too, mostly because she had no idea what she'd do without him.

Partly because she was hooked.

When she went a day or so without Bodhi, she became edgy, reactive, riddled with anxiety. Brandon — and the rest of Mother Libertas — told her it was a subconscious desire for further enlightenment. She'd seen withdrawal symptoms before, and there was nothing enlightening about them, but it wasn't enough to be aware that the stuff was terrible for her. Addicts know they're destroying their bodies and brains, but they do it anyway.

So she went back for Bodhi again and again, and dulled the side effects with follow-up doses.

The stuff was so damn good that she'd stopped feeling guilty about her silence. She had to be one of the only disciples aware of Bodhi's true purpose — the rest of them thought it was Gaia's nectar from Mother Maeve's tit. But if she *truly* enlightened them as to what they were doing to themselves, they either wouldn't believe her or would turn on her in their own denial. She was smarter than them all, so she could fake her devotion to survive.

But not for much longer.

Brandon tore her away from her thoughts when he said, 'There's Wyatt.'

The big man stepped out of his tiny corner office at the end of the motel, his belly swinging as it drooped over his belt. Under the fat he was solid as a lumberjack, but his knees were going and his face sported a new permanent wrinkle each time she saw him. Refusing to hire help might seem noble and stoic day to day, but in the long run it was obvious the sixteen-hour days were wearing him down.

Brandon got out of the pickup and gestured for Addison to follow.

She stepped down to the concrete and waited for him to round to the truck bed and take out a few items.

He handed her a bat.

She tried not to look at it, like denial would make it disappear.

They crossed the street through the fog hovering under the tepid streetlights and walked right up to Wyatt.

He handed Brandon a key labelled "46." They handed him his payment and his lifeblood.

Two glass vials of cloudy golden nectar.

An observer might shudder — two hits in exchange for the life of an innocent woman. If the observer *did* shudder, it meant they hadn't tried Bodhi. Nothing could resist it. All willpower wilted in the face of its wrath.

Brandon moved away and Addison followed him. Wyatt retreated back into the privacy of his office, where the first vial would remove all traumatic thoughts about what he'd done. The two disciples moved to the correct door, coated in shadow at the end of the building. The frilly curtains were drawn, but lamp light glowed within.

Brandon mouthed, 'You unlock it. My hands are full.'

He had a six-speed revolver in one hand and a hessian sack in the other.

Addison slotted the key into the lock with dainty finesse. Poor Karlie wouldn't hear a thing until—

'Now,' Brandon whispered.

Addison twisted the now-unlocked knob and shouldered the door open. Her frame was small, but adrenaline lent her strength. Brandon had taken a half-dose of Bodhi an hour prior, so adrenaline — coupled with the flood of chemicals — made him lose all concern for his physical wellbeing. He nearly twisted an ankle in his haste to barge into the room.

Karlie didn't have time to scream.

Brandon was at the foot of her bed in the first second, and had the revolver aimed at her head in the next. Karlie was a plain girl, pasty and chubby, with greasy hair and acne. Her soft eyes were overwhelmed with terror. She sat on the mattress, her back against the headboard, a faded paperback still gripped in her fingers.

Addison closed the door behind her, sealing them all in.

'Now, Karlie,' Brandon said. 'Don't you make a sound or I'll have to use this piece here. None of us want that.'

'W-what do you want?' Karlie stammered.

Brandon said, 'I'm going to put this bag on your head. Then we're going to take a little trip.'

'Is this about Jack?'

Brandon cocked his head and feigned confusion, but Karlie saw right through it. She closed her eyes to hide the tears. 'Please just tell me my brother's okay.'

'He's okay,' Brandon said, relenting. 'Don't you worry.'

Her eyes stayed closed, so she didn't see him round the bed and open the mouth of the sack. He yanked it down over her head and lowered her to the bed so she lay horizontal, sobbing into the coarse fabric.

He nodded to Addison.

She thought about running away from it all.

Then the half-year of conditioning and brainwashing combined with the physical Bodhi dependence. It all rolled over her in a wave, and she accepted her lot in life.

She walked over to the bed and swung the bat into Karlie's skull.

It connected with the *crunch* of cracking bone and the big girl went limp. Addison slammed the bat down twice more, an invisible anaesthetising wall separating her from her guilt. They dragged the body out of the motel, keeping away from the streetlights. They got her across the street without the interference of pesky witnesses and manhandled her into the truck bed.

Addison's stomach flipped end over end.

She got back in the cabin beside her brother and a groan escaped her lips before she could stop it. It was an inhuman, alien sound, signifying the loss of humanity.

She had nothing left.

But she could still feel good in an empty husk of skin and bones if she activated certain receptors, so she split another vial of Bodhi with Brandon and they drove away in unadulterated bliss.

They kept the silence at bay by reciting the mantras of the cause.

1

Nassau
The Bahamas

In a bare room gutted of furniture, Jason King seized Will Slater's right thigh, yanked it up above the man's hip, then stepped in with his lead leg and kicked hard.

Slater's left foot was the only point of contact with the wrestling mat beneath them, and when King kicked it aside he toppled over. All two-hundred and twenty pounds of King came down on top, but Slater bucked with the motion, utilising inhuman hip dexterity, and the pair rolled.

Slater ended up on top, and he sliced a leg through to full mount so he straddled King's stomach. King bucked, but he'd missed the window of momentum, and although he outweighed Slater by twenty pounds he went nowhere.

Slater simulated a pair of elbows, stopping them inches short of the bridge of King's nose.

Sweat poured off them.

King exhaled through pursed lips, sending perspiration flying, and gave a final animalistic effort.

He bucked again, this time twisting to his side in an attempt to send Slater toppling off-balance. Slater moved with it in the way only a jiujitsu black belt could, aware of every subtle ounce of balance and poise. With King bucking like his life depended on it, anyone else would have been hurled aside by the force, but Slater made sure to leech every last drop of energy out of King's muscles by rolling with it, staying composed in the face of King's aggression.

King ended up flattened out, sprawled on his stomach, with Slater now straddling his lower back.

And Slater was fresh.

King was heavy with lactic acid, still a force to be reckoned with, but vulnerable in the unforgiving realm of the black belt. Each subliminal mistake was amplified tenfold, and now Slater reached down and smacked a palm into King's ear, reflexively sending his face to the other side for protection, whereupon it met Slater's other arm.

Slater looped the crook of his elbow into King's exposed throat and locked the choke tight.

He didn't squeeze.

He didn't need to.

King tapped out of courtesy before it became a war of machismo. Grit and toughness are paramount in the field, but utilising the traits every day in training led to the accumulation of wear-and-tear.

Slater slid off King, pushing his face into the sweaty mat to accentuate the defeat.

King wiped strands of hair off his forehead as he got up.

'Lucky.'

'Uh-huh.'

Slater stopped short of rolling his eyes.

They reset three feet from each other, legs slightly bent, hunched over in the precursor to a wrestling bout, and

King's abdomen distended with a giant breath. He was sucking air in great gulps, hoping to feed his dead muscles with as much oxygen as possible.

Slater sensed blood in the water.

He shot in for a lazy double-leg, convinced he had King on his last legs.

King defended it with ease, and his laboured breathing vanished. An efficient bluff, because now Slater was out of position, scrambling to get back to steady footing before—

King got his hands locked behind Slater's back, giant shoulders around his waist, and picked Slater up like he weighed nothing.

Dumped him down, came down on top of him, and this time when Slater went to roll he was a little more flustered.

He left his arm out like it was on a silver platter.

He realised, but by then King had pounced on it, seizing Slater's wrist in a double-handed grip and feeding it between his legs. He locked in the armbar by extending the limb straight, then inched it past its physical limits, finally levering it into a position where the slightest pressure in the wrong direction would snap the whole thing like a flimsy twig.

Slater tapped.

They rolled away from each other, panting, sitting on their knees with their fists on the mat. Muscle sinew rippled, abdominal walls heaved, and the thin coating of sweat covering their bodies condensed at the ends of their elbows and jaws and dripped to the mats.

Slater said, 'Leave it at one apiece?'

King said, 'You should be a comedian.'

On his knees, Slater scooted over to his smartphone on the edge of the mats, connected wirelessly to the strap around his chest that measured his heart rate. He scrolled through metrics, taking note, then nodded in satisfaction. 'We're good. Twenty more minutes and we'll be overtraining.'

'I only need one minute.'

'Sure you do.'

King charged.

Slater fed him his leg deliberately, then reversed it and threw him down to the mats.

They grappled like their lives hung in the balance.

It was a perfect simulation of the real thing.

2

Violetta reflexively reached for the coffee grinder.
    She stopped short of gripping its rubber-coated handle.

She was still in the first trimester — it was only the seventh or eighth week of her pregnancy — but she figured there was no point putting off the sacrifices that would be necessary down the line. Now was as good a time as any to quit caffeine, and she'd braced for the headaches that would follow. With most of her work in her role as handler and co-ordinator involving deep focus at her laptop or desktop computer, coffee had become a staple of her routine. She used it as her anchor — when she made an espresso, it was time to get down to business. Rigorous analysis of intelligence documents followed, and now she'd have to substitute the black brew for water or decaffeinated tea. The very thought made her shiver.

In truth, she didn't have to quit cold turkey, but King and Slater were rubbing off on her.

It was either all or nothing, so she chose nothing.

The two men came through the sliding doors into the kitchen.

Sweat coated their bare chests, and their workout shorts were soaked. King went straight to the Italian coffee machine and switched it on, bringing the water to a boil as he ground beans into the metal portafilter, then pressed them down with the tamper.

Slater went to the fridge and pulled out a clear gallon jug filled with water tinged blue by electrolytes. He downed half of it, his Adam's apple convulsing with each swallow, and returned it to the shelf. Then he watched King use the machine to drip scalding hot water through the portafilter, culminating in an espresso you could put on a magazine cover.

He jerked his chin toward Violetta and said, 'Real considerate of you, King.'

Violetta rolled her eyes. 'I'm not going to go insane if someone drinks coffee in front of me.'

Slater shook his head. 'I'm not convinced. He's a terrible boyfriend. I think you should dump him and raise the kid on your own.'

King smirked as he sipped the crema off the top of the espresso. He turned to Violetta. 'Don't mind him. He's mad that I got the better of him.'

Slater fetched a bowl down from one of the cabinets and went back to the fridge for one of his prepped meals of grass-fed beef and collard greens. 'That's objectively false.'

Violetta said, 'Does it look like I care?'

'You should,' King said. 'If I beat Slater any worse there'd be talk of kicking him off the team. I mean, honestly ... pathetic performances recently.'

Slater said, 'I finished up 2-1. You want to make it 3-1 right here?'

King finished the espresso, put the empty glass on the kitchen counter and beckoned with a *Come on* gesture.

Violetta said, 'No.'

Slater pouted like a child.

King said, 'You're no fun.'

'Forgive me if I don't want four hundred pounds of muscle coming down on my belly.'

'We're not that stupid,' Slater said.

Violetta cocked her head. 'Debatable, Will.'

He said, 'How are you feeling?'

She shrugged. 'No different yet. It's a little surreal. It'll change things. Forever.'

Slater straightened up, realising he was positioned between the couple. 'I think we need to discuss the next nine months. We've been putting it off.'

King jerked a thumb at Violetta and said, 'We've talked. You're not privy to all our conversations.'

'That's a conversation I need to be privy to,' Slater said. 'It affects me.'

Violetta nodded.

King said, 'I never thought I'd be a father. I'm taking it more seriously than you might think.'

Slater said, 'How's that?'

'I'm thinking about going on hiatus for the next year. We both are.'

Slater turned to Violetta. 'I'd be mad if you still wanted to carry on with business as usual. But him?'

King said, 'Think about it.'

'I'm thinking about it.'

Violetta said, 'We've discussed this at length in private. Trust me, it's for the best.'

Slater said, 'You expect me to do this on my own?'

'If you and King go out to fight,' she said, 'and you get

taken, or wounded… I wouldn't be able to help myself. I'd go after you. I'd put the baby in danger.'

Slater shook his head. 'You wouldn't be that stupid.'

'Maybe it's stupid,' she said. 'Maybe I love that man beside you too much. But I can't change the fact that I do. I wouldn't sit back and let him get tortured and killed if I could do something about it.'

King said, 'So we're both out for the duration of the pregnancy.'

Slater shook his head. 'No you're not.'

King said, 'Will…'

Slater looked at him. 'Trust *me*. I know you better than anyone. You see someone in trouble, you're not going to be able to sit back. It's the same as retirement, and look how well that worked out for us both.'

King said, 'It's not retirement. It's a break. It'll be easier to cope with if I know I'll be back in less than a year.'

'And then you'll jump back in with a newborn at home? I don't think so. The same logic applies with a kid. You get compromised in the field, Violetta comes to save you, you both die. Then who looks after the baby?'

Violetta said, 'You do.'

Slater didn't respond.

Violetta said, 'I trust you and Alexis with my life. We both do. If something happens to us, we'd be honoured for you and Alexis to be his parents.'

A poignant silence elapsed, but Slater couldn't shy away from the questions.

'What about right now?' he said. 'Alexis is out there, doing work. What if she comes back with something?'

'Then you'll chase it up,' King said.

'What if it takes the both of us?'

King didn't answer.

A footstep sounded on the villa's porch.

They all turned.

Alexis stepped inside, her skin a deep bronze. She wore a loose sundress, and her black hair flowed down past her shoulders.

She said, 'Mickey Ream.'

No one spoke.

'That's his name,' Alexis said. 'He's going after Dylan Walcott's empire.'

3

Slater looked pointedly at King and Violetta, if only to hammer his point home.

They didn't react.

Alexis took in the room's atmosphere and said, 'What'd I walk into?'

Slater said, 'Actually, you came right on time. Better to discuss this now.'

She grimaced as her mood shifted. He could see the disappearing pride in her eyes, the satisfaction of successfully acquiring intel now dissipated by the dead mood in the villa.

They'd been tracking the aforementioned Mickey Ream for the past week. All they had to work with were scraps of information — an Australian expat causing trouble in Nassau, having fled his criminal past in Queensland to start anew in The Bahamas. Violetta had already found data from his past life in Australia. His real name was Raymond Doyle, but he wasn't using that identity over here. He was a ghost. He'd come onto their radar almost as soon as they'd touched down in Nassau because he'd gotten reckless. As far as they knew, he was a small-timer running an extortion racket out of coastal bars along the shoreline, with no fixed HQ. But he'd sensed a power vacuum at the top after news of Walcott's demise spread.

Now he was hunting for the throne.

'Tell us what happened first,' Slater said.

Alexis said, 'He's a good-looking guy, which helped. It was clear he'd never had trouble with the ladies before — I barely had to look at him before he came onto me. If he was less confident, he wouldn't have approached, and if I did all the work he would have been suspicious. So I did everything we planned. Sat across the table at his regular brunch spot, ordered the same thing he always did. That was what he first commented on. Our mutual affection for egg burritos. We chatted, he asked if I wanted to sit at his table, I said yes. We chatted some more. I got flirty. He told me his new name, offered to take me to some lobster restaurant tonight. I said it was out of my price range, he said I didn't have to worry about money, he had plenty. I started prying, but I kept it flirty. He gave away too much. Said he was already very successful, but had something in the pipeline that'd take him to another level. He said he's moving the pieces into place over the next few days. Said if he pulled it off he wanted to take me to every five-star restaurant on the island. I took him up on the offer, and agreed to a drink tonight at one of the bars he frequents. The one on Bay Street that's made to look like a speakeasy.'

'Holt's Saloon,' King said.

Alexis nodded. 'That one. I've got a date at eight tonight. How do you want to play it?'

Slater said, 'How hard did you sucker him?'

'He's already in love with me.'

Slater said, 'You got his number?'

'Of course.'

'Then you don't show. He'll call again and again. Send him a text saying you reconsidered and you don't like his vibe. That'll make him angry, and he'll drink. I can almost guarantee he'll go overboard. We'll take him when he comes out, and give him a stern talking-to about his future life choices. After that he'll never even think about touching what the Walcotts left behind.'

King said, '*You'll* take him.'

Alexis looked at King. 'Cold feet?'

Slater said, 'And here we are. Full circle. Back to what you walked in on.'

Her green eyes shone as she computed everything she'd heard, then her internal processor spat out an explanation.

She said, 'You both want out until the baby's here?'

She's prescient, Slater thought.

Violetta smiled. 'You know us better than Will does.'

'Not true,' Slater said. 'I suspected the same thing. I'm just not happy about it.'

King said, 'Doesn't sound like Mickey's the sharpest tool in the shed. Slater, you can handle this just fine on your own.'

'Maybe,' Slater said. 'But since when has that been our modus operandi? Since when do we do the bare minimum? The odds are a lot better if you're there alongside me.'

King opened his mouth to speak but Slater shook his head.

'You're in a Catch-22,' he said. 'If this is no big deal and I can take care of it myself, then there's no risk. Which means you can come along.'

King cut his retort off.

Slater said, 'He's a small-time crook who's got his wandering eye on the big leagues. All we need to do is intimidate him. Either you come along, or we let him do whatever he's going to do. And what if it works? What if he's powerful enough to have more men than we thought? Then he'll be in power within a week and this problem will be a whole lot worse.'

King said, 'I'm not making exceptions.'

'Come for the ride along,' Slater said. 'There's no harm in that. I'll do all the heavy lifting.'

King shook his head and turned away.

But Violetta nodded to him.

'Go,' she said. 'If anything it'll prove he can do it on his own. Indulge him.'

'Indulge me,' Slater said, winking when King turned back.

King mulled it over.

Slater said, 'This is part of the Walcott job. An epilogue to it. We keep the wolves at bay for long enough and Walcott's operation will fizzle out all on its own. Loans will go unpaid, contracts won't be met, and his empire will slowly be forgotten. Then you can take your hiatus.'

King looked at Violetta. 'If something goes wrong, don't even think about coming after me.'

She stared back.

He said, 'Better the kid has one parent than none.'

She didn't respond.

He said, 'Promise me that, and I'll go.'

'You have my word,' she said.

He knew she meant it.

The four of them didn't make promises lightly.

You couldn't, doing what they did.

4

Night fell on Nassau.

King and Slater drove their rented Ford Explorer away from their villa on Montagu Bay. The view of Paradise Island shrank in the rear view mirror. The island off the coast had a golf course to the east and the towering hotel/casino complex named Atlantis to the west. The silhouette of the enormous complex faded from sight as they took Bay Street west, passing the ferry terminal and bridges connecting the island to the mainland. From this angle, the sun set under the bridge connecting two of the towers, lending beauty to the gambling powerhouse, sucking tourists into its web.

'We didn't change a thing,' Slater ruminated. 'Business booms, no matter what we do.'

King looked over. 'What are you on about?'

Slater said, 'Dylan Walcott owned a handful of low-tier casinos, and look what he was able to accomplish. You think the big enterprises are any different? We might as well go after it all.'

'But we can't go after it all,' King said. 'That's impractical.

What we *can* do is target that low tier you mentioned. Mickey Ream might make it to the upper tier, and then he'll be a problem. We give him a talking to, and he'll never become a problem.'

'Or we get rid of him. That solves things fast. You can get back to Violetta. You can start your hiatus.'

King shot him a look as the sun melted into the horizon behind them. 'Don't start.'

'Don't start what?'

'You know.'

'You expect to carry on living with us, watch me go out to war, and sit back and be okay with it?'

King said, 'I never said I was okay with any of it. But I know where my priorities lie.'

Slater said, 'Right now, they lie with Mickey Ream. He gets into power, he starts loaning whatever Walcott's got left to all the same people. You *know* you don't want that to happen.'

King's face hardened to steel. 'Then let's get this done.'

They crossed the north face of Nassau, sticking to Bay Street the whole way, and arrived at Holt's Saloon at seven p.m., an hour before Mickey's scheduled rendezvous with Alexis.

They parked in the public lot across the street, facing the building and Cable Beach beyond. Out at sea, they saw the outline of Balmoral Island, rapidly disappearing in the gloom.

Holt's was a speakeasy, designed to look like it belonged in the Prohibition Era, with faux-Wild-West decor and an old-school façade. It mirrored the most popular bars and eateries on the island by taking a certain region's culture and ratcheting the cheesiness up to eleven. But it was busy enough. Customers flowed in and out through the swinging saloon doors, and the murmur of a packed house floated through the open windows. It was a perfect night — the air was hot and the purple remnants of the sunset were brilliant in the sky overhead.

Slater called Alexis. 'Break his heart.'

She said, 'I'll send the text now.'

They waited.

Not long, because trouble presented itself almost immediately.

It turned out Mickey Ream brought a few fellow Aussies along for the ride.

Three guys came out for a smoke break and lingered long after they finished their cigarettes. The whole trio were red-faced and thin-haired, but they were trying to look professional. They wore leather jackets and jeans despite the heat, and they cursed loudly and affectionately to one another, audible across the street. Their accents were thick but their tones were unsure, like they were pretending to be something they weren't. Slater sensed them personifying the "fake it 'til you make it" axiom, acting like tough henchmen when they were really nothing more than hangers-on.

But Mickey was smarter than your average player, so they'd need to be dealt with.

Slater said, 'We can't jump him if his boys are there to form a guard of honour.'

King said, 'What makes you think they're with Mickey?'

Thirty seconds later, the guy on the left spoke a little too loud. '*Nah, mate. We're better out here. Bloke got the cold shoulder from that bird. Let him drink on his own.*'

The words floated in through Slater's driver's window, which he'd buzzed halfway down as soon as they'd arrived.

Slater said, 'Plan's working.'

King said, 'They'll need taking care of, then.'

'Surely a group of tough guys is minimum-wage work for you. You can handle it.'

King looked over. 'Nice try.'

'I'm serious.'

'So am I. Go do what you need to do. I'll be here.'

Slater knew he wouldn't make any progress with King, and the opening was there. It was dark now, and there was plenty of room in the shadows for a beatdown. He grumbled as he unbuckled his seatbelt, but King saw right through it.

King said, 'You'll survive.'

Slater said, 'Maybe.'

He got out, crossed the street, and made to go inside. The trio parted, making way for him, but he pulled up short and stared daggers at the guy on the left. He'd been the loudest, and Slater targeted his ego. 'You got a boss?'

The Australian cocked his head. 'You drunk, mate?'

'Not yet,' Slater said. 'That'll come later. Business first.'

'What's your business?'

'Go inside and tell your boss he needs to do better than hiring three limp-dick morons to protect him. That's not going to cut it out here.'

Before the guy could stop him, Slater reached out and patted him on the cheek with a firm hand.

Then he turned and walked round the side of the building, out of sight of King and everyone else in Holt's Tavern.

It was a gamble, but he was confident in the outcome.

They had two options.

Go inside and deliver the message like obedient dogs — the smart move. Or massage their bruised egos and follow the mystery man into the shadows. There were three of them. They could teach him a lesson he'd never forget.

They followed him like he had them on a leash.

Either way they were puppies, but this made them think they had a choice.

Slater squared up as soon as they rounded the corner, keeping the beach to his back.

Ready for a fight.

They read the atmosphere, and the guy he'd patted on the cheek sprinted at him with sinister intentions.

5

Slater saw the punch coming from a mile away.

The guy's right cheek was redder than his left, the flush of alcohol accentuated by Slater patting his cheek seconds earlier. He was brimming with anger, seeing nothing but red, which helps you put all your adrenaline into the first punch but ruins your chances of fighting smart.

These guys had never fought smart in their lives.

The three of them were built, and that gave them confidence. Slater had seen it a thousand times before. The most dangerous person in a street fight is the one that understands they're outmatched and adapts accordingly. It's the skinny guy who's trained in a multitude of effective martial arts to make up for the fact that he risks getting dropped by the first punch.

These guys here usually won with the first punch against untrained brawlers, so the first Aussie swung like he was looking to knock Slater unconscious with one right hook. It probably would have worked if it landed, but Slater employed an iota of head movement and the fist lashed past like a whip.

He felt the displaced air on his cheek but then he was inches from the guy, fighting in a phone booth, and before the man could recalibrate Slater used his forehead like a battering ram to crunch into the bridge of the guy's nose. He delivered the headbutt with just enough force to shatter the septum. Considering the momentum of each party, it didn't take much.

The guy was tough.

He didn't go down.

He didn't even take a step back.

His head recoiled from the sharp shock of the pain, but apart from that he was still very much in the fight. He started swinging wildly, both fists clenched, refusing to aim and instead trying to hit anything he could get his hands on.

Which was the right strategy.

Sometimes stupidity benefits you by helping you accidentally make the correct decision.

Slater took three punches — one to the gut, one to the side of his arm, and one to the shoulder. The last two were meaningless, but the first left a sting. Nothing to be overly concerned about, but still impressive given the skill gap. It'd take a clean full-power strike to Slater's liver to shut him down — in the past he'd fought with broken bones, severe concussions, torn muscles. This was nothing in comparison, but it might have worked on someone less experienced.

Shame, Slater thought. *You did better than you'll end up thinking you did.*

The three punches bounced off him and he returned with a precise right hook to the guy's jaw, putting a little extra pop into it to pay the guy back for his successful hit. It broke the guy's jaw and the stunning reverberation of the *crack* in his head made him recoil harder. Now physics required him to take a step back to stop himself toppling over, so he did.

As soon as he was separated from the phone-booth style fight, understanding washed over him. He realised his nose and jaw were both cracked. He bent over, caved to the pain, and went down. Incapacitated not by the damage itself, but by his *acceptance* of the damage. Slater had learned to control that decades ago. If he hadn't, he wouldn't be standing here.

The other two Aussies saw their friend fall over and submit, which had a stronger effect than if they'd seen him get sparked clean unconscious. Giving up is a whole lot more demoralising than being taken out of the fight involuntarily.

But they were brave.

Or stupid.

Sometimes the two go hand in hand.

They charged at the same time, which was also the right idea, and Slater got the impression they were more than casual brawlers. You take the movie approach of attacking the hero one by one and — surprise, surprise — it doesn't work in your favour.

But Slater was physically stronger than both of them put together so he just grabbed the side of one guy's skull and used it as a bowling ball to smash against the second guy's shoulder. The first guy went down and the second guy stumbled off course from the impact, and Slater lined up a high kick like he had an invisible targeting system and threw it. Which is a terrible idea if you're evenly matched in a street fight, because as soon as you take one leg off the ground you risk getting taken down, where your adversary can beat your brains into the pavement, but Slater recognised a fight-ending sequence and went for it.

It landed, boot to jaw.

The guy walked right into it.

He went out cold with his feet still under him and collapsed at the knees, probably twisting an ankle as he went down.

It's hard to protect your joints when you're asleep at the wheel.

Slater took stock.

The first guy was done, the second guy was swimming in the unreality of semi-consciousness, and the third wouldn't have his senses back for hours. He'd wake up in thirty seconds — no one stays out for much longer than that unless they're comatosed or dead — but he'd be awfully confused for the rest of the night, dizzy and sick and disoriented.

Slater squatted by the second guy — the one he'd used as a makeshift bowling ball — and lifted his head off the pavement.

The guy stared up with unfocused eyes, but he was certainly more lucid than the other two.

Slater said, 'Here's what you do. You'll be back to full health first, before your buddies. They're both going to need trips to the ER. One's got most of his face rearranged and the other'll have a mean concussion. You'll have a headache for a few days, but you'll be fine in the long run. All of you will. That's unless you try to do the brave thing and go inside and tell your boss what happened. If it goes that way, all three of you will be in a ditch by the morning. I don't think you're ready to die, so I think you'll make the smart move. If Mickey's alive tomorrow and asks what happened, you show him your injuries and tell him an ambulance got to you before you could contact him. You throw your phones away and tell him your attacker took them. Then everyone walks away happy to be alive. My people and I are going to have a chat with Mickey later tonight, and if we get a whiff that he's onto us beforehand, all three of you are dead. Look me in the eyes and tell me you're not ready to die.'

The guy's lip was split where he'd bitten it in the clash of head against shoulder, so blood ran down his chin as he mumbled, 'I'm not ready to die.'

'Good. Tell me you're going to do the right thing.'

'I'll do the right thing.'

'Get to it,' Slater said. 'As soon as you start considering dialling Mickey's number, think of me.'

He lowered the guy's head back to the concrete and rounded to the front of Holt's Tavern.

A couple in their thirties were on their way out of the saloon doors.

The man nodded a friendly greeting to Slater.

Slater nodded back, and returned to the rented SUV across the street like nothing was amiss.

6

King gave him the evil eye as he slipped back into the driver's seat.

Slater closed the door behind him. 'What?'

'You just left them there? Round the corner.'

'Yeah,' Slater said.

King stiffened. 'Don't tell me you killed them.'

Slater rolled his eyes. 'Of course. I murdered three idiots who probably have no idea what they're really doing here.'

'So they're still there?' King said. 'I take it they'll get up, go inside, and warn Mickey.'

Slater shook his head. 'Not likely.'

'What'd you do?'

'Talked some sense into them. Just like we're going to talk some sense into their boss later tonight. It's as simple as that.'

'It's never as simple as that.'

'You need to change your mindset,' Slater said. 'If we're going up against insurmountable odds, then of course it's smart to sit it out given what you've got waiting back at home. But things like this? You can keep doing this as much as you like.'

'Says you.'

'We have a considerable advantage over almost everyone we go up against. You know it, I know it. If we leave Mickey alone and he ends up taking over Walcott's loan shark scheme, then it means we didn't help anybody. If we talk him out of it before he gets there, we've directly helped dozens, maybe hundreds, of hurricane victims who have nothing left. And all we have to do is rough him up in a dark alley and make him understand what's what. You're telling me you're not willing to do that? Low risk, high reward. I'll handle the high risk business.'

King stayed silent for a while, then said, 'Sometimes you're persuasive.'

'I know. One of my many talents.'

'You're starting to convince me … you and your bootleg therapy. Maybe you should take over from Dr. Phil when he calls it a day.'

Slater said, 'That'd go well.'

'You've got the face for TV.'

'And the personality for sending guests to psych wards.'

They waited thirty long minutes. No one materialised from round the side of Holt's. The guy Slater had spoken to must have deduced the entrance was being watched, and done what he'd been told. He and his buddies were probably in the hospital already, with their phones resting at the bottom of the ocean.

Truth was, Slater had no way of following up with them. He hadn't bothered sifting through wallets, finding IDs, taking notes for later. They weren't worth it, and anyway, he knew they'd listen to him. It would take an incredibly courageous and foolish person to ignore that warning. The three Aussies were tough, but deep down they knew what was best for them.

If they'd contacted Mickey, the small-time gangster would be long gone. He'd have slipped out the back, vanishing into oblivion.

Another hour passed. Conversation was sparse. They instinctively saved their energy in case something spiralled out of control later, which things had a habit of doing when they were involved.

Eventually Slater said, 'You ready to be a father?'

King didn't answer for a long beat.

Then, still staring forward, he said, 'Yeah, I am.'

'Was it planned?'

'No,' King said, then a look came over his face. 'Well…'

'You were open to the possibility.'

King nodded. 'We didn't expect it to happen. But we were careless with birth control, and that had to be deliberate. There aren't many things we're careless about. If we are, it's always for a reason. So … it wasn't discussed, which means it technically wasn't planned, but I think we both knew what we were doing.'

Slater said, 'What are you going to do when the kid's born?'

'Same thing we're doing now.'

'No,' Slater said, shaking his head. 'You're already on the fence. And this is the first trimester. When there's a living, breathing child in your arms, it's going to change everything.'

'Maybe,' King said. 'Right now, I don't know what that feels like. For a child to be … mine. And I'm not going to pretend I'll know what to do until the day comes. So what's the point of wasting time overthinking? I've done all the thinking I need to do, and the rest is in fate's hands.'

'You believe in fate?'

'I don't know,' King said.

The honest answer.

'I do,' Slater said. 'Guess I considered it wishy-washy bullshit before New York went dark. But of all the people who opened their doors for me when I was being hunted through that apartment building, it was Alexis. Of every situation that could have played out...'

King said, 'Every time I find myself thinking along those lines, I tell myself only fools see connections that don't exist.'

'Maybe,' Slater said. 'But in the end, all of this is just stuff we tell ourselves before we inevitably die. That makes it a little easier to believe. Helps me take life less seriously.'

'You're in this profession and you haven't gone insane,' King said. 'I'd say you've mastered the art of making light of turbulent situations.'

They went quiet again.

Then King said, 'You know what? I just missed out on a fight, and I didn't like it. Guess I have at least one addiction after all...'

Slater smiled in the dark.

King said, 'It's nearly been two hours.'

'If he's not out in fifteen minutes, I'm going in.'

'What if he's in there? You think it's wise to confront him in public?'

'I'm sick of waiting,' Slater said. 'We might not have a choice. And if he doesn't back down, he might have to disappear.'

King said, 'Fine. Wanting a hiatus doesn't mean I've lost my nerve.'

Slater nodded. 'Just checking.'

King turned his attention back to Holt's and grimaced. 'Here he is.'

7

Mickey stepped out of the speakeasy and swaggered east.

His stomach home to one too many beverages, he walked with the unique focus of inebriation, treating the rest of the world like it didn't matter. There was no concern for his blind spots, no pause to consider whether he should watch his back. He'd already been stood up on a date and lost contact with three of his buddies. He'd felt alone, isolated, and he'd turned to the drink to anaesthetise his mood.

Alcohol makes us far more carefree than we deserve to be, and that comes with a price if you work in Mickey's world.

King said, 'We take him now.'

Slater said, 'You sure?'

King said, 'You were right. This is a simple job.'

'That's what we always say.'

King looked over. 'No it isn't.'

He got out of the car before Slater could say another word — Mickey was disappearing fast, becoming a tiny silhouette between the seafront establishments and the dark blue ocean itself. It was a picturesque night, and Mickey slowly vanished under a blanket of stars, his clothes buffeted by a warm sea breeze.

King pursued on foot.

Slater reluctantly followed.

They didn't draw their weapons — they were sure Mickey was alone. He was a rote amateur in comparison to Dylan Walcott, and they'd outsmarted Walcott and his entire extended family only a couple of weeks prior. What did a gangster straight out of the Prohibition Era have to offer that a financial titan couldn't?

Nothing.

So King and Slater advanced, walking fast, bearing down on Mickey's drunken form stumbling left and swaying right across the sidewalk. The gangster stopped and put his palms on the seafront balustrade separating the street from a stretch of beachrock. At regular intervals, white foam washed upon the rocks, rearing up from the sea and spewing across them before receding in anticipation of the next wave.

Mickey watched the foam in a trance.

On the other side of the street, King made to cross.

Slater put a hand on his shoulder.

King looked over, but didn't speak. His expression asked the question. They were too close to Mickey to converse — there were only a dozen or so feet of asphalt between them, and the laughter and conversation from a nearby Italian restaurant was too muted, too distant, to serve as a distraction.

They were frozen in shadow, well away from the closest streetlights, which did nothing to illuminate the stretch of sidewalk they occupied. Dark silhouettes against a dark backdrop of trimmed hedges. If they spoke, Mickey would hear, but if the gangster turned around, he wouldn't see anything.

Slater hadn't yet responded, so King mustered the nerve to hiss *'What?'* under his breath.

Slater stared off to Mickey's right, where Bay Street followed the shoreline, twisting into the gloom. He gestured with his chin.

King studied the darkness.

A man stepped out of it on Mickey's side of the street.

Well, *barely* a man. The kid couldn't have been more than a couple of years out of his teens, at best, and he carried himself with all the anxiety of youth. It's hard for twenty-somethings to keep their intentions off their faces, and this guy was no outlier. He blinked a dozen times as he closed the gap, both hands stuffed in his pockets, his eyes darting in every conceivable direction with less than half a second's pause between each look. Mickey didn't notice, because Mickey was blind drunk. Drunker than King and Slater anticipated, because if he had a semblance of his wits about him he would have noticed the angry young man making a beeline for him along the promenade.

When Mickey finally sensed movement out of the corner of his eye, he turned.

The kid was practically on top of him by then.

Mickey saw the flowing brown hair, the pale skin, the strong cheekbones, the thin lips, and probably figured the kid was eighteen or nineteen.

He started with, 'The fuck you doing—?'

He didn't get any further.

One of the kid's hands came out of his pocket grasping a switchblade with white knuckles and he thrust it all the way to the hilt into Mickey's stomach.

Mickey looked down at the knife's handle, smacked his lips together, and looked back up at the kid. 'Shit.'

The kid's eyes were wide as saucers, fearing the worst.

Fearing that Mickey was invincible.

His words slurred, Mickey mumbled, 'What's that for?'

'F-f-from Mother Libertas.'

'What?'

The kid made to let go of the knife and run.

Mickey grabbed the boy's wrist with an iron grip and kept it on the handle of the blade lodged in his gut. 'Stay right here, kid. You ain't goin' nowhere. You committed to this, son. Best tell me what the fuck you're talkin' about.'

'You tried to take Dylan's throne,' the kid stammered. 'Dylan was funding us. You cut off our cash flow.'

'Oh,' Mickey grumbled. He let go of the boy's wrist, who backed away. Mickey turned back to the balustrade, now using it to keep himself standing. Blood ran down his legs and into his shoes. 'You know what? Fuck Dylan Walcott, and fuck you, kid. I didn't kill him. You got it all wrong.'

Across the street, King and Slater were frozen.

Mickey looked down at his shirt, now coated crimson. Slater hadn't seen the knife fall, which meant it was still wedged in his abdominal wall.

Mickey said, 'Guess right and wrong doesn't fuckin' matter anymore.'

He pitched forward and toppled over the railing.

Hit the beachrock and slid limply into one of the foamy crevasses between them.

∼

THE BOY STARED down with saucers for eyes, separated from

reality by a profound sense of detachment. Had he really just done that?

Wind blew off the ocean, whipping his face. It felt incredible. Everything did. His dopamine receptors were firing.

He heard the slightest sound behind him.

Chalked it up as another figment of his imagination.

Then a very real, very deep voice said in his ear, 'Looks like you lost your knife.'

8

The boy tried to run.

King caught him by the wrist and spun him like a top, and Slater grabbed his other wrist and slapped upon it the cable tie meant for Mickey. King fed Slater the other hand, and Slater cinched the plastic cable tight over his wrists, the coarse edges biting into the boy's skin, pinning his skinny forearms together.

They led him out of the streetlight and into the shadow.

King thought about sitting him down on the sidewalk in one of the empty streets between seafront establishments, but Slater shook his head. They walked him back to their car under cover of darkness and Slater manhandled him into the rear seats. Sat him up in the middle seat, made sure the cable tie wasn't going anywhere by cinching it tighter until it was just shy of cutting off his circulation, then frisked him.

In the boy's jacket pocket Slater found an old-school Ruger Speed-Six with a pair of extra moon clips for holding additional ammunition.

Slater held it under the interior light for King to see.

King shook his head. 'Why didn't you use that, kid? Would have been a whole lot easier.'

The boy smiled. 'Mother said make it personal. Mother said make it hurt.'

King didn't offer a response. Just looked at Slater with a wince.

Slater shrugged.

Trust our luck to wind up with a lunatic.

Instead of drawing further attention to themselves, King and Slater piled into the driver and passenger seats respectively, and King killed the interior lights as they slammed their doors. The darkness enveloped them all, so when they turned in their seats to look over the centre console at the boy, all they saw was a silhouette still smiling.

King muttered, 'What do we do with him?'

'You let me go,' the boy said. 'Or it'll be very bad for you both.'

No one spoke.

Slater elected to begin the makeshift interrogation. 'Who's Mother?'

The boy looked at him like he was stupid.

Slater said, 'The only way you'll get home safe, kid, is if you open your mouth.'

He relented. 'Mother is everything. The whole universe.'

Silence.

The kid said, 'Gaia.'

King said, 'Did the voices tell you to kill that guy?'

Even in the dark, the kid's eye-roll was visible, and suddenly he seemed a lot older.

Slater said, 'You think we're dumb?'

'You think *I'm* dumb,' the kid said. 'No, I'm not schizophrenic, if that's what you're wondering. Mother speaks to us through Maeve.'

'Who's Maeve?'

'Maeve Riordan. The messiah.'

'You're in a cult?' King said. 'That's what this is? Telling Mickey that Dylan cut off your cash flow while you had a knife in his gut. He was funding you, right?'

'It's not a cult,' the boy said.

'Sure sounds like one.'

The boy got starry-eyed. 'It's much more than that.'

'Where are you from?' Slater said. 'Can't place your accent.'

'Wyoming.'

'Doesn't sound like it.'

The guy's accent was halfway between Australian and American. It combined the guttural twangs of each, strangely pleasant to listen to.

The boy said, 'I was born in Wyoming.'

'Okay.'

'In my past life I lived in Sydney.'

King glanced at Slater.

Slater sighed. 'You mean you were born *again* in Wyoming, right?'

'Right. Reborn.'

'Where specifically?'

'Why?'

'Tell us, kid. You're not ready to die.'

'I am.'

Silence.

For an indescribable reason Slater believed it. Something about the tone...

King said, 'We're just curious. You tell us and we'll leave it alone. You keep stringing us out like this and we'll start digging. Protect your brothers and sisters.'

Reverse psychology, but the kid couldn't have been much older than eighteen, and he was susceptible.

He rolled his eyes like he was superior, like he wanted all this questioning to hurry up and end. 'Fine. Thunder Basin. Good luck finding it. And if you do go looking ... well, you'll see.'

King recognised the name. '"Thunder Basin." The Grassland? That's where this cult is?'

'Stop calling it that.'

'Or what?'

'Look,' the boy said. 'I'm eighteen, right? And it's plain as day you ain't gonna kill me. You're both like twenty years older than me.'

'You just killed Mickey,' Slater said. 'An eye for an eye. You heard that expression?'

'Course I've heard it. Doesn't make you any likelier to act on it. You work for Mickey, right, and you saw me do that, so if you were going to kill me you would have done it as soon as he went over that railing.'

'We don't work for Mickey,' King said.

The boy hesitated.

Saw his situation in a new light.

He said, 'Shit. What is this?'

Slater placed the Ruger Speed-Six on the centre console, in full view of the kid. No matter how fast he moved, he had no hope of picking it up and getting a shot off with his hands cable tied so tight they were turning white.

Slater said, 'You're in deep trouble. Start by telling us where you got this, and maybe we can work something out.'

'You from a rival gang?' the kid said, but he was fishing.

The boy had a narrow scope of experience in the world and, though he could kill, he couldn't hold his own in an interrogation. Slater watched him squirm in his seat, on the edge of breaking down. Negotiating for his life was something he had little skill at.

Slater asked another question instead of answering the boy's. 'What's your name, kid?'

'Jace.'

'Jace, how'd you get this gun into Nassau?'

'I didn't, obviously. I picked it up over here.'

'From who?'

'Some guy. I didn't plan any of this. Mother Libertas handled it. Maeve just told me where to go and what to do.' He stopped talking abruptly, trying to suppress all the emotions brought about by cortisol, and he looked out the windshield with damp eyes.

King said, '"Mother Libertas." That's what you said to Mickey. That's your cult?'

'Don't *fucking* call it that.'

King raised an eyebrow. 'Mother Libertas? I thought that was the name.'

'He means "cult,"' Slater said.

King twisted round further so he could look Jace right in the eyes. 'Listen. You don't get to tell us what we can and can't say. You're in more trouble than you think. Adrenaline's making you feel superhuman right now because you just killed someone, but it's going to wear off soon.'

Jace laughed.

There was something intensely strange about it, given his youth and his current predicament.

Each stab of laughter seemed to build on the last.

King said, 'Shut up.'

Jace calmed down, a smile on his face like all was right in the world. 'Here we go.'

Slater didn't speak. He was watching Jace's face closely.

The boy's pupils had swelled to twice their usual size.

Slater said, 'Did you take something?'

Jace cocked his head to one side, cracking his neck. 'Yeah, man. I took something. I'm telling you, let me out of this car.'

King said, 'You going to turn into the Hulk or something?'

'Not quite,' Jace said. 'I just won't give a shit about anything anymore.'

Slater said, 'I've met my fair share of people like that.'

'Not like this,' Jace said.

He threw his head back and smiled to the roof and let out a moan that was near-orgasmic.

Slater froze.

9

King said, 'You want to restrain him better?'

Slater said, 'Probably smart.'

Jace didn't hear a word they said. He was lost in ecstasy, hit by something he'd ingested prior to killing Mickey. Whatever it was, it came on fast.

Slater made to get out of the car.

The moment he moved, Jace took a deep breath, sucking in oxygen to the pit of his stomach, and strained like a madman. King saw every vein in the kid's skinny frame throbbing from the exertion, his muscles utilising every ounce of lactic acid.

And then some.

Because instead of breaking out of the cable tie he simply pushed and pushed and pushed until the skin on his wrists tore off, and he jerked his palms apart in opposite directions. His wrists slid out of the blood-soaked plastic, taking all of the skin off the tops of his hands with it. Jace didn't even recoil in pain.

King said, 'What the fu—'

Slater twisted and made to grip Jace by the throat and

pin him to the seat but he was lightning fast, aided by youthful athleticism and some devastating combination of substances racing through his brain, and he ducked under the arm and snatched the Ruger off the centre console.

King knew he should have moved faster, but your mind takes a second to compute the sight of a kid ripping his hands apart to get out of cable ties.

King roared, *'Put that down!'* as Jace's hand — now a mess of exposed muscle — snatched the gun.

His voice shook the car.

Slater dived over the centre console to crush the kid in a flying shoulder-charge.

He landed with all his two hundred pounds in the centre of Jace's chest.

Jace didn't notice.

Pinned in place by Slater's bulk, he brought the gun up and put it to the side of his head and blew his own brains out.

10

His head still down from the shoulder charge, Slater felt bits of blood and brain matter coat the back of his skull.

He froze, realising he wasn't hit.

He rolled off the body, sitting up beside Jace's corpse.

King stared back from the driver's seat, his face white.

He said, 'What just happened?'

Slater couldn't hear. His ears whined painfully. He managed to lip-read the words coming from King's mouth, but he couldn't muster the energy to respond.

King swallowed, blinked hard, looked all around to make sure he wasn't dreaming. Then he shook his head back and forth, swinging his jaw, bringing himself back to reality. Lucidity gripped him.

He grabbed the door handle. 'We're ditching this car. Now.'

Slater thought the stench of a corpse might make him sick for the first time in years. 'Yeah.'

He frisked the body with more care and came upon a concealed pocket sealed within the lining of the kid's waistband. He pried it open and withdrew two small glass vials filled with cloudy liquid tinged the colour of gold. Inscribed on each vial was a word indented in the glass: BODHI. Slater held them up for King to see.

King said, 'What is it?'

'Beats me. Must be the stuff that made him superhuman.'

'Which drugs are soluble?'

'Almost all of them,' Slater said, speaking from personal experience.

He pocketed the vials and continued frisking.

Came up with nothing.

'No ID?' he said. 'No keys? No wallet? No phone?'

'I don't think he was planning to make it back tonight,' King said. 'Those two vials were backup, in case he didn't have enough stuff coursing through his system to incentivise him to finish the job.'

Slater sat, still stunned. 'You think?'

The dead boy's eyes stared vacantly at the roof.

King said, 'This was going to happen, one way or the other. I'd wager we kept him alive longer by interfering. If we weren't there, he'd have killed himself as soon as he confirmed Mickey's demise.'

'But why?'

King said, 'Bodhi. That's Buddhist. It means knowledge, wisdom, enlightenment. Freedom from the banality of life. What does that tell you?'

'Not much. But it sure sounds like you're going somewhere with it.'

King said, 'Remember the Manson murders? He made them worship him using LSD. I'm sure he used similar jargon. You take buzzwords from Buddhist philosophy and combine it with powerful substances and you've got a kid that thinks his drug addiction is a message from the heavens.'

Slater said, 'That wasn't a psychedelic. Trust me. I've taken my fair share. That ... was like ten tons of crack to the brain stem.'

'It doesn't have to be exactly the same thing for the principle to apply.'

Slater soaked in the toxic silence. 'Let's get the hell out of here.'

They got out and walked away, moving as fast as discretion would allow. There was nothing in the vehicle to trace it back to them — they'd rented it under a false name, using fake documents generated for them by Alonzo back in the U.S. They hadn't brought anything to ambush Mickey besides themselves and the Glocks concealed in the holsters at their waists.

They didn't talk for at least a mile. It was three miles back to their villa, and Slater figured they might go the whole time without saying a word. The tinnitus from the unsuppressed gunshot going off inches above his head took the whole first mile to fade, and when he finally got his hearing back he let out a mighty exhale.

King took it as a cue. 'So if it wasn't a hallucinogen, what do you think he took?'

'Your guess is as good as mine.'

'I'd wager you're more of an expert on mind-altering chemicals.'

'I've taken almost everything,' Slater said. 'I've never seen anything do that.'

'PCP?'

'PCP's a hallucinogen,' Slater corrected. 'But I get what you're playing at, and no. PCP makes you lose your mind. He was all there. He had the cognitive skills to get the gun in his hand and his finger in the trigger guard before either of us could stop him. It's like it made him *more* lucid than he'd usually be, and it stripped away his concept of pain simultaneously. That's a mixture of a few different things. I can't put my finger on exactly what.'

'Can we test it?' King said.

Slater said, 'We can use our doc if we go back to the mainland.'

King nodded knowingly.

Their "doc" was the reason they could maintain their gruelling schedules. Dr. Noah Pressfield risked his medical licence to provide King and Slater with testosterone replacement therapy, human growth hormone, and accurate microdoses of the safest, most expensive steroids on the market. They had no medical reason for the supplementation, so the deal took place under the table — no scripts, no justification, just a pinch of missing inventory for Dr. Pressfield to clear up each calendar month.

The need for artificial enhancement was an unfortunate necessity of the industry.

Trying to survive using the capabilities of their bodies alone would never work, and that had been a fact since they'd first begun their careers in black operations. To do things the human body is barely capable of, you need help. Wherever they'd gone in their careers and their lives, they'd quickly acquired the connections necessary to keep the supplies flowing. In their previous lives the government had taken care of it all, but they knew the doses, knew the reputable substances, and they'd taken matters into their own hands as soon as they'd come out free. They only took the best stuff money could buy, and they paid Pressfield a premium to make sure it was all lab-tested when it showed up on their doorsteps. The concoction accelerated their recovery and kept their muscles firing when any other body would have collapsed under the workload.

Every professional athlete dopes, and they were professional athletes of a different kind.

More importantly, no one was drug testing them.

They could do what they liked.

And so could Pressfield.

Slater said, 'That would mean flying back with this stuff on us. We don't even know what it is yet.'

King said, 'How'd the kid get them over here? Look at that vial design. It's airtight. He swallowed them.'

'That's the route you want to go? We're becoming drug smugglers?'

'I haven't agreed to anything,' King said. 'I'm just listing options.'

They passed Holt's Saloon on their right, its steady thrum of country music like a bad dream, reminding them of what had happened since.

Slater pocketed the vials. 'What the hell are we going to say when we get back home?'

'What we always say,' King said. 'The truth.'

11

Violetta and Alexis stood shoulder-to-shoulder on the other side of the living room, their faces pale.

Slater bit his lower lip and chewed it absent-mindedly. He only realised he was doing it when the silence became too heavy, and he took his teeth off the skin so he didn't draw blood.

He shifted from foot to foot. 'I'd appreciate it if one of you responded.'

He'd laid out what happened, word for word, leaving nothing out, not even the explanation of the fine mist of blood coating the top of his bald head and the back of his skull.

Violetta said, 'Let me see the drugs.'

Slater fished them out of his pocket and handed them over. She twirled the vials around between her fingers, scrutinising them. Alexis looked on, her eyes swirling with discomfort.

Alexis said, 'You keep saying *boy*. How old was he?'

'Eighteen,' King said. 'So technically an adult, but that's no relief, I know. He had his whole life ahead of him...'

He trailed off, staring at the floor. He couldn't lift his eyes to meet theirs. He'd seen kids die before — the number of operations he'd undertaken, it was simply inevitable — but something about this time had him shellshocked. Maybe the proximity of it, the confined space of the rental car's interior, the horrendous noise, the fact that it was a suicide.

'Did you spook him?' Violetta said. 'Was it your fault?'

Slater smirked without a hint of happiness and turned away, as if he couldn't bear the conversation a moment longer. He went to the kitchen, took a shiny whiskey tumbler down from the top shelf of a glass cabinet, twirled it over in his hand, then put it back. He put his hands on the kitchen bench and breathed a sigh that came from deep in his core.

He said, 'I need a fucking drink.'

Alexis was fixed to the spot next to Violetta, but concern plastered her face. 'It's that bad?'

'Yeah,' King said, his stare vacant. 'It was bad.'

Violetta said, 'I hate to sound remorseless, but I take it he was going to do it one way or the other.'

'It's not that,' King said. 'It's ... I've seen brainwashing before, but that takes the cake. He didn't even consider an alternative.'

He trailed off, his gaze locked on the vials in Violetta's hand. He said, 'We need to test that stuff as soon as possible.'

Violetta said, 'Why?'

'I need to know what's in it,' he said. 'I need to know what it did to that kid.'

Her face changed.

She saw something in his eyes.

He was haunted.

Across the room, it clicked for Slater. They were both

considering that it could have been their own kid. Sure, Jace was technically an adult, but at that stage of life there's little room for independent thought. You do what you're told, and if everyone in the small hemisphere that encompasses your reality tells you the same thing, you listen. Add a chemical cocktail to the mix, and it speeds up the process, amplifies it tenfold in some cases. This was a more extreme version of what had happened to Melanie Kerr in Vegas a month earlier — roped into underage prostitution with the aid of drugs to squash any intrusive thoughts.

Slater could see King had abandoned everything he'd said earlier that day.

He would follow this to the bitter end.

Violetta was beginning to understand that, and the accompanying silence was overwhelming.

King said, 'Mother Libertas.'

Violetta said, 'What?'

'That's the cult he named. Dylan funded it. It's based in Wyoming. That was as much as we got out of the kid before he degloved himself. We need to—'

'He what?' Alexis said.

Slater sighed and pressed his hands harder into the countertop, sending veins bulging in his forearms. 'You skipped over that part, King.'

King realised he had. He *thought* he'd told them everything, but he'd only told them Jace had forced himself out of his restraints. He hadn't elaborated.

Violetta said, 'He ripped the skin off his hands?'

Slater said, 'The cable tie was tight. Tight enough to almost cut off circulation. He still got out.'

Violetta held the vial up to the light. 'What the hell is this, then?'

King said, 'I need to know. And we need to go to Wyoming.'

Alexis said, 'I thought—'

Slater said, 'I think we're past that now.'

He spoke to Alexis, but his eyes were on Violetta. She had newfound understanding on her face, and the last thing on her mind was discussing their agreement.

Alexis reached over and put a hand on Violetta's shoulder. 'Listen, I know this is fresh. But you need to think about this. What if we fly back home and you get cold feet? I say we sleep on it.'

King shook his head, but no one was paying attention to him.

Violetta was staring off into space, but she turned to face Alexis. 'What if there's kids younger than eighteen? We just had an opportunity fall into our laps we otherwise wouldn't have known about. I doubt Dylan kept records of his deal with Mother Libertas. If we don't put a stop to whatever the hell's going on over there...'

She trailed off.

King said, 'You don't think he kept records?'

'I'd wager he treated it like a start-up,' she said. 'An initial investment to help them gain momentum, unrecognised and unspoken. It sounds like a passion project for him. I don't think even someone as awful as Dylan Walcott would want a written record of his cooperation in something as evil as this. From what you explained, it's some sort of extremist cult. Gaia, Bodhi ... that Maeve woman. What was her name?'

'Maeve Riordan,' King said. 'That's what the kid said.'

'Jace,' Slater said. 'Let's stop calling him "the kid."'

He said it with a wavering pitch to his ordinarily atonic voice, like he was fighting for control.

King nodded. 'Jace.'

Violetta said, 'Whatever they're doing in Wyoming, it's working. You know what lies at the end of the road for violent cults. They either fizzle out, or they head toward an endgame event. Violent revolution in some way, shape, or form. We can't sit back and wait for something to hit the news we knew we could have prevented.'

Slater had to be sure.

He said, 'What you said earlier today...'

Violetta said, 'I've had a change in perspective. My baby is one life. What *this* is ... what it *could* be ... it outweighs any concern I have for my personal safety and the future of my child.'

Slater said, 'Are you sure?'

'Yes.'

She didn't hesitate.

Slater looked at King.

King maintained a calm facade, but underneath something burned. He wanted, more than anything else in the world, to find whoever was responsible for brainwashing Jace and rip them limb from limb.

Slater wasn't about to get in his way.

He said, 'Then let's get packing.'

12

After a stopover in Florida, they landed back in Nevada less than twenty-four hours after reaching their agreement in Nassau.

King half-expected to see their estate reduced to rubble when he turned into their street in "The Ridges," a private gated community in Summerlin, west of the Strip. He wasn't sure why — maybe it was inconceivable that life had gone on peacefully, with normality, while they'd been away. So much had happened in The Bahamas, such utter madness spanning nearly the entire archipelago, that it wasn't conceivable for things to be quiet and uneventful back home.

But the house still stood, untouched and unblemished, with its beautiful exterior facade and the water feature that usually flowed from the second-floor landing to a pool at the top of the circular driveway. Now it lay dormant, switched off in anticipation of a long stay in The Bahamas.

King closed the gate via remote control as soon as they were within the grounds, and had to wonder whether he was paranoid. Alastair Icke, Gloria Kerr, Keith Ray ... they were all gone. There was more to organised crime than just those individuals, but a certain vile subsection of the underground network had been reduced to ashes. No one had traced it back to them, and after a quick scan of local news Violetta revealed that their war against corrupt cops and judges never came to light.

Powerful people in the know had swept the grittier details under the table.

There were certain matters the public didn't need to know about.

Now they piled out of the car and went inside to see whether anyone had forced entry while they were gone. Before they'd left for Nassau, they'd placed stray hairs in surreptitious locations throughout the house, most importantly on the doorknob to the room that served as Violetta's intelligence centre. Every hair was still in place, exactly where they'd left them. Given their history, they had to be so cautious it bordered on paranoid. Their enemies were in the highest tiers of black operations, and the only thing that separated them from discovery was Alonzo. They trusted him, but he could be compromised at any moment, so they had to employ due diligence.

Satisfied the compound was secure, Violetta said, 'I'll get to work pulling up anything I can find on Mother Libertas. You two have work to do.'

King looked at Slater. 'A trip to the doctor's?'

Slater said, 'You read my mind.'

He dropped his suitcase on the sofa and fished inside a small sealed pocket for the two vials of Bodhi, which they'd already scrubbed clean of their saliva. He and King had tucked a vial each into their gums for the short trips through airport security on each leg of their journey back to Nevada. With body scanners unable to see through human skin — only clothing — all it came down to was their ability to act like everything was normal.

The number one giveaway of drug smugglers is nervousness, irritability, odd behaviour.

After the lives King and Slater had led, the pressure of a TSA screening was minimal, if nonexistent. They'd been their charming, charismatic selves, joking and smiling with the agents without so much as the slightest slur to their speech, and no one had given them a second look.

Now Slater said, 'I'll ring Pressfield, let him know we're coming.'

Violetta said, 'You sure he'll be okay with this?'

'You know what he's already doing for us, right?'

'I'm sure he has limits, no matter how nonsensical they might seem. Be careful not to overstep your boundaries. He's okay supplying you two. He might not like it happening the other way round. He might not want you bringing drugs to him.'

King said, 'You don't understand.'

She looked at him. 'What?'

'He'll do whatever we ask him to.'

'And why's that?'

'Because his reputation's on the line. The first time we approached him with our requests for performance enhancers, it was bribery. As soon as he accepted our offer, it became blackmail. Because if he refuses, we threaten to bring him down with us. He's carved out a nice life for himself. He's making a good living for his family. There's no way he's going to jeopardise that.'

'Is that fair?' Alexis said. 'I mean, ethically.'

Slater said, 'Come on. You should know by now you can't get anywhere in our world without compromising.'

He saw her eyes, watched her flashing back through her recent kills.

A mercenary in the upstairs bedroom of this very estate.

An enforcer on Grand Bahama who'd stormed their villa.

And finally a Bahamian labourer named Zidane. She'd killed him accidentally, punting him in the jaw with the toe of her boot after he'd tried to rape her. In suitably unpredictable fashion that was typical of the fragile human anatomy, her kick had found the right place on his skull to rattle his brain in just the right way to shut his lights off forever.

She'd killed three people in a surprisingly short time frame.

So Slater was right.

This world was messy.

She said, 'Do what you've gotta do.'

Slater looked at King and jerked his head for the front door. 'Shall we?'

'We've been home for ten minutes,' King said. 'Can't I make a coffee?'

Slater glanced at Violetta. 'He doesn't learn, does he? Some partner. Like he's rubbing the magic of caffeine in your face...'

She rolled her eyes.

Slater started for the door. 'The sooner I know what's in this Bodhi shit, the better. Make your coffee later. We'll swing by Starbucks on the way to Pressfield's clinic.'

He knew full well that King would rather make himself vomit than drink Starbucks.

King followed him to the garage.

13

The private practice was in Summerlin, only a five minute drive from The Ridges. It was a small but exclusive place, catering to the wealthiest residents who lived out west and wanted the fastest results and the most discretion.

King and Slater had a deal for a different sort of discretion.

They walked straight in, and Slater fed his name to the receptionist, who recognised him anyway.

The young woman said, 'Noah's finishing up with a patient now but he's on his lunch break in fifteen minutes. I'll let him know you're here. Is that okay?'

Slater nodded. 'That's fine. We're in no hurry.'

They technically were, but complaining about it achieved nothing and would only serve to make her stand-offish. Sometimes politeness is the key to expediency.

They sat in the waiting room, out of place amongst frail or overweight Summerlin residents riddled with a variety of medical issues, most of which could be relieved by actually paying attention to what went into their mouths instead of opening their wallets for the best medical care every time something went wrong.

Finally Dr. Pressfield appeared in the hallway. He didn't come into the waiting room and announce their real names, mostly because he didn't know them. Instead he met Slater's gaze and jerked his head toward his office, then disappeared back down the corridor.

King and Slater got up and bled past the reception desk, trying not to draw attention to themselves.

Slater still heard someone grumble. *'They just got here...'*

They didn't need directions — they'd been here before. Pressfield's office had his name on the door, and it stood apart from the rest of the doors in the clinic. Most of the doctors were GPs. Pressfield's expertise was a little more ... specialised.

Pressfield shook their hands as they entered, and King closed the door behind them. Pressfield was a small man with a no-nonsense attitude. He was in his fifties, with thick black hair shaped in a sharp widow's peak and a handsome wrinkled face.

He said, 'I must say I'm surprised you're here. I thought we were four weeks away from the next cycle.'

King said, 'We are. It's not about that.'

'What's it about? I don't have a whole lot of time today. I only just managed to squeeze you in.'

'With what we pay you, you'll squeeze us in whenever we ask.'

Pressfield said, 'What do you want?'

Slater took the vials out of his pocket and handed them over. 'We need these tested as soon as possible. Cancel an appointment if you have to. This takes priority.'

Pressfield took the vials and turned them over, one by one. 'What is it?'

King said, 'Why do you think we're coming to you?'

Pressfield narrowed his eyes. 'So you're really going to pretend you ordered this stuff off the dark web without a clue what was in it. I thought you'd at least know loosely what you were buying. Isn't that what you're using me for? To ensure the purity before you have a wild night?'

Slater said, 'We have no idea what's in it.'

'So sample it yourself.'

A still snapshot flashed like an effervescent nightmare in Slater's mind. Jace's eyes wide in splendour, bringing the gun to his temple with his skinless hand.

He said, 'We'd rather not.'

Pressfield said, 'Where'd you get it?'

Slater didn't respond.

King stayed mute, too.

Pressfield tutted. 'This is a highly unusual request.'

'We don't care how unusual it is,' Slater said. 'We're here to pay you to test it. Is there a problem? Should we go elsewhere?'

Pressfield smirked without lifting his eyes. 'I doubt you'll find a deal like ours anywhere else.'

'You think you're the only doctor in this city up for sale?'

Pressfield grimaced, like he didn't want to continue down this road. It was one thing to risk your medical licence, it was another to openly discuss it. 'I'll need to take it into the lab.'

'Can't you do it here?' King said. 'Surely you have the means to test it in this clinic.'

'I can test it here, but all I'll be able to say is, "Yes, these are drugs." Immunoassays — the methods we use here — aren't sensitive enough to pick out some of the higher-tier stuff. I'm guessing this is some designer shit.'

'Almost certainly,' Slater said, remembering Jace throwing his head back, struck by something otherworldly.

Pressfield nodded. 'Exactly. So I'll go do a Mass Spec on it.'

'What?'

'Mass Spectrometry,' Pressfield said. 'Its compound detection sensitivity is off the charts. And it can pick up multiple compounds in the same analysis, which basic methods like the ones we have here can't. Would you wager there's more than one substance in these vials?'

King looked unsure.

Slater said, 'Yes.'

'Then leave it with me. I should have the results before the end of the day. Then we can organise to—'

'After you test it, destroy it,' King said. 'We don't need it.'

Pressfield hesitated. 'Then why do you need to know what's in it?'

'Best we leave that unanswered,' Slater said.

He saw the glint in Pressfield's eyes.

Slater said, 'Take it yourself if you deem it safe enough. You're the expert, after all. Consider it payment.'

Pressfield said, 'What sort of degenerate do you think I am?'

King rolled his eyes, like that was self-explanatory.

Pressfield said, 'Give me a few hours. You sure you don't want this back?'

Slater said, 'We're sure. But no matter what the test shows, don't underestimate it.'

Pressfield zoned in on the truth. 'Did you see someone else take it?'

'Yes.'

'What happened?'

Slater could only shake his head. An explanation wasn't possible.

Pressfield grimaced and glanced at the vials in a new light. 'Might give them a miss, then. I'll call you when I know.'

King walked out, and Slater followed.

14

When they got back to the estate, they went to the kitchen and found Violetta hunched over the laptop, her eyes wide with strain.

King said, 'Where's Alexis?'

Violetta looked up. 'Where do you think?'

The *thwack* of a boxing glove smacking a heavy bag echoed down from the second floor. Their upstairs training room was at the very end of the house, separated from the kitchen by a labyrinth of rooms, a grand staircase, and ample insulation. But the impact of Alexis' punches still sounded sharp, like they were in the room overhead.

Slater said, 'That's my girl.'

Violetta said, 'You've created something you can't control.'

'You calling her Frankenstein's monster?'

'She's too pretty for that,' Violetta said, then looked Slater up and down. 'But you as Frankenstein, sure.'

King rounded the kitchen island, draped his arms over Violetta's shoulders, and kissed her on the cheek. There was more affection there now. A child was something that transcended the simple physical and emotional bond that most relationships consist of.

Slater didn't know the feeling personally, but he hoped some day he would.

He said, 'You look pale, Violetta. What have you found?'

She nodded, relieved someone had noticed the fact she'd blinked probably five times in the last thirty minutes. Now she turned away from the screen, her eyes nearly watering from the strain. 'Nothing.'

'Then what's the problem?'

'*That's* the problem.'

King stepped away from her, ran a glass of water under the sink tap, and drank half of it. He frowned as he looked out the window. 'The web is completely dark?'

'Completely,' Violetta reiterated. 'There's *always* something. I mean, look how much I found on Dylan Walcott before we even touched down in The Bahamas, and he had everything to hide. "Mother Libertas" is a dead keyword. There isn't a single mention on forums, message boards … nothing. "Maeve Riordan" is the same deal. Remember when Keith Ray tried to expunge his record from online databases so it looked like he never served as Clark County Sheriff? This is like that, but an *actual* blanket instead of the janky attempt Keith made. There was still so much I could dig up on the sheriff. Here there's … not a whisper.'

'So it's a tiny movement?' Slater said. 'It hasn't taken off yet?'

Violetta chewed her lower lip without realising. Her eyes were back on the screen, flicking over search results. King and Slater didn't need to pry. They knew she wasn't operating on the level of a simple Google search. She had methods of retrieving any scrap of data that had ever been placed on a cloud server. She was thorough, methodical, and she knew exactly how to dig in the right places. They didn't underestimate her, so they didn't doubt her confusion.

They shared it.

Violetta said, 'They have a drug they've seemingly bioengineered from scratch. They got funding from Walcott, which must have been some time ago. They have a kid they convinced to fly to Nassau on a kamikaze suicide mission just to send a message to anyone looking to fuck over their finances in future. So Jace was a throwaway. They must have plenty of fanatics. And they don't exist. Not even a morsel of information. That's not luck … that's careful planning. If I had to guess, I'd wager they have access to someone important. They've got a guy or a girl who's wiped every trace of them from view, but actually done a respectable job of it. Like their own internal KGB.'

Slater's phone rang.

He fished it out.

It was Pressfield.

He held up a finger, motioning for Violetta to hold her next thought, and answered. 'That was quick.'

'What can I say?' Pressfield said. 'I'm good at my job.'

Slater flashed back to every delivery they'd taken from the doctor, the comprehensive chemical breakdowns of the steroid microdoses that he didn't need to provide but included anyway, the professionalism with which he conducted his duties, no matter if they were legal or not. He had to concede that Pressfield was indeed talented, and a hard worker.

Slater said, 'What did you find?'

Pressfield said, 'It's a speedball — uppers and downers — but I'm confident in saying I've never seen anything like it before. It's engineered so precisely. There's Dextroamphetamine for intense focus and energy, pure MDMA — that's ecstasy, molly — for an added surge of euphoria, and Benzodiazepine to suppress pain and anxiety. The Benzos level the rush out and make it tolerable. You take this and you're on a one-way flight to cloud nine. And the dosage is massive. Whoever designed this ... if they got the amounts wrong, the consumer would be overwhelmed, barely lucid, lost in wonderland. But if I'm analysing it correctly, at these doses you'd keep your motor reflexes intact and still feel the biggest high of your life. You'd be superhuman for a short stretch. I can't imagine how addictive it'd be.'

Slater soaked in the words.

They perfectly mirrored what he'd seen happen to Jace.

He said, 'Is that all?'

'Seems to be,' Pressfield said. 'Like I said, you'd need a genius pharmaceutical scientist to concoct this. I don't know where you got it from, but if I were you I'd warn them not to produce too much. The authorities get their hands on one of these vials and there'll be a full-blown investigation. Warrants, searches, you name it. You hear me?'

'I'll be sure to give them a stern talking to,' Slater said. 'Thanks for your help.'

'You sure you don't want these back?' Pressfield said.

'Destroy them,' Slater said without hesitation. 'Or have yourself a wild Saturday night. It's none of our concern.'

'I appreciate your discretion.'

Slater hung up, knowing exactly what Pressfield would do.

We're all human, after all.

Violetta said, 'Well?'

'Dextroamphetamine, MDMA, and benzos. Engineered to perfection, he says. The most intense, most lucid high of your life. The sort of thing you could give someone and make them believe anything you say.'

He left it there, letting their imagination do the rest.

'If they've had access to Bodhi for some time,' King said, 'and the backing of Walcott's financial empire from the get go, then there's no chance they're still a tiny grassroots movement.'

Violetta said, 'Which means silence on the Web is far more sinister than it is coincidental.'

Alexis came downstairs and sauntered into the kitchen, coated in a thin sheen of sweat. She'd pulled her hair back in a tight bun, making her jade eyes shine.

She said, 'What have I missed?'

King said, 'There's something brewing in Wyoming, and there's nothing we can find on it unless we go there.'

Alexis turned to Violetta. 'You okay with that?'

'This is bigger than us,' Violetta said. 'This is an extremist movement who ordered the gutting of a gangster in public just because they suspected he was linked to Walcott's demise. If they're willing to do that, what else are they capable of?'

Slater looked all around. 'Well, it was good to be home for a few hours…'

15

Violetta had red-eye flights booked within the hour.

From Vegas to Denver International Airport, then a connecting flight to North East Wyoming Regional Airport, which would put them five miles north of Gillette, the closest city to Thunder Basin National Grassland. With a population of twenty-five thousand it was small in contrast to the metropolises of Las Vegas and New York, but big for arid Wyoming.

From there, it would be like trying to win the lottery off a single ticket.

Before they left for the airport, King stood in the estate's kitchen, mulling over their options. The Walcott fiasco had at least given them some breadcrumbs to follow — they had names, financial records, places to go, people to talk to. Here they had thousands upon thousands of square miles of arid plains, and not a single breadcrumb in sight. Jace had fed them a location, but he'd been right when he told them it wasn't enough. Thunder Basin National Grassland was impossibly vast and impossibly empty. If there was a cult out there, hiding in the steppe, all they had to do was bury their heads in the dirt when they picked up the scent of outsiders.

No, King thought. *We need a way in.*

Everyone else was packing — Violetta, Slater, Alexis, all upstairs. King snatched up his phone and called Pressfield.

Pressfield said, 'What?'

'Tell me you didn't destroy that stuff.'

Pressfield sighed for dramatic effect. 'Make up your damn mind. What — you got nothing to do this weekend?'

King said, 'Did you destroy it?'

'It's here,' Pressfield said. 'I was about to.'

'Sure you were,' King said. 'We need it back. It's crucial evidence. We'll swing by on our way past.'

'Your "way past"?' Pressfield said. 'Where you headed?'

'Not your concern, Noah. Get back to your clinic with the vials and we'll be past in the next hour.'

'You ask an awful lot of me, you know.'

King hung up. Best to give the doc something to worry about, make him believe his unofficial clients were pissed. It'd add urgency to his actions.

Slater came down the staircase, lugging a duffel bag in tow, a strange look on his face. He'd caught the last snippet of conversation. 'We're taking the Bodhi?'

King said, 'We need it.'

Slater raised his free hand in a *Stop* gesture. 'Count me out. I'm not ready for that much of a good time.'

King stared at him. 'You really think I'd take it?'

'I don't know what else you'd need it for.'

'Have you thought even twenty-four hours ahead?' King said. 'What happens when we land in Gillette? Where do we go from there?'

'One step at a time,' Slater said. 'Isn't that what we always say?'

'We'll spend the rest of our lives driving through Thunder Basin. That's not how we play it. What's the bet they've been using Bodhi to gain influence in all the right places? There has to be people in Gillette hooked on the stuff. If Bodhi really is some rare chemical magic like Pressfield says it is, then we follow that to the source.'

'You think it's manufactured in Gillette?' Slater said. 'That's a reach. They could cart it in from anywhere.'

'That's not the point.'

'What's the point?'

'Bodhi's their currency,' King said. 'Might be the most addictive currency in history. What could we do with two doses? What would people reveal to us?'

'We'll have to be *real* careful,' Slater said. 'You don't want to offer it to the wrong people.'

'Then we'll find the right people. It's a place to start. You got a better idea?'

Still hovering at the bottom of the staircase, Slater thought it over for all of three seconds. Then he said, 'Looks like we're swinging by the clinic.'

Violetta and Alexis were downstairs minutes later, having packed only the essentials, and they all took the same car they'd driven back from the airport. It was a second-hand Toyota they'd picked up from a used car lot months ago, one of the most common makes and models in Nevada. They didn't draw an iota of attention the whole drive, which was the point.

King went in to get the vial.

The receptionist said, 'Back so soon?'

King said, 'I'll only be a minute. He's got something for me.'

'He's not with a patient,' she said. 'Go right in.'

'Thanks,' he said, and brushed past the desk.

She said, 'Hey.'

He turned. Waited a beat, then raised an eyebrow.

She lowered her voice. 'Want my number?'

She was early twenties and drop-dead gorgeous. Full lips, curly brown hair, and a curvaceous physique. He held her gaze for a moment too long, then said, 'Wrong timing. You should have caught me at a different phase of my life.'

She used a hand against the side of her face to mask the slightest wink. 'Settled down, huh?'

'You'll do the same someday.'

'But when that day comes I'll still be up for a good time,' she said. 'You still want my number?'

He said, 'If I did, I never would have settled down.'

He left her sitting there, turning lazily in her swivel chair, a wry smile at her lips at the missed opportunity.

Pressfield was already hanging halfway out the door to his office, his right fist clenched around something.

King said, 'You're in a hurry?'

'Stop flirting with the receptionist,' Pressfield said. 'And I prefer to see you every four weeks, not four hours. Take this and get moving. I've got actual patients to see.'

King accepted the vials. 'We might miss our next appointment. We could be away for a while.'

'Where you headed?'

'Wyoming.'

'Why?'

King patted Pressfield on the shoulder. 'Best we end this conversation here, my friend.'

He closed his own fist around the vials of Bodhi, turned and walked away.

Halfway down the corridor, Pressfield said, 'You want to get a beer sometime?'

He spoke to King's back, but King turned to respond.

He looked the doctor up and down. '"My friend" was a figure of speech, Noah.'

Pressfield nodded glumly. 'Right.'

He disappeared back into his office.

King felt a twinge of empathy, but quickly disregarded it.

The last snippet of conversation had been within earshot of the receptionist, and as he passed her she said, 'That was harsh.'

She didn't mean it. Sarcasm dripped from her words. King got the sense Pressfield had made more intense advances toward her than the suggestion of a shared beer.

Still walking, King looked at her. 'Seems I'm a popular guy today.'

He walked out and got back in the Toyota.

Violetta said, 'How'd that go?'

King said, 'The receptionist offered me her number.'

She paused. 'What prompted that?'

King didn't answer.

From the front seat, Slater said, 'The way he looks.'

Alexis laughed, and it even made Violetta smile.

They headed for the airport, savouring the stillness and the camaraderie.

For all they knew, it might be the last morsel of normalcy before Mother Libertas swallowed them whole.

16

Domestic flights were more lax on security than their international counterparts, so hiding the vials in their gums was even less of a problem.

They passed through all the checkpoints without a hitch, using the fake IDs Alonzo had thrown a digital blanket over, which reminded Violetta to call him as soon as they touched down in Denver for their connecting flight. They passed the first flight in a variety of ways — Slater meditated, King and Alexis read paperbacks they'd picked up before boarding, and Violetta used her laptop and the outrageously expensive onboard WiFi to keep scouring for any trace of Mother Libertas.

From her disapproving grunts at regular intervals, King figured she wasn't making much progress.

As they came in to land in Denver, he looked over and said, 'Any luck?'

Violetta said, 'I'm going to call Alonzo as soon as we disembark. See if Uncle Sam has anything in the archives.'

King said, 'I highly doubt that.'

'Why's that?'

'They had dirt on Walcott, but they don't care about cheap business tricks, which is probably all they thought he was up to. It's our country's way of life, after all. We're merchants at heart. But an extremist cult? Someone who thinks they're the second coming of Gaia, who uses drugs to convert civilians into fanatics willing to die for the cause? That's a real threat. They'd take that very seriously. I assure you they'll have nothing.'

Violetta said, 'Can't hurt to check. They might not know the extent of it.'

King let her last sentence hang in the air, highlighting its ludicrousness. 'You think the people we used to work for haven't done their due diligence? They either have something substantial or nothing at all. And if eighteen-year-olds are flying to Nassau to kill gangsters and then themselves, I'd say Mother Libertas is still thriving, which means Uncle Sam has nothing at all.'

Again, Violetta said, 'Can't hurt to check.'

But when they landed and she dialled Alonzo, he confirmed exactly what King had posited.

'Nothing,' he said in answer to her question on what they had on Mother Libertas. It had taken him thirty seconds to respond. 'I've just run a quick sweep across all the intelligence agency databases. Those that publicly exist, and those that don't.'

'Is that normal?' Violetta asked.

Alonzo said, 'You sure it exists?'

'Very sure.'

'Then it's either comprised of less than a dozen members or someone's done an excellent job of keeping them invisible.'

'I'd guess it's the latter.'

'Based on what?'

'I shouldn't say.'

'In case I get waterboarded?' Alonzo said, mischief in his tone.

Violetta said, 'Would that surprise you?'

'It would,' Alonzo said. 'Because no one in this building is remotely aware that I'm still in contact with you. So while the waterboarding wouldn't surprise me, them being competent enough to find out about what I'm doing *would*.'

Violetta said, 'Can you run a name for me?'

'Sure.'

'Maeve Riordan.'

'Spell it for me.'

She did, and hoped there was no alternative spelling she was unaware of. Alonzo tutted for a few moments, then said, 'There's two Maeve Riordans in Wyoming. A thirteen-year-old and a thirty-eight-year-old. I assume your enemy isn't in their early teens.'

'Uh-huh.'

'Thirty-eight it is,' Alonzo said. 'She's ... well, she's a ghost.'

Violetta tensed up.

He continued. 'She was born Maeve Bowen in Dubois, a small town to the west of Wyoming. Current population somewhere around nine hundred. She embraced big city life in her twenties, and by "big city" I mean Gillette, population thirty thousand. She co-signed a lease with her now-husband, Dane Riordan, when she was twenty-eight, back in 2010. They lived in a small walk-up apartment for three years, and then in 2013 she fell off the map. She owns no property, isn't a tenant on any lease, has no bank accounts under her name. At least, not in the United States. Maybe she's living off-grid. Whatever she's doing, it's the right way to go if you don't want our noses sniffing about in your business. So Godspeed to her, I say.'

'I don't think you'd be saying that if you knew what she was up to.'

'Are you going to tell me?'

'No. For your own good. Deniability and all that.'

'Then Godspeed to you, too,' Alonzo said. 'Take care.'

He clicked off.

She stood in the centre of the airport terminal, letting waves of travellers stream past her. King noticed she wasn't speaking into the phone anymore and approached.

He said, 'Anything?' even though he knew from her face what the answer would be.

She said, 'We're hunting a ghost.'

He said, 'So I guess we're doing this the old-fashioned way.'

'Which is?'

'We try to storm this cult by force and they'll scurry away like ferrets. You know it, I know it. Slater might protest, but deep down he knows it too.'

She said, 'What are you getting at?'

'We need to pose as civilians and join the cause,' King said. 'It's the only way.'

She was aware of that, but she didn't want to acknowledge it. King and Slater were no strangers to deep cover — most of their operations serving the government had banked on the fact they were solo in the field, able to pretend to be anybody at the drop of a hat. But it had been some time since they'd gone this deep.

Especially with so many unknowns.

King saw her stewing. He said, 'Can I tell you something?'

She said, 'Of course.'

'I don't want you to have any part in this, but I know if I try to force you to bunker down in a motel while Slater and I handle business, you'll only revolt. And it's worse if you have to charge in with guns blazing to get us out of a messy situation. Better you're with us from the jump, even though the last thing I want is to put our kid in harm's way.'

She said, 'Why are you telling me this?'

'Because I want you to know that all I want is for you to get a one-way ticket back to Vegas and stay there. If you choose to do that, I'd be happier than anything.'

'But then you'd be reckless,' she said. 'And you might drop the ball.'

He said, 'I know.'

'So I'm staying,' she said. 'This is my problem, too. I'm still in the first trimester. Nobody will need to know I'm pregnant, no matter how deep into the cult we go. Let's infiltrate, sort out who's in the upper echelon, and take them all out. *Then* we go back home, and we stay there until this child is here.'

King smiled. 'I like the sound of that.'

They joined Slater and Alexis, who were standing politely off to one side, out of earshot, and the four of them went to board their connecting flight to Gillette.

But they split up well before they reached the boarding lounge. King and Slater peeled off, leaving Violetta and Alexis on their own.

All part of the plan they'd formed.

They had separate tasks to carry out in the town, separate covers to adopt.

And they didn't put it past Mother Libertas to monitor incoming flights, ensure potential victims were genuine.

They boarded in pairs, pretending not to know each other.

Game time, King thought.

17

King and Slater checked into the Arbuckle Lodge to the east of Gillette, beside Camplex Park.

The three-storey hotel was a rustic amalgamation of logs and wooden planks — vintage Wyoming. They'd landed in the early morning, and now it was just after ten a.m. They'd collected their luggage from the baggage carousel at North East Wyoming Regional Airport and bled out of the terminal without so much as a second look at Violetta and Alexis, who were on the other side of the small building, gossiping like the backpackers they were pretending to be.

Now, King and Slater secured one of the largest rooms, with two king-sized beds and plenty of space.

The old woman at the reception desk said, 'How many nights, sirs?'

Slater said, 'Can we pay for three nights now with the option to extend?'

She smiled. 'Of course, dear. Unsure how long you'll be in town?'

King put his elbows on the desk, keeping his face open

and warm. 'Just finished a tour overseas, ma'am. We're seeing which way the wind blows. Taking in as much of this beautiful country as we can. We've missed it.'

She instinctively responded with the necessary, 'Thank you for your service,' before tapping at her keyboard for a spell. Then she said, 'I've given you a thirty percent discount. It's not exactly the busy season right now. It's the least I can do.'

King said, 'Thank you kindly.'

Slater nudged him and said, 'Fuck's sakes, come on. Ain't got all day.'

The receptionist fought to stop her face hardening, thrown off by the rudeness.

Good cop, bad cop.

They couldn't both be polite. Their cover required them to seem slightly unhinged, after all.

She passed over a room key and looked over their IDs. 'Jason Rake. Will Cousins. Pleasure to have you both.'

'Happy to be here,' King said with a smile.

Slater grunted and made for the grand staircase. He could feel her eyes burning a hole in his back the whole way across the foyer.

Upstairs, they found their room and stepped inside. It was warm, lit by yellow desk lamps.

Cosy.

Slater cocked his head to one side with a grimace. 'I hate doing that.'

'I doubt you're the rudest customer she's had in the last week.'

'Even still,' Slater said. 'She was nice.'

King dumped his bag on one of the beds. 'We've got time to kill.'

Slater went over the plan. 'Stay in here all day like we're creatures of the night, and then tonight you head out?'

King nodded. 'You brought entertainment? It'll be a long, boring day.'

'Yeah,' Slater said.

King half-expected him to pull out a paperback he'd picked up from the airport when King wasn't watching, but instead Slater dropped to the carpeted floor and started hammering out push-ups on his fists.

King smiled and went to the bathroom to rinse off the grime from flying all night.

Over his shoulder, he heard Slater exhaling hard, already thirty-five push-ups deep.

18

Violetta and Alexis opted for the Budget Inn out west, opposite the Best Western on Rodgers Drive.

The taxi dropped them out front and they looked up at the building from the kerb, their small suitcases perched in front of them. The walls were off-yellow and cream, and the big sign out front advertised WEEKLY RATES, FREE BREAKFAST, WIFI.

It was a better representation of their financial situation than the Arbuckle Lodge. King and Slater were vets with money to burn, but Violetta and Alexis were backpackers on a tight budget, spending what little remained of their savings on this cross-country expedition.

They checked in, both of them polite and shy, avoiding small talk like it was cancerous and refusing to make eye contact with the receptionist for longer than a second or two.

Then they went to their room. It was tiny, rundown, with a single queen-sized bed for them to share.

Violetta said, 'I'll go for a walk for most of the afternoon, make my presence known about the town. Just in case we're being surveilled.'

Alexis said, 'Have you spotted anything?'

Violetta shook her head. 'No, and I doubt anyone knows we're here yet. But it doesn't hurt to be cautious. And the sun's out. It's a nice day for a walk, anyway.'

'I'll stay here,' Alexis said. 'Get in the right headspace for tonight.'

'You know what you need to do?'

Alexis nodded. 'Crystal clear.'

'You think it'll be a problem?'

Alexis said, 'Won't know until I try, but it shouldn't be too complicated.'

'You're more confident than you used to be.'

'I've been putting in consistent effort,' Alexis said. 'If that doesn't lead to confidence, nothing will.'

Violetta said, 'You ever think about what happened in The Bahamas?'

Alexis hesitated. 'In what sense?'

'You know what sense.'

Alexis shook her head. 'Not like the first time. But that's the case with everything, isn't it? The first time's the hardest. When it's all unknown. That great chasm of ... the unknown.'

'And now?'

'Now I could step out of this room and kill someone to save my own skin and not think twice about it.'

Violetta shook her head in bemusement. 'That didn't take long. You're all caught up.'

'Not quite,' Alexis said. 'Still got a lot of work to put in.'

'What will you do while I'm out?'

'Think about tonight. Train. There's a lot you can do with just your bodyweight.'

Violetta took in the words, let them digest, then said, 'You're Slater 2.0.'

'Not a bad label. I'll take it.'

Violetta smiled. 'Not a bad label at all.'

She headed for the door. 'I'll bring food back.'

Alexis was already completing a set of walking lunges across the tiny space. 'Thanks. I'll need it.'

Violetta walked out to enjoy the day.

19

As night fell over Gillette, Alexis sat alone at the bar of The Office Saloon, north of the city's main arterial street.

Neon lit-up Budweiser and Coors signs graced the walls above two pool tables with blue felt. A handful of blue-collar workers milled around the tables, shooting pool and shooting the breeze simultaneously. She overhead ample gossip about bosses, wives, kids, the political climate, and the state of the economy. The bartender had happily served her three Cosmopolitan cocktails in a row, elated to have something to put his mind to other than crack the tops of beer bottles and slide them over the counter to the regulars. He'd been courteous and pleasant for the hour she'd been here, making polite conversation but being careful not to linger.

He could tell she wanted her privacy.

Really, she just needed to talk to one of the regulars, and she was waiting for the inevitable approach. The bartender was in his early twenties, with a hint of stubble and long brown hair falling over his forehead. She doubted he had connections to the vein of Gillette's invisible gossip highway.

Then a guy in his early thirties dropped into the stool beside her.

He wore a flannel shirt and worn-in jeans above work boots. His demeanour was confident — he kept his shoulders back and his posture up — but he didn't make a direct advance. He signalled to the young bartender for another Coors, and the guy slid it across.

The thirty-something man finally glanced over at Alexis. 'Haven't seen you before.'

She met his eyes for a moment and smiled coyly. She couldn't deny the alcohol helped the facade. It wasn't hard to feign interest — beneath the stench of tobacco he was an attractive guy. White teeth — probably veneers, which must have cost half a year's salary — and a smooth, acne-free complexion. His eyes were green.

She hesitated for a moment too long, feigning social awkwardness.

He took the reins. 'I'm Brent. Pleased to meet you.'

'Alexis,' she said.

'You from around here?'

'No,' she said, sipping from her third Cosmopolitan. 'I'm not in town for long. Been drifting all over the place for a while.'

'I feel you,' he said. 'Spent most of my youth on the road. It teaches you things. Hard to put into words. I'm sure you know what I mean.'

She smiled again. 'That was my plan. Can't say it's working out the way I wanted.'

He finished a swig from his beer. 'How so?'

He was good, she concluded. Not overt, not overbearing.

In a different life, she might have taken this conversation seriously. He knew his way around an introduction.

But in this life, he was exactly the sort of easygoing gossiper she needed to spread word over town.

She said, 'I'm seeing a lot of places, meeting a lot of people. But I don't feel like I'm learning anything. I'm just ... lost. Feels like I've got no place in this world, you know?'

'How old are you?'

'Thirty.'

The truth.

He smiled. 'I'm thirty-five, and I didn't figure anything out until last year. Was working all over the place, labour job after labour job. No end in sight. Then one day it all just clicked. I guess I realised I'd picked up enough bits and pieces to understand how it works behind the scenes, so I started my own carpentry business. Right now I'm pulling in 100K profit a year. Not bad, hey?'

Too eager to impress, Brent, she thought.

Outwardly, she let her eyes widen. 'Damn. A man who knows what he's doing. Haven't met many of those lately.'

He couldn't hide his enthusiasm, no matter how much he tried. 'And I haven't met a girl like you in forever.'

She bowed her head, shy now. 'You don't mean that.'

'I do.'

Now, she thought.

She drained the last of her cocktail for dramatic effect and said, 'I'm useless. I know you think I'm pretty, but I'm just ... an empty shell. There's nothing below the surface. I don't know what I want from my life, I don't know what I'm doing. I'm a failure through and through. I'm thirty, and what have I got to show for myself? I might as well become a monk or something. I'm a waste of fucking space, Brent.'

He reached out and put a gentle hand on her shoulder.

'Hey, hey, hey...'

She bowed her head, blinking back tears.

He said, 'You know that's not true. You know you've got value. I can see it plain as day.'

'You're a great guy,' she said through a mask of turmoil. 'I'm sorry. You don't deserve my baggage.'

He said, 'We've all got baggage, don't we? Part of being human.'

He *was* a great guy. She felt bad about what she had to do.

She turned to him. 'Listen. I think you're very attractive. I want to see you again. I think we could have some fun.'

He was halfway through downing his beer, but his face lit up. He put the bottle on the counter and said, 'Well, Alexis, I'd like that too. What do you say we get out of here, find a quieter spot? Have some good conversation. I want to get to know you more. You ain't an "empty shell," I can see it.'

She stood up, and he mirrored her.

She said, 'Not tonight, sorry. I'm just ... look, everything came to the surface tonight. I'll be in a bad mood for a day or so. But you should call me. Take my number.'

She was already inventing a fake number in her head when—

'Come on,' Brent said, taking a step forward. 'What have you got to lose?'

He reached out to put his hands on her waist.

She inched back, millimetres out of range, so he grasped at thin air. His fingers were close enough to her belt to make him look foolish, putting him in an awkward spot. He'd either have to lunge forward, egregiously committing to the gesture, or admit defeat and step back.

He stepped back.

She stared right into his eyes. 'Did you hear me, Brent?'

Drink clouded his gaze. He smiled back. 'Oh, I heard you. But I know a girl like you is up for some fun. You're a wild soul at heart, ain't ya?'

He stepped forward again.

She lowered her voice and said, 'Get the fuck away from me before I cause a scene. I shit you not, I'll start screaming my lungs out, and you'll look like a predator. Is that what you want?'

He froze up. She doubted a woman had spoken to him like that in a long time.

He said, 'Well, I'm sorry...'

She said, 'Save it. You're just a scumbag like the rest of them. I was going to give you my number, maybe even sleep with you tomorrow, but you can forget about that.'

With a huff, she collected her purse off the counter and stormed out of the saloon.

He didn't follow her, didn't say a word to her back as she left. Probably just watched her rear end in the tight jeans and stewed with regret about what might have been...

When she stepped outside, she brought her emotions back down and coolly assessed the conversation.

Perfect, she thought.

He'd think she'd organically spilled her guts to him before things went south, and now he was jaded, full of resentment. Encouraged by the beers — she figured he'd drink plenty more tonight — he'd go and spread word of the gorgeous out-of-towner having a mid-life crisis, nearly crying over her drink. Pathetic, he'd say. Covering up for his unsuccessful pursuit.

Word would get out.

Hopefully, it'd reach the right ears.

She walked back to the Budget Inn.

20

King stepped into another saloon-style bar south of the main arterial, his mind already set on causing chaos.

You're a disgruntled, disillusioned, dishonourably discharged vet, he told himself. *Act like it.*

He slammed the door as he came in, sending all the regulars' heads shooting up like meerkats. King gave a couple of them dark looks, but most of his attention was fixed on the wall up the back. A closed door with a sign that read PRIVATE was positioned between a Polaroid collage of the bar's celebrity guests over the years and the mounted head of a trophy mule deer. Through a rectangular glass window set into the door, King saw four or five bearded men playing pool. They looked tough, they looked mean, and they looked no-nonsense.

Jackpot.

He went straight to the bartender and said, 'Whiskey.'

'Which one?' the guy said, not politely.

His tone radiated a message: *You bring this attitude in here, it won't do you any favours.*

King said, 'Jim Beam. Straight up. Two fingers.'

The guy poured it in menacing silence, because even though he didn't like the newcomer, he wasn't about to refuse business to a paying customer. The establishment wasn't doing well enough to discriminate.

King downed the glass in a single gulp, jerked his thumb at the door up the back, and said, 'What's back there?'

'Nothing that's your business,' the guy said, turning away.

King said, 'Either you tell me what's back there, or I go find out myself.'

The bartender wheeled back to face King. Then a sly smile played at his lips. He threw his hands in the air, took a step back, and jutted his chin. 'Be my guest, buddy. Go find out for yourself.'

King said, 'Another whiskey first.'

The guy thought about it, then shrugged. Probably thinking, *Well, you'll need it.*

As he poured he said, 'Who are you anyway?'

King said, 'A guy who doesn't like being told what his business is and isn't.'

The bartender rolled his eyes. 'I'm calling the cops as soon as you step away from this bar. Don't think you'll be getting beat half to death and then escape without getting held responsible for the damages.'

'So whoever gets their ass kicked is paying for damages?'

'Whoever instigates.'

'They'll throw the first punch. Just watch.'

'I'd tell you to get the hell out of here, but you're not going to do that, are you?'

King shook his head.

The bartender was tired, worn down from a long night.

He didn't have the energy to get involved in this. He said, 'Go on, then. They'll sort you out.'

As King walked away he heard the guy mutter, 'Fucking idiot,' under his breath.

He ignored it.

Went straight to the door up the back, copping stares of vitriol from the regular patrons the whole way, and thrust it open with a flat palm. It had no handle or lock, just swung in on its hinges. He walked through.

The pool game came to an abrupt halt.

They were either bikers or low-level criminals. King wouldn't be surprised either way. They looked like they took their hogs out on weekends, and they also looked like they distributed a bit of meth to the most vulnerable sector of Gillette's small population. Either way, they'd be fine in a few weeks. Even if they were good, upstanding citizens — which King highly doubted — sometimes ordinary people get in the way of the pursuit of evil.

King had to set a scene, otherwise their plan of approaching Mother Libertas would fizzle out.

The biggest guy squared up. And he was *big,* at least six-five and somewhere in the range of three hundred pounds. Most of it was fat, but there were great slabs of muscle under there, too. He had meaty hands that looked like they could tear a phonebook in half. His buddies — four of them — milled around him, sensing confrontation, relishing in it. They all had beards that reached their chests, and their eyes were cloudy with drink. King felt the warm burn of the Jim Beam in his own stomach, but ignored it. He'd needed to drink to appear unhinged — otherwise it'd look like a targeted attack instead of a random approach. It was paramount that he didn't raise suspicion when Maeve got wind of this.

The enormous man said, 'Where's your fucking invitation?'

King let the door swing shut behind him. 'What?'

'Off-limits here,' one of the smaller guys said. He looked just as mean as his buddies, but his words were softer. Like, *Come on, man. Save your own skin. Leave it.* 'Get out if you know what's good for you.'

King had to become something he despised, but he did it, because sometimes you have to act in the interest of the greater good. He pointed a finger at the smaller man and said, 'I can smell your fear, you hick fuck.'

That was all it took.

He'd taken a small spark and dumped gasoline on it.

All three hundred pounds of the big guy bull-rushed him.

21

No matter how seasoned a fighter you are, three hundred pounds is three hundred pounds.

If the big man collided with King shoulder-to-chin, it'd spark him unconscious in an instant. Those are the unavoidable laws of physics. So King went into full survival mode and reacted with all the fear he could muster. He needed it, because his life was very literally on the line. If he caught an unlucky shot and went out, all five of them would wail on him with punches and kicks before the collective anger subsided. The human brain is intensely vulnerable. One well-placed kick to the head when he was already out could cause irreversible damage.

The big guy closed the distance *fast,* like he'd played football at a near-professional level. King faked a massive overhand right with similar speed and physicality, which made the guy flinch as he came into range. He didn't slow down, but his centre of balance shifted, rocking his chin back to prevent getting clocked clean in the head as he charged in.

King pulled the right hand short and pivoted on his left leg and threw the right leg low, using everything in the gas tank. If he missed he'd sprawl off-balance and five testosterone-fuelled bikies would pounce on him, which lent him extra win-or-die strength. When his shinbone slammed into the outside of the guy's knee in mid-stride, it made the sound of metal striking flesh, and the guy's giant tree trunk of a leg pitched sideways. It had the successful effect of knocking both legs out from underneath him and instead of slamming into King, all his bulk slammed chest-first into the wood-panelled floor.

King recognised that it'd take a few seconds for the big guy to get back to his feet, considering the weight he was working with, so he forgot about him and lunged at the closest man still standing. It was the smaller guy, who'd pleaded for King to leave, so King just popped him with a teep kick to the left side of his ribcage, shutting his liver down and crumpling him. He'd be useless for the next ten minutes, but fine after that.

The other three…

One of them charged, throwing caution to the wind, and King reached out and grabbed his head in a vice-like grip between two palms. He brought it down on the edge of the pool table, the *thud* resonating off the thick polished wood, and threw him down. He was already limp.

The remaining two charged at the same time.

Smart.

It actually worked.

King threw a wild right hook to deter the guy on the right but he missed, swinging through air inches in front of the man's nose.

No one's perfect.

The guy ducked under it and blasted into a double-leg takedown. It was competent, and the guy was heavy and tall, and it worked. King wondered if his adversary had an NCAA background as he scrambled for balance. But he killed that train of thought quickly, because wondering about anything in the heat of battle is useless, and instead bucked at the hips as he went down. The guy was expecting an easy takedown, and the rapid switch in momentum threw him off, both physically and mentally. He literally tumbled off King, and the ferocity with which he'd been bucked made him freeze up.

On the ground, King twisted and threw a pinpoint right hand from his knees, breaking the guy's jaw by catching him on the point of his chin at just the right moment, when he was loose from the hurry to get back to his feet. His mouth hung open as King cracked him with the shot, which took care of his jaw in the same instant.

King was up a second later, and the last guy grabbed him and bundled him back to the edge of the pool table. He'd been sizing up his opportunity to pounce, waiting for King to get back to his feet instead of following him down to the unknown realm of ground warfare.

King figured these boys weren't Brazilian jiu-jitsu black belts.

So he took advantage of that, and when the guy pinned him against the pool table with all his bodyweight King reached down and looped both hands around the guy's forearm in a *kimura* grip and simply wrenched. Many of the traditional martial arts you see in movies are nonsense in street fights — you try to crane-kick someone or karate chop the arteries in their throat and you end up looking like an idiot. All those clichés about killing someone with a single strike, summoning your *ki* energy ... it doesn't work.

What *works* is jiu-jitsu, because it's all force and technique and physics. You bend an arm the wrong way and it snaps like a twig.

King snapped the elbow at the joint.

The guy gave up immediately. Howled and backed away like he'd been shot, his left arm dangling uselessly.

King thundered an elbow into his mouth, knocking two teeth loose as he sent the guy down for far longer than a ten count.

Silence for a beat.

Then the big guy from the start finally made his way back to his feet.

He limped like one of his knees was destroyed, which it probably was. Three hundred pounds going down on the joint the wrong way would spell disaster. He hobbled, his face white, and said, 'The fuck did we do to you, anyway?'

King said, 'Didn't accept my invitation.'

He stepped over two of the writhing bearded guys, got in the big man's face, and head-butted him.

Forehead to nose.

Crack.

The guy went down and stayed down.

King looked past him and saw the bartender in the doorway, leaning against the swinging door, arms crossed over his considerable chest, a cleaning cloth for the bar's surface hanging from his belt.

The man huffed and said, 'Cops are on their way.'

King said, 'Not here yet, though, are they? Bet you thought that'd take me longer.'

Echoing the big man's sentiments, the bartender said, 'What'd they do to you? Stole your girl or something?'

Stick to the plan, King thought.

He said, 'No. I just didn't like them. Privileged hillbillies who haven't served their country.'

'How do you know that?'

'I just know,' King said. 'Men like me, men who serve … we're different. We're better.'

He took a step forward.

The bartender didn't budge. His mass filled the doorway.

King said, 'You going to be a problem too?'

The guy flattened himself to the door, moving sideways to give King room to pass.

King walked by. 'Make sure people hear about this.'

'Don't you worry,' the bartender said. 'Word spreads fast. You're a dead man walking — vet or not.'

Good, King thought.

He said, 'Agree to disagree.'

A couple of patrons swore at him on his way out, hurling insults. He smiled at them, one by one, which he knew would only make them angrier. It tipped one man over the edge. He was there with his wife, big and heavyset, with the build of a labourer. He got up and stepped into King's way.

'A couple of those guys are my buddies,' he said.

'And you had a front row seat to that,' King said. 'You want to go the way they did?'

The guy didn't try anything right away, which was an immediate surrender. But he didn't want to back down for the sake of his pride. He said, 'Make sure you actually stay in town. You've got it coming.'

King whooped like he was deranged. '*Yes!* Let's see what you've got. I'll be here all week. Now get the fuck out of my way.'

The man did. He gave him the evil eye the whole time,

like he was milliseconds from throwing something. King knew he wouldn't.

He mock-saluted the patrons on his way out. 'Have a pleasant evening.'

They swore back at him.

He stepped out into the night.

22

Violetta sat at the kitchen table of their room at the Budget Inn, shifting restlessly.

Her phone rang.

King.

She picked up and said, 'I take it everything went well.'

'Everyone hates me,' he said. 'Word will get out.'

'You really think Maeve will hear it?'

'I can't see how she wouldn't,' King said. 'She'll give it some thought and realise she needs an anti-establishment enforcer. That's how she upgrades from getting eighteen-year-olds like Jace to do her dirty work. That's when she tries to bag someone like me.'

Violetta said, 'I hope you're right.'

'Is Alexis doing what she's supposed to?'

'She's out there now,' Violetta said. 'I doubt she'll disappoint.'

King said, 'Me either.'

'She's a natural, you know,' Violetta said. 'She hits harder than me already. She doesn't succumb to stress or fear. She was born for this.'

'And she added two tally marks to her body count in The Bahamas,' King said. 'She didn't seem affected, and Slater confirmed it. Seems like her first kill tore her up, but the subsequent ones didn't. I guess the brain is like a muscle after all. You tear it down, and it comes back stronger. I think she's already transitioning into an operative.'

'She is one,' Violetta said. 'Whatever she needs to do tonight, she'll do it. I have full confidence in her.'

'We were babysitting her two months ago,' King said. 'Where will she be a year from now?'

Violetta smiled at the thought. 'All I know is that I'll be left in the dust.'

'Maybe,' King said, as always refusing to deny the truth. 'But a year from now, that's what you'll want anyway. I'll want the same for myself, I'm sure.'

She said, 'Are you nervous?'

'About Mother Libertas? No. Not until I get a better sense of what we're going up against.'

'About the baby,' Violetta corrected.

Silence.

King finally said, 'Yes. Like it's my first operation all over again. It's all relative, isn't it? I'm so conditioned to danger, fighting, war … but fatherhood? There's no experience in the bank there. It's a new world.'

She said, 'You'll make a great Dad.'

'You'll make a great mother,' King said. 'We'll do it right.'

'Don't get complacent tonight. Get back to your room safe.'

'I will. Can't say the same for whoever tries to come after me.'

Violetta smiled again. 'Every thug in this town wants your head on a stick and you're more worried about having a kid in eight months.'

King said, 'The former is business as usual. The latter's uncharted territory.'

'I think you're adept enough at handling uncharted territory.'

'We'll find out, won't we?'

'I love you.'

'You too.'

A pause.

King said, 'Gotta go. Got trouble.'

Violetta said, 'Give 'em hell.'

She ended the call. It was strange — her life partner was seconds away from another violent confrontation, and she didn't feel an ounce of nerves for him.

Instead, she was worried for whoever he came up against.

23

King was two blocks away from the Arbuckle Lodge when he heard the truck crawling down the street over his shoulder.

He muttered a hasty goodbye to Violetta, killed the call, and slipped the phone back into his pocket.

The street was wide and the surroundings were dark. Camplex Park stretched out to his right, opposite the dormant facilities of the event space on the other side of the road. There was a horse racing track, a giant building with WYOMING CENTER AT CAM-PLEX for recreational sports, and a vast parking lot. All deserted, all quiet. It was late on a weeknight, and the good citizens were at home with their families.

The bad citizens were out for blood.

It was a tiny portion of the population, but that's the case everywhere.

Most people are good.

Some are bad.

Confront the bad, and they come after you.

The pickup truck pulled to a stop in the middle of the road, alongside King on the sidewalk. It was a new Dodge, black and shiny under the streetlights. Two beefy men leapt out of the rear tray, and the driver and passenger got out of the cabin. They were all bearded, just like the boys from the bar, and looked like truckers. All four had identical physiques, the same equal mix of muscle and fat. Size and strength seemingly weren't rarities out here. Two wore cut-off denim vests exposing slabs for arms, and the other pair wore big leather jackets over faded tees.

One guy from the rear tray had a pump-action shotgun.

A Mossberg 500.

King put his hands in the air right away.

The last thing he needed was catching an impulsive round to the chest. One tiny mistake right now, and he'd pay with his life. He'd leave Violetta to raise their child on her own, and the kid would grow up without a father.

That generated a determination unlike anything he'd felt before.

His emotions burned hot under the surface.

On the outside, he acted scared.

The guy with the shotgun spat on the ground and laughed. 'Not so tough now, big boy.'

One of the guys in the leather jackets said, 'You're coming with us.'

'Okay,' King said, making his voice shake. He looked at the ground. 'Fuck, I'm sorry. I was drunk before. I don't want you to—'

'Don't want us to *what?!*' the guy with the shotgun said, and let out a shrill laugh for no one to hear. 'We'll do whatever we want to you. What was it you called us? "Hick fucks"? Was that it? My memory might be failing me.'

'I didn't say that to you,' King said, on the verge of tears.

'Yes you did,' the guy said through gritted teeth. 'You said it to my best friend right before you shattered his nose. He's already in an ambulance. Word spreads fast. You're gonna pay for that. You're gonna wish you never opened your dumb mouth.'

King put his hands behind his head, trying his hardest to feign surrender. He kept his head bowed.

The guy with the Mossberg stepped off the road, up onto the sidewalk.

He jabbed the big barrel into King's chest.

King lifted his head. 'Looks like you're a dumb fuck just like your best friend.'

The guy's face flared hot and he went to put the barrel of the Mossberg against King's throat.

King grabbed the barrel and ripped the whole thing out of his hands. He gripped the barrel double-handed, swung it like a world-class pitcher and knocked half the guy's teeth out. He spun to the pavement, his mouth pouring blood, immobilised by the pain and the shock.

Two of the three still on their feet pulled their pieces. A pair of 9mm Glock 43s, optimal for concealed carry. The last guy didn't have a weapon. He stood there bristling, his bare hands clenched and shaking with adrenaline.

King already had the Mossberg trained on one of the Glock wielders. 'Don't.'

'You goddamn piece of shit,' the guy said. 'You're not going anywhere.'

King said, 'Says who?'

'This is a Mexican standoff, ain't it? We've got buddies on the way. You're a dead man. Do what's right and put that thing down.'

'This isn't a standoff,' King said. '*My* buddy's already here.'

A confused look spread across the guy's face.

Will Slater came up behind him and wrenched the Glock out of his hands.

24

The guy spun and Slater put him down with an elbow to the forehead.

The sound of a splitting watermelon echoed down the empty street.

It spooked the hell out of the other guy with the Glock, who spun fast, but not fast enough. He was crippled by indecision, unsure whether to keep his aim on King with the Mossberg or deal with this new threat, and he ended up in the anaesthesia of no-man's-land, between a rock and a hard place.

Slater was the rock.

He darted sideways and put everything he had into a body kick, using his shin like it was a murder weapon. He didn't hold back.

He connected.

Shin *slamming* into abdomen.

Massive internal damage made the guy fold over and drop like he suddenly weighed four hundred pounds. The Glock spilled from his hand, and Slater snatched it up and aimed both of them akimbo-style at the last man's face. He was still unarmed, fists still clenched, hands still shaking. The only difference was they were shaking with fear, not adrenaline.

Slater said, 'Get back in your truck, go find the rest of your buddies, and tell them they have a very serious problem on their hands.'

The guy nodded, his face pale beneath the thick beard.

Slater said, 'Tell them they should reconsider their approach.'

'Yes, sir.'

A beat of quiet.

Slater tilted the weapons in a shrug. 'What are you waiting for?'

The guy needed no further prompting.

He backed up, keeping his eyes on the barrels, ignoring his friends entirely. Two of them were returning from the depths of unconsciousness, and the other was rendered immobile on the ground, curled in the foetal position, clutching his stomach and riding out waves of unimaginable agony.

The last guy got back in his truck, slammed the door, and peeled away fast enough to make the tyres squeal in the night.

King said, 'Thanks.'

Slater said, 'Maybe you went too far.'

'Of course not,' King said. 'I went far enough to make sure this happened.'

'What if you didn't alert me in time? How'd you know they'd come at this exact moment?'

'Because I did,' King said, brandishing the Mossberg. 'And now we have guns.'

He tucked the Mossberg inside his jacket and Slater concealed the Glock 43s in his own waistband. They walked away from the scene before someone walked their dog past three crippled thugs and spotted the two culprits standing over them.

Slater said, 'What's the point? You really think they'll let us bring arms into the commune?'

'Of course,' King said. 'They're going to beg for our help.'

'Why?'

King laid it out. The movements, the sequences, the chain of events that would let them infiltrate Mother Libertas with minimal resistance.

Slater listened, digested, then said, 'That's banking on Alexis pulling it off perfectly.'

'You don't think she will?'

Slater smirked in the dark. 'I think she'll do whatever she needs to do. She might end up a better operative than the both of us before we call it a day.'

King went to say something, then stopped himself.

The Arbuckle Lodge loomed in the distance, its exterior lights bathing the surrounding area in warmth.

Slater said, 'Say it.'

'What?'

'I know what you were going to say. So say it.'

King said, 'When you met her, she had none of these abilities, and now she's closer to Ruby Nazarian than anyone else you could have met.'

Slater smiled, which wasn't what King was expecting. Any mention of Ruby in the past had brought up mixed emotions, a combination of regret and guilt, overlaid with a sad fondness.

Now he seemed at peace.

He said, 'I know. Sometimes I worry I'm the one making her do this. But I'm so proud of her.'

'She took the initiative on Grand Bahama,' King said.

'Without her going out on her own, we never would have found that logbook. We never would have found out about who Teddy really was.'

King could sense the pride radiating off Slater.

King said, 'You got lucky meeting her.'

Slater said, 'And you with Violetta.'

Now armed to the teeth, they snuck back into their room inside the lodge with newfound reassurance.

It felt good to be back in action.

25

The next morning, Alexis made her presence known.

She handed her location to any curious tails by stepping out of the Budget Inn first thing in the morning and covering a decent chunk of Gillette on foot. The sun hovered in a cloudless sky, adding a hint of warmth to the freezing air. She exhaled a cloud of breath, then set off east, passing auto shops and roadside takeout restaurants and a Ford dealership, all gleaming in the sunshine. Her surroundings were too industrial, too sparse and empty, so she veered north up South Burma Avenue and crossed the intersection separating Echeta Road and West 1st Street. She passed a hydraulics factory, a self-storage facility and a seemingly endless chain of warehouses on concrete lots until finally her surroundings became residential when she hit West Warlow Drive.

She turned east and walked a giant loop of Bicentennial Park, passing by a couple of high school sports teams conducting early morning training sessions, their soccer boots kicking up dewey condensation from the grass. Thoroughly warmed up now, she doubled back west, following the artery of Echeta Road. She passed a roadside drive-thru diner and ordered a bagel and a long black from the takeout window. The woman who served her was maybe fifty, plump, her face the texture of leather, her eyes kind.

She said, 'I haven't seen you before.'

Alexis said, 'New in town. Just visiting.'

'You like it so far?'

'So far,' Alexis said with a smile, accepting the steaming cup of coffee and the bagel wrapped in a paper bag.

She carried on west before finally turning north into a residential suburb and traipsing around until she hit a viewpoint called Overlook Park.

The park was aptly named.

The sun beat down on her face as she found a bench and sat down, taking some load off her feet after putting them to use for most of the morning. She found solace in looking out at the residential cul-de-sac and the prairie beyond. The hill sloped down past white houses with brown roofs sitting on freshly mowed lots and levelled out into the undulating grasslands that swept all the way to the horizon, so vast and so empty.

She enjoyed the weather, sipped the coffee, munched the bagel.

She and Violetta were early in their quest, and she figured the most important thing was making herself known to the residents of Gillette, spreading awareness of her presence through word of mouth. So she stayed on the park bench, and when the sun reached its peak in the sky she closed her eyes so she could tilt her face toward it.

The warmth calmed her, soothed her.

Almost made her forget the reason they were here.

Right now, life was beautiful.

When she lowered her head and opened her eyes to take another sip of coffee, there was a woman beside her on the park bench.

Alexis quashed her reaction before she could jump out of her skin. Whoever the woman was, she'd approached without so much as her heel scuffing on the sunbaked pavement. She looked like she was in her early thirties but could have been older. Her face was smooth and contoured and her eyes were crystalline. They were somewhere between blue and green, with flecks of both colours like an opal. She had frizzy brown hair falling in two big tufts on either side of her head, which served to frame her perfect face.

Alexis found her odd right away.

She was conventionally attractive, but the very nature of her being seemed artificial. She was intensely happy with nothing behind the eyes.

Alexis said, 'Hey. Nice to meet you,' like the easygoing wanderer she was supposed to be.

Good thing she remembered to keep up the act.

The woman beamed a smile and said, 'Hello. My name is Maeve. What's yours?'

26

Alexis' heart thudded for a single beat.

She felt it in her chest, more powerful than usual, but she didn't allow her heart rate to increase. She didn't allow any change of expression in her face. So all it turned out to be was a single *thunk,* then straight back to normal.

There wasn't a chance Maeve Riordan noticed.

Alexis smiled without a care in the world. 'Hi. I'm Alexis. You live here?'

'Not Gillette, I'm afraid,' Maeve said. 'I'm a ways out. But I like to visit every so often, make sure I'm keeping up to speed. What brings you here, girl?'

Alexis batted her eyelids and flooded her eyes with warmth, pretending it had made her day for this stranger to start a dialogue. 'Oh, I don't have a real good spiel for this part, I'm afraid. Some people I meet, they've got such nice stories ... so poignant and beautiful, you know? I'm just a bit of a nomad, and that's the truth. Grew up in Jersey but over there it's all so ... busy. Finished college and decided not to go straight into full-time work. Started backpacking across the country, and that would have been, what, eight years ago now? Ended up finding my best friend last year when I was passing through Ohio. She and I have been travelling together ever since.'

'What's her name?'

'Violetta.'

'And are you two ... together?'

Alexis scoffed and shook her head, lowering her eyes out of perceived shame. 'No, ma'am. It's not like that. Not like that at all.'

'You can tell me if it is,' Maeve said. 'Most people out here aren't what you think they are. There's no shame in it, girl. We're not going to persecute you for that.'

Alexis sighed. 'We're just friends. Honest. I'd tell you if it wasn't true. You seem like a very trustworthy person.' She laughed and looked around, like the ditzy girl next door. 'I mean, gosh, I've known you all of two minutes, haven't I? Thank you for listening to me talk. Not many people do. You're a good person, Maeve.'

Maeve said, 'Are you lost, dear?'

Behind the curtain, Alexis marvelled at Maeve's forwardness. The woman was getting right to the point.

But Alexis still had a role to play. 'I'm sorry?'

Maeve smiled, recognising she was moving too quickly. She looked out at the view and took in the ambience for a beat, then reached out and put a hand on Alexis' knee, 'I think we were supposed to meet.'

'Why's that?'

'This is a small town. Word gets around. I hear you didn't have much of a pleasant experience at the bar last night. Word reached my ears, like Chinese whispers. That man named Brent had some ... let's just say "impolite" things to say about you. About both your beauty and your wrath. But I heard about what you said last night. About how you weren't sure where to go next, or what to do, or even what the point of your life is. Now of course I'm awfully sorry that this personal information reached my ears, but it did, and we can't change the past, can we? All we can do is look to the future. And I think I'm in a unique position to offer you a bright future, Alexis. If you're interested…'

'I don't want to be rude, ma'am, but I hardly know you.'

'Which is a given when two parties have just met,' Maeve said. 'But I think over time, if we do get to know each other, we'll end up having more in common than you could ever imagine.'

Now she was staring right into Alexis' eyes, her hand still on her knee. Alexis didn't look away. She was struck by how transfixing Maeve's gaze was. It was seductive in its appeal. There was love and warmth in Maeve's eyes now, and Alexis couldn't tell if it was artificial anymore. She knew it was, but if she was truly a backpacker who'd met this woman, she would have bought it hook, line and sinker.

Alexis said, 'What's this opportunity?'

'Myself and my husband run … well, I guess you would call it a commune. We aren't fans of the regular way of living. As you can see, it's not very private. You had a few drinks at the local watering hole and opened your mouth and suddenly the whole town is talking about you. It's sad, to be frank. Very surface-level, very superficial. What we have is something pure. Out in the grassland, we've put together a little community of like-minded souls. We have an easygoing existence, and we champion love. Real, unrequited love. There isn't enough of it in this world. If you and your friend are interested, I'd be honoured to host you free-of-charge for a few days.'

Alexis didn't respond.

If she was too enthusiastic...

Maeve suddenly looked hurt. She cast her eyes away and took a small, fluttering breath. 'If not, dear, the last thing I want to do is annoy you...'

Alexis said, 'Why'd you come to me? I'm sure you see lots of people passing through town, ma'am.'

'And sometimes I talk to them on park benches like these,' Maeve said without missing a beat. 'If I don't like their energy, I never make the offer. We're a rather exclusive community, Alexis. I hope you understand how rare it is for me to offer an invitation so soon. But you're a pure soul. I can sense it.'

Sure you can, Alexis thought.

She looked all around like she was grappling with indecision, even though she had Maeve eating out of the palm of her hand. She stared vacantly off at the horizon, then allowed herself a half-smile and turned back to the woman.

'You know,' she said. 'That sounds like a fine idea, Maeve.'

Maeve beamed. 'You won't regret it, dear. I'm afraid we don't have everything set up to accommodate your needs — after all, I didn't know I'd be doing this so soon — but it won't take long. Shall we pick you and your friend up at eight tomorrow morning? At the entrance to Bicentennial Park?'

Alexis nodded, then paused. 'That's within walking distance of the Budget Inn. Did you know we were staying there?'

Maeve smiled, and Alexis could swear she was gripping her knee tighter. 'Perhaps. Word travels quickly, as I said. But don't be alarmed, dear. We have the best intentions in our hearts. Trust me, I think you are going to finally discover your purpose. Tomorrow will be the first day of the rest of your life. I guarantee it. And if not, no harm done. You and Violetta can be on your way. But life becomes magical when we open our eyes to new ideas, doesn't it?'

Alexis smiled back. 'It does. I'm excited to see your commune.'

Maeve said, 'We're all thrilled to have you. The rest of the community doesn't even know you're on your way, but they'll embrace you lovingly. Would you like that?'

Alexis teared up like she'd never had a place in this world. She shook her head in embarrassment and wiped her eyes, as if it were unintentional. She said, 'I would like that very much.'

Maeve took her hand off Alexis' knee and put it on her shoulder. 'You are loved, Alexis. I want you to know that. No matter what this life throws at you. You are loved. And there's a home for you out there. I have faith it will be with us.'

Alexis let the tears flow freely.

Maeve said, 'I'm sorry, dear. I didn't mean to make you emotional. We'll see you tomorrow. Have a pleasant evening.'

She got up and walked away, slowly, without hurry.

Alexis waited for her to go, then killed the tears. She wiped her face, impressed by the fact she could pull the waterworks out of thin air.

Then she headed back to the Budget Inn on foot.

27

In case the Arbuckle Lodge was compromised without their knowledge, King and Slater spent the night sleeping in shifts.

They got three hours of sleep each, twice over, going back and forth from midnight to midday. No one disturbed them. No one came for them. There wasn't so much as a peep from the corridor outside their room.

With six hours each under their belts, they headed outside in the early afternoon for a meal.

They'd already got word from Alexis that Maeve had approached her in Overlook Park.

En route to the closest eatery with Glock 43s concealed under their jackets, they kept an eye out for any signs of ambush, but it appeared their escapades the night before had deterred anyone from pursuing them. They knew if they hung around in town for too long and made their presence obvious, escalation was inevitable. But they couldn't maintain the roles they were playing and shut themselves up in their room from paranoia, so they strode for a twenty-four hour diner up the road from the lodge, aware they were probably under surveillance.

Slater said, 'That was fast from Maeve.'

King said, 'I'd wager she has her finger on the pulse of the rumour mill. It wouldn't have taken long for word to reach her.'

'You think she's heard about us?'

'I can't see how she hasn't.'

'Then why haven't we been approached yet? She should have been waiting for us downstairs.'

'She's not omnipresent,' King said. 'She can't be in two places at once. And we're wildcards in her eyes. Best to deal with the backpackers, get the easy job out of the way, before she figures out what to do with us.'

'Do Violetta and Alexis need us, then?'

King looked across. 'What?'

'They're already in. Their cover's intact, and they're getting taken to the commune tomorrow morning. Surely they can kill Maeve on their own.'

'You think Maeve's the only person running Mother Libertas? It's a serious cult. She'll have at least a handful of co-conspirators, and maybe hundreds of followers living in the commune. You think Violetta and Alexis can kill everyone in charge and escape without getting torn apart by the masses?'

'If they do it fast, and they don't hesitate … yes. Won't that shatter the followers' belief systems? If they see their invincible leaders killed?'

King shook his head. 'That's not us. We're not storming in there to kill anyone who seems like they might be in charge. What's to say Maeve hasn't brainwashed or threatened everyone she works with? We need more information on just how guilty the cult leaders are. Right now we know nothing. We barely understand how the cult operates or what exactly they tell their followers, and we don't know who's responsible.'

'You think we can stay here in town and find out?'

'We'd serve more of a purpose if we go there ourselves.'

'That's if this act works.'

'Then let's hope it does.'

They made it to the diner without incident, found no hostility in the faces of the patrons eating lunch, and concluded that they weren't in grave danger yet. They ordered huge meals and gorged on copious amounts of carbs in mutual silence. The old military adage: Eat when you can. You never know what the future might hold.

They finished, left a hefty tip, and figured it was best not to test their luck.

Slater said, 'I say we head back for the rest of the day. Keep in touch with the girls, find out what they're doing.'

King thought about it and nodded. 'We've done our job. The rest is in Maeve's hands.'

They'd been cooped up in their hotel room for the last twelve hours, so Slater suggested a detour through Camplex Park for a breath of fresh air amongst nature. They took Saddlehorn Road around the park, drinking in the sun, tasting the cool air in their throats. It was bliss in comparison to a stuffy room, no matter how luxurious the hotel was.

Trees were dotted intermittently through the swathe of grass constituting the bulk of the park. Slater took the lead, heading off the road, taking a direct diagonal route back to the Arbuckle Lodge.

King followed, but the emptiness rubbed him the wrong way.

There wasn't a soul about. The wind blew through the trees, whipping at their clothes.

A man with hunched shoulders and wide meth-crazed eyes stepped out from behind one of the trees with a gun.

It happened so fast that King couldn't shoot first.

He had his Glock out of his jacket in maybe a second flat, but the man already had his own barrel aimed at King's head, and he fired.

King wasn't there anymore though.

The instant he'd registered the hostile gun, he'd dropped to his stomach on the grass, hard enough to give himself a mild concussion if he wasn't careful. But a concussion was infinitely better than a bullet to the dome, so he took the risk. The guy's first shot blasted the silence away, and the displaced air of the bullet's flight path whipped over his head. It missed by a solid three feet, but the shooter was competent enough. He'd aimed for King's centre mass and instinctively squeezed the trigger before realising King's centre mass was now on the ground.

King fired back.

One shot to the head.

Almost unfair, given his skillset.

The junkie's neck snapped back and he slumped against the tree trunk and slid down to the base. His dead eyes were glazed as his chin dropped to his chest.

The noise of the twin reports echoed all the way through the vast grounds of Camplex Park, and faded away.

Slater stood deathly still.

King clambered back to his feet, already having suppressed his adrenaline response considering the threat was gone.

Slater looked all around. 'Shit. Let's go. Now.'

King said, 'Search him first.'

28

Slater figured a junkie hired by bikers to execute them in broad daylight wouldn't have much to offer in terms of important loot.

He reluctantly searched the corpse anyway.

Then realised he should never assume anything.

He went into the inside pocket of the body's oversized leather jacket, and felt the clink of glass between his fingers. He seized the contents of the pocket and came out with two full vials of Bodhi.

He held them up for King to see.

King's eyes widened. 'Where was he going with those?'

Slater went through the man's jeans pockets and found a phone and a tattered wallet, but no keys. He suspected the man was homeless. The smartphone was an ancient model with no passcode — typical junkie foresight — and the wallet held no credit or debit cards, just fifteen dollars in cash and an old ID that identified the man as James Fitch.

Thirty seconds had elapsed since the incident, and no Good Samaritans had emerged to investigate. Slater hoped they'd been far enough away from any ears to explicitly identify the noise as gunshots, but he doubted it. His ears were still ringing from the reports. Someone would come check it out eventually, so time was against them.

He finished patting down the body and said, 'That's it.'

King was already on the move.

They were back in their room within ten minutes, and only passed three people on the way back to the hotel, none within the immediate vicinity of the shooting. One of the three had nodded politely to them — the greatest threat in subsequent police interviews — and the other two hadn't glanced up from their phones.

Overall, a good result.

Slater sat on the edge of his bed, going through the would-be assassin's phone. There were multiple texts to a nameless contact — just a number in the phone — about drug deals for personal consumption. He disregarded them, kept scrolling, and hit the jackpot.

'Here,' he said.

King looked up.

Slater said, 'Most of the texts are the guy asking other people for times and meeting locations. For his own deals. But this one — contact name "Wyatt" — is the opposite. Wyatt asked for an ETA at ten a.m. this morning, and Fitch told him two in the afternoon. Guess he was optimistic about how quickly he could take us out.'

King stewed on the information. 'How'd he know we'd walk through the park?'

'Sometimes even junkies get lucky.'

'He's dead,' King said. 'Wasn't overly lucky.'

'But if he'd stepped out when our backs were turned...'

King nodded. He knew as well as Slater did how unpredictable life-or-death situations could be. All it took was one moment of complacency, one instant of dropping your guard, and a junkie with zero combat or firearms training could have a loaded weapon pointed at the back of your head. Then it's simple physics. One trigger pull, and you're gone.

Slater scrolled back through old messages between Fitch and Wyatt, and said, 'No specific address — Fitch must have already known it. But here, ten weeks ago, he says, "I'll be at the motel in five."'

'Doesn't help,' King said. 'I doubt he's staying there anymore.'

'Unless he works there.'

'Long shot. Besides, how many motels are there in Gillette?'

'Plenty,' Slater said. 'But...'

He opened the maps application on Fitch's phone. The three most recent addresses entered into the search bar showed in the immediate history. The very first was the address for a budget motel in the south-east of Gillette, almost outside the city limits. It was at the edge of the city closest to the Thunder Basin National Grassland.

Slater said, 'Got the address.'

King shrugged and said, 'Still...'

Slater looked up. 'This Wyatt guy probably owns the place. You don't want to know why he's receiving regular Bodhi drops from a junkie?'

King said, 'Use your head. We go there, we speak to him, maybe pretend we're new delivery guys, and he gives that information straight to Maeve. It's the most basic security check he could do. Then there's no way we can go into the commune. We'll blow our cover.'

Slater said, 'What if he knows everything about how the cult operates? That's information too valuable to pass up. And like I said, Violetta and Alexis already have a way in...'

King said, 'So you want to interrogate Wyatt, ruining our hopes of infiltrating Mother Libertas, and abandon the girls once they're deep inside. We have no idea what protocol is out there. Is there even cell service? If they're in danger, and we're stuck here in Gillette, will they even be able to contact us?'

Slater said, 'Or Wyatt spills his guts and gives us information that incriminates everyone at the top of the cult's food chain. Then we can dispense with the bullshit cover, take that Mossberg, storm the commune, and put one in the heads of everyone out there.'

'That's assuming this Wyatt knows anything.'

'Only one way to find out,' Slater said. 'And I doubt Maeve's reckless with the Bodhi she disperses. So he's important.'

King mulled on it for a long time. The silence was thick in the room, and Slater cleared his head and went through a thirty-minute yoga routine to give King time to think. His mind was already made up, his logic falling to the eternal Patton quote: *A good plan violently executed now is better than a perfect plan executed next week.*

He'd found that applied to almost every aspect of life.

When he finished, coated in a thin sheen of sweat, he looked back at King.

Who said, 'Okay. You're right. All four of us don't need to be there in disguise. If it ends up that way, great, but it's not a given.'

A pause.

Slater said, 'So?'

King said, 'Let's go talk to Wyatt.'

29

They went on foot to a car rental shop, hired an old sedan with their false IDs, and drove it south-east, straight to the motel.

They parked across the road, got out, and made for the reception office like they had a thousand things to do that day and no time to waste.

Wyatt sat behind the desk as they stepped into the small space, their presence made known by a small bell jangling above the doorway.

He was a great slab of a man with broken capillaries in his cheeks and tufts of reddish-brown hair that had receded a couple of decades ago. He wore an enormous polo shirt that looked like a bedsheet on his body, with a name badge reading: WYATT NELSON.

He looked up with tired eyes and said, 'Can I help you boys? Need a room?'

'We can help you,' Slater said. 'We're Fitch's replacement.'

Wyatt didn't get up, or even react. His face just creased with wrinkles of confusion.

'Huh?' he said.

Slater didn't know whether he was playing dumb or honestly didn't know his dealer's last name.

King said, 'We've got what you need.'

Wyatt stewed restlessly, small beads of sweat moistening his upper lip. Then the confusion dissipated and he said, 'Oh, Jimmy?'

'Jimmy, James, Fitch, whatever,' Slater said. 'You understand why we're here?'

Wyatt nodded, but he was still apprehensive. 'They ain't mention a replacement. Y'all cops?'

Slater rolled his eyes. 'Yeah, we're cops. You're not dumb, Wyatt. Would cops have this?'

He took out all four vials of Bodhi — the two they'd smuggled into Wyoming, and the two they'd taken off Fitch's body. He laid them on the countertop, letting the amber liquid shine under the overhead light.

Wyatt couldn't help himself. He was deep in the grasp of the substance's power. Desire rippled behind his eyes. He said, 'Four?'

Slater said, 'Four.'

'Jimmy was bringing me the usual top-up. Why you giving me extra? I ain't got the money for it, if that's what you want. I dunno what y'all know about the arrangement, but I don't pay for this shit. I do certain favours for—'

King held up a hand like he was scolding a child. 'Yes, Wyatt. We're all very grateful for what you do. Others might find it dirty, but we see the world differently, don't we?'

Slater tapped a finger beside the vials, highlighting their presence.

Wyatt gulped. 'Okay, well, thank ya very much. Anything you want from me?'

'Nothing yet,' Slater said. 'We figured we'd make this an introductory session. Anything you want to know about us?'

Wyatt shook his head. The beads of sweat were fatter now, more obvious, and Slater couldn't tell whether they were due to nerves or withdrawal symptoms. He wondered how long it had been since Wyatt's last dose.

Wyatt looked all around, like there was the slightest possibility of eavesdroppers, then leant his considerable weight forward onto his elbows. He looked up at Slater. 'Y'all want the body? Maeve said she'd send people. That you?'

King didn't miss a beat. 'That's us.'

Wyatt nodded. 'Got her out back. She put up a damn good fight.'

Slater said, 'Don't they always?'

Inwardly, he burned.

Wyatt levered his fat frame out of the chair. It groaned underneath him, protesting the load it was forced to bear every day. He waddled round from behind the desk and jerked a thumb at the lone door up the back of the office. 'This way.'

Slater couldn't respond at risk of letting his anger blow his cover, so he nodded, his mouth a hard line.

Wyatt stared at him. 'Somethin' wrong?'

Slater said, 'Why would something be wrong?'

'You look funny. You boys new to this sort of work?'

King said, 'We've done tours. We're fine with a little blood.'

Wyatt smiled, his teeth so yellow they were almost brown. 'That's good. That's real good.'

He swaggered to the back door, opened it, and stepped down to a stretch of bare land behind the main building. None of the rooms faced out back — all windows faced the street. It was a dead zone for witnesses. But there was nothing incriminating, just dead grass and patches of dirt.

Wyatt led them to a corrugated shed that looked like a garage.

'My tool shed,' he explained. 'A little bigger than most, but I do all the repairs here myself.'

Slater couldn't fathom the disconnect — how lackadaisically the man discussed regular maintenance as he took them to a body.

Slater said, 'Where is she?'

Wyatt cocked his head. He didn't turn around, kept walking toward the side of the shed, but his tone changed. 'You're a grumpy one, ain't ya?'

King said, 'First job jitters. He'll be fine.'

Wyatt approached the door and took a small ring of keys out of one of his pockets. He fiddled with the old lock. 'Well, ain't you two lucky, then. Maeve gets people like you to do this sort of business ninety-five percent of the time. But there's the odd set of circumstances that sometimes means I've gotta get my hands dirty. This broad ended up renting a room by coincidence, and the Riordans had no one in the area. Picked up the phone and asked me to choke her out. Isn't that funny? That sort of thing being discussed over the phone ... I don't know, maybe I'm old-fashioned...'

He got the door open, pushed it in, and stepped into the musty shed.

Slater didn't budge.

He didn't know how to control himself and maintain their cover.

King walked past, clapped a hand on Slater's shoulder, and said, 'Shame we didn't get to gut the pig ourselves, hey, partner?'

It worked.

The disgusting remark helped dissipate some of the anger, spread it away so it wasn't solely concentrated on Wyatt. Slater knew King didn't mean it, and it was strange enough to shock him out of his rage.

He erected a mental wall, took a deep breath, and followed them into the shed.

30

King went in first, behind Wyatt, so he saw her first.

A thin middle-aged woman, naked, her face mutilated, her corpse dangling from a crude meat hook fixed to the roof.

Around her were shelves of tools and a couple of disassembled shells that were previously old cars. King didn't notice any of it. All he saw was the woman, and Wyatt staring up at her with a smile on his face.

King said, 'Well, that's something. Who is she?'

Wyatt turned, surprised. 'Maeve ain't told ya?'

King shook his head. 'It's the first we're hearing and seeing of this. But Maeve'd send us back for the body eventually, so we might as well take it off your hands now. So, who is she?'

'Journalist,' Wyatt said, returning his gaze to the corpse. 'One of those independent ones, I dunno the term. She was sniffing around in places she didn't belong. I can seem harmless enough when I'm just the simple fat man behind the desk, ya know? People tell me things. I struck up a conversation with her when she checked in. She said she was looking into a number of ... uh ... "unexplained disappearances." I think that was it. But y'all must know how many of those "disappearances" take place at this here motel, so I ain't like it when I heard that. I told Maeve, and she gave me the order. So there we go.'

King said, 'You said she put up a fight?'

'I asked for her help out back here,' Wyatt said. 'She didn't like it. Came into the shed, but then she musta sensed something was off 'cause she tried to run.'

Silence.

Wyatt smirked. 'I know what you're thinking. I'm fast over short distances. Pinned her to the wall and beat her stupid head in. Not sure what exactly killed her, but ... doesn't matter, does it?'

King said, 'Maeve gets you to do that often?'

Wyatt shrugged. 'Usually Dane gives the orders. This time it was Maeve. I've had to do it ... I dunno ... half a dozen times? They kinda blur together.'

'Who's Dane?'

Wyatt took a long time to answer. 'You sure you work for them?'

'Who's Dane?'

'They ain't introduced ya, yet?'

'No.'

'Well, you didn't hear it from me,' Wyatt said. 'He's her husband. Them two run the whole setup.' He paused, ruminating. 'Hey, you tried some of that Bodhi yet?'

'No,' King said.

Wyatt's face lit up. 'It sure is something. Don't be afraid to, either. Them Riordans have convinced all their "disciples" that it's the key to spiritual enlightenment or some shit, but it's just damn good. You don't get sucked into their fancy words and just take the Bodhi and you'll have yourself a grand old time. I guarantee *that.*'

King nodded. 'Who else runs the cult?'

Wyatt grimaced. 'I wouldn't call it that in front of them. They're sensitive, you know. But who you met so far?'

'Just Maeve.'

'That's it,' Wyatt said. 'Maeve's the big show and Dane's like the … secret police. Does all the security and shit. But they don't let anyone else up top. Maybe you two will be the first to get promoted, who knows.'

'Thanks,' King said. 'We have all we need.'

Wyatt looked up at the body, grinned, and turned back. 'You want to know—?'

King pulled his Glock and trained it on Wyatt's face.

'No,' he said. 'I don't.'

31

Wyatt didn't seem to compute.

His lips flapped as he stared down the barrel.

He said, 'I'm sorry if I said something that offended you, sir.'

King said, 'Really?'

Behind them, the body dangled limply on the meat hook.

Wyatt said, 'Killin' me would be a bad idea.'

'Would it?'

'Maeve'll find out. I'm one of her best resources. Y'all ain't want to get on her bad side.'

King said, 'That's where you're wrong. We most *definitely* want to get on her bad side. And I'm not going to do anything to you. I'm just holding you in place.'

'For what?'

Slater pushed past King, grabbed a handful of Wyatt's hair, and kicked his legs out from underneath him. The big man offered feeble resistance. His knees were weak and rubbery. His face was already bright red.

Slater held him down on his knees, all three hundred pounds of flesh and bones quivering. 'Where's all that strength you used to kill her?'

Wyatt mumbled, 'Get off me.'

'Come on, big guy,' Slater said. 'Where's your heart? Where's your courage?'

Wyatt's face turned purple as he tried to burst back to his feet. Slater slapped him hard in the face, spun him round, and locked a forearm under his chin, constricting his airways. He cinched the choke tight and tilted Wyatt's face up to look at the corpse.

Slater said, 'You're going to die. Adrenaline's pumping through you right now but I need you to understand that before I do it. This is it for you. You're done.'

Wyatt struggled, but all his weight was futile against Slater, who might as well have been made out of steel.

Slater said, 'Come on, buddy. You're almost there. When's it going to sink in?'

Wyatt tried to look away from the corpse.

Slater didn't let him.

The big man started crying, great sobs wracking his body. He was terrified beyond description. Slater had forced him into an existential crisis.

'There we go,' Slater said. 'Now say goodnight.'

He squeezed with the grip of a boa constrictor. Wyatt's face went a deeper shade of purple, his cheeks close to exploding, spit flying out of his mouth.

Wyatt let out a final pathetic cry.

Slater locked the choke even tighter, crushing his windpipe, cutting the blood flow to the brain.

Wyatt was still crying as he went out, one of the most pathetic deaths imaginable.

Which was Slater's intention all along.

Slater held the choke at full strength for another thirty seconds, counting them under his breath. When he was sure the man was dead, he let go and pushed him to the floor.

Slater spat on his body.

King said, 'I figured you'd do something like that.'

'It wasn't enough,' Slater said. 'Nothing would have been enough.'

'Would you have done it slower?' King said. 'If we had time?'

He needed to know.

Slater shook his head. 'That's not who I am. I cave to those instincts and I'm no better than a sadist. But he deserved that. You can't tell me he didn't.'

King sighed. 'Guess our cover's out of the picture now. We'll have to take the commune by force.'

'You don't like that?'

'I hate it,' King said. 'For all we know, Maeve has a suicide pact with her followers. What did Wyatt call them — disciples? She gets suspicious, she takes dozens if not hundreds of people with her. It's the ultimate psychopath move. Make your enemies pay by making their efforts futile.'

Slater said, 'Then we get her and her scumbag husband before they can do that.'

'Won't be so easy,' King said, surveying the shed, lost in thought. 'Unless...'

Slater understood immediately. He saw a red pickup truck up the back of the shed, burrowed behind the disassembled cars. It was shiny, kept in good condition. Wyatt's car.

King said, 'You know what I'm thinking, right?'

Slater smiled. 'Of course. She'll buy it. Hook, line and

sinker.'

'We won't know until we try.'

Slater grabbed Wyatt's body by the collar and started dragging it across the shed.

32

The next day, they came at eight on the dot to collect Alexis and Violetta.

Not Maeve. Not her husband.

A boy and girl in their early twenties, if not younger. They were adults, but only just. They drove an old Toyota Land Cruiser pickup — four-door, not two — with room in the back for Alexis and Violetta.

The women stood shoulder-to-shoulder in front of the backdrop of Bicentennial Park, with its beautiful green lawns home to soccer and baseball fields. A couple of teams of elementary school kids conducted early morning practice.

A world away from what Alexis and Violetta were about to step into.

Alexis saw the truck approaching, and out of the corner of her mouth she muttered, 'Last chance. Protect yourself and your baby.'

'You need me,' Violetta muttered back. 'You saying you'll go in there alone?'

'Gladly. If this makes you uncomfortable, don't do it.'

'It's always uncomfortable. That's the job.'

'Look at them,' Alexis said, staring through the grimy windshield at the driver and passenger. 'They're kids, just like Jace.'

'Easily susceptible,' Violetta said. 'Prime targets for manipulation. And they're young. They've got no money. They're vulnerable. Like we're pretending to be.'

Alexis said, 'I'll remember this when I'm standing across from that bitch.'

Violetta said, 'I'll be there alongside you.'

Conversation ceased abruptly as the Toyota pulled up and the pair got out. Up close they resembled each other like mirror images. The same flat faces, small eyes, asymmetrical jaws. They both had pale skin and bad complexions. The guy was younger, taller, lankier, and the girl was short and squat. They both had an eerie detachment in their eyes, a faded milkiness like they were high. Alexis guessed they were brother and sister, and also guessed they had a mutual affection for Bodhi.

But they certainly weren't on a potent dose right now or they'd be rolling around in the grass, incapable of operating a vehicle.

The guy said, 'You're Violetta and Alexis?'

He addressed them in the correct order, first looking at Violetta, then across to Alexis.

Violetta said, 'That's us.'

'Pleased to meet you,' the guy said. 'Brandon.'

He spoke with youthful indifference, and Alexis guessed he was eighteen or nineteen. His sister hadn't opened her mouth yet, which didn't seem abnormal. She was quieter, more reserved. Her eyes were the same as her brother's, but there was something else in them. Not uncertainty ... but she definitely wasn't as comfortable in this role as Brandon.

Alexis kept her gaze on the girl and said, 'What's your name?'

'Addison,' she mumbled.

Brandon said, 'Sorry. She's a bit tired. Can I throw your bags in the tray?'

Alexis nodded politely. She wanted to use her social skills to take over the conversation, fill the awkward silences, make Addison more comfortable, give Brandon something to respond to. But none of those avenues would align with the image of a wandering backpacker, still a little awkward from lack of societal integration. So she shut her mouth and let the silence play out. Violetta kept quiet, too, acting the shyest of them all.

They got in the back of the pickup's cabin and found the long footwell littered with fast food wrappers, empty Gatorade bottles, and a couple of empty vials with the odd drop of leftover amber liquid inside.

Alexis froze, wondering if this was all a setup.

They were being so blatant with it...

But you don't know what Bodhi is, she reminded herself. *The vials mean nothing to you.*

Brandon got behind the wheel and Addison got in the passenger seat. They drove away, manoeuvring through Gillette until they took I-90 out of the city limits. They stayed on the highway for close to an hour, passing through Wyodak and Rozet. The sleepy towns showed little sign of life as they went by outside the window.

Finally, when they turned off I-90 into the small town of Moorcroft and headed south toward the Thunder Basin Grassland, Alexis pretended to get the courage to ask questions.

She said, 'So how long have you two been living with Maeve?'

'We don't live with her,' Addison answered immediately, anxious to respond to any queries after such a prolonged silence. 'We live in the bunkhouses.'

'That's not what she meant,' Brandon said. 'She meant how long we've been in the commune.'

'Oh,' Addison said, hunching over in disappointment.

She didn't enjoy being the fool.

Brandon said, 'Just over six months now.'

He sounded like he wanted to say more, but he didn't. He must have been instructed to keep information sparse. As far as the newcomers were aware, it was just rural living, away from civilisation. Like-minded people collaborating to create a peaceful existence.

There was far more to it than that, and before long the new arrivals would be converted…

But they weren't yet.

Violetta said, 'Do you like it there?'

Brandon said, 'It's the best place on earth.'

Violetta said, 'Addison?'

Addison twisted in her seat to make eye contact. Either she was an impressive actress or the unease she'd shown earlier was truly gone. But her eyes were honest and frank as she said, 'There's really no place I'd rather be.'

Alexis said, 'What makes it so good?'

Brandon said, 'You'll see.'

He said it fast and sharp, allowing a trace of hostility to creep into his tone. Alexis knew why. Addison was being uncharacteristically open, even turning to meet the eyes of the strangers in the back, and she might get too complacent with her newfound behaviour and say something she wasn't supposed to.

They sat in silence for the rest of the journey, driving deeper and deeper into the desolation. The plains were staggeringly empty. There was so much land in every direction, panning as far as the eye could see. If you ran out of fuel out here, you'd probably die of dehydration before you stumbled on a trace of human life.

It was perfect for Maeve Riordan.

Out here, you could make your own rules.

33

Brandon took the pickup truck down an unpaved trail, and it led them around the perimeter of a long shallow hill that gave the landscape its undulating look.

On the other side of the broad landmark, nearly a dozen buildings were burrowed into the base of the hill in a tight cluster. They approached from the east, but the commune was visible from close to half a mile away given the nature of the terrain.

Brandon said, 'Home sweet home. Welcome.'

'Does this place have a name?' Violetta said.

'Our group is—' Addison started.

'The commune doesn't have a name,' Brandon interjected sharply, shooting a dark look at his sister. 'Our community has branded ourselves with a name, but that's not important. You two might just be passing through, after all. You don't need to know what you don't need to know.'

Silence elapsed, and he cocked his head in irritation at the haste with which he'd had to come up with the spiel. It hadn't sounded right, and everyone in the car knew it.

Alexis watched the buildings get closer through the windshield. The commune was centred around two structures that were far larger than the rest — a grand building with a conical spire that could only be a church, and a big rectangular building that looked like a mess hall for troops stationed overseas. Around the centrepieces were around ten long low buildings that had to be accommodations, a couple of enormous garages, and finally a simple two-storey farmhouse further away from the rest, up a long driveway that finished a third of the way up the hill.

The farmhouse was like a king's throne, elevated above the commune, looking down on its subjects. It was old and constructed with remarkable care and attention to detail, whereas the rest of the buildings appeared to be thrown together with modern materials. A byproduct of rapid expansion, Alexis figured. With the followers growing in droves, they had to be fed and clothed and given somewhere to sleep. Depending on how long Mother Libertas had been in operation, Maeve might soon have command of a small city's worth of devotees if she kept her current recruitment pace.

Men and women moved between the buildings, like ants from this distance, but rapidly growing larger in the windshield. As far as Alexis could tell they were normal. They dressed simply and made no strange movements, just carried on about their day like serenity was their main priority.

She said, 'Are you going to introduce us to all your friends?'

'Not yet,' Brandon said. 'You've got an appointment at the big house.'

'The big house?' Alexis asked, but she knew.

Addison pointed at the farmhouse. 'Maeve's place. She

asked us to bring you there first. There's some introductory stuff to go over.'

Brandon said, 'You need to know how things work here.'

Violetta said, 'Can't you tell us?'

She saw him mask a smile in the rear view mirror.

'No,' he said. 'No, I can't.'

34

The pickup kicked a plume of dust off the previously undisturbed driveway as it pulled up to the farmhouse.

Alexis said, 'She was expecting us?'

Brandon said, 'Of course.'

Maeve stood at the top of the steps leading up to the porch, clad in a farm dress, every part the humble, simplistic commune leader. It was an impressive act, given what they knew about her true nature.

She descended the porch steps, lifting the hem of her dress as she stepped down. She walked across the driveway to them as they got out of the car. Like automatons, Brandon and Addison bled into the background, walking away silently. When Violetta looked over her shoulder, they were already halfway down the decline to the commune, having abandoned their vehicle.

Probably because it wasn't theirs.

Must be one of the communal rides.

Maeve stepped forward and embraced Alexis in warm arms, curly hair framing her face. Violetta realised how good of an actress Alexis was when she bowed her forehead to Maeve's shoulder and sighed in her arms, as if the hug was what she'd been searching for all along.

After a long silence Alexis stepped out of the embrace and said, 'This is my friend, Violetta.'

Maeve turned to Violetta and smiled. 'I've heard so much about you, dear. Oh my, you two are a sight to behold together, aren't you? Such gorgeous creatures.'

Violetta squirmed uncomfortably, playing shy.

Maeve said, 'I'm Maeve. Maeve Riordan. This is my commune.'

Violetta cleared her throat. 'Sorry, I know. I suppose not saying anything was mighty rude of me. I'm happy to be here, Maeve. Thank you so much for the invitation.'

They could see the excitement barely suppressed in Maeve's eyes. Two polite, shy nomads, ripe for exploitation. She thought they'd bend to her every word.

Maeve said, 'Come inside. I've prepared tea.'

Falling in behind Alexis as they went up the porch steps, Violetta felt like she'd been transported to the Wild West. It truly was a different life out here. She wondered how the commune generated power, and what sort of system they had for maintaining a steady train of supplies. Mostly she found herself flabbergasted at how a community of this magnitude could fly so effortlessly under the radar. She'd seen the number of buildings. There had to be at least a hundred people living here, if not more.

How had no one back in civilisation acknowledged it? Not even with something as small as an online post?

Because people who hear about it disappear...

Maeve led them through the screen door into an old-fashioned sitting area with rattan chairs, a faded leather sofa, and ornate side tables. A royal blue rug covered most of the floorspace, making the room feel cosier than if the wooden floorboards underneath were left exposed. A soft breeze blew in through a handful of windows that were cracked open, circulating fresh air from one end of the ground floor to the other.

Maeve gestured to the sofa. 'Please, sit.'

They sat.

Alexis said, 'This place is lovely.'

'One second, dear,' Maeve said, disappearing into the kitchen.

She returned with a kettle that looked as if it had come off a charcoal burner moments previously. Steam crawled out of the spout. It was then that Alexis noticed the teacups already on the low table between the sofa and the armchairs. There was a measure of fine powder — bright green, in the distinctive matcha style — in each cup. She poured near-boiling water into each mug of fine china, then took a whisk from beside the cups and stirred the contents into thin green tea. She handed them over, one by one.

Alexis sipped hers.

It was *very* good.

'Did you have a pleasant journey?' Maeve said as she took her own cup and sat delicately in the rattan chair across from them.

Both women nodded.

Alexis sat forward. 'I guess we don't know exactly what to expect. But we're coming in with open minds.'

Maeve swirled the tea in the mug and took a soft sip. 'That's fantastic news. Really, that's all you need to make the most out of life, isn't it?'

Alexis shrugged.

Violetta stayed quiet.

Maeve cocked her head. 'Did I say something offensive?'

'No,' Violetta said, speaking for the first time since they'd sat down. 'Definitely not. Sorry ... we're shy, is all. Don't do well with small talk.'

She looked over to Alexis, who nodded her confirmation.

Maeve said, 'Shall we get straight to the point then?'

Alexis said, 'Which is?'

Maeve sipped from her teacup, settled back in the chair, and watched them.

Alexis and Violetta shifted restlessly on the sofa.

Maeve said, 'Do you think there's more to life?'

Silence.

35

Alexis said, 'I'm sorry?'

'Have you ever looked back on your life and thought, "What if...?"'

More quiet.

But Alexis started to open up. 'I guess I have.'

Violetta nodded, mute but understanding.

Maeve said, 'Isn't that a fascinating concept, though? That in every moment we have in time, we choose what action to take. It draws parallels to quantum physics. In each moment there is limitless possibility, infinite choices, and therefore there are limitless versions of ourselves. In some parallel universe, there's a version of you that has made *every* choice correctly. Imagine where that person is now. Imagine the sorts of things they've accomplished. Imagine ... your ideal self.'

Alexis said, 'I couldn't begin to picture...'

Violetta's gaze went far away, the concept dawning on her.

Maeve said, 'That's why we're here in Thunder Basin.'

'I'm sorry?'

'To become what you *could be,* you must do something out of the ordinary. Wouldn't you agree? Isn't that the very definition of ordinary? Choosing to remain within the walls of your old life...'

Alexis said, 'Yeah, I guess.'

'That's why we're away from civilisation,' Maeve said. 'We're mastering our destinies, to use a cliché. But it's true. Here ... you're alleviated of all the responsibilities of that dreaded rat race that takes place back in the real world. We come here and we breathe the pristine air and we ... evolve. We become the people we should have been all along, through a series of practices and habits and mantras.'

They took in the words.

Alexis realised that if she had no idea who Maeve was or what the cult leader truly did to get results, she'd fall for it.

That terrified her.

Maeve carried on. 'Think about this rationally, then, and ask yourself what's stopping you from living the rest of your life by this ideal? In every *single* moment, you make the right choice. You tap into some primordial consciousness, you grow connected to this earth, to all other living beings, to Mother Earth herself. You liberate yourself from mediocrity and complacency. You achieve unimaginable things, and you do it effortlessly, because you make the determined, conscious, committed *choice* to do it. Does that sound like something you two might be interested in?'

Violetta said, 'Hell yes it does.'

Maeve laughed. 'I like your spirit. And you, Alexis? Are you willing to find out what you're capable of?'

But Alexis hesitated, unwilling to dive in so fast it'd seem suspicious. She let her face turn overcast. 'I wouldn't know where to start. That's not ... who I am.'

Maeve stood up, rocketing out of the chair. Her voice

rose. 'Don't you *understand,* girl? That's what this place is. That's why you ended up here. It was Mother Earth, Gaia, guiding you to a better future. I've studied the power of the human spirit my whole life. I've found ideas, actions, habits ... that make you unstoppable. I want to share these gifts with you, Alexis. And you, too, Violetta. I want to open your eyes to a new world. Where every action you take, every step forward, is *charged* with purpose. Every time you make a decision it's bursting with *relentless energy.* It comes from this ground we live on, this bubble we inhabit. It's right there for the taking. I would like to show you how to take it. If you'll let me.'

Violetta said, 'Yes,' without hesitation.

Alexis said, 'What does it involve?'

Maeve sat back down and smiled warmly. 'Nothing crazy. But now I feel comfortable sharing some things with you. This commune is a liberation movement. We call it "Mother Libertas." We're unlocking human capacity, becoming the optimal versions of ourselves, finding purpose in a cold, sad world. I warmly extend an invitation to you both. If you'd like, join us. If not, carry on with your travels. But I want you to give it some real thought. You might choose to leave too hastily, and end up back in the aimless wandering you're already sick of, and then you'll most definitely look back on your life and ask yourself ... "What if?"'

Alexis said, 'It sounds too good to be true.'

'Maybe because it is,' Maeve said. 'For something to be "true" or "acceptable" it must coexist peacefully with a functioning society. But our society is broken. People are torn between the useless see-saw of the political spectrum. They're fat, tired, overworked, undernourished, chemically addicted, broken in the soul. We offer something purer. We offer hope.'

"Chemically addicted," Violetta thought. *That's rich.*

But the scary part was Maeve had a point.

The movement made sense. There was something romantic and poetic about detaching yourself from the world, starting anew in an exotic location, stripping yourself down to your basic instincts so you could change your automatic habits. Violetta knew King and Slater were masters of the concept. It worked. They made the hard choices in every moment, and it had carried them to where they were today. But sometimes concepts are *so* appealing that they're ripe for exploitation. That's what Maeve was doing.

Speaking some fundamental truths about the world, sucking in her audience, and then using that initial devotion to make them servants to her every whim.

Hell, Violetta thought, *every salesman does it.*

She was taking the practice to its extreme.

And succeeding.

Alexis broke the silence. 'I'm in. I guess it takes courage to admit you're lost. And I'm lost. I'll try anything.'

Maeve looked at Violetta.

Violetta said, 'I was in from the moment you started talking.'

Maeve smiled. 'I'm thrilled to hear it.'

Alexis said, 'What now?'

Maeve waved a hand dismissively. 'Nothing. You've been here half an hour. The first step is understanding our way of life, integrating with the community. I assure you it won't be difficult. Everyone here is accepting. You'll feel right at home. So I'll get Brandon to show you to your room, and then over the next few days we can practice some of the strategies I've discovered about how the human mind really works.'

The women nodded.

Maeve jutted her chin. 'Go on, then. You'll find Brandon at the bottom of the hill. I instructed him to wait.'

Alexis said, 'You knew we'd accept.'

Maeve shook her head. 'You'd need to be shown to your rooms anyway. It's a common courtesy.'

'If we refused,' Alexis said, 'you wouldn't have kicked us out?'

'Of course not, darling,' Maeve said. 'Do you think I'm a monster?'

Yes, Alexis thought. *Yes, I do.*

36

In one of the outbuildings on the other side of the commune, Elias practiced close-range elbow strikes.

The sequence was part of Biu Ji, "Thrusting Fingers," the third form of the traditional Chinese martial art Wing Chun.

He slammed an elbow into the *mu ren zhuang,* a wooden dummy designed specifically for Wing Chun practice. As he threw the strike, he made sure he was aware of every atom in his muscle chain, using the supreme control of his body to harness his *ki,* his energy.

Elias had practiced Wing Chun his whole life. An outcast in his home town of Cheyenne due to social awkwardness and lack of conversational timing, he'd retreated into a shell at the age of fourteen and never really left. He'd spent hours every evening after school watching videos on the martial art, practicing on a wooden dummy he'd built himself. That first dummy had been a cheap imitation of the real thing's craftsmanship, but it did the job. After school he'd drifted from manual labour job to manual labour job, which helped harden his thin, tall frame. He continued to devote his life to Wing Chun, mastering each of the forms in turn, working on his close-range strikes until he achieved a breakthrough at the age of twenty-five. It was then that he was able to tap into his *ki* at will, giving him the strength of ten men in brief bursts.

Elias had never been in a fistfight before.

It had simply never materialised. Here in the commune he'd been forced to use his talents in macabre ways, but he'd never come up against a resisting opponent. He feared for his adversary on the day he did. Devoting his entire life to a single focus had sharpened him in ways he could barely fathom.

That's how the Riordans had found him eight months ago.

He rarely trained in public, but on one of the occasions that he brought his *mu ren zhuang* to the local park in Cheyenne, a couple of passersby had spotted him and watched his hand speed and dexterity in awe. As chance would have it, one of those bystanders would go on to join Mother Libertas, and one night they mentioned what they'd seen to Maeve. She'd sent a couple of scouts to Cheyenne to track him down, and they'd found him easily enough.

Then she'd approached with an offer.

The rest was history.

He hadn't left the commune in eight months, and he relished the role of "enforcer" for Mother Libertas. It charged him with a true purpose, something his past life distinctly lacked. Modern times create soulless, socially inept shut-ins, and that's what he'd been until Maeve had set him free.

It had been difficult to shake his conditioning at first, considering his social ineptitude and inability to hold a conversation with a stranger. But over time he'd come out of his shell as he got to know the Riordans better. It'd have to be enough — he couldn't get close to any of the disciples, for they came in with increasing frequency and the few that wanted out obviously couldn't return to society and spill their secrets, so Elias was tasked with silencing them.

Which reminded him of the work he had to take care of tonight.

He charged his *ki* and delivered ten more consecutive strikes to the wooden dummy. It was built with expert craftsmanship, but it nearly splintered all the same. His power was becoming frightening, each ounce of muscle serving a kinetic purpose. He'd recently passed the ten thousand hour mark that symbolised mastery — an average of three hours a day training Wing Chun for the past nine years. Now twenty-eight, he had the physical abilities of a man in his athletic prime, and would doubtless become better and better with time as Mother Libertas expanded into its new role.

He was more than ready.

Sweat soaking his traditional Chinese outfit, he stepped away from the dummy and conducted fifteen minutes of transcendental meditation in the corner of the room that served as his training facility, lowering his heart rate to baseline. Then he rose, padded barefoot to the door, and opened it to survey the commune.

He spotted two newcomers.

They were following Brandon toward one of the bunkhouses on the opposite side. He caught their side profiles as they passed by. They were women in their early thirties, jaw-dropping to look at, carrying themselves with a grace that meant they were athletically gifted and took exceptional care of their bodies. After devoting his life to the same practice, Elias knew disguised power when he saw it.

He made a mental note to find out more about them — by studying their movements and their anatomies as they walked past, he concluded they could hold their own in a fistfight against most of the male followers of Mother Libertas.

That was impressive, and might reveal more about who they claimed they were.

It was Elias' job to sniff out liars.

Which, again, brought him back to the job that awaited him tonight.

He closed the door, sat back down in the corner, and returned to his meditative state.

He needed all his energy harnessed for the evening.

37

Brandon showed Violetta and Alexis to their room.

Everyone they passed was polite and respectable, but kept their distance. There was a clear understanding amongst the followers that the newcomers hadn't been initiated yet. Until then, the followers would be wary of the invisible bubble. They wouldn't get too close, wouldn't grow too attached. They were devoted to the tribe of Mother Libertas, and nothing else.

They were a mixed bag. En route to one of the bunkhouses, Alexis nodded a wordless greeting to four Caucasians, an Asian-American couple, and an African-American woman. They ranged from their twenties to their forties, but no older. That was clearly a result of the screening process for potential victims, and revealed that eventually Maeve would put her devotees to use in ways that the elderly wouldn't be able to manage.

Like a violent revolution, for example.

But that was a long way off. If Mother Libertas was a start-up company, it was currently going through one of the early stages — the accumulation of capital. More followers were more hands were more resources. And if all of these people gave Maeve and her husband their money under the guise of being "reborn" out of their old lives ... well, that was a nice nest egg to fall back on.

That wasn't to mention what Maeve could get from the outside world in exchange for Bodhi...

Wherever the drug was made, it wasn't here. There were no facilities for lab work, unless they were somewhere else in the grassland, but purchasing those quantities of equipment would raise red flags. The more likely option was a pre-established lab in one of the major cities, paid gross sums of money under the table to manufacture and bottle.

Brandon reached the bunkhouse furthest to the east of the commune and said, 'Through here.'

They went inside and found themselves in horrid conditions.

The air reeked of unwashed clothes — stale sweat and the hint of tobacco. Wet garments were strung up on coathangers in doorways, people moved in and out of their rooms like silhouettes in the poor lighting, and the walls smelled of damp rot, only adding to the disrepair.

Alexis didn't mind.

In fact, she felt great.

She didn't know why.

Brandon said, 'Here's your spot. It's your lucky day, girls. You've got your own room.'

He pushed a door open and gestured for them to step inside. The bedroom was practically a closet, claustrophobic in design, with a twin bunk bed frame nailed to the opposite wall. There were thin cheap mattresses on each bed, and fitted sheets folded neatly on top of their pillows.

'Thank you so much,' Violetta said, and it seemed she genuinely meant it.

Brandon nodded. 'No problem. I'll leave you to settle in. Come find me if you need anything, yeah?'

'Will do,' Alexis said.

'Anything at all,' Brandon said. 'I mean it.'

He gazed at them for a little too long.

Again, Alexis didn't care.

Which was odd.

Brandon nodded to himself, stepped out and walked away. He left the door open — closing it might highlight how small the space truly was.

Alexis wouldn't have cared either way. She didn't think anything could ruin the mood she was in.

Violetta put her bag on the bed and said, 'Let's take a walk. Get some fresh air.'

Alexis said, 'Really?'

'The scenery's stunning,' Violetta said. 'We might as well look at it.'

Because the room's bugged, Alexis realised. She scolded herself for being so stupid, but she couldn't stay frustrated. Instead she found it funny.

She masked a giggle and said, 'Sure, why not?'

They went out through the same door they'd come in, leaving their phones in their bags. The devices were useless, anyway. There was no service this far from civilisation. Their building marked the very edge of the commune, and out back it surveyed the endless landscape, like an alien planet of grass and dirt.

Violetta walked a few dozen feet away from the building, until they were out of earshot of any eavesdroppers, at the tip of the vast emptiness.

She turned to Alexis and said, 'Do you feel it?'

'Feel what?' Alexis said.

Violetta said, 'Inside you.'

Alexis cocked her head, confused. 'I feel good, I guess. Maybe we needed some fresh country air after all.'

Violetta said, 'Are colours brighter?'

Alexis hesitated.

She looked all around.

The prairie was magnificent. It was so empty it practically glowed, a well-preserved frontier, a world away from the chaos of modern city living. It was how humans were supposed to live. It was glorious...

Violetta said, 'Alexis.'

She snapped out of it. 'Yeah. Colours are brighter. Do you think—?'

'The tea.'

'Oh.'

'It was a tiny dose,' Violetta said. 'But holy shit, I feel good.'

Alexis fought through the dopamine spike and used an iota of common sense. She said, 'This is how it works.'

'What do you mean?'

Alexis stared into Violetta's eyes. 'Right now, my brain's telling me to listen to whatever Maeve says. If life feels this good out here, why put on a cover? Why not *actually* live out here? That's what's going through my head right now...'

'You don't honestly—?'

Alexis said, 'No. I can detach myself from it. But if I was any weaker ... maybe all those months ago, before I met Will, maybe I would have fallen for something like this. I was still a smart woman back then. I had my head on my shoulders. I wasn't gullible. But this — the setting, the chemicals, the words Maeve uses — it's a different level of persuasion. It's incredibly good.'

Violetta said, 'I know.'

Alexis looked into her eyes.

They were twice as blue. She wasn't sure whether it was her own perception, or the Bodhi in Violetta's system.

Then something broke through the elation, and Violetta's face went dark and she said, 'Fuck.'

'What?'

'That's how good this stuff is,' Violetta said. 'For an instant, I forgot I was pregnant. The baby…'

Alexis' own joy fell away. 'Oh, shit.'

Violetta shook her head. 'It's a microdose. Barely perceptible. Just a mood elevator. That's not enough to harm the child.'

All went quiet.

Violetta looked out across the plains and said, 'If Maeve slips me some again, I'll cut her throat.'

Alexis listened to the determination in her voice.

She was telling the truth.

38

That afternoon, Dane rapped his knuckles lightly against the wood of the farmhouse's office door.

Even though his wife had requested his presence it still didn't feel right. These were her "deep focus" hours, early in the afternoon between congregations, when she locked herself in the office and let her grandest visions spill onto the page. He'd seen the aftermath of what had to be a hundred sessions by now. Every time, the result was pages and pages of handwritten scrawl, written in the loose style of her free-flowing train of thought. They were notes for her eyes only, and sometimes Dane's. Plans for the future, broader aims and goals for the movement, and ideas for new nefarious methods of infecting the disciples with feverish hatred and devotion.

She'd been doing these isolated brainstorming sessions ever since she'd morphed into a destructive charismatic

"Destructive charismatic," he thought. *Giving your soulmate a label like that...*

But it was true. He'd stumbled upon the definition online, sitting up late one night. A destructive charismatic bent followers to their will with a bombastic, unabashed personality. They were masters of persuasion, refusing to recognise their flaws and doubling down whenever anyone criticised them. It created an aura of achievement and accomplishment, like it was effortless, like the world fell into their lap the moment they opened their mouth and spewed their rhetoric.

That was Maeve Riordan, through and through.

That late night Googling session had been a rare moment of self-reflection, when Dane finally realised what his partner had become. In those moments he realised what they were, *who* they were. They didn't come often, but when they did they hit him hard.

He'd always known he was a monster — his childhood had made that inevitable. Universal qualities of empathy and compassion come from the correct development of a baby's brain. An infant needs love, care, nurturing. Dane had received exactly the opposite of those three things, and had identified himself as a psychopath in his early twenties after giving it a couple of minutes' thought. He'd spent most of his life dangerously paranoid, but he figured it was unique that he was able to acknowledge it instead of vehemently ignoring it like Maeve did.

But just because you understand why you're conditioned the way you are, doesn't mean you can change it.

He'd certainly changed Maeve.

Morphed her into what she was now.

She used to be a normal, easygoing woman. He'd given her a life of her own, then let her stoke her own fire.

Now he entered the room. She was hunched over her desk, closer in resemblance to a crazed philosopher than the straight-backed omniscient deity she pretended to be. She looked up from the pages and fixed him with a stare.

He said, 'I don't want to disturb you.'

She said, 'It's fine. We have to talk.'

'Is it about the new girls?'

'How'd you know?'

'I can't see what else it'd be.'

'Besides you and I, they're now the most important people in this commune.'

Dane hesitated, thrown off. 'What?'

'Did you not hear me?'

'That's ... not what I was expecting to hear. I thought you'd have a problem with them.'

'Why would I?' Maeve said. 'I mean, just look at them. I'm sure you want to stick your dick in both of them, preferably at the same time. Am I right?'

In his early twenties, Dane thought psychopaths were devoid of all emotion. That's how it seemed for him, years ago. But it's not true. Psychopaths are indifferent to anyone other than themselves, but they can worry about their own thoughts, their own emotions.

Like he was doing now.

He'd never felt more uncomfortable.

There was a dark glint in Maeve's eyes.

He said, 'That's not true.'

She said, 'I know it is, darling. Like I said, *look* at them. But don't you see the potential? I mean, fuck *me*. How did we get so lucky? They're already eating up every word. They'll be fully converted as soon as we dose them with a full hit of Bodhi, and then *imagine* what they can do for us.'

He said, 'You mean recruiting?'

She rolled her eyes. 'Come on, Dane. Are you really going to stand there and play the moron?' She stewed, chewing her lower lip with a rabid quality. 'You know ... you've been doing an awful lot of that lately.'

'Of what?'

'You're wishy-washy. You were hesitant about killing that girl at the motel, too. What was her name? Krystal?'

'Karlie.'

'Karlie,' Maeve said, lifting a finger in recognition. 'You didn't want her killed.'

Not even the mob talked so brazenly and soullessly. They'd say "disappeared" or "got rid of" or "dealt with." Maeve, as always, cut straight to the chase. *We killed that girl.*

He said, 'I don't give a shit about the girl. You know that. It was about letting our body count run unnecessarily high.'

'I'd argue it was very necessary. This commune requires anonymity. Are you losing your spine?'

He stood there, hands clasped in front of him, practically squirming. He looked over her head at the wall behind her, like a soldier standing at attention.

She tutted, filling the silence with her derision. 'That's not the husband I know. That's not the man I married.'

Dane tried to mask a deep inhalation, then said, 'Back to the point. You want to groom those new girls to lead entire legions of our disciples because they look like supermodels and it's easy to believe they're reincarnations of Gaia's beauty. If we put them in leadership positions, anyone with a penis will worship them, and the women will serve them out of fear and envy.'

Maeve's eyes seemed to glow. '*That's* the man I married.'

Dane said, 'I always understood that. I thought it went without saying.'

Silence.

Horrid silence.

Maeve put down her pen. 'What are you saying, baby?'

He forced himself not to let his internal squirming show. 'Just that—'

'You're arguing for the sake of arguing these days. Something's changed in you.'

He went quiet.

She got up and rounded the desk, her dress frills bouncing with each step. She walked right up to him, cupped his face in her hands.

She said, 'Right now Mother Libertas is like a space shuttle trying to break out of orbit. Do you know a shuttle burns through more fuel in the first couple of minutes of flight than the rest of its trip combined? That's what we've been fighting for all this time. We're on the cusp. I can't have you getting cold feet now.'

He said, 'I'm with you all the way.'

He knew what she was doing, but he could do nothing to stop it. She was using her rhetoric on him, her allegories and her persuasions, the same way she spoke to the disciples.

Suddenly it all clicked for him.

Why he'd been so discontent lately, why he didn't think the same as her anymore.

When they'd started the cult, they'd been on the same wavelength. They understood it was all a ruse, a front for amassing power, and they both relished it. He still loved that side of it. Nothing made him happier than plotting, scheming, looking for better methods of converting new disciples. But Maeve Riordan was starting to believe her own bullshit.

That was the missing puzzle piece.

A destructive charismatic can only use their powers of persuasion for so long before they start convincing themselves. She truly thought she was omniscient, above the rest of humanity, just because she could spin a good tale and lead a cult of worshippers. She'd spent so long feeding them her lies that they'd festered in her own mind.

She was speaking to her husband, the man who knew her down to her core, like he was a newcomer that needed brainwashing.

Despair filled him as her fingers dug harder into his cheeks, because he realised there was nothing he could do.

How could he resist? How could he make an enemy of her? She had two hundred rabid followers on this land that would tear him limb from limb if she so much as asked them to restrain him.

And he could see in her eyes that she was fully aware of that.

She said, 'Are you going to do what I say, baby?'

'Yes.'

'How can I be sure?'

'What choice do I have?'

Her eyes blazed. She let go of his cheeks, gave one of them a condescending pat, then took a step back. Smiled like she was in the grasp of a Bodhi hit, even though she'd never touched the stuff.

'None,' she said. 'None at all.'

39

The mess hall was enormous, and everyone in the cult ate three communal meals a day.

At dinner — their first meal in the commune — Alexis and Violetta got a true sense of the scale of Mother Libertas.

The movement was two hundred strong already, a small army. No wonder the bunkhouses were cramped, the conditions poor. Looking out at the sea of followers as she munched on a serving of chicken casserole and rice, Alexis realised what was going on.

Maeve was implementing a literal version of "growth hacking," which were the strategies implemented by modern companies to acquire customers fast and cheap, and she'd used Dylan Walcott's capital to do it. Alexis could imagine the pitch Maeve made to Dylan.

'I'll combine my persuasive speeches with chemical compounds to suck in as many lost souls as possible. Then, when I have enough members, I'll get them all dependent on Bodhi, and use my ever-increasing sphere of influence to amass more and more of their money. I'll use that money to pay off those in

important positions who have the ability to shut us down, get them hooked on Bodhi too, and from there we'll spread like the plague.'

Walcott would have handed over as much money as she asked for.

Now, beside her, Brandon said, 'How was your first afternoon?'

Addison sat on the other side of him, head down, eyes on her food.

'It was great,' Alexis said. 'Everyone here is so nice.'

'There's word going around that you've decided to join us.'

Alexis bowed her head. 'That's correct. Maeve is incredible. I can't imagine a future without her wisdom in it.'

Brandon leant forward to look past Alexis. 'And you?'

Violetta looked up from her plate. 'Oh, yes. It's wonderful.'

'You don't sound so convinced.'

'What would you like me to say?'

'I don't know,' Brandon said, 'but I expected a little more enthusiasm than that.'

Violetta's face shifted. 'Are you doubting my commitment already?'

Brandon said, 'I—'

Violetta sat forward, too, so they were talking across the space in front of Alexis.

Violetta said, 'Are you jealous of us or something?'

'What?' Brandon said.

'Stop pretending you're some big shot here,' Violetta said. 'You're nothing. Maeve already trusts me and she sure wouldn't like to hear about one of her followers intimidating the new arrivals.'

The colour drained from Brandon's face, and his eyes

went dark — a potent blend of fear and anger. He said, 'Listen—'

Violetta said, 'I swear, I'll go talk to her right now. I'll tell her all we're trying to do is assimilate and this farm boy keeps harassing us, asking us too many questions, trying to get in our pants, and it's really turning us off the whole movement. How do you think she'll feel about that?'

Violetta spoke in a measured, even tone, not once raising her voice. It created an aura of total control, and it had an immediate effect on Brandon.

He sat back in his seat and stared at his food, his lips sealed.

Beside him, Addison grumbled, 'Idiot.'

Directed at her brother, not Violetta.

Violetta settled back, satisfied…

…then pain seized her abdomen.

She squeezed her eyes shut and hunched over. Alexis knew exactly what it was, and sat still, eyes fixed forward. Brandon was emotionally wounded, focused on his food, so he didn't notice. But Addison leant forward to get a good look at Violetta. There was concern on her face.

'Are you … cramping?' she asked.

Through the discomfort, Violetta opened her eyes and fought for control. She smiled and waved it off. 'No, no, it's not that. I'd know if it was that, honey. Trust me. I think it's just digestive issues.'

Addison nodded and returned to her food. Brandon hadn't joined the conversation, but his eyes sharpened with clarity.

But he took it no further, and Violetta recovered enough to slip back into a jovial mood.

The tension now dissipated, Alexis scanned the mess hall and spotted a man hovering in one of the exit doorways, staring back at her with unrestrained curiosity. He was in his late thirties, Caucasian, with thick brown hair cut short and a neatly trimmed beard. His frame was thin and tall. His shoulders were stooped like he was self-conscious of his height, and his eyes were intense. They didn't blink once as they watched her.

She figured he was Dane Riordan.

She mouthed, *'Can we talk?'*

Above the heads of a sea of devotees, he nodded once.

She got up.

Violetta said, 'Where are you going?'

She said, 'I'll be back.'

She tried to minimise the attention she drew as she weaved between the long benches and tables, but it was impossible. She was brand new in the commune, and stunning to look at. Half the male eyes in the room were fixed to her backside as she moved to one wall and went around the perimeter of the hall. She kept her eyes fixed straight ahead, refusing to return any long gazes.

The unwanted attention made her think about what Maeve wanted with her and Violetta.

The cult leader was probably frothing at the mouth thinking about what she could use them for.

Any man would listen to them.

Any man would serve them on the off chance they returned the affection.

They could recruit hundreds for Mother Libertas.

Maybe thousands.

Dane could see it too.

She approached him and stared up at him in the doorway. 'Hey.'

'Hi,' he said.

His voice was quiet and reserved. He was more introverted than his wife. It seemed Maeve was the performer and he was the director, but Alexis knew Maeve was too smart to simply fulfil the role of the air-headed actress getting fed lines. Maeve probably wrote most of them herself.

Dane said, 'Everyone's staring at you. Should we talk outside?'

'They're not staring at you?' Alexis said, not taking her eyes off him.

'No,' he said. 'They're not.'

She let him lead her out through the corridors that framed the perimeter of the mess hall, and they stepped outside into a crisp cold night. The blanket of stars overhead was mind-boggling in its intensity. Weak exterior lights cast a dim glow around the mess hall and the church, but the bunkhouses were shrouded in darkness.

Alexis put her hands in her pockets and exhaled a cloud of breath. 'I'm Alexis. Pleased to meet you.'

'Dane. Likewise.'

'My friend and I are interested in staying here permanently. That's if you think we're a good fit, of course.'

He said, 'So I've heard. My wife says you've got great potential.'

'We do?' Alexis said, batting her eyelashes.

Dane said, 'I know what you're doing.'

40

She didn't outwardly react. 'Do you?'

For the first time he smirked, and it was like his face opened up. He crawled out of his shell, if only for a moment. 'You get what you want from men.'

She said, 'Sometimes.'

'Tell me about the last time you didn't get what you wanted.'

She let the silence unfold. 'Well, I'm not exactly important, if that's what you're asking. I'm broke and lost. Seems like you think I'm some sort of manipulative mastermind when I can't even figure out what I want in life.'

'That's by your own choice. Now you've made the choice to be here. Now you can start getting what you want.'

She said, 'Will you help me with that?'

The smirk was still plastered on his face. 'You trying a hostile takeover on Maeve? Out with the old girl, in with the new?'

She said, 'You're getting the wrong idea from this. I'm just a—'

'A simple wanderer,' Dane finished. 'I know. Maeve

heard it, but she didn't believe it either. We think you have potential. You and your friend, but moreso you.'

'Potential for what?'

'That'll come in due course,' he said. 'Right now it's our intention to make this as pleasant as possible for you. So if there's anything you need, anything at all, come see us. If your room isn't good enough, or you're lacking in any supplies, tell us.'

You could do it now, Alexis thought.

Dane's guard was down, and she could take his back and lock in a rear naked choke before he understood what was happening. She could choke him out right here in the dirt, go up to the farmhouse and get the jump on Maeve before she could arm herself.

But if at any point in that long sequence she made a single mistake, someone would raise the alarm and two hundred fanatical disciples would descend on her and Violetta.

So instead of killing him she said, 'There's one thing.'

He raised an eyebrow.

She said, 'A suggestion. You might want to look into it. Unless I'm speaking out of turn. If you don't want my advice, I understand.'

'Why wouldn't I want your advice?'

'Because I'm just a—'

'I thought we dispensed with that,' he said.

He was being careful with his words, and so was she. She figured she'd put out the first proper feeler. It might win his trust, or it might make her a prime target for suspicion.

But it was a gamble she figured she needed to take.

She said, 'Okay. If you're willing to dispense with it, I am too. I sort of understand what you're doing here. Or, at least, I think I do. I want to help you spread the cause, but I'm not overly concerned about "the cause" itself. Does that make sense?'

After a long, painful silence, Dane said, 'You say that in front of any of the followers and they'll execute you for heresy.'

She doubled down. 'Then it's a good thing none of them are around to hear it.'

He put his hands behind his back and stared at her, trying to squeeze the weakness out of her. She didn't give an inch. She stared right back at him.

He said, 'Yes. That is a good thing.'

Inwardly, the tensed coil relaxed again.

He said, 'What's your advice?'

'I met two guys at a bar a couple of nights ago,' she said. 'I think they might be of use to you.'

'How so?'

But his eyes were already alight.

You already know about them, Alexis thought. *And their exploits in Gillette.*

She said, 'They were loose cannons. But I think they'd be perfect for your operation, if you can convince them. I don't think they're the sharpest tools in the shed, so they should cave pretty easily to Maeve's persuasions. They're ex-military, and they were running their mouths off about how they'd just roughed up half the town's criminal population. I don't think they like mainstream society all that much. They don't mesh with it. If they were telling the truth about their exploits, and you brought them in, they could make you practically immune to dissidents. And they'd bring the security of this commune to another level.'

He soaked in her every word, pensively quiet.

She continued. 'I don't know much about them. One was white and the other was black. They were both massive, like two hundred pounds of muscle each. I got the vibe they were telling the truth about what they've done, what they're doing, what they want. I think they'd be a perfect fit.'

He didn't say a word.

She kept going. 'I'm going to be blunt here, and I hope you forgive me. You're going to need a militia to take this thing to the next level. Like your own private paramilitary force. I think those guys are the perfect place to start. Just an idea. If you think I'm being too forward, well ... I guess now I have a vested interest in the growth of this community. If we're on the same page...'

He scratched the stubble along the base of his jaw.

Instead of responding, he turned and surveyed the settlement. Looked out at the buildings, at the darkness beyond them, then turned his gaze back to Alexis.

He said, 'From what I gather, you're implying this whole commune — and the beliefs it was founded on — are nothing but a sham, a parlour trick.'

Alexis said, 'Interpret what I said however you wish. And respond to it however you wish. I'm at your mercy.'

He liked that.

After years of what could only have been an impossible relationship with a literal psychopath, he liked having a beautiful woman subservient to him.

He said, 'Anything else you can tell me about these men? For example, the true reason you want them here.'

She cocked her head.

He said, 'Two big strong tough guys? Potential partners for you and your friend, maybe?'

Alexis scoffed and shook her head. 'They're empty-headed.'

'Then why would I want them here?'

'Let me clarify,' Alexis said. 'Their brains are empty in

the areas that would make them optimal romantic partners for me and my friend. But in the areas that would make them ruthless killers for you and your wife ... those parts are full to the brim.'

'You took all this from a single conversation?'

'I'm perceptive,' Alexis said. 'Just like how I've not even been here a day, but I've already made more progress with you than any of those morons in that shed.'

Dane could have killed her for that, and faced no consequences. This commune existed outside the realm of the law, a hidden fortress of ardent worshippers, and he could bury her for seeing the cult for what it really was.

But he didn't.

He just nodded, turned and walked away.

'Enjoy your evening,' he called over his shoulder.

He vanished up the trail to the farmhouse.

41

In Maeve's office, Dane said, 'What do you think?'

Maeve sat back in her chair, mulling it over. 'I want your opinion before I make mine.'

'We could use them.'

'We already have Elias.'

'Elias is one man. He's done good work, but I doubt his methods would work out in the real world.'

She raised an eyebrow. 'You doubt his abilities?'

Dane thought, *He's full of shit in the same way we're full of shit. How don't you see it?*

To voice his concerns would be sacrosanct, though, so he said, 'No matter how talented he is, Elias can't be in two places at once. That's my point.'

She nodded, pensive. 'Still no word from Wyatt?'

'None. You know why.'

'Do I?'

'He killed Fitch and skipped town.'

'You said that,' Maeve said. 'But no matter how many times I go over it in my head, I can't see him doing that.'

'You can't?' Dane said. 'He was so dependent on Bodhi

he would have exchanged his family for a single hit. You think Fitch was incapable of fucking things up? It was probably something as stupid as not showing up on time. Wyatt would have been getting withdrawals, and he just snapped. Killed the junkie, took his stash of Bodhi, and ran.'

Maeve said, 'He wouldn't *do* that.'

'Why not?'

'Because then his supply is finite. You said he'd exchange his family for a hit, but he'd also exchange his pride. He'd get on his knees and beg Fitch if it meant that junkie rat kept sending him vials of the stuff.'

'Well, now they're both AWOL,' Dane said. 'You tell me what to do.'

Maeve kept thinking.

Behind her, the grandfather clock ticked.

'You're right,' she finally said. 'We need extra muscle. I don't see what they'll do here that Elias can't, but out there … they'll be additional manpower. And we're expanding, so that's what we need.'

Dane nodded. 'Want me to head into town tomorrow?'

She shook her head. 'No. I'll go tonight. There's shit to do tomorrow.'

'Tonight?' Dane said. 'How will you find them?'

Maeve smiled. 'I already know where they are, baby.'

'That's news to me.'

'I don't tell you every scrap of information I hear.'

You should, Dane thought. *That's my job. I'm the director. You're the preacher.*

He knew Maeve was starting to shirk her role, though.

It unsettled him to his core. *What happens when I become unnecessary?* he thought. His every waking moment had to be spent ensuring he knew too much to be replaceable.

Husband or not.

He said, 'What do you know about them?'

'Between them they put eight people in the Campbell County Memorial Hospital. A few of the bikers that sling meth, and their associates. No matter how hard I press, I can't find a reason why they did that. I think they're angry, disillusioned, lashing out at the world the only way they know how. I think that anger can be channelled into crushing our opposition. Don't you?'

Dane said, 'That means they're unpredictable. That's never good.'

Maeve rolled her eyes. 'No one stays here and remains unpredictable. That's why we do what we do, isn't it?'

Dane shrugged.

Maeve said, 'Do you disagree?'

'No,' Dane said hastily. 'It's just ... what if your methods don't work on them?'

Her eyes burned as she sat forward and stared at him. 'My methods *always* work. You know that better than anyone.'

Unfortunately, he did.

He nodded, turned on his heel, and made to leave. He could tell she wanted him out.

'Don't wait up,' she said to his back. 'I might not be back until the early morning.'

'Do you need someone to drive you—?'

'No,' she said. 'I'll do it myself. And besides, you and Elias have that matter to attend to, remember?'

Oh, yes, Dane thought. *Of course.*

He nodded his understanding, then walked out and went upstairs to the bedroom, uncertainty twisting his stomach.

42

Elias entered the bunkhouse like a ghost.

To those who saw him moving through the lowlight, his presence would invoke mortal fear. He didn't mind that at all. Deeply introverted, he neither wanted nor cared for an abundance of friends. The Riordans were enough, and if the rest of the commune considered him a nightmarish spectre, then so be it.

There was something about it he almost enjoyed.

He moved through the narrow corridor, opened the right door, and found the right bunk.

He lowered a hand softly onto the shoulder of the sleeping form curled up on the mattress.

The disciple's name was Hudson, and he opened his eyes in the near-darkness.

Elias whispered, 'Come with me, son.'

Hudson was trembling before he stood up. But he complied, because he didn't know what else to do. It was an age-old dilemma. If he panicked and ran, that'd seal his fate one way or the other. It'd make things black and white. If he behaved and begged for mercy, it offered the chance of redemption.

So he followed Elias meekly as they went outside and walked away from the handful of exterior lights that stayed on all night. The darkness closed in and the yellow light receded, but Elias didn't take the man all the way out into the black. He hovered at the edge of the commune, out of earshot of the rest of the sleeping disciples.

Dane Riordan came out of the shadows.

In many ways, he and Elias were alike. Tall, thin, wiry with corded muscle. If they were professional fighters, their reach and length would be a sizeable advantage. Not an ounce of their weight was wasted — both were devoid of fat. But Dane wasn't a fighter. He left that messy realm to seasoned practitioners. His advantage was his mind.

They put a hand each on Hudson's shoulders and pushed him to his knees. Now they could see the fear on his face. Up close, he was an ugly sight to behold. Long blonde hair the colour and texture of straw, a pockmarked sallow face, and kind eyes that didn't belong in this world. He'd taken Maeve's words at face value and joined Mother Libertas out of the goodness of his heart.

It hadn't taken Hudson long to see what the movement really was.

Dane said, 'You betrayed us, Hudson.'

Hudson shook his head, those kind eyes riddled with terror. 'No, sir. I would never.'

'Are you sticking with that argument?'

'I don't know what you mean.'

'I'll give you one opportunity to tell the truth,' Dane said. 'Only one.'

'I don't know what you're accusing me of,' Hudson said, but the fear in his eyes said otherwise. 'I swear, sir.'

'You told Brandon you were going to steal one of the cars, make your way back to civilisation. I believe the words were, "Everyone's going to know the sick shit they get up to out here."'

Hudson shook his head emphatically. 'I never said that.'

Dane said, 'Brandon, step forward please.'

The young disciple had been waiting in the darkness, just out of range of their mutual field of view. Now his silhouette materialised as he took a few steps forward. Hudson twisted on his knees, saw the new arrival, and his face fell.

He said, 'Okay, okay, okay. I take it back. I said it. Fuck, I'm sorry.'

'Too late,' Dane said. 'You had your opportunity and you lost it. That's on you.'

'No,' Hudson said, his face twisting. 'Please.'

His shoulders rounded and he sunk deeper into himself, staring at the dry ground beneath him.

Dane said, 'Brandon, did Hudson say those words?'

Quietly, Brandon said, 'Yes.'

'Thank you,' Dane said. 'Go back to bed.'

Brandon bowed his head and trudged back to the commune, fully aware of what he'd just done.

Dane stopped him as he passed by, lifted his chin with one hand — Maeve's specialty — and turned Brandon's head to face him.

Dane said, 'Open your mouth.'

Brandon complied.

Dane came up with a vial of Bodhi in his other hand and poured its contents onto Brandon's tongue.

He said, 'Enjoy.'

Brandon shivered with delight and crept away, not yet feeling the effects of the drugs but warmed by marvellous anticipation. It would be the best night of his life, just as every night with Bodhi became. Each consecutive experience seemed to trump the last. It was glorious.

When Brandon was gone, lost to bliss and suppressed memories, Dane said, 'I can't let you go, Hudson.'

Hudson said, 'I'll do anything for you. I'll become your most loyal subject. I'll devote my entire life to this place. Please. Don't do this, sir. I'm ... I'm all messed up inside. I don't know what I'm saying half the time.'

Dane said, 'You'll pretend you're devoted, to curry my approval. And then the first chance you get you'll run, because now you know what we're capable of.'

'No,' Hudson said, but his eyes were squeezed shut as he shook his head. He couldn't bear to look up at Dane. 'No, no. Please, sir.'

Dane nodded to Elias.

Elias had been harnessing his *ki* the whole time, and now he lashed out with a strike that used the side of his hand in a chopping motion. He smashed the hand into Hudson's throat, crushing his windpipe and carotid artery. The subject of the blow always lost consciousness immediately.

This time, though, he botched it. He hadn't mastered his *ki* tonight — something had thrown him off.

Hudson stayed conscious and fell back spluttering.

It took him two minutes to die.

When it was finally over, Elias looked over at Dane. 'Sorry.'

For the first time, he saw unrestrained disgust on Dane's face.

Dane lifted a new vial of Bodhi to his own lips, drank half, and closed his eyes. When he opened them again, he'd composed himself.

He said, 'It's fine. This never happened. Take care of the body. I'll see you in the morning.'

Elias had never felt so uncomfortable.

Dane Riordan was a vicious psychopath, devoid of anything resembling empathy. So what the hell had Elias just seen on the man's face?

It made *him* feel guilty, which couldn't be right, because every action undertaken in the name of Mother Libertas was divine and just. This was the perfect reality, where every choice made was the correct one, so why did Dane look like he regretted what just happened?

Dane walked away.

Elias dragged Hudson's body out into the plains.

43

At midnight, someone knocked at the door.

Slater sat bolt upright in bed, his hand already wrapped around the hilt of the Glock 43 on the bedside table. He looked across the room and saw King's silhouette grabbing the Mossberg shotgun off the base of his bed.

Still silent, Slater listened.

No footsteps. No rustling. A sixth sense is always flawed by nature, but he got the sense there was only one person on the other side of the door. Still, it wasn't enough to rely on intuition, so he padded across the room and pressed his eye to the peephole for less than half a second.

The best way to get the jump on someone inside a hotel room is to press a barrel to the peephole, wait until you hear them looking through it, and pull the trigger.

He wasn't about to be a statistic.

But all he caught was the briefest glimpse of an unarmed woman in a peach-coloured farm dress.

It rattled him more than if it had been an armed hostile.

He gestured to King, who flipped the bedside lamp on. In the timid glow, Slater mouthed, *'It's her. She's unarmed.'*

He watched King mask a shiver and lower the Mossberg to the other side of the bed. They were both fully dressed, anticipating an ambush by one of the many parties they'd pissed off in Gillette, so Slater opened the door right away.

In character, he said, 'Do you know what the fucking time is? Who are you?'

Maeve was like a robot wearing human skin. She smiled through the insult, not fazed in the slightest. 'That's not how you should talk to a potential employer.'

'What?'

'I have a job offer for you,' she said. 'It's incredibly lucrative. I suggest you hear me out. If not, I'll walk away and you'll spend the rest of your life wondering what might have been. Your call.'

She was good.

He pretended to think about it, then said, 'What's the offer?'

'You expect me to deliver it to you out here?'

'That'd be preferable,' he said. 'I need my beauty sleep.'

'No you don't, dear,' she said. 'You're a specimen. Those eyes...'

She winked at him.

She was *good*.

He lowered his guard and stepped aside. 'Come on in, then.'

He opened the door wide and she sauntered through, where King sat on the bed he'd already made. He looked up, his hair tousled and shaped by the pillow. 'What is this?'

She said, 'I have a job offer for—'

'I have ears. You think I didn't hear that?'

She smirked. 'You two are a sight to behold, aren't you? Look at you both.'

King didn't react. It was the first time he'd laid eyes on Maeve Riordan, and he understood the appeal. She had flawless features for a woman in her late thirties, and under the dress her curves were voluptuous. It no doubt added to the mythical temptation, and would help convince her followers she was Gaia reincarnated.

You couldn't sway people effortlessly unless you were beautiful.

Something she clearly understood, judging by how her face lit up when she looked at them.

Slater said, 'Answers, please.'

She said, 'This job, if it's right for you, will make you richer than you can ever believe. Think of it as paramilitary work for a wealthy benefactor.'

'Paramilitary?' Slater said, eyebrows arched. 'You run a militia, do you? You look like you run a stable.'

The tightrope he had to walk was thin. If he was too eager, Maeve would see right through it, and back at the commune Alexis and Violetta would be in dire jeopardy. But if he was too standoffish and ended up insulting this woman who thought she could bend every man, woman and child to serve her ... well, she might become enraged.

She maintained her composure. 'One of us has to get to the chase, don't we? Otherwise we'll be going around in circles all night, teasing each other.' She glanced at King. 'Actually, I might like that...'

She was doing everything right. If they were testosterone-fuelled ex-soldiers like she thought they were, they'd bite at her flirtations.

So King did.

He pushed his hair off his forehead with one hand and

said, 'Maybe we should get that out of the way first, then. What were your words? *"You'll spend the rest of your life wondering what might have been."*'

She thought she had him in the palm of her hand. She smiled. 'Not just yet, darling.'

She turned back to Slater. 'So?'

He said, 'Go ahead. We're all ears.'

She said, 'Do you hate your country?'

Silence.

44

Slater said, 'Interesting way to start.'

'You haven't answered the question.'

'There's no easy answer.'

'Are you angry about what they made you do overseas?'

Slater hesitated. Then said, 'Maybe. How'd you know we were overseas?'

'You stirred up your fair share of trouble in town,' Maeve said. 'One of you mentioned that you served. Gossip made its way to my ears. I consider myself somewhat switched on, so I put two and two together. I see a pair of disgruntled veterans furious about the state of the world, taking it out on the small-time criminals here in Gillette. Am I far off the mark?'

'"Disgruntled" could be construed as an insult,' King said.

She scoffed. 'Spare me the sob story. You want to know what I know?'

'What's that?' Slater said.

She said, 'I know what you two are *truly* capable of. Given the right motivation, I know what you could accomplish. And all it'll take is stepping away from this ridiculous illusion we call civilisation.'

She left it there, allowing their imaginations to run wild in the ensuing quiet.

King said, 'Sounds extreme. What if we're not interested?'

She shrugged. 'Not my problem. I'm simply here to show you a path. It's your choice to walk down it or not. And I can see, plain as day, that you are men of extremes. So this offer is perfect for you.'

She's good, Slater thought again.

He said, 'What's the path? What's the offer?'

'I lead a movement in Thunder Basin, away from society. It's grown faster than I ever could have imagined, and we're onto something. We've stumbled upon solutions to humanity's problems, and we're gaining new members faster than we can handle. That comes with a smorgasbord of security issues. The powers that be are going to have a vested interest in oppressing us, but I'm ready to tell them to stick their concerns where the sun don't shine. To do that I need muscle. I need men that know their way around confrontation.'

'A "movement"?' King said.

'I'm not here to sell you on our beliefs,' Maeve said. 'I respect you both, so I won't pitch it to you right away. I'm simply here to offer you jobs, independent of the movement. But at the same time I know eventually you'll see how beautiful our message is. One step at a time, my dear.'

Slater said, 'What sort of work will it involve? I don't want to get there and find out you're going up against the police and the military.'

'Do you think I'm stupid?'

'I don't know. We've only just met.'

She said, 'We wouldn't last a day if we were that overt. No — we are subtle. Exposing ourselves to the masses right now wouldn't be smart. But there's always risks, doing what we do. I'm planning in advance, expecting more resistance in future. There's already some trouble brewing here. Two of my contacts have gone radio silent on me — I suspect one of them has fled town. I can't reveal more until I know I have your loyalty, but just know you'll never be asked to do anything outside the range of your abilities.'

'How do you know the range of our abilities?'

'I made an assumption based on how many people you put in the hospital.'

Slater said, 'The pay?'

Maeve said, 'We'll get to that.'

'That's what everyone says before revealing it's dog shit.'

'First I need an expression of interest. Tell me you're interested, and you stand to make more money and do more fulfilling work than anything you've seen in your lives. That I *guarantee*.'

King said, 'I'm interested.'

They looked at Slater.

He nodded slowly.

She said, 'We live in a commune in Thunder Basin. The facilities are excellent. Will you come out and see them? We can discuss all the details out there.'

Slater looked hesitant.

Maeve lowered her voice and said, 'Want to know something else? Your friends are with us.'

King said, 'We don't have friends.'

'Maybe not yet,' Maeve said. 'But wouldn't you like to get to know those two beautiful girls from the bar better? Alexis and Violetta, I believe it was…'

She trailed off, flashing a sly look.

Neither of them spoke, but they both made it appear they were tantalised.

Maeve put the nail in the coffin. 'To them, you'll be gods. If you take my offer, you'll have power over all of my followers. You'll be my security team. They worship me, so they'll worship you. What sorts of things could you get up to with the women who love me? You can have them all. Whoever you want, however you want.'

Silence.

King said, 'I'm in,' knowing there was a special place in hell for Maeve Riordan.

45

In the back of her pickup truck, King and Slater sat quiet and stoic.

At close to one in the morning, after finalising specifics, Maeve drove them into the darkness. It was absolute, all-encompassing — the grasslands swallowed them whole. They had their hands in their laps and their duffel bags between their legs like they were off to military boot camp.

Maeve had already asked them how many nights they'd booked at the Arbuckle Lodge, and they'd told her it didn't matter. When they were in, they were all the way in, and they had no attachment to anything other than their own destinies, so they'd be coming with her now instead of waiting out their stay in Gillette.

She liked that.

Now, Maeve said, 'I need to make a few things clear.'

Slater said, 'Sure.'

'You're not hired just yet, obviously. We wanted to snatch you up before anyone else could get to you, so we made our move prematurely, but that's okay. We're all professionals here. If you don't like our setup, or we don't like your attitude, we go our separate ways. No harm done.'

King said, 'What's going to be surprising about your setup? I thought you already covered everything.'

Maeve shook her head, the back of her skull wrapped in shadow as she stared out the windshield into nothingness. 'I haven't even scratched the surface.'

Slater knew, between himself and King, he was the bad cop. So he sat forward and said, 'What exactly is going on here?'

Maeve said, 'The movement I run ... no matter how hard I try, I can't explain what it is. You're just going to have to see for yourself.'

Slater said, 'You think we're suckers?'

King said, 'Will...' like he was scolding a younger brother.

Fulfilling the role of "good cop."

Maeve said, 'It's quite alright, Jason. Both of you relax. You're going to stay with us for a few days as we get to know each other. Right now we hardly know a thing about each other. How can we know if we'll work well together if we don't click?'

King said, 'That sounds fine.'

Slater shook his head in the darkness. 'Are we getting paid for this time?'

Maeve looked over her shoulder, her face stern. 'If you don't like it, Will, I'm happy to take you back to your lodge. But if at any time you're unclear about the dynamic, then let me make it clear right now. This is *my* setup. *My* commune. You are welcome guests, but until I fully trust you, that's all you'll be. Everything I said in the hotel room still stands, but you wouldn't have come with me if I simply asked you to visit. If everything goes well, you'll have jobs — and lucrative ones at that — but that's dependent on whether or not we click.'

King said, 'We'll click.'

Slater said, 'Maybe.'

A long period of quiet elapsed. Slater stared out the window, pretending to think it over. There wasn't much to look at. Just the gaping chasm of the frontier at night.

Slater said, 'I'm fine with it. You keep saying "we" though. Who runs the commune with you?'

'My husband,' Maeve said. 'Dane. He'll want to talk to you tomorrow.'

King said, 'We'd be happy to.'

Maeve said, 'Not you. Just Will.'

King didn't respond.

Maeve said, 'Is that going to be a problem?'

Slater said, 'Why me?'

'Dane is our head of security,' Maeve said. 'He's very particular about who we recruit. He'll interview you one by one. And you're first, Will, because something tells me you'll have more questions than your friend.'

Slater said, 'Something tells you right.'

King said, 'Who are we replacing?'

Maeve said, 'What?'

'I assume you already have some sort of security measures in place. Who are they?'

Maeve said, '"They" are Elias.'

Slater said, 'One man?'

'He's talented in specific areas,' Maeve said. 'I won't go into detail. Don't want you running your mouth around town if you decide to leave.'

No one answered.

Slater understood what she'd done. By hinting at illegalities, she'd put both King and Slater at risk. Even though she hadn't revealed anything concrete, she'd said too much. Now they'd better accept her offer, or they wouldn't be allowed back into society with what they already knew about Mother Libertas.

It was already all or nothing.

They either devoted their lives to the cult or were silenced forever.

The truck bounced on a pothole as it surged further into the grasslands.

46

King saw the cluster of buildings first as the soft lighting broke up the darkness.

There were only a couple of exterior lights switched on, but it was enough to make the commune look like a homing beacon, especially surrounded by such emptiness.

Maeve rounded the outskirts so as not to wake everyone in the bunkhouses — at least, that's what King assumed they were — and drove up the incline to where the farmhouse lay dormant. No lights blazed inside the two-storey house, and the porch lights were off too. The headlights from Maeve's pickup lit up the wraparound porch with stark white lighting.

Exposing someone sitting on an outdoor rocking chair.

He was long and spindly, and he rose off the chair as soon as the light hit him.

Maeve said, 'That's Dane. I don't know what he's doing out of bed, though.'

They all got out of the pickup as Maeve killed the engine. The headlights took another few seconds to die, but when they did they plunged everything into total darkness. Dane's silhouette had been watching them silently, and now it disappeared.

King stood fixed to the spot, thoroughly unnerved.

Maeve called through the night, 'Turn a light on, would you?'

The porch creaked as Dane moved across it. Slater was on the other side of the vehicle, and King suppressed a shiver, shaking the feeling of being starkly alone. He regretted leaving the Mossberg and the Glocks back in Gillette. Maeve had forced them to dump their weapons and then frisked them both carefully before letting them into her truck. They'd gone along with it. He was coming to realise she had a way with words, a certain inflection of tone that made you grateful she was even paying you attention.

He'd gone into this knowing exactly who she was in her core, and still he had to fight not to be put under her spell.

There was a reason Mother Libertas was growing so fast.

The porch light came on, and revealed Dane Riordan in better lighting. He was far taller than his wife, his shoulders slightly stooped from the shame of being the centre of attention due to his height. But he was all thin muscle and bones, and probably weighed no more than a hundred and seventy pounds.

He said, 'Jason and Will, is it?'

Looking up from below the porch, they both nodded.

Dane descended the porch steps and extended a hand. 'Dane. Pleasure.'

They shook his hand one by one.

Maeve drew up alongside him, completing the subtle two-on-two face-off.

Dane said, 'Obviously there's a lot that's still up in the air. I'm sure you can both understand.'

King said, 'Same goes for us. But we're interested. Whether this works out or not, I think we've got more in common than you think.'

'Is that right?'

King nodded.

Dane looked at him for a beat, then said, 'You might be right. Can I speak my mind?'

'Please,' King said.

'I'm not the type to make small talk and skirt around the point. Nor is my wife here. If you two have a problem with operating outside the parameters of the law, I suggest you enjoy our hospitality tonight then make your way back to Gillette tomorrow. If you stay, you'll be asked to do things that will make you uncomfortable. Is that going to be a problem?'

King said, 'No problem. We're both war criminals if you judge what we've done within the "parameters of the law." Is *that* going to be a problem?'

Dane smiled. 'No. It certainly won't.'

He turned to Slater. 'You don't talk much.'

Slater said, 'You're right.'

'Dinner,' Dane said. 'Tomorrow evening. You and I.'

Slater glanced at Maeve, who smiled knowingly. Her eyes said, *See? I know my husband.*

Slater said, 'Sure. You're buying.'

Dane laughed.

He turned to Maeve and said, 'I like them.'

Still facing them, Maeve said, 'I'm afraid we need sleep. But Elias will show you to your room.'

'Elias?' Slater said. 'The guy we're replacing?'

'No,' a voice said behind them.

47

They turned.

Elias was blonde-haired, blue-eyed, fair-skinned. He was tall and wiry like Dane Riordan, but his poise was more athletic, more graceful, less laboured. His posture was impeccable underneath the simple garments he wore. He was a baby compared to King and Slater, somewhere in his mid-twenties, but his eyes were intensely confident.

Slater could see through them, though.

He saw false confidence. A kid who'd never been in a street fight. Slater guessed, just from the posture, that Elias was trained in some Eastern martial art. More about looking good and flowing smoothly, less about being able to destroy someone's face with a barrage of strikes.

You never know...

Elias said, 'You'll be working alongside me. Not replacing me.'

Slater squared up to him, brash and unashamed. 'And how does that make you feel, kid?'

Maeve darted in behind him and seized his wrist in an iron grip.

Slater turned.

Maeve said, 'You don't talk like that to him. You don't talk like that to any of us. Is that the example you want to set before we've hired you?'

'No,' Slater said. 'I'm sorry. He just snuck up on me, is all.'

His tone smug, Elias said, 'Scared you? Sorry, friend.'

His wrist still in Maeve's grasp, Slater said, 'I'm a little jumpy. Quick to defend myself. Two tours will do that to you, make you check every corner. I'm sure you can relate, Elias.'

Elias said nothing, brushing off the thinly veiled insult to his lack of worldly experience.

Elias said, 'Do you practice Wing Chun?'

Slater paused at the question's strangeness. 'Is that a requirement? Being a *ninja?*'

Elias pursed his lips, looking Slater up and down. 'It would help. How will you defend us from threats?'

'With my combat training,' Slater said. 'There are other martial arts.'

'They're inferior.'

Slater didn't answer. What he wanted to say was '*There are other martial arts that actually work*' but he refrained. He'd antagonised the man enough for one night.

The air bristled with tension as Maeve said, 'You two have made friends already. Jason, stay back for a moment, please. Elias, show Will to his bunkhouse. And leave each other alone. I can't stand this alpha male dynamic.'

Elias nodded respectfully. No matter his opinion, Maeve's word was clearly law.

He folded his arms behind his back again and glided down the trail, expecting Slater to follow.

Slater looked at King. 'You good?'

Maeve responded. 'He's good.'

There wasn't much Slater could do.

He nodded, bid them goodnight, and followed Elias down the trail.

48

Maeve sat King down in one of the rattan chairs in the sitting room and shooed her husband away.

Dane melted into the background and disappeared through a doorway, and then it was just the two of them, alone.

She said, 'Tea?'

King said, 'I'm okay, thank you.'

'You must be tired,' she said, 'so I'll keep this brief. I hope you don't mind me sending your friend away. I think he needs rest. I wanted to speak freely without hearing retorts to my every word.'

'He's cold until you get to know him,' King said. 'Then he's the loyalest person you'll ever meet. He'll do great things for your ... movement.'

She hesitated. 'Why did you pause?'

'I was thinking of the right word.'

She smiled, and he couldn't detect any hint that it was a performance. She was damn good at her job. 'Were you going to say "cult"?'

He shook his head.

She said, 'It's okay. I won't bite. You can be honest with me.'

He said, 'I don't know what to call it. But that's not the word I would have chosen.'

'It may seem like a cult from the outside,' Maeve admitted. 'I wouldn't judge you if that's what you thought. It's a valid concern. But you only found out about this world hours ago. I want you to know that the principles and philosophies I've discovered are life-changing. With time, I'm sure you will take advantage of them. And ... do you mind if I speak freely?'

'Please.'

'You have incredible potential. More than your friend. Working in harmony with Mother Libertas and its principles ... there's no telling how far you'll go. I can't imagine the man you'll be a year from now. All it requires is your commitment.'

If King hadn't gained control over his ego long ago, he might have actually bought it.

She made you feel special, like you were the centre of the universe and everything revolved around you.

It was seductive.

Intoxicating.

For the first time he noticed an oak humidor on the table. She reached out and lifted the lid, revealing ten Cuban cigars lined neatly within. The box had already been there, so she'd known from the moment she left Thunder Basin she'd be returning with King and Slater. That took genuine confidence.

Maeve said, 'Care to indulge?'

'It's late,' King said.

'That wasn't a no.'

He settled back in the armchair and smirked. 'You're right. It wasn't. Will you be joining me?'

She looked up into his eyes. 'You've got to have a little fun in this life.'

She handed him one of the massive cigars. 'This is from Hoyo de Monterrey. It's a "Le Hoyo de Río Seco." The thickest cigar to come out of Cuba in regular production. They cost a pretty penny.'

He said, 'Is this my first week's payment?'

'No, my dear. That'll come in time.'

She used an Alfred Dunhill cigar cutter — lavishly expensive in its own right, engineered to perfection — to snip the end off her own Cuban, then King's. Then she lit her end with a metallic double torch lighter and passed it over to King. He touched the flame to the end of his own cigar and the tobacco flared orange. He drew the initial smoke into his mouth.

It was incredible.

They smoked slowly, relishing the process, and King realised it was a genius manoeuvre on Maeve's behalf. A cigar of this size would take over an hour to finish, and the nicotine buzz would build as time passed, stripping him of his inhibitions.

She was adept at using substances to get what she wanted out of people.

As the alluring scent of expensive cigar smoke circled the sitting room, she said, 'I expect you want to know what this place is all about.'

He said, 'If it's good money, I don't care.'

'That's my point,' she said. 'You should care. Close your eyes.'

He complied.

Now that his world was dark the nicotine had a greater

effect. His body tingled, and he figured this was a far lesser version of what she usually did with Bodhi.

Her voice was all-encompassing now. Closing his eyes heightened his other senses. He took another draw on the Cuban as she started to speak.

'Breathe in through your nose and out through your mouth.'

He did.

She said, 'Slower.'

He went slower.

She said, 'Feel your heart rate going down. Feel the oxygen coming in, the carbon dioxide going out. In with peace. Out with unease. In with stillness. Out with stress.'

Even though he knew what she was doing, it still had an effect on him.

He was tranquil before he knew it.

Then she started to speak.

'Mother Earth is alive, Jason,' she said. 'Do you feel it beneath you? Always in motion. You can't fathom its power, but it's there, and it's waiting for someone to harness it. You may not believe me yet, but bear with me. I want to try a visualisation exercise. I want you to imagine the power of the earth, of Mother, of Gaia, moving through you. Coming up through the floor, starting with your toes. Feel them tingle. Feel the power work its way to your calves, your thighs ... your hips, your stomach ... your chest, your arms ... your head.'

King sure felt something.

Now he got it.

She combined powerful substances with meditation and her own rhetoric to put her followers in a heightened state. Then she fed them what they wanted to hear, building their confidence, their mood, their devotion.

After enough sessions, they'd do whatever she wanted.

She was a drug.

Mother Libertas was an addiction.

And he couldn't deny it felt good.

She kept talking in her own soothing way, relaxing him, coaxing him into a state of ecstasy. When she finally told him to open his eyes, the world flooded in. Colours were brighter for a beat. It took his eyes a moment to adjust.

He sat bolt upright in the armchair and decided to shiver for dramatic effect.

She said, 'Do you see what Mother Earth has to offer?'

He nodded, then drew on the cigar one final time and tamped it out in the ashtray on the table.

She said, 'You're going to do fantastic things for us, Jason. Your limitations are perceptions. Together we're going to liberate the world.'

He said, 'I can't fucking wait.'

'Tomorrow,' she said, raising her hands in admittance of the late hour. 'We'll speak tomorrow. Thank you for your time. Elias is out front, and he'll show you to your room.'

'Thank you,' he said. 'I mean it.'

She lowered her voice like she didn't want her husband to hear. 'I'm excited to get to know you better.'

She put a look on her face like she wanted to tear his clothes off right there.

He knew it was just her way of gaining his devotion, but the primal part of his brain believed it all the same.

He nodded to her, got up, and walked out.

Before he reached the front door, he took stock of his own mood. He was buzzed from the cigar, relaxed from the guided meditation, and had to admit her words were soothing. He was more in touch with his body, aware of every muscle, his movements smooth.

Vivid memories flashed in his mind. First, a naked woman suspended from a meat hook. Then a kid ripping the skin off his hand so he could get out of his restraints and commit suicide.

He met Elias on the front porch and the blond man led him wordlessly down to the commune.

49

Slater lay on the bottom bunk in a room that was barely larger than a supply closet.

The walls were damp in places, the floorboards chipped and faded, and the bunk frame creaked every time he shifted his weight.

He calmed himself. *We're in. Not long to go.*

All they had to do was assess the routines, find an opening, and execute the Riordans.

Deep down he knew it wouldn't be as simple as that. There had to be over a hundred people living here, religiously devoted to Maeve and Dane, and they wouldn't take an upheaval of their life lightly. There's a time and place for all-out war, and with this many potentially innocent lives in the mix, that time wasn't the present.

The door opened and Slater tensed up in anticipation of an attack.

King stepped in. He was calm as ice.

Slater said, 'How'd it go?'

King mouthed, '*Bugged,*' and swept a hand around the room.

Slater nodded knowingly.

King said, 'That was some crazy shit. They're onto something.'

'What do you mean?'

'Maeve told me about what they're doing here. Showed me a few of the practices. I ... can't even explain it. It was fucking wild. You're going to love it.'

'You reek of smoke.'

'We had Cubans.'

Slater grumbled like he was discontent at being left out.

King said, 'Start showing more appreciation and she might want to involve you.'

'We hardly know a thing about this place.'

'Now I know more than you do,' King said. 'Because I'm pleasant to be around. You should try it.'

Slater said, 'I'll give it a crack tomorrow.'

Their fake conversation completed for the benefit of any microphones that might be listening, King turned out the light and vaulted into the top bunk.

They lay there in silence, wanting to say so many things but not being able to.

It made the atmosphere crackle, and as a consequence it took them an eternity to fall asleep.

50

Alexis woke at dawn.

She listened, waiting to hear Violetta stir, but heard nothing. Eventually she peeled herself off the thin mattress and stood up, at eye level with Violetta's bunk.

Violetta opened her eyes and swept blond hair off her face. 'Hey.'

'Hey,' Alexis said. 'I'm taking a walk.'

Violetta opened her mouth to ask a question, then remembered the room was probably bugged and clamped it shut. She nodded quietly, and mouthed, '*Careful.*'

Alexis nodded back.

She stepped outside into the cool morning air. A fine layer of mist swept slowly away from the commune as the sun rose over the prairie. It was a scene straight from the Wild West. The community was already alive with people, most of them trending younger — mid-twenties or early thirties. Everyone had a place to be, something to do. The disciples operated as a well-oiled machine, an amalgamation of parts tasked with some divine manual labour job to keep Mother Libertas running smoothly. Supplies were carried between buildings, clothes were washed and hung up to dry, loose dirt was swept off pathways. Each of the followers moved with purpose, like their every movement mattered, which they probably thought it did.

With this level of coordination and synergy, Mother Libertas would never stop growing.

Alexis turned in a half-circle and saw Slater across the commune.

She froze.

He noticed her at the same time, and their eyes met with sharp understanding.

She didn't outwardly react, but relief flooded her.

They made it. They're here.

She realised she could go talk to him without ruining their cover. She'd been the one to recommend them to Dane, after all, and she'd told him she'd met King and Slater at a bar, so it made sense that they'd be familiar with each other.

She started for him.

Addison stepped into her path.

The young woman had materialised out of nowhere, as if she'd been waiting for an opportunity to catch Alexis alone. Her face was still shy, and Alexis could tell it made her uncomfortable to approach a stranger.

'Hi,' she said softly.

Alexis stopped in her tracks, because to do otherwise would have seemed suspicious to anyone watching. She took her eyes off Slater and trained them on Addison. 'Hi. Nice to see you again.'

'Could I...?'

Addison trailed off and looked over her shoulder. She was clearly paranoid of being overheard.

Alexis said, 'What is it?'

'Could I speak to you somewhere private?' Addison said. 'It won't take long.'

Alexis looked from her to Slater, who hadn't moved.

Addison said, 'Please.'

There was desperation in her tone.

Alexis ushered her round the back of the bunkhouse, to the perimeter of the commune. It made no sense for the building's exterior to be bugged, and the grasslands swept out endlessly, capable of snatching their words away.

Alexis put a hand on Addison's shoulder. The girl was trembling.

'What's going on?' Alexis said.

Addison looked left and right, then mustered her courage and said, 'I need to get out of here.'

51

King stepped outside into the morning light and found Slater standing motionless, staring into the distance.

The disciples flowed smoothly around the commune, attending to their tasks.

King walked up beside Slater and muttered, 'You good?'

Slater said, 'They're here.'

'Who?'

Slater hesitated. 'The girls from the bar.'

King looked around, assessing their surroundings. He lowered his voice. 'You think they're listening to everything?'

Slater turned and raised an eyebrow. He mouthed, '*Not worth the risk.*'

They looked away from each other like nothing had happened.

King felt it. The cold tendrils of paranoia, slowly enveloping his world. That's when it struck him — how hard it would be to break free from a cult. The lack of control, the uncertainty…

Not knowing who was listening, and when.

It was so much easier to obey.

King raised his voice to full volume and proclaimed, 'I'm going for a walk.'

Slater shrugged. 'Be my guest.'

Then it clicked.

King thought, *If they're listening, they'll stop me.*

Slater nodded when he realised.

King strolled through the commune, passing the church and the mess hall, heading in the general direction of the farmhouse.

He rounded a corner and Dane was there.

Waiting for me? King thought. *Or just a coincidence?*

'How did you sleep?' Dane asked, leaning against the side of an outbuilding. His hair was perfect and his eyes were sharp.

Like he'd been up all night.

Plotting.

Scheming.

King said, 'Like a baby. After two tours you can sleep anywhere.'

Dane shrugged off the insinuation that the living conditions were terrible.

Dane said, 'There's a congregation this afternoon. You can see how Maeve runs it.'

King said, 'Can't wait.'

'What are your plans this morning?'

King thought, *He knows.*

He decided to test the man by sticking to his guns.

'Thought I'd go for a stroll.'

Dane shook his head. 'You don't want to do that. There's nothing out there. You're better off staying here, meeting the disciples, getting to know them.'

'How'd you know I didn't mean a stroll around the commune?'

Dane quashed a wry smile and said, 'There's not much of it. I figured you wanted to walk in the prairie.'

'I do.'

'I wouldn't.'

'I'll be okay. It'll be good to clear my head.'

'Clear it from what?'

King hesitated, made up his mind, then pressed forward. 'Listen. I'm not here to be a follower. I'm looking for employment. If you have a problem with me doing things that the disciples aren't allowed to do, then *I'll* have a problem, too.'

Dane raised an eyebrow. 'Oh?'

His eyes were steel.

King had seen the worst of humanity. He could deal with a withering gaze. 'You heard me.'

Dane thought about escalating it. King could see it in his eyes. He was drunk on his own power, considering mustering reinforcements. If he called thirty followers over to prevent King from leaving, then King's only option would be to break free with brute force. Dane wanted to call King's bluff.

But he didn't.

He said, 'Go on, then. But we're going to have a proper discussion about who the boss is when you get back.'

'I know who the boss is,' King said, subtly de-escalating the tension. 'I'm just very particular about my own freedoms.'

'Mother Libertas is the true freedom,' Dane said. 'Remember that. Remember what you felt last night with Maeve. There's so much more of that to come. If you listen. If you obey.'

Compared to Maeve's subtleties, Dane was like a sledgehammer.

But King wasn't fazed. 'Sure. Just let me have a walk.'

'Are you asking permission?'

Silence.

King said, 'Yes.'

Dane smiled. 'There we go. Of course. Don't wander too far, though.'

King knew the last thing Dane wanted was losing track of the newcomers, but the power trip had him in its grasp.

King nodded respectfully and walked away, heading west.

52

As soon as Addison spoke, Alexis' stomach knotted in fear.

She tightened her grip on Addison's shoulder, raised her eyebrows, and waited for the girl to look her straight in the eyes before she shook her head vigorously.

Addison lowered her voice. 'What?'

Alexis leant in close and whispered, 'Don't say that to anyone other than me.'

'That's why I asked to speak over here. And that's why I asked to speak to *you*. You're not—'

She stopped herself short.

Alexis whispered, 'I'm not what?'

Addison's eyes were wet. 'You're not in too deep. Yet.'

'Listen to me. Addison, *listen*. You need to be very careful. I don't want you ever repeating this to anyone. You hear me?'

Addison said, 'That's what you just said.'

'I need you to understand.'

Addison chewed her lower lip, thinking. 'You know they're evil, don't you?'

'Who?'

'You know who.'

The Riordans.

Alexis opened her mouth to respond, then froze. She had a sudden, overwhelming urge to walk away. It wouldn't surprise her if Maeve or Dane had put Addison up to the task of ensnaring traitors. She was barely an adult, easily influenced, and she'd obey anyone in a position of power. They could take advantage of her.

No, she told herself, looking into the young woman's eyes. *No.*

Addison wasn't faking it. She'd have to be an Oscar-worthy actress to do it, and the fear in her eyes was palpable.

After a long rumination, Alexis said, 'Yes. I do.'

It made her heart hammer. If she'd judged the girl wrong, now was the time for Addison to walk away, report her findings to the Riordans. Then Alexis would be taken, overwhelmed by the sheer number of followers, maybe imprisoned and tortured and killed for her dissidence.

Addison didn't walk away.

She nodded slowly, shocked that she'd found someone who didn't worship the Riordans, then her brow furrowed. 'Then why are you here?'

'We know what's going on,' Alexis said. 'We're here to put a stop to it.'

Addison's eyes widened.

Alexis said, 'You need to stay put.'

Addison shook her head, her face white. 'No. I can't. Not anymore. I need to get back to Gillette.'

'To speak to the police?'

Addison went even paler. '*No.* I can't do that.'

There was still terror in her eyes, but now there was something else.

Guilt.

Alexis thought, *What did they make you do?*

Now was not the time to find out.

Alexis said, 'Does anyone suspect you're seeing things differently?'

'I don't know.'

'Have you been acting differently?'

'Maybe.'

'You need to stop doing that. It's only temporary, but you need to fit in. Don't draw attention to yourself. You don't know what they're capable of.'

Addison clammed up.

Her eyes turned wet.

Alexis said, 'What?'

'I know what they're capable of. They've made me do things...'

Alexis touched a finger to her lips.

Addison squeezed her eyes shut, blinked back tears. 'Maybe I don't deserve to get out of here.'

'You do.'

'I didn't protest. I didn't refuse to do anything they told me to do. I'm ... I'm a terrible person. I deserve to die.'

'You were scared. You knew what they'd do to you if you refused.'

Addison didn't nod, but Alexis saw agreement in her eyes.

'Go back out there,' Alexis said. 'Act normal. Don't even think about what we just spoke about. Don't treat me any differently. Let us do our thing.'

'Who's "us"?'

'There's a few of us.'

'The two new guys?' Addison said. 'They're with you.'

'Don't worry about it. Nothing happened here. Go about your duties. Don't act suspicious.'

Alexis had enough experience now to know her advice was unproductive. Telling someone not to act suspicious makes them act suspicious.

Addison nodded, trying to stop her lower lip quivering.

Then she turned to walk away.

Alexis said, 'Addison.'

The girl looked over her shoulder.

Alexis said, 'Not a word of this to your brother.'

Addison nodded again.

Her face said, *No shit.*

Alexis figured Brandon's brainwashing was beyond salvation.

Addison walked away, leaving Alexis alone on the outskirts.

She took a deep breath and steeled herself.

For the first time, the consequences of failure properly hit her.

Victims like Addison will die.

It put an invisible weight on her shoulders, crushing down on her, and there was nothing she could do to remove it.

53

The commune shrank away as King walked into the grassland, but it never disappeared entirely.

Such was the nature of the land. Aside from the hill that the Riordan farmhouse was positioned on, the prairie was flat in every direction for dozens of miles. There were slight undulations, but they were few and far between. King knew he would draw the ire of Maeve and Dane for disobeying, but it wouldn't do him any good if they trusted him implicitly. He wanted to methodically rattle them, put them on the back foot, see how they reacted. It was all part of gathering intelligence. If they verbally assaulted him when he got back, he'd know they were volatile, unable to keep their emotions in check.

He crested one of the slight rises in the landscape and started to descend the other side.

He stopped.

Elias was fifty feet in front of him, lowering a corpse into a hole.

There was no blood. The body had previously been a man, maybe in his mid-twenties, with long hair and pale skin turned even paler in death. His neck was swollen and bruised — a mixture of purple and black. His lips were blue. Rigor mortis was already setting in.

Elias was sweaty with exertion. His blond hair was matted to his head and his face glistened. He looked up and saw King, but he didn't pause. With a smirk he continued lowering the corpse until he could dump it into the grave. He'd dug the hole himself — a shovel covered in dirt lay beside it.

He brushed the dirt off his hands as he let go of the body.

Without looking up, he said, 'You're not supposed to be out here.'

King's head and heart fought a silent battle.

His heart told him to kill Elias right there. Expedite the process. Go back to the commune, deal with the Riordans, and get the hell out of Wyoming. He'd seen more than enough to know that everyone in charge here deserved death. But his head told him to wait. Maintain the cover, look for weaknesses and openings in the Riordans' defences so they could get the job done efficiently, without butchering it and enraging all the followers.

His head won.

Just.

He shrugged and said, 'Does it matter if I am? You don't think I've seen a body before?'

Elias seemed to appreciate the honesty and the straightforwardness. He straightened up, opening his shoulders, becoming warmer. Showing camaraderie. He said, 'Well, I think they were waiting to reveal what this job requires.'

King said, 'They never would have approached me if it was something simple.'

Elias nodded.

King said, 'Who was he?'

Elias put his hands on his hips, stared into space. Thinking hard. Then he said, 'I shouldn't say. You should go back, pretend you didn't see anything.'

'I will,' King said. 'I'll pretend not to know.'

Elias looked at him.

King said, 'So?'

It swayed Elias. He said, 'The outside world isn't ready to find out about us. Not yet. It'll happen in due time, but right now anyone wanting to speak up are whistleblowers. You saw what our government wanted to do to Snowden.' Elias gestured into the hole. 'I did what I had to do before he could flee our borders.'

King tried not to look at the corpse at risk of showing his infuriation. He battled down disgust as he said, 'What was he going to do?'

'He was weak,' Elias said. 'He knew what he signed up for but he changed his mind when he got here. Maybe the living conditions weren't as luxurious as he hoped. Who knows ... but he was going to steal a truck and head back to civilisation. He was going to alert people who absolutely need to stay in the dark.'

King glanced at the body, noting the swollen, bruised neck. 'How'd you kill him?'

'A Wing Chun strike,' Elias said. 'To the throat.'

'Impressive.'

'I know. That's why they keep me around.'

Because you can beat helpless unresisting hostages to death, King thought. *Very impressive.*

Elias stood there, smug.

King said, 'Well, I'll leave you to it.'

Elias' face changed.

Imperceptible, but it shifted.

He said, 'You're not going to say anything about this, are you?'

'I thought we already went over this.'

'Just don't get any ideas,' Elias said. 'I know what you're thinking. You and I aren't so different.'

Oh, but we are, King thought.

He said, 'What am I thinking?'

'That it was a lapse of judgment to do this where you could stumble across it,' Elias said. 'You could take that to the Riordans, convince them I'm inept. Persuade them that the job's not right for me, that it's right for you.'

King smirked. 'Your secret's safe with me, friend. Trust me.'

As soon as he turned his back and walked back to the commune, the smile vanished from his face.

Dark stoicism replaced it.

He felt Elias' eyes on his back.

54

With the body buried under six feet of hard-packed dirt, Elias tried to wind down in his living quarters.

But he couldn't.

He sipped green tea from a fine china mug — a luxury he'd only been permitted because of the power he wielded as the Riordans' enforcer — and sat cross-legged on the hard wooden floor. He'd never used cushions or padding to meditate. He considered them weak. Strength was voluntarily enduring discomfort.

Right now, though, he rippled with discomfort that was entirely involuntary.

He'd been stewing on the chance encounter with the newcomer all morning. First name "Jason," last name unknown. And that was all Elias knew. He knew even less about his dark-skinned, quiet, permanently angry compatriot.

Around an hour ago he'd decided to do something about it.

There was a knock at the door to his quarters.

Elias got up, put the empty teacup on the small side table, went to the door and opened it.

He ushered the young man in with haste.

The guy's name was Grayson. He was twenty-four, previously a construction worker with a lacklustre work ethic and no real promise in life. He'd stumbled across Mother Libertas much the same way everyone did, and Maeve's whisperings had converted him within days. Elias had heard rumours — that Grayson's sister, Karlie, had been scouring Gillette for signs of him, and instead of dispatching Elias, Maeve had sent a brother and sister out to deal with it.

It rubbed Elias the wrong way.

Maybe that's why he'd chosen Grayson for this task.

Grayson's plain round eyes were alive with desire. Elias had promised him something in exchange for this clandestine meeting...

Grayson said, 'Where is it?'

Elias said, 'In the tea.'

He handed Grayson a fresh cup of green tea that he'd prepared minutes earlier.

Grayson said, 'A full dose?'

'And a little extra,' Elias said. 'It'll put you on cloud nine. Just make sure no one notices you're tripping. That much Bodhi is like a never-ending orgasm.'

Grayson said, 'When do you want it done?'

'At the afternoon congregation,' Elias said.

'That's not far away. I've got a knife, but it's not sharp enough to—'

Elias pressed a razor-sharp switchblade into Grayson's hand.

Grayson clutched the knife, took a deep breath, and downed the entire cup.

Elias said, 'Make sure you do it fast. And if you get caught, you know what to do.'

Grayson feigned drawing the blade across his own throat.

It always flabbergasted Elias how quickly Maeve could get her followers to sacrifice their own wellbeing for the good of the cause.

Then again, that was the whole point of cults.

Elias thought about asking, *Why are you doing this? Why did you agree to stab a man you don't know in church for a single hit of Bodhi?*

But the second question contained the answer.

The stuff was that good.

So he didn't say anything. Just motioned to the door and gave Grayson a look like they were brothers in arms, fighting the good fight against a perceived common enemy.

Grayson nodded back and walked out.

In an hour he'd be on top of the world as the Bodhi flooded his brain.

55

King got back to find Dane waiting for him outside the mess hall.

The followers were piling into the building for the first communal meal of the day — a hearty breakfast to fuel them for the workday. There was endless work to do on the commune — renovations, construction, repairs, the thousand odd administrative tasks that are required to coordinate two hundred people living together in the middle of nowhere. It was paramount that the living conditions, while poor, never devolved into squalor. With an intermittent stream of Bodhi, the disciples could put up with simple living (their pleasures coming from elsewhere), but they needed basic necessities to survive.

Drugs fuelled productivity, which kept the commune's resources and assets growing, and it allowed the disciples to attend their daily congregations and practice their meditations without worrying about where their next meal would come from, or where they'd sleep at night.

Dane pulled King aside and said, 'Happy now?'

King slapped him on the shoulder. Despite his impressive height, the man was frail. 'Very.'

Dane said, 'Don't touch me.'

'You're going to need to drop the ego,' King said. 'It'll make us work better together.'

'We don't work together,' Dane said. 'Not yet.'

'So when are we figuring that out?'

'You've been here eight hours,' Dane said. 'You haven't even had your first meal yet. Settle in. Talk to some people. Get a feel for the place.'

'I'm not signing up for your cult. I'm getting hired to protect it.'

All the warmth vanished from Dane's eyes, replaced by cold calculation. He looked over King's shoulder, but his lizard-like tension uncoiled as he realised none of the followers streaming past had been in earshot. He waited for the last few stragglers to enter the mess hall, leaving them alone outside.

In an entirely new tone, Dane said, 'You use that word again in public and I'll have you executed. Don't test me.'

King froze.

How would the man I'm portraying respond?

He backed off and nodded respectfully. 'Understood. I apologise.'

Dane said, 'I'm putting you on the next ride out of here. You're not fit for the job.'

King's heart thudded.

'Dane, I'm sorry,' he said. 'Really, I am.'

'I don't want to hear it.'

'I'll do what you need.'

'No, you won't.'

'I'll prove myself.'

Dane thought about it.

'Okay,' the man said. 'After breakfast you sweep floors and scrub toilets until the afternoon congregation. Should be five or six hours of work.'

King nodded immediately, reverting to recruit mentality. 'Yes, sir.'

Dane paused. He hadn't been expecting that. He smiled. 'Might have some use for you after all.'

He dismissed King with a wave.

King walked into the mess hall, realising that the Riordans' intent all along had been to employ psychological warfare to make King and Slater subservient.

Then they'd protect the commune free of charge.

After they were converted.

56

King and Slater ate across from Violetta and Alexis on one of the tables in the mess hall, but they couldn't discuss anything substantive.

It was infuriating.

They chit-chatted about the imagined night they'd met in the bar. They discussed what future plans they'd had before coming here. They talked about how much they liked the community, the sense of belonging.

Slater wouldn't dare say anything else.

As soon as he'd started chowing down on his thin bacon, overcooked eggs and slightly burnt toast, he'd realised they were being surveilled. The disciples on either side of them ate in silence, focusing hard on their food, their ears open. Paying attention to every word. Maeve or Dane must have put them up to the task.

When he and King finished eating, they got up without incident, bidding a muffled goodbye to Violetta and Alexis, who nodded disinterestedly back.

They didn't so much as hold eye contact.

Someone would notice.

When Slater turned to leave, as a few of the disciples were already doing, Maeve was at the exit doors.

She stood beside a trolley with multiple tiers, each tray sporting a grid of see-through plastic cups, barely larger than shot glasses. Roughly two ounces of water were poured into each small cup. She wore her trademark peach farm dress, and her face was open and warm.

As each disciple left, she handed them a cup, watched them drink it, and returned it to the tray.

Slater didn't need to sample the liquid to know it was a Bodhi microdose.

The key to productivity for the coming day.

There was no way to avoid or refuse it without drawing attention, so Slater steeled himself.

It would be the first substance in his veins since he'd quit drinking half a year ago in New York.

Somehow it frightened him more than a live firefight.

He knew his brain, knew its finer intricacies. If he wasn't careful, this would spiral him back to where he'd been.

You take this, he thought, *and that's it.*

No matter how good it is.

When you get back to the outside world, you don't touch a drink.

A harsh ultimatum, but one he knew he needed.

Or he'd cave, over and over and over again.

He went straight for the exit, despite King's concerned gaze.

King muttered, 'Are you sure—?'

Slater shushed him and said, 'Yes,' as he went past.

Maeve was watching him like a hawk.

Slater went to walk past her.

She put a hand on his arm. There was no force behind it, but her grip carried invisible weight.

She said, 'Drink this.'

She handed him a disposable cup.

He looked down at the water. It seemed normal, innocuous.

He said, 'What is it?'

'Gaia's spirit,' she said. 'Mother will be with you throughout the day.'

Slater raised an eyebrow.

Maeve said, 'See for yourself.'

He couldn't say *I don't do drugs anymore* because she hadn't revealed it was drugs. And if he refused on the grounds of suspicion, he'd insult the very nature of Mother Libertas.

He couldn't blow his cover here, with two hundred people around him.

Not unarmed.

He drank the liquid down, worried it was a full dose. But that would be ludicrous. In the Bahamas, Jace had lost his mind on a full hit, awash in ecstasy, uncaring of the consequences of his actions. That wouldn't lead to a productive workday here in the commune. No, it was definitely a microdose.

He handed the empty cup back to her.

She smiled at him, gripped his arm a little tighter, and whispered, '*Mother awakens.*'

He walked out, thoroughly unnerved.

Behind him, King downed his own cup without complaint or hesitation.

They moved outside, into the chilly air.

King was pale.

Slater's heart skipped a beat.

He looked around, checking for signs of Dane, but the man was gone.

Slater turned back to King and said, 'What is it?'

'Violetta,' King hissed under his breath. 'The baby.'

Slater muttered, 'Fuck.'

57

Violetta's heart was in her throat the whole way to the exit.

She'd seen Slater and King drink their cups.

She couldn't do it.

Two doses, she thought, and it filled her with terror for her unborn child.

No matter how small, drugs were drugs. Not to mention their potency.

Dexedrine, MDMA, and benzodiazepine.

She'd already been subjected to a microdose without her knowledge. Now she'd have to accept a second. In all likelihood there'd be no consequences, but she wasn't willing to accept even the slightest risk.

As she advanced toward Maeve, she thought, *Can I control my own physiology?*

King and Slater could. They could put themselves into heightened states in an instant, conjure up all sorts of unpleasant sensations if it fuelled them to fight harder.

But could she?

She was a handler, not an operator.

She took a breath to centre herself, then focused all her attention on her stomach. She tried to imagine the food inside it — she'd eaten plenty — churning, breaking apart, digesting.

She tensed her abdomen as hard as she could without letting it show on her face.

She imagined putrid stenches, disgusting tastes, the grossest visions her mind could conjure.

She pictured her gag reflex spasming.

It spasmed.

Vomit swelled in her throat.

She kept the feeling at bay for just long enough to reach Maeve. She had to queue up behind nearly a dozen disciples, and she feared she'd started the process too early. But the line moved quickly, without interference. Maeve didn't need to pay attention to the regular followers. They were hooked. They'd drink Bodhi without thinking twice.

Violetta reached the front of the line.

She tried to drain the colour from her face.

She thought it worked — she felt terrible.

Maeve offered her a cup. 'Here.'

Violetta said, 'What is it?'

'Gaia's lifeblood,' Maeve said. 'You'll be astonished.'

Violetta let herself look intrigued, then told herself, *Now*,

She envisioned biting into a fetid, rotting corpse.

It worked.

She retched, doubled over, and threw up on the floor.

Maeve darted back.

'I'm sorry,' Violetta coughed between retches. 'I'm so sorry. I don't know what came over me. Maybe I ate something... oh, no. I'm sorry.'

Maeve said, 'It's no problem. Here. Drink this. It'll make you feel better.'

Violetta retched again.

Maeve's mouth creased into a hard line and she gestured to a couple of nearby disciples. One supported Violetta under her arm and helped her out of the mess hall. Another darted for cleaning cloths and set to work mopping up the vomit.

The floor was clean and disinfected in less than a minute.

The disciples were desperate to please.

Maeve resumed her position like nothing was amiss and gestured Alexis forward. 'Drink, my dear. Unfortunately your friend missed out.'

Alexis downed her cup, gave Maeve a smile of gratitude, and went out.

Violetta, you genius, she thought.

58

King watched one of the disciples help Violetta out of the building.

The morning sun struck her face. It was drained of colour. There were flecks of puke around the corners of her mouth.

King couldn't help himself.

Silently commanding himself to maintain his cover, he darted forward. 'Are you okay?'

She looked up, and there was relief in her eyes.

It made him pause.

He'd been ready to go to war with the whole commune.

She waved a hand dismissively. 'I'm fine, I'm fine. Had a spell of nausea before I made it to the exit. A real shame. I didn't get to try that water.'

King breathed out.

He unclenched his fists.

'Rest up,' he said. 'Make sure you stay hydrated.'

She smiled at him like a shy stranger. 'Of course.'

The disciple led her away.

When King turned around, Slater was right there, his own fists balled up.

He'd been just as ready to fight.

King's eyes said what he couldn't vocalise.

Thank you, brother.

Slater returned the gaze, injecting the same weight into his own look.

They turned and saw Dane coming down from the farmhouse. He weaved around followers, putting a hand on their shoulders one by one, then worked his way over to King and Slater.

His eyes on King, he said, 'Ready to get to work?'

'Of course.'

'Your friend will help you.'

Slater said, 'What?'

Dane let the question fade into nothingness. He didn't take his eyes off King the whole time. 'I suggest you explain.'

He was at the end of his tether, sick of being talked back to, and Slater recognised it.

King said to Slater, 'I was a prick. It's my bad. We're going to do some grunt work to prove we're taking this job seriously. That okay?'

Slater shrugged. 'Work is work.' He turned to Dane. 'Where do you need us?'

It disarmed Dane, provided him some much needed respite. 'You'll be scrubbing floors and toilets.'

Another test.

Slater said, 'Fine by me.'

Dane relaxed. He was satisfied. 'Follow me. And don't forget our dinner tonight, Will.'

'I'm looking forward to it.'

Dane paused, thrown off by the sudden change of demeanour. 'You two might be the men for the job after all.'

King said, 'That's what we're here for.'
Dane led them away from the mess hall.

59

A bell tolled above the church, signalling the imminent afternoon congregation.

King and Slater pounced at the opportunity.

The noise gave them the window they needed. They stood up from the scrubbed floorboards in one of the bunkhouses, their shirts spotted with sweat stains, and went out back where there was no one watching. The bell clanged incessantly, over and over again, but they knew it wouldn't last forever.

So they talked fast.

Slater said, 'Bodhi is fucking incredible.'

He'd been zoned in with unnatural focus all morning and afternoon. Scrubbing floors and toilets and stripping beds of dirty sheets felt like purposeful work, and he'd relished every moment of it. The feeling had never overwhelmed him, but the chemicals in each compound seemed to co-exist in mutual harmony. He'd never felt all that different, but his mood had elevated ever so slightly and then stayed there all day, without fail. It was a beautiful stream of artificial energy, and he couldn't imagine what a full hit of the stuff would feel like.

King said, 'Right?'

'That was a microdose,' Slater said. 'What would a full dose feel like?'

'Maybe a microdose is the optimal dosage.'

'Maybe.'

Slater took a breath. 'So what are we waiting for exactly?'

King said, 'We need to figure out whether Elias is their only security.'

'You think they're that stupid?'

'I don't think they're stupid,' King said, 'but they might be naïve.'

'They might really think he's some Wing Chun master?'

'Don't get it twisted,' King said. 'He *is* a Wing Chun master. That's just impractical in actual combat.'

'You don't sound so sure.'

King shrugged. 'This whole fucking place gives me the creeps. I don't know what to believe. But I say we do it tonight. After your dinner with Dane. We isolate Elias and kill him, then go for the Riordans when they don't suspect a thing.'

'Kill Elias?' Slater said. 'Does he deserve it?'

King remembered the anguished expression on the face of the corpse Elias had buried.

He said, 'Yes. I saw him with a body.'

'Body?' Slater said. 'Whose body?'

The bell tolled a final time, and the background noise faded.

King scanned the building beside them for signs of bugs, but he knew if they were there they'd be concealed well.

And he couldn't take Slater out into the grassland to speak. Someone would see. Suspicion would arise.

King gave Slater a look, saying, *Trust me.*

Slater nodded back.

They went back through the bunkhouse, out its front door, and made a beeline for the church. The last of the disciples were filing in. Their mutual excitement bristled in the air. It was like a fever, originating with a small expression of elation and then spreading fast through the ranks.

King heard whoops, hollers, and shouts of camaraderie.

Clearly Mother Libertas didn't require respectful silence during their congregations.

Respect didn't mesh with a movement built on the foundations of mind-bending drugs.

He and Slater merged with the rear of the flank and followed them through the giant double doors into the church. Neither of them had been inside yet, and they realised searching for Violetta and Alexis was pointless. The women would be somewhere in the sea of two hundred followers, ferried into one of the long pews.

King and Slater moved down the nave, the long rectangular base of the cross-shaped church layout. They could have shuffled into one of the empty pews up the back, but the disciples were disciplined in their quest to fill the seats at the front first. So King got caught up alongside Slater in the flow of traffic, and found himself naturally guided toward a pew with three spaces on the end.

A young man with considerable athleticism forced his way between King and Slater.

King stopped in his tracks. 'You good?'

'Yeah,' the guy said, his face glistening with a thin layer of sweat. 'Sorry.'

He was panting with nervous energy.

He stared at King for a little too long.

There was nothing King could do without causing a scene. He stepped into the pew and shuffled down to the furthest available seat.

The young man crammed in beside him, and before Slater could take the space closest to the aisle, another disciple wormed his way in.

Slater stared silently at King.

King stared back.

Slater walked off to another pew on his own.

The young sweaty guy stared at King without blinking.

His pupils were swollen.

60

King faced forward, trying not to react, but he soaked up details in his peripheral vision.

The guy was big and thick, maybe six feet tall and two hundred pounds. Beefy muscle and fat from eating at a calorie surplus coupled with long days of manual labour. Maeve seemed to go for a particular type with the young men she recruited. They all seemed physically powerful yet mentally lost, either not intelligent enough to know where they were headed, or burdened by an abundance of options with a nihilistic outlook on the future.

It was the perfect recipe for a place like this.

Mother Libertas simplified everything, made life straightforward, gave lost souls a trajectory.

That alone was appealing, and that didn't include the Bodhi or Maeve's skills as an orator and a persuader.

Altogether it was the perfect storm.

The young guy was high on Bodhi. Almost too high. He had abandoned all social niceties, staring unashamedly at King without concern.

King said, 'Hey. What's your name?'

'Grayson.'

'Jason,' King said. 'How's that? They rhyme.'

There was a moment's delay, too long to be natural, then the joke computed. Grayson laughed — shrill, discordant, detached from reality.

His face fell and he awkwardly faced forward, waiting for the sermon to begin.

The only sound came from the murmuring of the masses.

King stood rigid, and for the first time he tensed up. He didn't like this. Slater was long gone, sucked into the crowd, and Violetta and Alexis were too short to be distinguishable amidst the sea of heads. The church stank of body odour and dirty clothes, but the electricity in the atmosphere overrode the smell.

Everyone was thrilled to be here.

Maeve appeared from a door that must have led to the sacristy — the private rooms behind the altar where the priest prepared for their service. She still wore her patented farm dress, which had a disarming effect. There were no robes or official garments. The beauty of the movement was in its simplicity. Maeve walked gracefully up to the altar and spread her arms wide.

The room fell silent.

She said, 'We begin with the creed.'

Her voice naturally echoed through the nave. The space was engineered to perfection, an architectural wonder.

Maeve said, 'Mother, lift me from despondency.'

Two hundred voices parroted in unison. *'Mother, lift me from despondency.'*

King jolted at the synchronisation. The noise was tremendous, then faded back to quiet.

It was unnerving.

'Mother, free me from complacency.'

'Mother, free me from complacency.'

It boomed off the walls, off the ceiling, then the echo dissipated.

'Mother, bloom my power.'

'Mother, bloom my power.'

The disciples were getting more energetic each time they recited the creed, as if they were drawing real strength from each command.

King stood stoically, refusing to join in, merely observing. Amidst the deafening voices, he looked to his right and saw Grayson had broken out in a full sweat. Perspiration ran down his face, down the sides of his skull.

'Mother, bloom my spirit.'

'Mother, bloom my spirit.'

Grayson looked to his left. Directly into King's eyes. His pupils had been swollen before, but now they were almost doubled in size. There was barely any colour left in his eyes — his pupils swallowed his irises. His cheeks were red and beading with sweat.

A massive dose of Bodhi was hitting him.

'Mother, give me strength.'

'Mother, give me strength.'

King didn't move a muscle.

When the congregation rallied to return the creed at an indescribable volume, Grayson reached into his waistband and came out with a knife.

'Mother, be with me.'

'Mother, be with me.'

Some of the disciples were screaming the creed.

Grayson kept his movements hidden as he jerked at the waist, bringing the switchblade around low, aiming for King's stomach.

Aiming to tear his intestines, rupture his stomach, disembowel him in the church pew.

'Mother, awaken.'

'Mother, awaken.'

King slipped into survival mode. As the word, '*Awaken!*' boomed through the church he caught Grayson's wrist and stopped the blade inches shy of ripping his guts to pieces. He used animalistic strength, every vein pulsing with the exertion. Thankfully his determination went unnoticed amidst the communal fervour.

'Mother, awaken!'

'Mother, awaken!'

King broke one of Grayson's fingers by snapping it back, successfully pried his hand open, and ripped the switchblade free.

'MOTHER, AWAKEN!'

'MOTHER, AWAKEN!'

As soon as the knife was clear, King brought Grayson's wrist down, bent his knee, and brought it up. The two limbs clashed, and the knee emerged victorious. It was a shockingly fast movement, and it was lost in the midst of the disciples shouting and screaming, raising their arms to the heavens, some of them openly crying with joy.

Grayson wrenched his broken, mangled hand out of King's grip and stood bolt upright, at attention, facing forward.

Like nothing had happened at all.

King folded the switchblade in and palmed it before anyone could see.

He faced forward too.

His heartbeat throbbed in his neck, every sense heightened, his brain transported back to the fight-or-flight mentality of hunter-gatherers on the ancient plains.

Grayson blinked sweat out of his eyes and ignored King.

Like it would all go away if he pretended it hadn't happened.

King couldn't stab him without making an enemy of two hundred rabid cult members.

He felt sweat welling on his forehead and under his arms at the exertion of fighting for his life, and the sheer strangeness of what had just happened.

There were ten people behind him, ten in front, and seven to the left, and all of them were transfixed on Maeve, unaware of what had unfolded nearby.

King stood shoulder-to-shoulder with his would-be assassin and waited for the service to come to an end.

He was alone.

61

Maeve spoke for close to two hours.

King barely heard a word.

The chants of '*MOTHER, AWAKEN!*' had subsided after increasing sequentially in volume for what felt like forever, and then the frenzy of emotion had given way to stillness and the disciples had taken their seats in the pews.

King sat down beside Grayson and muttered, 'What was that for?'

Grayson stared forward. Didn't blink, didn't respond, didn't so much as recognise that King had spoken. He was riding a wave of Bodhi unlike anything he'd experienced, and the failed assassination attempt had left him mentally depleted. Now all he could do was surrender to it and pretend that reality didn't exist.

Pretend that the man he should have murdered didn't have his knife, wasn't sitting beside him, entirely unharmed.

King muttered, 'Don't go anywhere after this is over.'

He could see Grayson contemplating what he should do.

Run, fight with his bare hands, alert the Riordans. None of them seemed like the right call in the middle of a sermon.

So he sat there and surrendered to the Bodhi.

Sweat ran from all his pores, despite the afternoon chill. The pain of his broken wrist and fingers must have been hitting him.

Maeve ranted about the philosophy and teachings of Mother Libertas. She spoke of the mind-body connection, the ability to choose a new reality in each moment in time, the connection to Gaia, how the maternal love the earth spewed could be harnessed, shaped, mastered, channelled into a new life and a new existence and a new universe.

It was powerful stuff if you were vulnerable.

King, on the other hand, didn't pay attention at all.

All his critical thinking was focused on planning what would happen after the service concluded.

Grayson shifted and cracked his neck, rolling through the pulsating waves of the Bodhi experience, trying in vain to sit still. A couple of people noticed, and a woman in her mid-thirties sitting behind them put a hand on Grayson's shoulder and whispered for him to relax.

He nearly jumped out of his skin.

But Maeve's words drowned out the tension. She was an incredible orator. King could admit that much. Even though he wasn't listening to the words, the way they floated through the church was something to behold. Her rhetoric captured the attention of every disciple.

When it was finally over, everyone recited the creed for a second time.

They all stood up to shout the final commands.

Grayson was on the comedown, his skin clammy instead of flushed. Going through the mother of all hangovers.

King said in his ear, 'Don't you move a muscle.'

As the final bellowing chant of *'MOTHER, AWAKEN!'* rippled through the ranks, concluding the service, Grayson powered past the man beside him and stepped out into the aisle prematurely.

If he'd timed it a little worse, everyone would have stared at him for moving too soon.

Instead, a handful of disciples on the aisles followed suit, and suddenly everyone was streaming for the doors.

'Fuck,' King muttered.

He shoved past the guy on his aisle, who still hadn't moved.

'Hey,' the guy started. 'What the—?'

King was already gone, out in the aisle, shouldering past the disciples who were in his way.

Grayson made it to the exit. The back of his shirt sported an enormous sweat patch, a dark oval that encompassed most of the material. He stepped out into the late afternoon light and strode fast for one of the outbuildings, hoping to lose King in the maze.

King made it past the first few disciples closest to the exit doors and broke into a light jog, like he had somewhere to be but wasn't in a huge hurry to get there. It was a calculated risk, but Grayson hadn't been willing to go there. He didn't want to run at risk of arousing suspicion, so by the time he made it to one of the bunkhouses on the perimeter King was on his tail.

Grayson ducked into the shadows.

Behind the building, the sun melted into the prairie.

The commune glowed orange.

King ducked into the building after the young man who'd tried to kill him.

62

Slater found Alexis and Violetta out the front of the church, amidst the few dozen disciples still milling around in the shadow of the building.

Aware of keen ears all around them, Alexis made it seem nonchalant when she asked, 'Where's your friend?'

Slater scanned the commune, looking for any sign of King.

He came up empty-handed.

He tried not to sound overly concerned. 'I don't know.'

Violetta said, 'What's his name again?'

It meant nothing, but it added to the believability that they'd only met once in a bar.

Slater turned to her. 'Jason.'

He masked the worry in his throat.

63

Damp with stale sweat, Grayson shouldered a door open and hurried through into one of the rooms, guaranteed to be empty.

Its occupants would still be milling outside the church, and there was no reason for them to return to their quarters before finalising their daily tasks.

King saw the man go in and took a deep breath.

Subdue, he told himself. *Don't overreact.*

He ran down the hallway.

Subdue.

The door had swung back closed, so he pushed it open again, refusing to allow Grayson a moment to compose himself.

Subdue.

Grayson had another knife. It must have been hidden under his mattress, or tucked into his meagre belongings, because he'd only been in the room for a few seconds. In that time he'd managed to retrieve the backup weapon — a crude cutlery knife that would do the job regardless — and he swung it at King with desperate abandon.

All notion of minimising the damage fell aside.

King's life was on the line.

He threw himself back into the door frame and narrowly missed the blade hacking into his face. The only light in the room came from a tiny window beside the bunks, and the metal glinted in the lowlight. King rebounded off the doorway and snatched hold of Grayson's knife hand. The other arm was useless, hanging limp by his side, the wrist broken.

King tried to simply smash the intact limb into the bunk frame and spill the knife from his grip.

Grayson ripped his hand free with surprising strength.

Inhuman strength.

Bodhi was firing all his nerve endings, tunnelling his focus. He was tapping into the primal survival instinct, and he used it to break free from King's hold.

He geared up for another wild slash.

Enough, King thought.

He backed up a step, putting himself just out of range of another swing, and pulled Grayson's first switchblade from his own pocket.

He flicked it open.

Grayson lunged.

Eyes wide, face oily, teeth clenched together.

He came down with the knife from ceiling to floor, an effective approach to a two hundred and twenty pound target in a confined space. There was little chance he'd miss.

King dropped to the floor, as if cowering away from the stabbing attempt, which he effectively was. The key to survival in life-or-death situations is abandoning your ego. It might look exciting to try to parry the lunge with his forearms, but there was a significant chance he'd lose a hand in the process.

Grayson's knife slashed through the air inches above King's hunched back.

Missed by next to nothing.

But it doesn't matter if it's an inch or a mile.

A miss is a miss.

King rolled and swept Grayson's legs out by slamming his shin into the delicate ankle joint, sending the disciple spilling to the floorboards. The man landed on his back and came close to knocking himself out by lashing the back of his skull against the hard floor, but he stayed lucid. He scrambled, coming up into a sitting position for another slash of the—

King shoved the switchblade into the left side of his chest, tearing through into his heart.

Grayson's pupils swelled to a crescendo and he broke a couple of teeth from their gums by clenching them in his death throes.

King left the knife in his chest to prevent massive blood loss. That way, the room would avoid the crimson pools of a crime scene. King kept pressure on the stab wound, his hand wrapped around the hilt, and looked into Grayson's eyes as the man died.

Under his breath, he muttered, 'What is it about this shit that makes them kamikazes?'

He wasn't expecting a response.

Grayson sucked in a deep, rattling breath, then blood ran out through his teeth as he said, 'Because dying doesn't matter when you feel like this.'

He smiled as he slipped away.

64

The sun was close to touching the horizon as King went into overdrive.

There might be witnesses around within seconds, so he wasted no time. He burst into action, slipping Grayson's unblemished kitchen knife under the mattress of the lower bunk, then returning pressure to the switchblade in his heart.

He got his hands under the body's armpits.

Grayson was close to two hundred pounds, but it was light work for now.

Adrenaline was a potent stimulant.

King steeled himself and dragged the corpse out into the hallway. He looked left, then right. The door facing the prairie was closed tight. An orange glow spilled through the window set above the door handle. The door facing the commune was still half-open from where Grayson and then King had thrust it open. King could see a sliver of the central buildings, and a decent chunk of the open space between them, but so far no one had populated it. All it would take was a single disciple stumbling onto the scene and King's cover would be shattered.

The vein in his neck throbbed double-time as he dragged Grayson down the hall.

He found a door set between two of the rooms and tried it, hoping it was unlocked.

It swung open.

Supply closet.

There was barely enough space for the body, and someone would find it eventually, but it was the best on a list of bad options.

He dumped Grayson beside a large mop in a five gallon bucket of dirty sudsy water. The bucket hadn't been emptied yet from the day's labour, and someone would do that eventually.

Leaving the building with the dead man was out of the question. The bunkhouse was positioned on flat ground, distanced from its surrounding buildings, and any exit he took would expose them to anyone on this side of the commune. They'd be seen. There was no way around it. And the rest of the rooms were bedrooms and bathrooms, which would be populated well before someone checked the supply closet.

The corpse was a ticking time bomb.

King looked down into Grayson's wide eyes, unseeing and unfocused.

Who put you up to this?

Dane?

Maeve?

Elias?

Or any of the other two hundred followers, potentially envious of the newcomers, jealous of the attention they were receiving despite the lack of work they'd put in on the grounds.

He had endless questions, and zero answers.

So he forgot about it. What he couldn't control didn't matter. Right now all he could do was stay alive, regroup with Slater, Violetta, and Alexis, and figure out when to strike.

They'd have to do it fast.

Aim to overwhelm.

King elected to go find the others and swung the supply closet door closed, sealing Grayson into darkness.

Revealing the rest of the hallway leading out to the commune.

There wasn't as much light anymore.

King looked over.

Dane Riordan filled the corridor.

65

King's heart jolted but he didn't outwardly react.

Without missing a beat, he ran through a mental image of what he'd seen in the supply closet, focused on what *wasn't* there, and said, 'Looking for a dustpan and brush. You know where I can find them?'

Dane watched him closely.

Scouring for any hint of deception.

King wasn't fazed.

He couldn't allow himself to be.

Dane said, 'They should be in that closet.'

Were they there? King thought. *Did I miss them?*

He stuck to his guns. Retreat was surrender. Surrender was death.

King said, 'I looked. They're not there.'

'Check again.'

King rolled his eyes and reached for the handle.

Dane smirked. 'I'm messing with you. You're off the clock.'

'The workday's not over.'

'You're right,' Dane said. 'But you're still off the clock. You've earned it.'

King nodded his satisfaction. 'Appreciate it. What's planned for tonight?'

'I've got dinner with your friend,' Dane said. 'That should be interesting. After that, we'll talk business.'

'Not before?'

'You're in the clear. You're the man for the job. Will … he's a wild card. I want to sort him out before I move ahead.'

'What's Maeve's opinion?'

'Why?'

King held up his palms in an attempt to disarm. 'That wasn't supposed to be an insult. I've insulted you enough and you've held strong. In my book that makes you an ally. I hope you understand it was never personal. I was just … wondering if she had input in this decision.'

'No,' Dane answered bluntly. 'Not for this. She's in charge of the narrative, I'm in charge of protecting us.'

'"The narrative"?'

Dane winked. 'Our little secret. Don't spoil it for your friend. I'm going to indoctrinate him tonight.'

King found that hard to believe.

Slater wouldn't buy the philosophy of Mother Libertas for a second.

Dane didn't move, like he was calmly playing the waiting game, like he knew…

King didn't have a choice.

To save face, he had to act like he didn't have a care in the world.

He walked out of the building, past Dane, leaving the man alone in the bunkhouse.

66

Dane waited until King was out of sight, then sauntered down the corridor.

He came to the supply closet and paused in front of it.

Reached out, twisted the handle, and slowly opened the door.

Grayson's blank glassy eyes stared up at him. His mouth was agape, and a trickle of blood ran from the corner. A switchblade was shoved up to the hilt into the left side of his chest. It would have killed him in seconds, plunging straight into his heart.

What the fuck? Dane thought.

The kid was new. They'd gone to great lengths to make sure he assimilated well. His nosy sister had been making too much noise in Gillette, so they'd sent Brandon and Addison to silence her. Grayson had been a disciple with strong potential, easily exploitable, buying into every word that came out of Maeve's mouth.

And now this.

Why?

Dane realised raising the alarm would be unwise. He'd already harboured suspicions about the newcomers, but he hadn't had the chance to pry deeply yet. Tonight was his chance. Isolate Will, the more unhinged of the pair, and get the truth out of him. That wouldn't happen if he turned this into a war. There were questions that still needed answering — namely, how had Jason silently killed this man a minute after the service had concluded? — and if they were experienced combatants, he didn't want to lose a dozen disciples to the pair before the sheer numbers overwhelmed them. Casualties weren't something they could afford right now. Each man and woman here was an important building block of the foundation.

Dane stared at the body a moment longer.

This was something different. This was a new level of skill. Something he hadn't seen in the flesh before. Whoever had trained Jason ... they'd been undeniably brilliant.

And who has those sorts of resources?

He had a call to make.

So for now...

Sleep well, Grayson.

Dane closed the door on the corpse.

67

Dane found Maeve in the sacristy behind the church's altar.

It was the same room she'd converted Grayson in only a week earlier. That felt like an eternity ago. Dane realised his mistake: expanding too quickly. They'd done zero proper background research on the new arrivals, their attention consumed by how perfectly Jason and Will fit the description of who they needed.

But perhaps that's what the newcomers had been going for all along.

Maeve looked up from her desk. 'What is it?'

Dane expunged all memory of the body in the supply closet from his mind, then scolded himself for his idiocy.

She can't read your mind.

But she was looking at him with a dark glint in her eye. 'What is it, baby?'

He said, 'I'm going to test Will. At dinner.'

She raised an eyebrow. 'You think that's the way to go?'

'He's unstable, unhinged, angry at everyone. But any

obstacle can become an advantage. It's all a matter of the right perspective. We're chipping away at Jason, and he's already close to being on board, but it's a smooth slope for him. His head's screwed on right. With Will, it's going to be zero to a hundred. I want to turn it up to a hundred.'

Maeve nodded. 'Very well.'

'And I'm going to call Connor.'

'Why?'

'I need a deeper background check on them before we trust them fully.'

'A background check from *Connor?*' Maeve said, perplexed. She put her elbows on the desk so she could lean forward and stare into his eyes. 'What do you know that I don't?'

'Nothing.'

'You're lying.'

'I'm not,' he insisted. 'But I get that vibe from them. You read the report that came back from the hospital. You saw what they did to those boys in Gillette. That's not normal. Ordinary veterans don't do that. I think they're a cut above.'

'There's a big gap between soldiers and Connor's world,' Maeve said. 'They'd have to be several cuts above.'

Dane remembered the knife buried in Grayson's chest, the smile on the corpse's face. 'I think they are.'

Maeve shrugged. 'Suit yourself. But I trust my intuition. I'm telling you they're clean.'

'How do you know?'

'I sense it in the earth. Mother speaks to me.'

He looked at her.

She was dead serious.

And she was ready to put up a fight if he mocked her for it.

He walked out with his stomach sinking.

She's in deep now, he thought.

A terrifying thought struck him.

You're on your own.

Out in the church now, he stood at the altar so he could overlook the dozens of empty pews. Every footstep echoed in the colossal space. It had taken two laborious years and thousands of hours of manual labour to build. They'd had to swear the building team to secrecy, and then killed a couple of them at the end anyway because they didn't trust they'd keep their mouths shut.

But Maeve had stressed its importance.

'*We need it,*' she'd said. '*Every religion relies on monuments that inspire awe. We're the same. It'll help the image.*'

He'd said, '*We're going to be a religion?*'

Her eyes had widened, alive with excitement. '*Baby, you have no idea how big this is going to get.*'

Back then she'd known the Mother Libertas rhetoric was made-up nonsense.

Nowadays, the lines were blurring.

He missed the old times. The simple times.

He fished out his sat phone and called Connor.

The young man took a few rings to pick up. 'Hey. Sorry.'

'No problem,' Dane said. 'Work got you on your toes?'

'It's crazy right now. More ops than ever that need intel.'

Dane said, 'I'm going to provide you with the exact physical description of two men. I believe they might have been involved in your world, once upon a time. I want you to scour the system for them.'

'I can't do that without triggering alerts.'

'Then find a way around,' Dane said. 'I hope you understand what's on the line here.'

Connor inhaled.

Dane knew the man would do anything to follow through.

A monthly supply of Bodhi hung in the balance.

68

Slater was en route to the bathroom when King came out of nowhere, grabbed him by the wrist, and hauled him aside.

They moved silently through the building, went out the back door, and surveyed the landscape again.

The sun was halfway hidden below the prairie.

The grasslands glowed gold.

Slater lowered his voice. 'What?'

'I killed a guy.'

Slater looked over his shoulder out of paranoia, checking for eavesdroppers. Satisfied, he turned back. 'You *what*?'

'That man who wormed his way between us in church,' King said. 'He tried to stab me in the middle of the fucking sermon.'

Slater became aware of a familiar sensation.

Crippling uncertainty.

Who was coming for them? Why? Was their cover intact? Did Maeve suspect something? Did she *know* something? Was it simply a random, disgruntled disciple?

He forced the questions aside and fixated on what was in his locus of control. 'Where's the body?'

'Supply closet in one of the bunkhouses. I think Dane found it.'

Slater's stomach dropped.

King said, 'Yeah, I know...'

'Why haven't we been outed yet?'

'I don't know.'

'What do you mean he found it?'

King said, 'He sprung me in the hallway as I was closing the door. We had a bullshit conversation, and he lingered. I had to leave. To do otherwise would have been suspicious. But all he had to do was open the door and have a look once I was gone.'

'Why did you let him do that?'

'You wanted me to kill him?'

'Yeah,' Slater said, clenching his fists one by one, rolling his neck. 'That's exactly what I fucking expected. Now we have one more person to worry about when this all goes haywire.'

King said, 'Do we pull out?'

Slater stared at him.

King raised an eyebrow. 'Do we?'

Slater said, 'When have we ever retreated?'

'When it's tactically sound to do so,' King said. 'I have. Plenty of times.'

'This commune is unarmed nutcases,' Slater said. 'You really want to run?'

'Two hundred bodies is two hundred bodies. Trained, untrained, armed, unarmed. It doesn't matter. They all sink a vial of Bodhi and come after us, we're fucked. Even if we got our hands on weapons, we'd run out of bullets.'

'So we make sure it doesn't come to that.'

'How?'

'If you're so sure Dane found the body,' Slater said, 'then he hasn't sounded the alarm. Deliberately. He doesn't want this powder keg to blow, just like us.'

'Why wouldn't he?'

'Some of the disciples might not be all the way in. It's a fairly new movement. They probably don't want to put everyone to the test so soon. They don't need their devotion questioned. They need to be coddled, further indoctrinated. You know they do.'

King thought about it. 'So you go to dinner?'

'I'll see what happens,' Slater said. 'I'll take part in whatever conversation he's planning to have with me. If I see a window of opportunity, I'll take it.'

'What opportunity?'

Slater spoke softer, so it was barely a mutter. 'You know.'

'Are we prepared for that?'

'We have to be.'

King had deliberately tested the plan with incessant questions, but now he nodded, jumping on board. 'I don't think I'll be able to get my hands on weapons before then. They'll be locked up somewhere safe. Possibly in the depths of the farmhouse.'

Slater shook his head. 'We won't need them. We take out Maeve, Dano, and Elias ... then the Judas goats are gone.'

King raised a questioning eyebrow.

Slater said, 'The goat that leads the sheep to slaughter. Without them, the sheep don't know what to do with themselves. Don't know where to go. They're rendered useless.'

The sun melted away, but the sky stayed gold.

Rapidly fading to dark.

King said, 'So it's go time?'
Slater nodded.
King said, 'Enjoy your dinner.'
He walked away, heading for the mess hall.

69

The bell tolled twice, signifying the workday had come to a close and it was time to eat.

King moved through the small clusters of disciples heading for the mess hall, and found Violetta and Alexis loitering in front of the entrance.

A big young man stood beside them. His build was tall and lanky, but he had big hands and feet that offset his thin limbs. His nose was squashed, adding to the flatness of his face, and his hair was already receding. He was an ugly guy with an intense stare that he wasn't smart enough to recognise as confronting.

King nodded to Violetta as he approached, which drew the ire of the young man.

King looked into her eyes.

She was intensely uncomfortable.

So was Alexis.

Both of them were squared away, trying to face as far away from the man as they could without being impolite. It was likely he couldn't take social cues, but more probable that he'd been put up to the task of sticking with them.

King came to a stop in front of the trio and looked at the young guy. 'Hey. I'm Jason.'

'Brandon,' the guy said. 'You know them?'

He jabbed a finger at the two women.

King said, 'I do.'

'That's cool.'

King turned to Violetta. 'How are you holding up?'

'Just fine,' she said with a smile and a look in her eyes that revealed she was far from fine.

Brandon said, 'What else you got to say?'

King turned slowly. The differences between them were obvious. King had forty more pounds of muscle, twenty less pounds of puppy fat, and stood around three inches taller. On top of his physical attributes, he looked like he could tear a phonebook in half with his bare hands. That took something more than physical prowess. It required experience and confidence and a vibe that was subdued yet unhinged.

But Brandon's pupils were swollen with Bodhi. Maeve had allowed the young man more than a microdose, stripping him of all his inhibitions. He would pick a fight with anyone she asked him to without regard for his own safety.

And she'd tasked him with making sure no one bothered the new girls.

Whether they wanted him there or not.

King said, 'I'm just asking some questions to my friend.'

Brandon said, 'You rudely interrupted. That's what you did. She was talking to me.'

'No she wasn't.'

'Take a hike.'

'Where to?' King said, looking around. 'I'm waiting for dinner just like everyone else.'

'Away from us. You're not welcome here.'

King said nothing.

Brandon got a smug look on his face. 'This is above your pay grade, buddy.'

'Is it?'

Violetta gave King a look that said, *Not here.*

King knew why. There were close to a hundred people around them, talking amongst themselves but ready to fight for Maeve until their dying breath. If King flattened Brandon, and the Riordans disapproved, it'd spell disaster.

King turned and walked away.

Brandon laughed at his back.

King could feel Violetta and Alexis stewing, intensely uncomfortable. He was more worried about Alexis. Seasoned operators can put aside their egos, ignore the insidious emotions that can make them abandon their cover, but civilians can't. You insult a civilian to their face and nine times out of ten they'll absorb the negativity rather than letting it brush off them.

Across the crowd, King turned back and looked at Alexis.

She was seething, but she had the wherewithal to turn her face away from Brandon, pretending the disgusting man wasn't there.

She looked out across the commune with her teeth clenched.

She'll make a damn fine operative.

70

Dane led Slater on foot to an old-school log cabin nearly a mile away, tucked in the crook of a slight rise in the grassland.

It was deliberately separated from the commune. It gave Slater a dark premonition about what went on here, away from prying eyes. The cabin itself sported a renovated interior with central heating and LEDs instead of relying on a fireplace and candlelight. It had been prepared in advance for the occasion, the central table set with cutlery and bowls of food covered with lids.

This time of year it got dark early, and by six p.m. the sky was a royal blue, turning the trees scattered across the plains to spectres. Slater couldn't shake the sensation of vast emptiness, complete isolation. It accentuated Dane's movements, like all his gestures were more notable in the silence.

They sat down.

Dane poured some red wine out of an aged bottle, brought his glass to his lips and sipped from it. Slater had a thin cylindrical glass with lemon-scented water in place of a wine glass. He'd already informed Dane he didn't drink.

Dane said, 'Did you ever?'

'Ever what?'

'Drink.'

Slater smirked. 'Yeah.'

'Bet you didn't look like that when you were drinking.'

Dane tilted his chin, gesturing to the musculature beneath Slater's beige corduroy jacket and white shirt.

Slater drank down a third of the water. It tasted faintly of lemon, too, and he wasn't sure if he approved or not. It was a courtesy in formal settings to tinge plain water with various fruits, but he'd always preferred to keep things simple and unblemished.

He said, 'Actually, I did. I was very good at balancing my obsessions.'

'How's a man with that sort of dedication end up out here?'

'What do those two things have to do with each other?'

Dane's fingertips were touching in a gesture resembling prayer, but now he separated them, asking a question with his open palms. 'You and your friend are ... what did you say ... wandering?'

Slater nodded. 'Call it a personal revolution.'

Dane smiled and sipped at his wine. '"Personal revolution." I like that. And now you want to join *our* revolution.'

Stick to the cover, Slater thought. *There's a chance he didn't find the body.*

'I like what you're doing here,' Slater said. 'I want on board.'

Dane's eyes narrowed ever so slightly. 'On board?'

Slater sipped more water. 'You heard me.'

'I was under the impression you were here seeking enlightenment. Truth is an elusive gift, and we only offer it to the souls we think are prepared to bear the burden. It can be ... confronting.'

Slater said, 'Did you forget that back in Gillette Maeve offered us jobs? I think you've already put it together that me and my companion are a little more switched on than your average convert who comes wandering in.'

'Don't patronise the disciples.'

Slater said, 'We're not just ex-military. We're ex-SF. I waited to tell you that because I didn't want you to get your back up. But I think if you drink a little more wine you might get more creative, and I'm sure you could come up with a number of ways to put the two of us to use.'

Dane said, 'What makes you think we need two soldiers working for us?'

'The fact that Maeve told us she did.'

'We might have been bluffing. To get you out here. To get you to see the light.'

'You need to protect the interests of the cause.'

Slater's words were veiled in sarcasm.

Dane's smirk shifted slightly. It was no longer co-conspiratorial; now it was as if Slater was a true outsider, his words falling pathetically on deaf ears.

Dane said, 'I think your ego is in the way.'

Slater paused. 'What?'

'You think because you've got some combat experience you deserve more than your fellow disciples. You think you should be put on a pedestal, maybe armed with weapons, allowed to lord over the peasants as the right-hand-man to myself and Maeve. You think the privileges that come with your manipulation of Mother Libertas royalty are fully deserved. But I suggest otherwise. I suggest you are lost, adrift in this beautiful country with no fixed purpose. You have a collection of jigsaw pieces in your hands but no idea how to assemble them into anything resembling a cohesive narrative. So this is what I propose. We will not recruit you as equals. You do not deserve to go unenlightened. What we shall do instead is convert you, and then you'll provide those services to the cause with no expectation of reward or recognition. Because the success of the cause is the ultimate reward, and its spread across this planet is enough recognition for a million lifetimes.'

Slater saw, up close and personal, how rhetoric could be used by a master wordsmith to give them a biblical aura. He saw right through each of Dane's thinly veiled persuasions, and didn't lend the shtick any weight.

But he had to get this conversation back on track, or all their work would be for nothing.

Slater said, 'Cut the shit. I'm not some hillbilly you feed a few fairytales to and expect them to slave away for you. I have very particular skills and they come with a price. Same goes with my friend. So either we enter negotiations or the two of us pack up shop and hike out of here.'

Dane said, 'If you came with the assumption of negotiation I'm afraid you'll leave empty-handed.'

His eyes blazed now, alight with splendour.

Slater shifted uncomfortably.

'You taste the honey?' Dane said.

Slater looked down at his glass, and suddenly it seemed unfamiliar. 'What?'

'The water,' Dane said. 'It's scented.'

'I tasted lemon instead of honey.'

Dane shrugged. 'Doesn't matter either way. It's time for your awakening, brother.'

Slater sat deathly still.

Every minuscule sound in the cabin echoed, far more than before. If Slater's drink had been spiked, it'd take time to kick in. Drugs don't work instantaneously, unless he was snorting cocaine or injecting heroin directly into the bloodstream. Oral consumption took longer. He had time.

He went for the knife beside his plate.

'No,' Dane said.

It might have been a trick of the mind, but Slater could swear the man's voice boomed louder than humanly possible. He said it quietly, but it somehow reverberated off the cabin walls.

Is it kicking in already?

He remembered the kid, Jace, almost degloving himself, his eyes swollen in frenzy.

Was there Bodhi coursing through his own veins?

He realised too late his hand was hovering inches off the knife. He hadn't committed to the gesture. He figured Dane had something he needed to hear.

Dane said, 'I'd suggest you reconsider your decision. You could kill me, sure ... I don't doubt that. But in about fifteen minutes you're going to get hit by a wave you've never felt before. All the vehicles are locked up, so you'll have to flee on foot, and at night the grasslands are a *bad* place to lose your mind.'

Slater thought he'd mastered his fears.

Tamed his animal instincts, put himself in so many life-or-death situations that the concept of danger barely registered anymore.

But this was a whole different beast.

This would be a trip to the edge of insanity.

He said, 'Fuck you.'

His voice quivered. It shocked him.

He'd never lost control like this, and the drugs hadn't hit him yet.

Dane said, 'Good. Let it out. You came here with rage,

my brother, a deep rage in your soul, and you and I are going to get to the bottom of it tonight. This cabin is our therapy booth. And I took your story on board before we came here. I sensed your power ... both you and Jason have it radiating off you. You are strong men with strong minds. It'll take some effort to break through that barrier. That's why I dosed your water with six hits of Bodhi. You've had half your glass, so that's three full doses. One dose is enough to send a disciple into a new world. But you are prepared for this, my brother, and you will emerge a new man. We will confront your demons here tonight. We will find your truth, find your peace. You will emerge a fanatic of the cause. I'm sure of it.'

Slater couldn't speak.

Not from the drugs crippling his motor senses; they hadn't even hit him yet.

The fear, the uncertainty, the endless falling sensation in his stomach...

It was fear he'd never grappled with.

Before he began to spiral he was already flashing through an internal kaleidoscope, watching a slideshow of all the horrors he'd witnessed throughout his life, all the terrors that made him turn to the bottle in the first place.

He put his head in his hands and said, 'Shit.'

Dane smiled.

Slater could hear the man's lips tilting upward.

Dane said, 'Are you ready for the war inside your head?'

71

Violetta and Alexis ate in Brandon's shadow.

He loomed over them, taking his assigned role as their guardian very seriously. Whoever had put him up to it, they'd been serious, because he wasn't even bothering to make it look like his presence was genuine. He chewed noisily beside Alexis, their shoulders touching, and stared daggers across the table at Violetta.

Violetta couldn't remember the last time she'd despised someone more.

Finally Alexis broke, but Violetta couldn't tell whether it was part of the cover or not.

Alexis jerked a few inches across the bench away from Brandon, and said, 'Could you leave us alone, please?'

Brandon smirked through a mouthful of cajun chicken stew.

'Why?' he said with his mouth open, chunks of chicken in his teeth. 'What's wrong? You don't like me?'

'Not really,' Violetta said. 'Could you give us some space?'

Brandon fell silent. He kept chewing, staring at her, refusing to blink.

Alexis said, 'Did you hear us?'

Brandon said, 'You're guests here. You know what that means? It means you do what we say.'

'Are you in charge?'

'No,' Brandon said, smiling. 'But those who *are* in charge told me to watch you. So I'm going to watch you.'

'I don't like that,' Alexis said. 'It makes me want to leave.'

Brandon didn't take the bait. 'Does it look like I care?'

Violetta stood up.

Brandon said, 'Where are you going?'

'To the bathroom,' Violetta said. 'You're not going to follow me there, are you?'

'I'm thinking about it.' He winked at her.

She suppressed a shiver of disgust and walked away.

Alone with Brandon now, Alexis stared at her food, refusing to acknowledge his presence.

Out of the corner of her eye she noticed Brandon craning his neck to scan the mess hall.

Finally he said, 'Where's that big guy?'

Alexis said, 'What?'

'The big guy who came up to you two earlier. He's not here. Do you think—?'

Alexis interrupted. 'You must be close to Maeve to get trusted for an important job.'

Brandon's pride overshadowed his suspicions, and he turned his attention to her. 'I've been a loyal disciple for a long time. She thinks I'm trustworthy.'

'Wow,' Alexis said, pretending to be transfixed. 'What do you think she has in store for you down the road?'

Brandon started ranting about positions of power, a slave to his own ego.

Alexis wasn't listening.

She'd put up with this if it meant Violetta had bought time to speak to King.

72

Slater needed Alexis.

More than anything he needed her by his side, to ride out whatever was to come.

Or King, his brother-in-arms.

But the very thought of getting up and fleeing the log cabin made him freeze in fear, and he realised Dane had impeccable foresight. There was a reason he'd brought Slater all the way out here, roughly a mile from the commune. Any attempt to find his friends would lead to him blindly stumbling through the dark, and if he lost control of his sanity out in the shadowy plains he might never get it back. In contrast, the warmth of the cabin and the dim glow of the overhead lights was like a sanctuary.

As soon as he realised he wasn't going anywhere, he buckled in for the ride.

'You're okay,' he muttered to himself under his breath. 'Walk in the park.'

'Yes,' Dane said. 'It's a walk in *a* park. But it's not any park you know.'

Silence.

Slater worked his jaw, staring acid hate across the table the whole time.

Dane said, 'Do you see?'

'See what?' Slater said. 'A degenerate who drugs his guests against their will?'

Dane started, 'Bodhi is no drug. It is a—'

Slater tuned out his next words and told himself the truth to drive a wedge between his own thoughts and Dane's persuasions. *Bodhi is a potent blend of Dexies, molly, and benzos. I'm aware, you piece of shit.*

The Dextroamphetamine would get his heart racing, the MDMA would drill dopamine into his receptors, and the benzodiazepine would level everything out to keep him calm and numb and stop him panicking. But that was what one dose was supposed to do. A single hit was expertly crafted to deliver maximum euphoria, but three was beyond overkill. What if he'd ended up finishing the whole glass? How would that have gone down?

Slater made the first violent movement when he lashed out and swiped the rest of the Bodhi-laced water away.

Dane shot to his feet, as if the hit had triggered the start of his sermon.

'Yes!' he shouted, his voice booming. 'Feel that anger! Feel that hate you have toward us! Realise it is not directed at us, and in fact is aimed outward, at all of humanity, at the uncertainty that ripples through your being.'

Slater thought, *This'll be easy not to listen to him. The guy's a lunatic.*

Then it began.

It started with a soft numbness behind his eyes, like the sharp edges were taken off everything in his field of view. The lights overhead glowed brighter, and Slater found himself staring at Dane's face as the man spewed his delusions.

His stare accentuated every capillary in Dane's cheeks, every bead of sweat squeezing their way out through his pores, the flecks of spittle on his tongue as it darted in and out of his mouth.

Every crack of dry skin on his lips, every speck of dandruff in his hair, every morsel of food in his beard.

Dane said, 'Turn within, Will. Look for the source of your anger. Look for the well. Envision it. Accept it.'

Slater waited a second to reply.

It dragged out for all eternity.

The room hovered in stillness, the very definition of the calm before the storm.

Slater said, 'Fuck you.'

Brilliant colours exploded in his vision, making the cabin pulsate. It wasn't a hallucinogen like LSD or mushrooms, so he could still make out his surroundings without slipping into a different world entirely, but the furniture in the cabin shifted dramatically. It still looked the same but it felt like a realm he'd never touched before.

Panic swelled in him with dark fury.

He gripped the edges of the table. His touch was different, heightened. He could sense every sliver of wood in the table, imagine where the logs had come from to make the cabin itself, smell the forest and the grass and the musty aroma.

Dane was there, looming over him.

'Listen, Will. Listen to my voice. You are in its grip.' His voice boomed like he was omnipotent. 'Do not fight it. You have fought everything in your life, but if you fight this, you will lose. Let it in. Embrace it. Love it. Cherish it. That is the only way to victory here. Your combat experience means nothing now.'

Slater put up a steel wall in his mind, and realised if it weren't for meditation he would be lost.

The key principle of meditation is detachment and observation. When you sit there with your eyes closed, your purpose isn't to think *nothing*. It's to observe your thoughts as they enter your mind, watch them with a keen eye, and let them float on by. It allows you to separate yourself from the rash impulses of anger, greed, fear, envy. In everyday life you can catch those thoughts better, realise they aren't *you,* let them go...

He did that now.

As the reality he knew slipped away, he didn't give in. It would be so easy ... he felt so damn good. Just accepting Dane's words would open the floodgates and he'd slip into unimaginable pleasure, but if there was one thing on this earth Will Slater was accustomed to, it was denying himself pleasure. Every neuron in his brain pleaded with him to let go, to give himself over, to tear down the walls in his head and become one with what he was experiencing.

He wanted more than anything to fully embrace the compound, let Dane become the messiah.

He held strong.

Dane whispered the mantras of the cause for what might have been ten minutes, but felt like ten years.

Slater let the words come in, watched them try to attach themselves to his heightened subconscious...

Watched them fail.

He imagined himself as a rock golem, impenetrable, detached from the world around him as it morphed and twisted and pulsed and throbbed and—

In his ear, Dane whispered, 'Let me in. Become one with the creed.'

Slater looked up at the man, smiled and winked. The gesture took focus like he couldn't comprehend, but he did it.

Dane stood there, his face kind and benevolent, but the eyes never lie.

Slater saw every atom of his irises, every detail in his pupils.

There was frustration there.

He latched onto Dane's irritation and managed the words, 'Keep trying.'

Dane bent down and gripped his throat.

73

Violetta intercepted King in the exterior corridor, outside the door leading to the male and female bathrooms.

There was no one else in sight, but the window might not last long.

She kissed him briefly on the lips, more to steady herself. His presence warmed her. His touch spread calm in her.

She stepped away and saw he was pale.

She said, 'What is it? I saw the look on your face from across the room.'

He filled her in with a brief summary of what had unfolded. She soaked it in without emotion, then mulled it over, her handler side kicking in.

She said, 'So what's changed? You were okay before dinner.'

'There's no way Dane didn't find the body,' King said. 'That's what I've realised. Believing otherwise is idiocy.'

'He hasn't done anything yet.'

'But he will. Don't you see? This is his last stand. I never should have given Slater the go-ahead.'

'You think Dane will try to kill him?' Violetta said, stepping closer to King. 'Think about that for a second. Stop and take a breath. That would go disastrously for him.'

'No,' King said, shaking his head. 'Dane's switched on. He knows his limitations. I think he'll use Bodhi.'

'How?'

'By slipping it to him.'

Violetta considered the ramifications, the mental destruction that might ensue. And Slater had been uncomfortable taking a microdose for the sake of his cover. What would a full dose do to him?

'You're just guessing,' she said. 'It'll be fine. He'll be back in no time.'

King said, 'Something tells me I'm right.'

Violetta went quiet, considered the consequences.

She said, 'If he doesn't come back, we move tonight.'

'Yeah,' King said. 'Maybe.'

Distant footsteps drew closer.

Violetta said, 'But where's Dane taken him?'

King's jaw was tense as he said, 'I have no idea.'

He walked into the bathroom before anyone spotted them together.

74

Slater's heart thudded, and it was all he could concentrate on.

The more he worried about it, the worse it got.

130 beats per minute.

140 beats per minute.

150…

160…

Dane said, 'You're sweating.'

His voice was like thunder.

Dane said, 'Listen to my voice. Feel its weight. Feel me moving the earth beneath you. *Feel.*'

The earth moved.

Slater knew it was all in his own head, but just because you know something's not real doesn't make it any less terrifying. The cabin shook, glowing and pulsing and swirling.

Somewhere in the overworked pleasure centre of his brain, a voice of reason pushed through.

If you can show lucidity now, Slater thought, *you will break him.*

All it's going to take is one massive push.

Do it.

Do it right now.

All of him screamed to lose himself to the pleasure. To loll his head back, listen to Dane's words, and allow them to change him. It was beyond enticing.

But he'd built his life on denying himself pleasure.

What Dane hadn't taken into consideration was Will Slater's ability to embrace pain. Right now, it hurt his mind to keep the effects of the drugs at bay. It hurt so goddamn much.

But that's where he lived, day in, day out.

He went towards it.

Dane grabbed him by the throat again and looked down into his eyes. 'See, my child. See the light.'

Slater stared back.

He opened his mouth to speak.

He saw Dane's eyes swell with excitement.

Slater said, 'Do you know how fucking stupid you sound?'

Dane's face fell.

Slater smacked his hand aside, got up, and walked across the room. It took unbelievable effort. Everything swayed. Disassociation made his legs feel like jelly, demanding that he stumble and fall and come to rest on the floor, relishing the sheer stimulation of the drugs.

He refused.

He absolutely refused.

He made it to the door and threw it open.

Behind him, Dane's voice filled his head. 'You're not going to go out there. It's dark. Think of the unknowns. You'll be terrified.'

Slater stared into the void.

The darkness warped then constricted, throbbing like it

was alive. His mind ran through the possibilities — wild animals stalking him in the shadows, disciples hunting him across the prairie.

It's not real, he told himself. *None of it is real.*

Dane said, 'Come back to me. Back to the warmth. Take a seat, put your feet up, enjoy the moment. Listen to what I have to say. I'll show you how the world really works.'

How the world really works?

It works by confronting your fears.

Slater smiled to himself. He didn't allow Dane to see.

All you have to do is get through the night.

Simple.

And impossible.

A paradox.

He stepped out of the cabin and walked off into the grassland, embracing his deepest terrors.

75

King paced the bedroom.

There was little else to do.

It was past ten p.m. The commune had wound down for the night. The disciples of Mother Libertas were on nature's sleep cycle — sleep when it gets dark, rise at first light. It was a pleasant way to live. No phones, no social media, no overthinking, no incessant thoughts ... just the calm, peaceful completion of daily manual labour surrounded by the stillness of nature.

Wyoming's grasslands were the perfect location for a cult like this.

King had contemplated it all day.

Now he could think about nothing other than the fact that Slater hadn't returned.

He went over his options, thinking quickly, aided by isolation. He could set off into the darkness in search of where Dane had taken Slater, but that was an approach destined for failure. He'd be walking in circles without any light, unless he wanted to bring a torch and alert the entire commune to the fact he was out there, doing something he shouldn't be doing.

He could go to the bunkhouse where Alexis and Violetta slept, rouse them from sleep, determine what to do next.

That would destroy the cover.

Expose them immediately.

King realised they should have moved that afternoon, before dinner, but indecision had stymied their drive. They were spread out, unable to talk to each other aside from hushed whispers in hidden corners. They didn't know enough about the inner workings of the cult. Infiltrating Mother Libertas under the guise of civilians was the smart move, but it needed time.

Dane, it seemed, was expediting things.

So do I move now?

Without weapons?

Without a plan?

Slater could handle himself. King knew it, but the fear of the unknown was oppressive. To combat it he lowered himself into his bunk, closed his eyes, and attempted to meditate.

It didn't work.

His eyes flew open and he lay there in uncomfortable silence.

Fearing for his brother-in-arms.

76

The last thing Dane Riordan expected was for Will to follow through with it.

The big man stepped out of the cabin and disappeared.

Dane's stomach twisted.

He lunged forward, rounding the table, passing the food that hadn't been touched. He made it to the door, which had naturally swung closed, and threw it open.

Will was gone.

Dane felt cold. He'd told Maeve that security measures weren't necessary, that Elias could be put to better use elsewhere. There was no way a man could withstand such a mammoth dose of Bodhi. That's what he'd thought.

He can't withstand it, he reminded himself.

The Bodhi would tear Will's world apart, but the man had resisted its initial effects, held it together long enough to take the situation into his own hands.

And I just stood there.

Let him walk out, because I didn't think he'd do it.

Dane tried to be honest with himself, tried to admit that

the reason he'd hesitated was because he was scared. He had a suspicion about who the newcomers truly were, and if he was correct, then Will and Jason could kill him with their bare hands.

No more games, he told himself.

Time to put them in the dirt.

He killed the lights and left the food and cutlery on the table. A disciple could clean it up in the morning. He stepped out of the cabin, now nothing more than a dark husk, and set off for the commune. The settlement was a beacon of light in the blackness of the plains, and he knew Will would avoid it. The man would try to ride out the Bodhi away from prying eyes, protected by solitude.

It'd break him, but he wouldn't be disturbed if he stayed out in the prairie.

That was a tall order, but Dane now knew the man was up to it.

Dane walked fast, striding it out over the terrain. Involuntary shivers ran through him. He imagined Will ignoring the Bodhi, quashing its effects, and proceeding to stalk his prey. Every time Dane turned his head he pictured the big man leaping out of the night, teeth bared, hands wrapping around his throat…

'Fuck this,' he muttered for no one to hear.

He was sober, and he still couldn't stop the intrusive thoughts.

He wondered what Will was going through.

77

Slater fought not to lose his mind.
It would be so easy. If he lay down in the cold dirt and let go, he'd have the best few hours of his life. But he'd also lose all spatial awareness, vulnerable to any of the disciples walking up to him and slitting his throat.

To stay cognisant under the effects of so many drugs would be the toughest test of his life.

Being hunted in this state, being a wanted man ... it was horrifying.

He stumbled without seeing, walking away from the distant light of the commune. In his heightened state the glow was heavenly. He ignored it. If he stumbled into the commune in this state, the mental burden would be overwhelming. Trying to act normal under the watchful eye of strangers...

No.

He needed solitude.

A dark monster reared up out of the ground.

He jolted, nearly falling over, and the anxiety made his

vision spin. Unreality closed in, but he pushed back against it, keeping it at bay. He composed himself and stared ahead.

It was a giant cottonwood tree, alone on the plains. He'd nearly walked right into the trunk.

He circled it, barely able to keep his feet, putting the trunk between himself and the commune. That way, even if a search party came out this way, he'd see their torch beams before they saw him.

He sat down against it.

The bark felt alive, each touch of the wood rippling across his back. As soon as he came to rest, his sensations heightened even further. Stillness exacerbated the effects of the drugs.

'Holy shit,' he breathed.

The night expanded, becoming endless and infinite.

'The morning,' he told himself. 'It'll fade by then. You just need the morning.'

Monsters in his head came to the surface, hitting him like punches.

Memories of endless killings and beatings. Blood, bullets, gore, steel, broken bones, torn skin.

He tried to force himself out of the thought loop.

He couldn't.

So he went toward it.

'Try it,' he said out loud to himself. 'Try and break me.'

He went deep into his own head, gave himself over to the traumatic memories, and the rest of the world fell away.

The Bodhi seized him, and he felt the full power of it.

Three substances, combined in perfect ratios.

A whole new world.

He rested his head back against the tree trunk and fought to maintain his sanity.

78

In the bowels of the farmhouse, Dane's phone screen lit up with an incoming call.

It was three in the morning now. Dane had locked himself in his office, plotting, scheming. A plan was coming together. All he needed now was confirmation.

He answered the phone. 'Connor.'

'Sorry,' the voice said back. It was youthful yet experienced. 'Work's been chaotic.'

'Did you do what I asked?'

A pause. 'You're going to love me.'

'I already do,' Dane said. 'Gaia runs through us, and she flows to you. You know what that feels like. If you have good intel, I'll permit you to ascend to the next level. And the Bodhi will flow forever.'

Connor sucked in a breath in nervous anticipation.

Then he said, 'Jason King and Will Slater. Those are their real names.'

Dane sat forward in his chair, eyes widening. 'They're in the system?'

Connor nearly laughed. 'To put it mildly. You ready for this?'

'Of course.'

Connor told him a long story.

79

In the early hours of the morning, just before the sun started rising over the plains, Violetta stirred.

There was someone in the doorway.

She jolted and sat up, and the movement rattled the bed frame. She felt Alexis stir in the bunk underneath.

Violetta composed herself and said, 'Yes?'

It was Elias.

He said, 'Maeve wants to speak with you.'

Silhouetted by the weak hallway light, they couldn't see his face, so Alexis assumed he was talking to both of them.

She grumbled, 'Right,' and swung one leg off the mattress.

'Not you,' Elias said.

His voice was soft, but there was something unhinged in it.

Alexis froze, halfway out of the lower bunk.

Elias said, 'Get more sleep. There's nothing to worry about.'

His shadowed head tilted upwards to the top bunk. 'You. With me. Now.'

Violetta had no choice but to comply. Refusing would mean compromising the entire cover, and they were too early in the process for that. The communication they had with King and Slater was also more difficult than they'd imagined. So for now, obedience was key.

She got dressed, put her hair up in a bun, and followed Elias outside.

It was freezing. Her breath clouded in front of her face as she tucked her hands into her armpits to encourage circulation. Elias, dressed in a loose cotton tee and corduroy slacks, didn't seem to notice. He walked in the Asian style, with his arms folded behind his back, like a pensive philosopher out on a late night stroll.

He made her uncomfortable.

With the night hanging thick over the commune, they headed for the farmhouse.

Violetta said, 'What does she want with me at this hour?'

Elias shrugged. 'That's neither my business nor my concern.'

'Thanks for the help.'

Elias bristled. He turned to look at her as he strolled. 'Maybe it's something to do with that attitude.'

'What attitude?'

'This is a community of love,' Elias said. 'We all lift one another up. Being curt and smug won't get you anywhere.'

'I meant no disrespect.'

'That doesn't automatically mean none was received,' he said. 'I'd be careful with your words in future.'

Every part of her wanted to fire back, but she didn't.

Maeve was waiting on the farmhouse porch. A couple of the exterior lights were on at each end of the porch, petering out into a long shadow in the centre, where the front door hung open.

Maeve stood in front of the door, her dress silhouetted.

She said, 'I apologise for the hour, Violetta. But there's something we need to discuss.'

'Sure,' Violetta said.

Her heart beat a little harder than usual in her chest. She tried to quieten it.

Maeve gestured for the door. 'Come on in.'

Elias said, 'Do you need me?'

'Wait out here,' Maeve said.

It doubled the tension.

Elias bowed his head. 'Yes, ma'am.'

Violetta followed her into the house. They sat in the same sitting room where she and Alexis had first been initiated, but the setup seemed far more sinister at night with minimal lighting than on a beautiful sunny day with fresh air flowing through the open windows.

Now it was cold and still.

Maeve sat down in the armchair and let the silence draw out.

As soon as Violetta started to squirm, Maeve sat forward and said, 'You should have told me you were pregnant, dear.'

80

Alexis stewed in her bunk.

Indecision had her in its grasp, clouding her judgment. Was Violetta in danger? Should she get up and investigate when she'd been explicitly told to stay where she was? Was it worth blowing her cover on the off chance it was already compromised?

As she lay there, wondering what to do, she started to drift back into sleep. The stress of pretending to be someone else got to her, making her bone-tired in the moments of quiet respite. Against her best interests, she began to fade away, slipping into much-needed additional rest.

Then she woke up again to a gun barrel in her face.

Brandon stood over her, his bulk filling her field of view, trapping her in the bunk.

He held a semi-automatic pistol with a serious lack of trigger discipline — his finger was inside the trigger guard, an inch away from sending a round through her skull. If she made any sudden movements or startled him in any way, he'd probably accidentally pull it.

She froze, the weight of the situation striking her.

Like a giant fist around her throat, obstructing her breathing.

She tried to inhale and said, 'What are you doing?'

'You were good,' he said. 'You did well. But now it's got to come to an end. Sorry.'

She said, 'I have no idea what you're talking about, Brandon. Can we talk? Does it have to be like this?'

'Yeah,' he said, 'unfortunately.'

Real fear outweighed the performance, and when she spoke it came from her true self, not the role she was playing. 'Is this it?'

He said, 'Not just yet. Maeve wants answers. No use killing you if she finds out the other bitch knows nothing.'

He winked at her.

She said nothing.

He said, 'You could be the mastermind, after all.'

'You're not going to believe me,' Alexis said, 'but you've got this all wrong. Someone's fed you bad information. The truth will come out eventually. Don't do anything stupid until then. And trust me, I'm not mad at you for this. I understand you're suspicious, but I'm not who you think I am.'

She spoke with conviction, and it actually made him hesitate. By reversing the confrontation to make him appear the guilty party for training a gun on an innocent woman, he was shocked out of automatic behaviour. He had to think hard about what he was doing.

But she couldn't make a lunge for the weapon, couldn't take advantage of the confusion.

Not with his finger inside the trigger guard.

He said, 'Get up. Come with me.'

'Where?'

Anger flickered in his eyes. 'You don't get to ask questions.'

She was already dressed, unwilling to strip to her nightwear in a place as alien as this commune, so she simply got up and slipped into her shoes and let him lead her out of the bunkhouse.

He said, 'To the church.'

It loomed over them, the spire piercing the night.

She trudged toward the building with her head bowed.

She didn't know what to do.

81

King saw Dane Riordan walking through the commune in the early hours of the morning.

The tall man moved slowly between buildings, and King only caught a glimpse of him out his bedroom window, but it was enough.

It was the straw that broke the camel's back.

He decided to abandon his cover.

He was done with games. Slater hadn't returned from the cabin, his bunk lying empty all night, and he couldn't go check on Violetta and Alexis without drawing the attention of half the commune. There'd no doubt be watchers, disciples tasked with keeping a keen eye on the newcomers before they could be trusted, and they'd raise the alarm the instant they saw King approaching two women in the early hours of the morning.

To hell with it, he thought.

Dane was here, and Slater wasn't. That alone was reason to raze Mother Libertas to the ground. If Dane had somehow got the upper hand on Slater…

King would tear this whole place down.

He stepped out of his bunkhouse and made a beeline across the commune, weaving between buildings. He felt naked without a pistol at his waist, but there was no chance of finding where the Riordans stored their arsenal, let alone breaking in and acquiring firepower. For now, he'd have to get this done with his bare hands.

Cortisol flooded his system as he walked hard for Violetta's building.

Crunch time.

The door leading into their bunkhouse was already open, and he went to walk straight in.

Dane stepped out into the weak light.

King came to a halt, facing the spindly man. 'What are you doing here?'

Dane said, 'What are *you* doing here?'

'Get out of my way.'

'You sure that's a good idea?' Dane said. 'Think about what you're doing.'

King hesitated.

Dane said, 'Do you really understand this place? What it is. What sort of resources I have access to. Have you ever fought two hundred people at once?'

King backtracked immediately. 'What are you on about?'

'You tell me. You're the one that decides what this is.'

'I need to piss,' King said. 'The toilet's clogged in our bunkhouse.'

Dane smiled knowingly. 'Is it?'

'You want to go see for yourself?'

'I just might.'

'Be my guest. In the meantime, let me relieve myself. I don't know what you're on about, but I'd watch your mouth. I'm your new head of security, remember?'

Dane's smile dissipated into a slight smirk. 'Are you?'

King didn't like the atmosphere one bit. He didn't respond.

Dane said, 'Don't use this building. You'll wake everyone up. There's a bathroom in the mess hall. I'll take you to it.'

'No thanks.'

Dane raised an eyebrow. 'No?'

'You heard me.'

Dane gave him the once over with his gaze, and came away satisfied. 'You're not armed.'

'Neither are you.'

'But you'll still do as I say. It's not a request. It's a command.'

'No one in this place is commanding me to do anything.'

'You work for me.'

'Do I?'

They were going round in circles, and they both knew it. Skirting around the unspoken truth.

Does he know? King thought.

Dane sure seemed different.

All that was left to do was take a risk. 'I need this building, not the mess hall. Violetta wanted to speak with me.'

Dane hesitated before responding, letting the words hang.

'At four-thirty in the morning?' he said. 'What on earth about?'

'I don't know. That's why I'm here.'

'How did she contact you?'

'We spoke at dinner.'

'You're new here. This isn't the right timing to be sleeping with the disciples.'

'She's not a disciple yet,' King said. 'She's as new as I am. And I'm not sleeping with her.'

Dane smiled. It was sinister. 'Everyone here is a disciple, my friend.'

'I'm going to need you to get out of my way,' King said. 'Respectfully.'

'"Respectfully,"' Dane parroted.

He left it at that.

King said, 'Dane.'

Dane said, 'Jason.'

'You know what I'm asking.'

'She's not here,' Dane said. 'She's up at the farmhouse. Speaking with Maeve.'

Now it was King's turn to parrot. 'At four in the morning? What on earth about?'

Dane said, 'That's not your concern.'

Make a decision, King thought.

He was done with games.

He said, 'Yes, it is.'

He turned and strode for the trail leading to the farmhouse.

Dane didn't call after him, or protest, or give chase. He just watched quietly as King walked away, which was somehow more uncomfortable than if he'd become angry.

King felt eyes drilling into his back all the way across the commune.

82

Every footstep in the empty church echoed.
Brandon walked Alexis down the central aisle and directed her to sit in one of the pews. Then he stood over her, keeping the gun trained on her face. He was calm and poised in the midst of heightened tension, and she was sure there was a small dose of Bodhi flowing through his veins.

She said, 'Do you know what you're doing?'

'Shut up.'

He was still too far away to make a lunge. Bodhi was helping him stay calm and composed in a risky situation, and it nullified most of the beginner mistakes he would have made if he was sober. If his youthful anger was free to control him, he might step in and put the gun to her temple, which would allow her to jerk to the side and break his fingers as she disarmed him. Although she had to accept that might not work either — King and Slater could do it, but they both weighed north of two hundred pounds, and had powerlifted their whole lives. That sort of explosive strength simply wasn't replicable.

So she fell back on persuasive methods. 'You know, I've always thought there was something about you...'

He didn't say anything.

She continued. 'Ever since you picked me up ... I don't know. It's like I haven't been able to take my eyes off you.'

'Shut up.'

'I might as well tell you,' she said. 'If you're being serious and my life is really in danger. I might as well say what's on my mind.'

He didn't repeat the phrase. He fell quiet, looking at the space above her head, trying to feign that he wasn't listening despite every part of him wanting to hear what came next.

She said, 'If this is my last night on earth, then so be it. What Mother Libertas deems as necessary is always right. I won't put up a fight. But I damn well want to enjoy what time I have left.'

'Would you be quiet?' he said. 'No one said anything about killing you. I have to hold you here.'

'But if Maeve decides it's not in the best interests of the movement to keep me alive ... well ...'

She trailed off.

He lowered his head in a slight nod, encouraging her to keep talking.

She skirted half a foot across the pew, inching closer to him. She lowered her voice and said, 'No one's around. They won't see what we get up to.'

Silence.

She said, 'I want you, Brandon.'

'Why?' he said. 'No one wants me.'

'I do.'

In her peripheral vision, she watched his jeans grow tight around the crotch area. In his head, two opposing impulses fought for control. The subservience to the Riordans, screaming at him to do his job and not get caught up in this foolishness. Then the animal, primal part of his brain, relishing power over this gorgeous creature, desperate to satiate his desires.

He finally looked at her — her green eyes, her pale skin, her luscious curves.

He said, 'What do you want with me, exactly?'

She touched her lips with her tongue. 'To get those pants off, for starters.'

'Go on, then.'

He was still holding the gun, but his finger came out of the trigger guard as he sauntered forward.

She was seconds away from ripping the weapon — which she now identified as a Beretta — out of his hands when a voice broke the silence from the other end of the church. 'What's going on?'

It was a female voice, timid in tone, but it echoed.

Brandon wheeled around, and Alexis looked over her shoulder.

Addison stood there, her hair tousled from sleep, her eyes half-closed. 'You weren't in the bunk when I woke up. What are you doing?'

Brandon stepped away from Alexis and returned his finger to the trigger, aiming it at his hostage again. 'This isn't your business, Addison. Go back to bed.'

Addison met Alexis' eyes and then lifted her gaze to Brandon. 'Who told you to do this?'

'Maeve.'

'I hope so,' Addison said. 'I really hope so.'

'You think I'd hold her at gunpoint for no reason?'

'What's the reason?'

'Confidential,' Brandon said, then his face began to redden as he turned hot. 'Go back to bed!'

Addison said, 'Fuck off, Brandon. If Maeve is telling you to do this, then I'm just as involved as you are. We came here together, in case you forgot.'

'She didn't ask you, did she?'

Addison didn't reply, but she didn't retreat either. She looked at Alexis again.

Alexis mouthed, *Help me.*

Addison didn't react.

But when she turned her attention back to Brandon, she said, 'Let's stop this shit, okay? We're taking this too far. I should have said something earlier...'

Brandon said, 'About what?'

'This isn't the life for us, Brandon.'

'What are you talking about?'

'We don't belong here.'

Now Brandon's eyes were hot along with his face. Rage burned bright behind them.

He trained the gun on his sister.

'Blasphemy!' he shouted. 'Who got to you? Who fed you lies? Was it this bitch here?'

Addison froze, her face paling. 'You're insane. You're not my brother. Not anymore.'

Brandon tensed up with rage.

Alexis lunged for the Beretta.

83

Violetta managed to quash the panic in her chest and save face.

She didn't outwardly react, just furrowed her brow in confusion. 'Pregnant?'

Maeve said, 'Don't play stupid, girl.'

'I'm not...' Violetta said, trailing off into introspection. 'This is the first I'm hearing of this.'

'No it's not,' Maeve said. 'I'm not going to punish you. You don't need to worry. In fact, I have good news. Exceptional news. It's going to change your life. It's going to change us all...'

Violetta didn't answer.

Beneath her facade, she was crippled by fear.

Maeve said, 'I was told you were pregnant. Gaia spoke to me, whispered to me in the middle of the night. And I can see on your face that it's true. You don't need to deny it anymore. There's nothing to be afraid of. You're safe here, my dear.'

Violetta had no idea how to play it.

Deny? Stick to her guns? Admit it? Act grateful that Maeve was aware?

How does she know? she thought.

Her head reeling, she said, 'I'm sorry. I wasn't familiar enough with this place to admit it. I was going to tell you, as soon as I was comfortable here.'

'You're not comfortable?'

'I'm getting there,' Violetta said. Her voice shook. She didn't need to fake it. 'Just … it's a lot to handle right now. I didn't know if I belonged here. Now I know I do.'

Maeve beamed. 'That's lovely to hear, Violetta. And really, there's no need to be alarmed. I have a deeper connection to Mother Earth than anyone on this planet. When she delivers me a message, I listen dutifully. And she told me that your child is special. In more ways than you will ever know. He has warrior blood, warrior mana. A warrior spirit. He is the future of Mother Libertas, Violetta. That is what I was told. That is what I believe.'

Violetta's head spun.

Does she know who I am? she thought. *Does she know my real identity?*

It was eerily coincidental if she didn't. Almost too coincidental. The child of Jason King, one of the most devastating government operatives in history, coupled with Violetta's athletic prowess and genetics…

If warrior blood was real, the baby growing in her womb had plenty of it.

But does Maeve know? Or is she making it up as she goes along?

Maeve said, 'I'm afraid your place here is no longer voluntary. Your baby has been chosen by the Earth. It will be raised here, boy or girl, and it will lead Mother Libertas into upheaving society. It will bring a new world into existence, Violetta.'

Violetta needed air.

Now.

She got to her feet.

Maeve said, 'Sit down, dear.'

Through sharp breaths, Violetta said, 'I need some fresh air. I'm sorry. I'm panicking.'

'Your head is panicking,' Maeve said. 'Your heart and soul see clear...'

But her words wouldn't work this time.

Violetta knew if she kept playing along, she might very well be imprisoned until her baby was born. King and Slater couldn't protect themselves from two hundred disciples with their bare hands, and if Maeve sent them into a frenzy, preying on their groupthink and tribalism, they would attack the newcomers with no regard for their own lives. In the face of those numbers, whether the disciples were trained or not, King and Slater would succumb.

This was the endgame.

If Violetta stayed and tried to play along, she could wind up in a cell, helpless.

Your child is in mortal danger.

It made her forget the risks, forget the cover. Nothing mattered but her baby's safety, and it overrode her.

She walked away from Maeve without a second look.

84

King made it almost all the way up the trail before he realised there was someone waiting for him.

A tall lanky silhouette, standing with the restrained poise of a lifelong martial artist.

Elias stared at him as he approached. 'Has Maeve requested your presence?'

King nodded. 'Yeah. It's urgent. Step aside.'

Elias shook his head. 'If you were telling the truth I'd already know about it. I'm still the head of security, you see. Nothing from Maeve gets past me without my knowledge. What are you really doing here?'

'Kid,' King said, 'if you don't move, I'm going to beat the living shit out of you.'

Elias bristled. It was the first outward threat any of the newcomers had made, and although he'd suspected they weren't who they seemed all along, the confirmation was still shocking all the same.

Elias adopted a Wing Chun posture, loosening his muscles. 'If you really want to try…'

King sighed.

He didn't have time for this.

And the unknowns were palpable. Dane was somewhere below in the commune, doing who knows what. Maeve was inside with Violetta. Alexis could be anywhere. Slater was still AWOL.

Fighting this moron would achieve nothing, and might end up making things a hundred times worse if Elias raised the alarm.

Then the front door of the farmhouse burst open and Violetta hustled out onto the porch. She was breathing hard, the colour drained from her cheeks.

King stared at her. 'Are you okay?'

Elias said, 'You two know each other?'

'Shut the fuck up.'

Elias darted at King and threw a palm strike at incredible speed. King had underestimated Elias' ferocity, because the kid came at him so fast he barely saw the strike before it whistled through the air at him. But he hadn't pioneered a black-ops division for no reason. His reflexes were just as superhuman, and he sidestepped and shoved Elias in the chest. The man lost his footing and tumbled away from the house, tripping on a stray rock and collapsing into a ditch. He was more dangerous than King had anticipated, but following him into the ditch was a terrible idea.

With so many unknowns in the mix and the entire commune bristling like it was a pinprick away from bursting, every move had to be smart and calculated.

Which sometimes meant retreat.

King repeated, 'Are you okay?'

Violetta's voice was barely audible, but King read her lips. 'She knows I'm pregnant.'

Ice ran through King's veins.

He thought, *Fuck.*

He said, 'Come on.'

'Where are we going?'

'We find the others,' King said. 'Then we get out.'

'But the Riordans...?'

'Your safety trumps the mission,' he said. 'Now let's go.'

Elias was scrabbling out of the ditch, his clothes dirtied and his morale wounded, when Violetta ran down the porch steps and took King's outstretched hand.

Maeve stepped out onto the porch behind them.

Her voice flooded the night. 'Where are you lovebirds going?'

King ran with her, down the trail.

Elias and Maeve watched them go in menacing silence.

85

Elias turned to Maeve. 'You want me to go after them?'

'They have nowhere to run,' Maeve said. 'Dane will handle it. I want you to go find the other one.'

'Slater?'

Maeve nodded slowly. 'Now we know he's King's brother operative. We know their history. There's no chance he ran away. He's out there, at the perimeter, waiting for the Bodhi to wear off. Go find him.'

'What do you want me to do with him?'

She stared down at him from the porch. 'What do you think?'

He nodded. 'Yes, ma'am.'

He charged his *ki,* prepared himself to deliver a fatal strike.

It would mark the first time he'd used his skillset against a resisting opponent.

He couldn't wait.

86

Brandon didn't see it coming.

He'd anticipated many things, but Alexis being able to hold her own in a fistfight wasn't one of them.

She tackled him to the church aisle, and his skull struck the concrete as it whiplashed. The Beretta came out of his hand, but Alexis had no chance of snatching it. Reality never works with precise coordination like in the movies — it's inherently random.

So the gun skidded under one of the pews and stayed there.

Brandon was nearly fifty pounds heavier than her.

If they ended up in a neutral position, he'd beat her to death. That's physics. There's no way around it. Fifty pounds is fifty pounds, and it's distributed across muscle and bone structure to provide an incredible advantage. If they were standing up, and Alexis punched him in the face, it'd maybe break his nose. If he punched her in the face, she'd snap out of consciousness instantly, maybe for a long time. There was every chance he'd put her in a coma.

All she had to rely on was the advantage of surprise.

She'd managed to take him down simply because he hadn't been expecting it. Now she was on top, in mount position, and he was possibly concussed from his head bouncing off the stone floor.

Aside from that, she had nothing.

So she made full use of her advantage.

She targeted his forehead with the point of her elbow and dropped her limb hard, aiming to slice instead of strike. It worked. Her elbow ran a jagged line across the skin of his brow, splitting it, sending blood flowing down his face.

She lined up another elbow...

...but he bucked her off like she weighed nothing.

She realised she'd massively miscalculated. Drawing blood had both brought him back to his senses and enraged him. It had put him in fight-or-flight mode, and now he was fighting like an animal. Alexis tumbled across her back as she spilled off him. One of the pews stopped her momentum and she started scrabbling to her feet.

Brandon was already on his feet.

He charged her, grabbed her around the waist and picked her up.

Terror seized her.

She was out of control, no limb in contact with the ground, and her life was in Brandon's hands.

He could do whatever he wanted to her.

He kept lifting, then changed direction and slammed her down on the pew.

On her neck.

An inch or two to the left or right and she would have been paralysed forever, but she recognised which way she was going in mid-air and tucked her chin to her chest in anticipation. Brandon drove her into the wooden seat across her upper back, bruising the muscles and maybe tearing something in one of her shoulders, but that was preferable to unconsciousness, paralysis, or death.

She spilled off the long bench and tumbled to the floor, squashed against the back of the next pew. Brandon stood over her, and raised a foot to stomp her face to mush.

Alexis' heart sank and through the pain she suppressed tears.

This angry kid, his teeth gnashing together in rage, was about to stomp her to death.

And there was nothing she could do about it.

A voice said, 'Don't you fucking dare.'

It took Alexis a moment to realise who'd spoken. She'd never heard the voice say anything with confidence.

Addison's timidity was gone.

She was in the aisle, out of sight, so Alexis couldn't see what she was doing.

Brandon sure could.

He slowly lowered his boot and stepped back out of the pew.

Alexis clambered to her feet, her upper back screaming.

It was agony, but when she saw Addison, pride overwhelmed the pain.

Addison aimed the Beretta at her brother.

Her finger was less than an inch off the trigger.

Brandon said, 'You dumb bitch.'

Addison's eyes were wet. She composed herself before she spoke. 'Do you even know who you are anymore? Do you realise what you were about to do?'

Brandon was beyond reproach. Anger drowned out any chance of introspection. 'Addison, listen to me. Shut the fuck up and put the gun down before someone comes in and sees you aiming it at me. You know what they'll do to you? I'm a loyal disciple. You've been hit and miss since you got here. Who are they going to side with?'

'You'd get them to kill me?' Addison said. 'That's what you're saying you'll do?'

Brandon said, 'Trust you to act high and mighty. Remember Karlie?'

Her throat spasmed as she gulped.

He nodded, his eyes crazed. 'Yeah, you remember Karlie. Acting like I'm the devil for hurting this bitch here when you took a baseball bat to an innocent girl's head. Why don't you think about your own actions for a while? In the meantime, put the fucking gun down.'

Addison's hand trembled.

Brandon's voice became monotonic. He knew exactly where to press. 'Karlie. You killed her.

'Karlie. You beat her brains in.

'Karlie. She was only looking for her brother.

'Karlie...'

Addison screamed, 'Shut up!'

Brandon said, 'Karlie's corpse is in the ground. There's dents in her skull where you swung that bat. I mean, you really gave it your all, didn't you?'

Addison squeezed her eyes shut and dropped the gun. She sank to her knees, clamping her hands over her ears, giant sobs wracking her body. A confused, lost, innocent young woman, twisted into something she couldn't comprehend by Maeve Riordan.

Alexis felt sick.

It took Brandon a second to compute the fact there was no longer a gun trained on him.

That's what did him in.

Alexis lurched out of the pew and leapt onto his back, locking in a body-triangle with her legs, clamping to him like a backpack. He spun, arms flailing as he threw punches, but nothing worked. He reached back to gouge her eyes but she already had a forearm around his throat, and she locked the rear naked choke in and wrenched tight.

That's the only scenario where fifty pounds of weight difference doesn't matter.

It took him fifteen seconds to go out.

Impressive, considering he should have been down by ten.

But the end result was the same.

He went limp and collapsed, falling forward, face ricocheting off the stone. There was a *crack* as his nose broke, but he didn't react. He was already unconscious.

Alexis clambered off him, and already he was beginning to resurface from unconsciousness, but he wouldn't be cognisant for at least a couple of minutes.

She walked over, picked up the Beretta where it had fallen by Addison's sobbing form, and pulled the girl to her feet.

'Listen to me,' Alexis said. 'You're not a monster. You're not.'

'Can you do me a favour?' Addison mumbled between sobs.

Alexis nodded.

Addison said, 'Kill me. I don't deserve to live.'

Alexis bowed her head.

She hated Maeve with every fibre of her being.

87

The afterglow made Slater superhuman.

When he finally came down from the high, there was a hint of daylight in the Wyoming sky. It was the same shade at pre-dawn as it was at dusk — a dark royal blue. The aftereffects of the abundance of chemicals made the colours brighter, but they also sharpened his senses. Reality seemed different — clearer, crisper, in focus.

Slater worked his way back up the tree trunk, stood on shaky legs, and re-calibrated.

It took all the effort he could muster.

The night had lasted both minutes and years. Moments dragged on for all eternity, then whole hours passed in the blink of an eye. He'd experienced the full emotional spectrum, turbulence rattling behind his eyes, but he never let it show, despite the fact there was no one around to see. Briefly, when he gained lucidity amidst the haze, he understood that the commune wouldn't be the same in the morning. Covers would be blown, confrontations would play out, all while he was forced to sit in the dark and grapple with his mind. He wouldn't be heading back into the same world he'd walked out of.

But now he had control of his motor functions and his reflexes, and he breathed in pure elation as he rolled his wrists and they responded.

Two things happened at once.

The distant wail of a siren startled him, made him jump, and he realised something was very wrong back in the commune.

Then a hand clamped down on his shoulder and pushed him back down to a seated position.

Slater settled his heart rate, then looked up.

Into the eyes of Elias.

He said, 'Oh. Hey, kid.'

Elias' gaze bore into him, scrutinising him, studying him for signs of mental destruction. That amount of Bodhi ... it had to have crippled Slater permanently. Elias' hands were rigid and straight, and Slater knew he was trying to charge his *ki,* his energy.

He could see all of Elias' demons, all the man's insecurities and beliefs.

Elias believed unconditionally in the power of Wing Chun.

That's why he was unarmed.

Slater said, 'Are you here to kill me?'

Elias said, 'Took me forever to find you. Dane told me to put you out of your misery. He butchered it last night. Gave you a dose that was a little too heroic. Then he found out who you really were.'

Still seated, knees tucked up, Slater waited for Elias to trail off before he said, 'Kid, why are you still talking?'

Elias hesitated, then composed himself. 'Because you're helpless.'

'Yeah?'

'The Bodhi hasn't worn off yet, so your wires are scrambled. Your brain's fried. And even if you can put up a fight, you know you can't possibly match me.'

'Is that right?'

'Why don't you find out for yourself?'

'Are you charging your *ki?*' Slater said. 'Is that what's happening?'

He said it with such mocking derision that goosebumps appeared on Elias' neck. His anger rose to the surface. The kid wasn't able to suppress it.

His voice shaking, Elias said, 'You've thrown a few punches and kicks and you think you know what combat is?'

Slater said, 'I've been *in* combat my whole life. I know what works and what doesn't.'

'You're not making this any easier for yourself.'

Slater leapt to his feet, every sense primed, anticipating exactly what was going to happen.

It happened.

Elias, with all his belief and devotion and focus, finished charging his "*ki*" and threw an open-handed strike at Slater's neck. It was fast, and decently impressive, and if the side of his hand connected with Slater's throat it might have done real damage. But Slater implemented an ounce of head movement he'd picked up from boxing, and executed a shoulder roll. He leant back against the tree and took the blow on the meat of his deltoid muscle.

It stung a bit.

That was all.

Elias' hand darted back like it had been caught in a bear trap, and a look of pure shock crossed over his face. It was either disillusionment at the effectiveness of Wing Chun, or terror at what Slater might be capable of.

Or both.

Slater said, 'Try again.'

88

King and Violetta hustled all the way down into the centre of the commune, listened hard, and heard nothing.

Through laboured breaths, Violetta said, 'Should we steal a ride?'

'They'll be locked up,' King said. 'Let me think.'

A wailing alarm ruptured the early morning quiet.

They nearly jumped out of their skin.

Shouts that were practically war cries emanated from the bunkhouses.

King's stomach dropped.

Dane emerged from one of the distant buildings, hands behind his back like a monk. Above the piercing alarm, he shouted, 'Where do you think you're going?'

'Get Alexis,' Violetta said in King's ear. 'She's still in her bunk. We need to get Ale—'

Disciples began pouring out of the bunkhouse that contained Violetta and Alexis' room. They were rabid, barely human, possessed by the hatred and paranoia that Maeve had instilled in them.

In that moment King realised Maeve had succeeded.

The siren song of brutality ran deepest through Mother Libertas in times of crisis. Violetta posed no harm to the movement, but they didn't understand, nor did they care. The wailing alarm had turned them into savages, reduced them to their primal instincts, instincts that had been expertly shaped by Maeve.

They were all hungry for blood.

They didn't care where it came from.

Now King recognised why he hadn't acted sooner. Because of this. Two hundred members could be activated with the touch of a button, the alarm sending them into a frenzy. They didn't need Bodhi for this. This came from deep in their souls.

They would do whatever the Riordans commanded.

King stood frozen to the spot as Dane plucked useful followers out of the pack with hand gestures. He ushered nearly a dozen of the fittest, strongest men into a tight cluster, then silently commanded the rest to hang back.

The air went still.

Dane pointed at Violetta and said something to the pack. King couldn't hear what was said above the noise of the alarm. Then Dane's finger point moved over to King, and Dane drew a line across his own throat.

Message received.

King didn't hesitate. He took Violetta by the hand and ran with her into the mess hall, slamming one of the entrance doors open and spilling into the perimeter corridor circling the main cavernous space. They ran down the hallway in the dark, the shadows swallowing them.

Violetta panted with fear and struggled to control her emotions.

As they ran he said, 'What happened with Maeve?'

She filled him in.

His insides twisted.

The fear was insidious on Violetta's breath. 'Jason...'

'I know,' he said, forcing himself to remain stoic. 'I know what this means.'

Outside the building's walls, distant cries echoed across the grassland.

Of elation, of ecstasy, of purpose.

Violetta said, 'What do we do?'

Each syllable wavered.

He found an unlocked door leading into the giant main space and ushered her through. The mess hall was spotless, every speck of dust and residue cleaned away by the disciples. The long tables shone under the overhead lights that stayed on all night. The benches were empty. Not a soul about.

King led her to the other end of the hall, hoping to find an exit they could slip out of before the disciples surrounded the building. He came to a door set beside the long countertop where meals were served. He tried it. Locked.

He swore for no one but Violetta to hear.

She said, 'We can't blow our cover. We can talk our way out of this, I'm sure of it. It's understandable that you got spooked, that I got spooked. We can explain...'

King looked at her. He knew his eyes were steel.

He said, 'No way.'

'Jason...'

'Fuck the cover,' he said. 'Fuck all of this. The cover's blown anyway, isn't it? Why else would Maeve say the baby's the second coming of Gaia?'

'How *would* she know?' Violetta said. 'It's highly goddamn improbable that she knows our identities considering our own government doesn't know where we are ... there'd be nothing in the files that revealed I'm pregnant.'

'Have you told anyone?' King said. 'Anyone at all?'

Violetta racked her brains. He could see the memories flying past behind her eyes. She stopped on one of them. Her face cringed.

King said, 'When?'

'I cramped in front of Brandon and Addison,' she said. 'On our first night here, in the mess hall. But that could have been anything. Period pains, stomach bug, you name it...'

'They told Maeve,' King said. 'And Maeve guessed. She bluffed, and you didn't call it. But I think she also knows who we really are. That's why she's acting this way. I think she believes her own delusions.'

'It's not a front,' Violetta agreed. 'She honestly thinks my child is a sign from the gods. How does she lead these people if she believes what she's feeding them?'

'I think her head's a mess. She doesn't know what she believes.'

'We need to get out of here,' Violetta said, trying not to hyperventilate. 'Bunker down, lay low, regroup. Otherwise...'

King tensed up, staring over her shoulder.

She froze.

King said, 'Looks like it'll have to be "otherwise."'

She turned.

Disciples bled into the mess hall through the twin entrances on the other side of the space. They moved in silence, their hands bare. No one was armed. Even though Maeve and Dane might know who the newcomers truly were, the message hadn't been passed down to the followers just yet.

They thought they could do this through sheer force of numbers.

And maybe they could.

King counted eleven disciples stepping in.

All men.

The de facto foot soldiers.

89

Bodhi had Slater zoned in like nothing else.

At massive doses, the compound was insane.

Now, with the afterglow of a heroic dose coursing through him, he was twice as focused.

Elias stood there, completely vulnerable, trying to harness his invisible energy. It didn't seem to work, because he threw the next strike dejectedly, aiming for Slater's centre mass, hoping to wind him.

Slater tensed his chest and took the blow where it was intended to land.

It bounced off his pectorals.

It did nothing.

Slater said, 'You've only used this on helpless hostages, haven't you?'

Silence.

Elias threw another strike, harder than the second, putting his whole being into it.

Slater jerked into another shoulder roll and the side of Elias' hand smacked off his shoulder again.

No factor.

Slater said, 'This is a fight, Elias. I can fight back.'

Elias kept valiantly attempting to master his *ki* and he stepped in for a close-range elbow, a move he must have practiced well over ten thousand times. He executed it fluidly. His cocked right arm swung with impressive speed.

Slater stepped aside.

The elbow missed.

Slater said, 'How many dissidents have you killed for the Riordans?'

Elias swung again with the same elbow.

Slater shoulder rolled.

Took the blow across his upper arm.

Slater said, 'How much power did that give you? How did it make you feel?'

Elias' eyes were burning, his face twisted. He threw a barrage of punches and elbows, treating Slater like a Wing Chun dummy, emptying his gas tank on the *mu ren zhuang*. He did everything right, everything that martial arts had taught him. He didn't allow his emotions to take over, didn't let the rage creep in and affect his composure. He threw his attacks with pinpoint precision, using the full extent of his anatomy.

But he overlooked one critical aspect.

He always had.

The fact that he'd never trained against a resisting opponent.

Slater caught one of the elbows and threw it aside and got right up in Elias' face. He kept the knowledge that Elias had murdered defenceless followers in the back of his head, so he didn't hold back. He headbutted the guy in the jaw, cracking the bone, which put Elias in a dark place the kid had never felt before. It's easy to stay within the confines of your comfort zone and never train to face adversity, and that's what Elias had done his entire life. He was fast and sharp and could hit hard after relentless practice on the *mu ren zhuang,* but that's about twenty percent of what you need in a fight to the death.

There's so many more intangibles.

As Elias stumbled back with a broken jaw, Slater kicked him low in the calf, causing the muscle to seize up, and Elias went down on one knee.

Slater lined up a kick that ordinarily would have slammed into the body, but instead cracked into the side of Elias' skull because of his kneeling position.

Elias splayed into the dirt.

Slater said, 'Get up.'

No movement.

Slater said, 'Come on, get up.'

Elias got to his knees, then worked his way shakily back to his feet. His mouth and nose poured blood. His eyes had watered up, and his jaw hung open unnaturally. He couldn't shut it. It was broken.

Slater said, 'Harness your *ki.* Like you do before you kill those who betray the movement.'

Elias was statuesque, defeated.

'Come on,' Slater said. 'You've tapped into some higher ability, haven't you? You can fight better than any of these MMA fighters you see on TV. You're a master. Prove yourself.'

It touched the right nerve.

Concentration swelled in Elias' face as he tried to shut out the pain and summon ten straight years of practicing Wing Chun in privacy. All those hours, all that hard work.

Slater learned long ago that smart work beats hard work any day of the week.

Elias threw a final, all-out hand strike, aiming for Slater's throat.

His eyes were rabid with desperation.

Slater slapped it aside, drilled a calloused fist into Elias' nose, then seized the back of his neck and held him in place as he smashed three consecutive elbows into the guy's throat. Each impact caved in muscle and tissue and bone. Elias' eyes rolled up, exposing the whites, and he fell unconscious to the dirt.

He died choking.

Slater thought of all the people he'd killed for the Riordans, and figured Elias deserved worse than that.

Unfortunately there was no time to be cruel.

Standing over the body, Slater muttered, 'Shame.'

He rolled the corpse over so it was face-down, lifeless eyes burrowed into the dirt.

He went to find Alexis.

90

One of the disciples in the mess hall took the lead and said, 'Where do you think you're going?'

King put a hand on Violetta's shoulder, conveying the need for her to stay where she was, and he stepped forward, using himself as a human shield. There were still a few dozen feet of empty tables and benches between him and the first disciple.

He said, 'Let's all cool it. We need some breathing room. We'll work this out later, okay?'

The first man shook his head slowly, each swing of his chin menacing. 'That's not how it works, I'm afraid. You heard what Mother said. You are chosen, Violetta. You can't shy away from this.'

King pined desperately for calm and peace, but those concepts were long gone.

His stomach knotted as he realised he might have to blow the cover by force.

But he had to be sure.

He said, 'What are you going to do with her, exactly?'

The disciple's eyes flared.

The dark silence said everything.

But the man spoke anyway. 'You heard the command. She is priceless, and it looks like you two don't want to hang around. That's not acceptable. The baby will usher in a new era for Mother Libertas. If the lady doesn't want to stay, then we'll make the lady stay.'

King sensed every ounce of the danger his unborn child was in.

It changed him in his core.

He sensed the darkness rising in him, matching the energy in the air.

He said, 'Is that right?'

The first man smiled, relishing the confrontation. He'd been moving closer this whole time, sidestepping the long tables, and now King could see the swollen pupils. A low dose of Bodhi, enough to strip him of inhibitions, remove fear, elevate excitement. King stared past the man to the other ten followers, and all of them had the same glint in their eyes.

They were separated by mere feet now.

King hadn't lifted a finger in anger his whole time in the commune.

That was about to come to an end.

He said, 'You sure this is the way you want to go?'

The first man said, 'You're making the choice. Not me.'

'We're going to walk out of here,' King said, giving him a final chance. 'That's within our rights.'

The guy smiled devilishly. 'Not anymore.'

King said, 'Fine.'

A couple of dozen feet behind him, King heard Violetta quietly say, 'No.'

He ignored it.

Nothing would endanger his child.

Nothing.

King sized up the first guy. He was tall, big, strong, with pale skin and sandy hair. A farmhand in a previous life, maybe. Now a devoted convert.

Given a purpose, an identity, a tribe.

In that moment, King properly soaked in the disciple's behaviour for the first time. All the man's doubt and hesitation was gone, replaced by ardent commitment to the cause, leaving him free to commit any atrocity he desired in the name of the movement.

For the first time, King truly understood the danger of Mother Libertas.

Then King became an automaton. Stripped himself of his own inhibitions for the following minutes, until Violetta and the child inside her were safe. Adrenaline fused with relentless determination and overrode his senses.

Violetta said, 'Jason, no.'

He ignored it.

He walked straight at the first guy and said, 'Okay. We surrender.'

The guy cocked his head. 'You do?'

King's demeanour didn't gel with his words, and he was closing the distance fast.

King nodded. 'Yeah, man. We screwed up. I'm sorry.'

'Stay right there—'

Too late.

King darted into range and unleashed a colossal uppercut into the base of the farmhand's jaw.

The other ten disciples charged at him, their rage as dark as their souls.

91

The alarm didn't stop.

The blaring noise had filled the church for minutes now. The building's thick stone walls muffled most of the din, but some sound snuck through, which was enough. The whine reverberated, echoing off the walls and the high ceiling.

Addison's eyes were wide, depression giving way to terror.

Brandon was already stirring, crawling through semi-consciousness, the alarm lurching him awake like a walking zombie. Alexis realised that was neurological conditioning. The Riordans must have practiced the panic drill over and over again with their disciples until it was muscle memory, making them the equivalent of sleeper agents snapped into activation with a coded sound. The alarm was a distress signal. A threat to the foundations of Mother Libertas.

Even through the church walls, Alexis heard the rally cry of the disciples as they tore from slumber.

'Shit,' she said.

Addison said, 'Maeve has private quarters. Behind the altar.'

The girl could barely get the words out. Her face was aghast. Alexis could see she wanted to run. Addison was torn between the familiar comforts of the group, and doing the right thing.

She was brave enough to make the hard choice.

She said, 'Come on. We can hide there. I'll show you.'

Brandon clambered shakily to his feet and took a step toward Alexis. Alexis lifted the Beretta and aimed it at his face. He stopped in his tracks.

He said, 'All I need to do is scream.'

'Then you'll be dead.'

'And so will you.'

His eyes were glassy and his nose was swollen and misshapen, but she saw the processing going on in his head.

Am I ready to die for the cause? he was asking himself.

'You know you're not,' Alexis said, answering a question that hadn't been vocalised.

Brandon didn't scream.

He said, 'What do you want?'

The question came out muffled, distorted by the blood in his mouth. It was pouring from both his nostrils, running over his upper lip, staining his teeth.

She jerked the gun toward the altar. 'Walk.'

Addison shuffled past them, leading the way, refusing to even look at her brother.

Brandon said, 'Hey...'

Addison wheeled around. 'Shut up, Brandon. Shut up.'

She started for the altar. Alexis made Brandon go next so she could keep the gun trained on his back.

The church doors slammed open.

She jumped in her skin, looked over her shoulder, and saw her worst nightmare come true.

A search party filed into the nave of the church. Five men, all well-built. They spotted her at once, and cheers of elation rippled through the church.

Alexis knew she couldn't shoot them. So far there were five, but if she fired an unsuppressed weapon in a space like this, there'd be two hundred surrounding the church.

Those were impossible odds.

She turned back and kept her aim on Brandon, who was giddy with joy at the sight of his friends.

'Help me, brothers!' he shouted.

The five men broke into a sprint.

Alexis said, 'If you're not in the sacristy in ten seconds I'll blow your brains out.'

Brandon grimaced.

Then he turned and reluctantly ran after his sister, leaping onto the altar and down the other side, heading for the closed door up the back of the church.

Alexis followed with her heart in her throat, rapid footsteps closing in behind her.

92

Everything was surreal.

Like walking through an alternate reality.

Slater made it to the edge of the commune and came face to face with two disciples out the back of one of the bunkhouses. A man and a woman, both Caucasian, in their forties. They looked like a couple, standing too close together to be mere acquaintances. They were the oldest people Slater had seen in Mother Libertas. Despite the chaos going on around them, their faces were kind, and Slater pitied them for allowing Maeve to prey on their weaknesses.

They looked at him, both dumbfounded.

The man said, 'You're supposed to be dead, son.'

Slater said, 'Those are old plans. You're misinformed.'

'Where's Elias?'

'Not here right now. He put me in charge.'

'He did?'

'Maeve told him to. She had a revelation. Apparently I was chosen by Gaia.'

'Wow,' the woman said, genuine awe on her face. 'Where

are you headed now?'

'To find a friend. Are you two going to stop me?'

They shook their heads.

The man said, 'Do what you need to do.'

Slater walked straight past them, through the empty bunkhouse, and out the other side. Now he was in the open, but strangely he felt no fear. He was in touch with his own mind, so he recognised it was still affected by the Bodhi. His fear was gone, replaced by channelled confidence, and he remembered why he'd become addicted to substances — both legal and illegal — in the first place. The good ones strip you of your inhibitions, and if you use that to channel positivity and forward movement it can be incredible for—

No. He cut himself off from the thought. *Not again. Don't go down that road.*

He felt his demons rising, and he battled them down.

Out in the open now, members of the commune stared at him, but there was no instant animosity. In the strange dawn light there was still confusion rippling through the ranks. The disciples had been roused out of bed by the panic alarm, but someone else must have been labelled as the enemy, because they were unsure about Slater. And there was no sign of Dane to direct them, to highlight their enemies.

These people couldn't think for themselves.

That's how they'd bought into the cult in the first place.

The Riordans' screening process, victimising the easily influenced.

Where is *Dane?* Slater thought. *And, more importantly, where's King?*

The mess hall and the church loomed ahead.

He chose the church.

He wasn't sure why.

93

One down.

Ten up.

King understood he was dealing with men who wouldn't use common sense. No matter how many of them he beat down, they'd keep coming. They wouldn't retreat, wouldn't waver, wouldn't falter. Not when Maeve's creed was charging them with inhuman energy, fixing onto the chemical compound of Bodhi to make them savage.

King didn't need drugs to become a savage.

He leapfrogged one of the tables, coming down on top of one of the disciples who'd broken into a sprint to try and flank King from the rear. King shouldered him into the bench behind him, which took his legs out from underneath him. The disciple sprawled onto the opposite table and King dropped an elbow into his unprotected face, sandwiching his head against the metal tabletop. The guy rolled to the side, lost in semiconsciousness.

King heard footsteps behind him, so he spun and lashed out with a body kick that was guaranteed to hit the centre mass of a target he couldn't yet see. The toe of his boot slammed home against the new arrival's solar plexus, crumpling him, and King slammed a left hook into the side of his forehead as he bent over. He grabbed the collapsing body and drove it down into the bench, breaking a couple of limbs with the downward pressure.

Three down.

Eight up.

He left the two crippled followers there and dived back over the same table. The frantic move isolated two new disciples who'd tried the same flanking measure, to no avail. But they weren't deterred in the slightest, and they charged. No matter how talented, he couldn't defend two strikes at once. He didn't exist in the Matrix.

He rolled away from one punch and caught another on the side of his neck.

It was a hard hit, rattling his skull. He felt no pain, but that's a bad indicator of punishment absorbed in the heat of a fistfight. Adrenaline makes you largely immune to pain unless an injury impedes your movement, so a better test of whether you've got your wits about you is a quick equation, computed in milliseconds.

Seven times eight.

The answer came immediately: *Fifty-six.*

He was all there.

No need for a tactical retreat.

Resolute.

He grabbed the guy who'd hit him by the collar with one hand and returned the favour with the other. Drilled a big right fist into his Adam's apple, holding back so he didn't destroy the guy's windpipe and suffocate him. A breath exploded from the man's lips and he dropped, but King had already let go of him and spun and swung an elbow with reckless abandon. The second guy had jerked sideways, though, so the point of King's elbow hit him on the shoulder.

It still knocked him off his feet, sending him spilling onto one of the benches. He scrabbled upright and King kicked him in the face and sent his unconscious body sprawling under the accompanying table.

Five down.

Six up.

This was the part where everything usually changed. Realising they were dealing with a man far stronger, faster, and more precise than any adversary they'd faced before, most people would sense the tide shifting and run away.

Most people weren't dosed with Bodhi, though.

All six of the remaining disciples came at him, practically frothing at the mouth.

Then two of them peeled off, ran down a parallel aisle, intent on cornering Violetta.

King saw flaming red.

Dived back across the table, abandoning all concern of differentiating between strikes to incapacitate and strikes to kill. That no longer mattered. Protecting his family was everything.

Family.

The word struck him.

Something he'd never considered.

He came down in a heap behind the two guys who'd peeled off, but they didn't turn around or slow down. They were zoned in, their tunnel vision focused on Violetta hunched in the corner of the mess hall. She was trying to minimise her presence, make them focus on King, but it wasn't working.

King sprinted after them, closed the distance with

relentless athleticism, and seized one of the men around the waist from behind.

He weighed about one-sixty.

He might as well have weighed ten pounds.

King unleashed all his fast-twitch muscle fibres and picked the guy up and hurled him down into the closest bench. The guy landed on his upper back, taking most of the impact across his rear deltoids, stunning him into submission. The other guy finally wheeled around and King fired an uppercut into his stomach, tearing muscles, then grabbed him by the collar and jerked and brought him down on top of his comrade.

The pair clashed heads, stunning them both.

King grabbed the head of the man on top, lifted it up, and smashed it down like a bowling ball on the forehead of the guy underneath.

Two more immobilised.

Four up.

The last four had their sights set purely on King, the biggest threat, which was fine by him.

In fact, he relished it.

They scrabbled over tables, all four of them coming down in his aisle.

He went statuesque, planting his feet down, forming a human barricade between them and Violetta.

He lifted a hand and beckoned them toward him. 'Have a go.'

They all came forward.

They had a go.

King's muscles were flooded with lactic acid from dishing out so many devastating shots, but he gave thanks for all those gruelling combat simulations in training as his conditioning kicked in.

He figured he could go at this pace all day.

The most athletic of the four remaining disciples charged, all pent-up aggression fuelled by the substances in Bodhi. King diligently recognised the threat and brought his guard up, bringing a forearm vertical alongside each ear. He absorbed the guy's first full-power punch on his forearms, dissipating the power through his muscle chain. The guy's energy fizzled out as King nullified his first attack and he hovered in place for half a second, sucking up momentum for another swinging punch.

Half a second was all King needed.

His hands were already up in a boxing-style guard, so he lashed out with a one-two combination. His first punch was a jab, half-power, that landed square on the man's unprotected face and broke his nose, which stunned him and froze him in place for just enough time. King followed through with the "two," a brutal right hook, looping around his flabby arm and slamming his knuckles into the side of the guy's skull.

Out.

King felt his heart *pounding* now, at his maximum heart rate, and he knew he was in the red zone. Fighting at this pace for much longer would gas him out, riddle him with fatigue, so he sped things up. You can use maximum effort or maximum time. If he slowed down and brought his heart rate down, he could dance with the final three disciples all day, but he didn't want to do that.

He wanted this over.

The last three came in all at once and actually fared well.

Two of them shot for takedowns in unison, each going for a separate leg, like they were connected cognitively. King wondered if they were the only pair who'd planned their avenue of attack in advance before stepping into the hall. If one of them went for his legs he could have thrown a knee toward the ceiling, catching him on the jaw, but not when both went for it. They actually got hold of his thighs — two arms wrapped around each leg — and drove him down to the concrete.

Shit.

Sprawling on his back, King grabbed a handful of one guy's hair and wrenched his head up from where it was burrowed into King's hip. Then, with his adversary's face exposed, King sliced an elbow off his back, opening a horizontal cut all the way along the guy's forehead. Drops of blood rained down on his face but he ignored it, threw the guy off, and made to deal with the second man.

Who dropped a fist into King's face, crushing his jaw, and King felt a tooth rattle in his gums. It didn't break off, but it was close.

You'll pay for that.

He grabbed the guy and rolled over so he was on top. It didn't take much effort — King outweighed him by fifty pounds. A third-degree black belt on the ground, he slipped into mount position and dropped a fist twice consecutively into the guy's face, slamming his head back against the concrete, separating him from lucidity.

The very last disciple came up from behind and seized King in a rear naked choke.

Again, it was well executed. The guy had some sort of jiu-jitsu training, because his squeeze was good and his technique was crisp. But again, he weighed a hundred and fifty pounds soaking wet, so King simply stood up and bent over, and the guy was forced to leap onto King's back to maintain the choke.

King turned around, carrying the guy's whole weight,

lined up his aim, and leapt backwards off his feet, dropping the man's spine into the closest bench.

The choke came loose and the guy spilled off, hurt bad.

King spun in place and punched him once, twice, three times in the face, then finished the combination with a staggering elbow to the forehead.

He stood up, chest heaving, lungs burning, muscles screaming.

Eleven down.

None up.

94

They only made it to the sacristy entranceway.

Addison got the door open and spilled through, but Brandon was moving deliberately slowly, and it took him a few more seconds to reach the door. By then Alexis could sense the pack of rabid disciples right on her heels.

If she pressed forward, all she'd achieve was taking the standoff to an enclosed hallway with no chance of slipping out an exit.

So she overtook Brandon, grabbed him by the collar, spun him around and shoved the Beretta into his skull.

'*Stop!*' she shouted.

The disciples skidded to a halt. Most of them were up on the altar. One man had leapt down, closing in on them, now only six feet away. Brandon could almost reach out and touch him. His hair was tousled from sleep. He was heavy-set, with pale skin and freckles covering his bare arms. He was wearing a wife-beater.

Alexis said, 'I'll kill him.'

She pressed the gun harder into Brandon's head.

The disciple up front smiled. It was sickening.

'He's not the priority,' the man said. 'You are.'

She felt Brandon tense up, as if he couldn't believe what he was hearing.

She understood.

He'd thought Mother Libertas was everything. He thought he was special. Now he realised he was just a pawn. No one was more important than the Riordans and their demands.

Alexis had faced close to a dozen life-or-death situations now. They were becoming bearable, allowing her to think coherently even at the height of fear.

But now she couldn't.

Now she just felt sick.

Because Addison was behind her, cowering in the doorway, and if they captured Alexis they'd know that Addison had helped her. The young girl would be tortured and killed, made an example of.

Alexis wanted to vomit.

Then she blinked, refocusing on the altar. She'd taken her eyes off the raised platform to speak to the disciple who'd leapt down, but something had changed in the interim.

There was a sixth disciple in the party.

95

Slater hovered in the back for only a moment, long enough to identify that Alexis was in trouble.

Then he exploded.

Dropped the first man with a massive right hook. Pivoted to the second and kicked him in the chest, sending him careening back off the altar. The guy fell hard, dropping from the platform, and bounced his head off the stone floor. Slater seized the third by the collar and smashed his own forehead into the guy's nose, snapping it clean, then used the double-handed grip to heave him off his feet and throw him into the fourth man. The fourth guy stumbled back, thrown off but not incapacitated.

Slater only needed a moment of hesitation, though.

He shoved the third guy aside, who was busy cupping his brutalised nose in his hands. He closed the gap and kicked the fourth guy in the calf, making the muscle seize up, and the guy went down on one knee. Slater grabbed a handful of his hair and brought the guy's face down onto his own knee.

The man who'd leapt down to confront Alexis was the only one left standing.

He was frozen in hesitation, now thoroughly outnumbered.

'Allow me,' Brandon growled.

Alexis paused.

Brandon shrugged the gun away from his temple, knowing she wouldn't shoot. He took a couple of steps forward and pummelled the messy-haired disciple until the man was unconscious. Punches, kicks, knees. They were devoid of competent technique, but Brandon had natural power. When he was finished, he stood over the unconscious man and spat on him.

From the sacristy entranceway, Addison said, 'What the hell are you doing?'

He looked like a deer caught in headlights. 'They were going to kill me.'

Addison pointed to Alexis. 'You were going to kill her.'

'That's different.'

'How is it different?'

He went quiet.

Slater leapt down from the altar.

96

Addison stammered, 'What's going on?'

Alexis quickly turned to the girl. 'It's okay. He's with me.'

Eyes bloodshot and cheeks streaked with tears, the girl put her head in her hands and sobbed with relief.

Slater gripped Alexis' hand. He didn't pull her into a hug — she was still aiming the Beretta at Brandon.

She stared Slater in the face.

He looked ten years older. His eyes were bloodshot, his skin was plastered in dried sweat, and his forehead was etched with deep stress lines.

She said, 'What the hell happened to you?'

'Later,' Slater muttered. 'What are you doing with these two?'

'He held me at gunpoint. She saved me.'

'Was he going to kill you?'

'No,' Brandon said.

Slater got in his face. 'Did I say you could fucking speak? You aimed a gun at her?'

'You two ... were pretending you didn't know each other?'

He was putting it together. Slowly.

'Yeah,' Slater said. 'You're lucky you're not dead.'

'Why haven't you done it yet?'

Groans and whimpers floated softly through the church as the search party clawed their way unsteadily back to their feet. No one else arrived. It made sense for now. There were roughly two hundred disciples, but almost half of them were women, and more than half the men were weak and timid, with no combat experience. They'd cower and cry if they were antagonised. Mother Libertas' philosophy coupled with Maeve's persuasiveness was slowly honing them into servitude, but they weren't there yet. There were maybe forty men in the commune with the size and strength to be able to handle adversity, and not all of them had the fight in them.

These five had been ready to fight.

They'd be useless for a few hours, minimum.

The odds were getting better.

Slater looked at Brandon. 'Because we're not like you.'

'I told you I wasn't going to kill her.'

Slater grabbed him by the collar and hurled him toward the sacristy. 'I don't give a shit.'

Alexis and Slater led them down a windowless hallway and into Maeve's office, complete with robes she donned on special occasions. Slater forced Brandon down to his knees and used all the robes to practically mummify him, tying them tight around his frame. They pinned his arms to his sides, pinned his legs together. Stretched out prone, he wasn't going anywhere.

Now they were in the safety of privacy, Alexis stepped right up to Slater and whispered, 'What happened to you?'

Slater muttered, 'Three hits of Bodhi,' into her ear.

Her eyes went wide. She held him at arm's length and stared into his eyes, probably checking whether he was still all there. He looked back at her, let her make her conclusions, because honestly he wasn't sure himself.

She said, 'You look okay. Holy shit. *Three?* My whole mood changed off a microdose, which was probably a fifth of one dose.'

Slater said, 'It's been a crazy night.'

'Why on earth did you do it?'

Slater stared at her. 'You think it was my choice?'

Silence.

She said, 'Dane?'

Slater nodded. 'He spiked the water. Six doses. I drank half of it before I realised. I can't imagine what would have happened if I drank it all.'

They realised they weren't keeping their voices down.

From across the room, Addison said, 'You had three hits of Bodhi?'

Slater looked at her. 'Who are you?'

Alexis said, 'This is Addison.'

'I've seen her around,' Slater said. 'She's one of them.'

'She's not,' Alexis said. She jerked a thumb at Brandon on the floor. 'He is.'

Slater looked from one to the other. 'You two related?'

Addison nodded. 'My brother.'

Slater turned to Alexis. 'Where's King?'

'I don't know.' Alexis' eyes were taut with stress and fatigue. 'This is chaos.'

'Maybe not. Maybe the tide's turned. Elias isn't a problem anymore.'

Alexis froze. 'He found you?'

'Unfortunately for him.'

Addison seemed to get the message. 'That wasn't Elias, then.'

'Yes it was, kid.'

'Did you shoot him?'

Slater said, 'I beat him to death, if you really want to know.'

A long pause elapsed. Addison didn't have the strength to respond immediately.

She said, 'No you didn't. Elias is a Wing Chun master. You wouldn't have been able to touch him.'

Alexis whispered in Slater's ear. 'She's had a change of heart but she's still indoctrinated. Don't judge her. She's nineteen.'

Slater ignored Addison and said, 'We need to find King and Violetta. Now.'

Alexis nodded. 'I don't know what to do about—'

Slater finally turned his gaze to Addison. 'Kid, are you going to untie your brother?'

Addison shook her head. 'I held him at gunpoint to save Alexis. She'll tell you.'

Slater looked at Alexis.

Who nodded.

Slater said, 'Can you make sure he doesn't go anywhere? We need to leave for a while.'

Addison shrugged. 'I'm in too deep, aren't I?'

'Who knows? Slater said.

Alexis gave him a dark look.

Addison said, 'If you're asking me whether I'll let my brother go, the answer is definitely not. He would have killed me for the cause. I saw it in his eyes.'

Slater glanced down at Brandon.

He was conscious, staring vacantly into space, oblivious to any and all criticism.

Protected by the belief system in his head.
Slater believed Addison.
He said, 'Okay. Let's go.'

97

Before they left, Alexis combed through the drawers. It didn't take her long to find an identical Beretta tucked under a pile of papers. She took a brief look at the documents. They were new speeches, ready for delivery at the next congregation, handwritten by Maeve in cursive.

She read the first page.

Imagine life without guilt.
Without doubt.
Without fear.
Now close your eyes, my children. That's it. I want slow, deep breathing. I want you to harness the power of your mind. Recognise its connection to the universe. Understand that your limitations are mere perceptions. You have the power within you, right this moment, to strip yourself of all your inhibitions. Live like Mother commands you to.
Live free.
Open your eyes. Breathe the air.

Where has this power been all your life?
Inside you.
Everything you ever wanted ... Mother has always been within.
Awaken her.

On paper, the words were empty.

Self-improvement shlock.

Out of Maeve's lips, they would be powerful. Alexis had seen it first hand. She imagined Maeve reading the pages, commanding devotion from her followers. It would be easy for a lost soul to pledge allegiance. Maeve had those qualities she described in the speech — lack of guilt, doubt, fear, empathy — because she was a psychopath. In times of turmoil, psychopaths are appealing. They provide clear direction in the face of uncertainty, because they're not burdened by the emotions that cripple most of us.

Alexis saw it clearly.

She put the pages down and handed the spare gun to Addison. 'Make sure he stays put.'

Addison said, 'Will you come back for me?'

Tears welled in her eyes. She'd been promised things before.

The world had let her down every time.

Alexis said, 'I promise.'

She tried to convey how much she meant it.

Addison seemed to understand. 'Okay, I'll stay here.'

It sounded like she was reassuring herself.

They couldn't loiter any longer. Each extra minute the Riordans spent pumping their followers full of their doctrine was a minute they couldn't afford. Alexis handed Slater her Beretta. He was a better shot, and denying that was counter-productive.

Together they moved out of Maeve's office and closed the door behind them, leaving Addison standing over her restrained brother, shaking involuntarily.

98

Across the mess hall, Violetta said, 'Your tank's empty, isn't it?'

King couldn't respond.

He had to double over as fatigue hit him. As soon as the threat of death is nullified, your brain catches up to your body. He could barely lift his arms. He'd maintained his maximum heart rate for the entire length of the brawl, and now he was paying the price. Between deep gulping breaths, he lifted his head and said, 'Yeah.'

Already, three of the disciples were on their feet.

They were no threat.

Blood streamed from noses, mouths, foreheads. They wobbled on shaky legs, their balance disrupted as their brains spun in their skulls, searching for an equilibrium they wouldn't find for hours. Like walking zombies, just without the groaning and raised arms. They were silent as they worked their way to their feet. Bodhi couldn't override cognitive damage.

They'd be okay tomorrow, aside from superficial injuries, but tomorrow was a long way away.

They trundled for the exits, struggling for each step.

King walked back to Violetta. His legs burned from the effort required with the kicks and the explosive movements, the lunges across tables and the exertion of hurling the disciples' bodyweight around.

Violetta's face was overcast when he reached her. She got her shoulder into his armpit, supporting his weight so he could take a load off his legs.

'I'm fine,' he said.

'You're not,' she said. 'And now the cover's gone.'

'It was already gone.'

Across the room, one of the disciples reached the exit in the right-hand corner. He took one step into the darkness, his limbs still shaky, and a fist shot out of the shadows and cracked him across the jaw, knocking him out all over again.

He collapsed.

Slater stepped into the mess hall, a Beretta in his hand.

King had never been so happy to see a gun.

Across the hall, Slater cast wide eyes over the mayhem.

'What'd I miss?' he yelled.

Violetta shouted, 'We're okay. We're not hurt.'

Striding fast across the space, ignoring the disciples all around, Slater watched King like a combat sports referee keeping a keen eye on a compromised fighter. He took in King's behaviour and said, 'He's not okay.'

King realised his face had paled. 'I'm fine. Pushed myself too hard.'

'Did you get hit?'

'No,' King said, then caught the withering glare from Violetta and reconsidered. 'Once. At the start. But I'm all there.'

'Did you do the times-table test?' Slater said.

'Yeah.'

'Doesn't always mean you're good to go. You could be compromised.'

'I'm *fine,*' King repeated. 'Just tired. As soon as I get my breath back…'

Violetta said, 'Where's—?'

She cut herself off when she looked over Slater's shoulder and saw Alexis step in through the same doorway Slater had emerged from.

Violetta exhaled. 'Okay … we're okay.'

Slater said, 'For now.'

Alexis cautiously sidestepped one of the shuffling disciples, who was cradling his broken nose, walking blind. 'What the hell happened here?'

Slater said, 'King happened here.'

They rendezvoused in the middle of the hall.

Reunited.

There was no time for elation. They were in a death trap, probably surrounded on all sides by Mother Libertas, who the Riordans would be in the process of arming.

But at least they had a gun.

King said, 'Where'd you get that?'

'Long story,' Slater said.

King looked over his shoulder, and froze. 'Shit. Give it here.'

'What?'

King took the Beretta out of Slater's hands and shouldered past him.

Five more disciples had stepped into the hall.

99

King fell back on his military career, recalling everything they'd drilled in basic training to steadily transform him from an emotional civilian to someone right at home amidst chaos.

These followers — all men, all tough-looking — were still emotional civilians, no matter how badly they wanted to pretend they weren't.

More importantly, none of them were armed.

King aimed the Beretta at their faces and screamed at the top of his lungs. '*All of you get the fuck out! Now!*'

They froze in their tracks.

The animalistic volume of the shout cut through the Bodhi that was protecting and coddling them. A couple got shaky legs right away, and looked like they were a hair's breadth from retreating.

King kept his voice at the same volume. '*I will shoot you! Turn around and fuck off! Three seconds! Two! One—*'

He could see all five of them going to war in their own heads.

All their conditioning fought to control them. The

drugs, the brainwashing, the Mother Libertas creed — it all demanded they go forward, even in the face of insurmountable odds. It was better to die for the cause than retreat like a coward. But that only worked in principle. In reality they were staring at an unhinged two hundred plus pound man, armed with a semi-automatic pistol, threatening to blow their heads off if they didn't do what he said.

Reality won.

The five men bled back into the shadows.

King let the adrenaline out in a mighty exhale.

He turned and saw Slater practically shaking, ready for a fight to the death.

This wouldn't stop.

Right now the commune was in turmoil, still bleary in the early hours of the morning. The disciples would be confused, lacking clear instructions. But soon that would all change, and they would unify under the Riordans and simply overwhelm the imposters, whether they were armed or not.

King knew it.

He hoped Slater did too.

He said, 'We need to move. Now. And we stick together or we're fucked. Force our way out of this hall, find a ride, and get out.'

'Then come back for the Riordans?' Slater said.

'That's not important right now.'

'Yes it is.'

King could see the burning desire in his eyes.

He said, 'Let's go.'

King led from the front, hustling past the incapacitated disciples within the mess hall. He reached the exterior doors and swept the outside corridor with the Beretta up, clearing every corner.

The building was deserted.

And the alarm had stopped.

For the first time he recognised the eerie quiet. He didn't like it. He made sure Slater, Alexis and Violetta were close behind him, effectively glued to his back, before he continued. He ignored the main entrance/exit and ran down the sparsely furnished hallway until he came to a side door marked: EMERGENCY EXIT.

He kicked it open and waited.

Dawn light flooded in, then the horrid blast of a gunshot ruptured the silence. The bullet thwacked into the door frame, half a foot from King's centre mass.

He realised it was the first shot fired on the commune since they arrived.

Distant screams rose like banshee wails. King ignored the terror now rippling through the commune's population, waited for another shot to impact the door frame, then leant out and sized up his target in milliseconds.

The disciple was holding a pistol with shaky hands. He was older, maybe forty, but there was no humanity left in him. He had given himself so completely to the cause that he was determined to murder these newcomers for the cult.

That was enough for King.

It wasn't an easy decision, but in the end it was simple.

Him or me.

King shot him in the forehead before the guy could get a third round off.

He didn't watch the body fall to the dirt. He hated the choice, hated what the Riordans had forced him to do, but there was simply no way he could talk reason and common sense into a man firing on them. And behind King was Violetta, carrying their child. That stifled his remorse.

He surveyed the landscape.

There were three isolated clusters of disciples in sight. No one was armed. Half the followers were women, and the men were terrified. They were all fleeing in separate directions, startled into panic mode by the gunshots close by.

King let them go.

When push came to shove, Mother Libertas was timid. A few more months, maybe these people would have been stripped of their souls, completely brainwashed to ignore danger.

Now, however, they were still human.

Maeve hadn't stripped them of everything yet.

King looked across this side of the commune and spotted Dane. The tall man was empty-handed, hovering in the doorway of a low rectangular building with wooden walls.

His face was stoically set, but there was terror behind it. King could see it even from this distance.

King swept his aim over to centre on Dane's chest.

Dane sucked in the cool morning air through gritted teeth and retreated into the building at a sprint to avoid getting shot.

King said, 'Stay on me. Ready?'

Three grunts of affirmation came from behind.

If they were all armed, the smart move would be to split into teams of two to prevent them all getting bottlenecked in a trap. But three of them were unarmed, so staying in a tight unit was paramount.

As they raced out of the mess hall, Alexis stopped over the body of the forty-year-old disciple and bent down. King refused to look. He didn't want to see what he'd done.

Besides, his entire concentration was focused on the building Dane had fled into.

Alexis caught up and the four of them swept through

the doorway, King still leading the charge. They stepped into a lavishly furnished entranceway, done up with the same decor as the Riordans' farmhouse. There were rattan chairs on bearskin rugs and mounted deer heads on the wooden walls.

Dane stood next to a doorway up the back of the big lobby, hands in the air, his face pale.

Surrendering.

100

King said, 'Don't fucking move.'

Dane's lower lip quivered.

King ignored it.

Slater said, 'He's faking it.'

King said, 'What?'

'He's not scared. He's never scared.'

With inhuman athleticism, Dane leapt out of sight, sprinting through the open doorway into the next room like an Olympian coming off the starting blocks.

It's unbelievable what fear can do.

King roared, 'Stay with me!' as he ran across the room, his footsteps muffled by the artfully placed rugs.

It would be suicide to charge into the unknown on his own, leaving Slater, Violetta, and Alexis stranded with no weapons. On the off chance he lost a battle of reflexes or ran into a trap, it was better for Slater to be right behind him, ready to scoop the Beretta off his corpse and finish the job.

They barrelled into the room.

It was pitch dark.

Lights flared to life overhead. Harsh white bulbs, leaving

no room for shadow, exposing an entirely bare room. Every surface was concrete — the walls, the floor, the ceiling. There were brown stains on the floor. King knew immediately it was blood.

There was no sign of Dane.

He ground to a halt and twisted and caught Slater as the man sprinted in behind him. He spun Slater around like a top and shouted, '*Out!*'

Slater understood in milliseconds.

Violetta got it a second later.

It took Alexis a moment longer. She still had subconscious civilian tendencies, and reacting on the fly in a life-or-death situation takes longer than a few months to become ingrained in your DNA. You have to override your human instincts.

She was slow to catch up, and King and Slater hung back for a beat to make sure she got out with them.

Rapid footsteps sounded in the lobby, and the door swung shut on them.

Not Dane. The man couldn't teleport.

One of the disciples, waiting in the wings, ready to pounce.

The back of the door was cold steel.

A bolt slid across the door on the other side.

All those tiny details you don't notice in the heat of combat catch up to you. King should have seen the door was modified, the situation was abnormal, Dane was baiting him. But he couldn't. Despite his reflexes and experience, there's a limit to what the brain can process in milliseconds. Half the battle of staying alive in warzones is refusing to hesitate, but sometimes it's a Catch 22. You hesitate, you see clearly. You go, you don't. But if you don't go, you die.

King's heartbeat spiked as he stood motionless, looking

around the room. He gripped the Beretta tight as sweat ran down his back, condensing in his armpits, forming rivulets down the side of his head.

He was still panting for breath when reality set in.

There were no exits.

The only feature of the room was a tinted glass window running halfway across the right hand wall. King didn't need to shoot at it to know it was bulletproof, and the shot would destroy their eardrums in such a confined space. He needed every sense firing on all cylinders if he hoped to get them out of this alive.

Slater said, 'We still have guns.'

He didn't sound confident.

King held up the Beretta. 'Gun. Singular.'

Alexis twitched, but King barely noticed.

A silhouette passed behind the tinted glass, its features darkened. King recognised the gait.

Dane watched them patiently, studying his prey.

101

King saw the building for what it really was.

A jail.

A torture chamber.

On the other side of the glass, Dane spoke to them through a grate of fine holes identical to those in prison visitation rooms. 'Sorry about all this.'

King said, 'No you're not.'

Dane looked at him. 'Jason King.'

King froze.

Dane turned. 'Will Slater.'

He turned again. 'Alexis Diaz.'

And again. 'Violetta LaFleur.'

Silence.

Dane said, 'You boys are outcasts from a black-operations division of our government. You are two of the most feared and most successful field operatives in this country's history. Violetta, you were their handler, and then you followed them when they split. And you, Alexis ... you're a wild card. I don't have as much information on you. Supposedly, you're an ordinary civilian who got sucked into their cult just as badly as you all pretended to get sucked into mine.'

No one spoke.

King said, 'You're reaching,' despite there being close to zero chance of that.

Dane raised his eyebrows. 'Am I? I must say, that'd have to be one of the more accurate guesses in the history of guesses. I should buy a Powerball ticket.'

Slater said, 'Someone fed you bad intel.'

Dane laughed. It echoed through the air holes. 'Someone fed me very, very good intel. We've had our hooks in an intelligence asset in Washington for months now. He's been helping to keep us out of the media, put a suppression blanket over unexplained disappearances, turn everyone's attention away from the Thunder Basin grasslands. Everyone with common sense, that is. He lets the naïve ones wander in and fall into our trap.'

'So you finally acknowledge it's all bullshit?' King said. 'I never thought I'd see the day.'

Dane said, 'Did you take me for an idiot?'

'I don't know what to take you as.'

'I get it,' Dane said. 'This chat of ours will stay between us, so I don't mind venting to the four of you. My wife, it seems, has fallen victim to the timeless mistake of believing her own lies. I keep everything functioning smoothly when she goes off the deep end ... when she really thinks she's Gaia.'

King said, 'You know what she's doing. You know how dangerous that could be.'

Dane said, 'I do.'

'Then put a stop to it.'

Dane shook his head. 'I can't. And even if I could, I wouldn't.'

'We can help you,' King said. 'We can work with you to end this.'

'Did you not hear me?' Dane said. 'Why would I? Do you understand the trajectory of this movement? Do you know where we're headed? We own all the right people now. No one's going to investigate us. The beauty of the way the outside world is structured is that if you have power, you're untouchable. And if you know the right ways to entrap people, accumulating power is … easy.'

King said, 'I figured you'd say that.'

Dane smiled. 'Good for you. Now put the gun down and kick it across the room or I'll leave you here to die of dehydration. That's not the way to go, believe me. You'll be begging for a drop of water through split, cracked lips. Or you can die with dignity. Your choice.'

King put the Beretta on the floor and punted it with his boot. It skittered across the concrete, came to rest in the far corner of the room, and lay still.

Dane signalled off to the side, to someone out of the line of sight.

The steel-core door opened and one of the disciples stepped in, brandishing a fearsome assault rifle. It was a military-issue M4 carbine, brand new and shiny, and King figured the weapon had never been used. Whichever intelligence asset Dane controlled had probably sent a crate of them to Mother Libertas free of charge in exchange for a never-ending supply of Bodhi. The arsenal was tucked away somewhere, maybe buried in the bowels of the Riordans' farmhouse, and that's where Dane had disappeared to in the early hours of the morning.

King thought about lunging across the space.

He wouldn't make it in time.

The disciple was a guy in his thirties with a plain build

and a plain face. His greasy hair was matted to his forehead in a bowl cut. His pupils were swollen with Bodhi. He'd do anything Dane commanded, and he was already bringing the carbine up to aim at them. This wasn't the movies, so he wouldn't deliver a spiel before he shot them. He was the grunt, carrying out the Riordans' every wish.

King felt sickening helplessness.

He realised he was about to die.

Then Alexis' hand came up holding the Beretta she'd taken off the body of the forty-year-old disciple. She'd had the pistol tucked into the small of her back, and now she fired once and blew the newcomer's brains out the back of his head.

He slumped in a widening pool of his own blood and the rifle spilled from his hands.

The door hung wide open behind him.

Alexis turned to look at Dane, frozen in the window.

He couldn't move, paralysed by how fast everything had unravelled.

She said, 'What were you saying?'

He turned and ran.

King couldn't believe it. If Dane had simply walked away from them, left them there to rot, they wouldn't have been able to get out. They would have died of thirst before they got through the steel door or the bulletproof glass. But hubris and sheer human idiocy and impatience had led to the man wanting to make a statement. If he sent one of the disciples in to pump them full of lead, their bodies could be strung up on poles in the centre of the commune for all to see. A grotesque morale boost for Mother Libertas, showing the disciples what happens to their enemies.

Impatience and a need for dramatics lead to the deaths of many men.

Quiet professionals don't take those risks.

Slater said, '"*Gun. Singular.*" Nice touch. Like we'd ever forget to take a dropped weapon.'

King scooped up the carbine, checked it was loaded with a full mag and ready to fire, and nodded to the other three.

Slater fetched the Beretta that King had kicked away, then they left the room. They swept the whole building, but Dane had already abandoned it.

Slater said, 'I know where he's going.'

Alexis said, 'You do?'

He nodded. 'What will you do?'

'I'll go to Addison,' Alexis said. 'She needs someone there for her when the cult is destroyed.'

Slater nodded.

He turned to King and Violetta. 'What will you do?'

King said, 'Destroy the cult.'

102

The log cabin wasn't as terrifying without Bodhi crippling his emotions.

Slater strode across the prairie, keeping a tight grip on the Beretta. He expected resistance, but not a lot. The world Dane had so carefully built out here was coming down on his head.

There was no cohort of disciples standing guard around the cabin. No one at all. Just the wind and the dawn light and the stillness.

But the lights were on inside.

They'd been switched off last night.

Someone had repopulated the cabin.

Slater grappled with something he could only liken to post-traumatic memories. Laying eyes on the cabin sent a bolt of fear through him, making his stomach drop. His brain connected it with the mind-boggling Bodhi trip, and pleaded, *No.*

Slater had spent a lifetime mastering his fears.

He wasn't about to change that.

He advanced.

As soon as he got within fifty feet of the cabin, the small door opened and Dane stepped out. His eyes were hollow and sunken, his forehead was lined with stress marks, and his teeth were clenched.

He held a switchblade knife to his own carotid artery.

Slater stopped in his tracks. 'What are you doing?'

'I'll end it,' Dane said. 'Right here. Then you'll never get what's in my head.'

Slater stood motionless, aiming the Beretta at the dry prairie ground.

He didn't raise it.

He simply raised an eyebrow.

It forced Dane to elaborate, to fill the silence. He was the one pleading, after all.

He said, 'Wouldn't that drive you mad? All this madness I've created, all these people I've killed, all this damage I've done to my followers. I would never repent for it. I'd just be dead. By my own hand, too. There's a satisfaction in that. You want me alive. You want to hurt me for what I've done. I can see it on your face.'

Slater said nothing.

Dane pressed the blade tighter into his throat. 'So what's it going to be?'

'You're going to give this a moment's thought,' Slater said. 'And you're going to realise how stupid you are.'

Dane went tight-lipped.

Wind whistled across the grasslands.

Slater said, 'Go on. Do it. I won't stop you.'

Dane said, 'We can negotiate. There are some things I want.'

'You're not going to get them. Go ahead and kill yourself. See if I care.'

Checkmate.

Dane didn't take the knife away, didn't admit defeat, but he didn't break the skin either.

He stayed frozen.

Slater said, 'It's just you out here. No one else doing your bidding. And you don't have a damn clue what to do.'

Dane said, 'There are things I know. About the movement outside of this commune. You think this is it? This is a training ground for new recruits. You have no idea who we've bribed, who we've hooked on Bodhi. I can name names that would blow your mind. If I die, you'll never get them. This thing will spiral out of control and there won't be a thing you can do about it.'

Slater let him talk, let him get it out of his system.

He waited a long time to respond.

Then he said, 'You're a master manipulator, Dane. You wouldn't tell me. You'd send me on a wild goose chase and you'd do everything in your power to save yourself. That's who you are.'

Dane shook his head, but he was rattled by the tension, and he couldn't lie as effortlessly as usual.

Slater said, 'And there's one other thing.'

'What's that?'

'No matter what I tell you to do, or what you think is right, you're not going to cut your own throat. Because that takes incredible strength of character and your spine is weaker than glass.'

Dane's face paled.

Slater said, 'For example…'

He put the Beretta down and walked straight at Dane.

Who took the knife away from his neck and made a wild lunge at Slater.

Slater caught his wrist, bent it until it was inches away from snapping, and ripped the switchblade out of his hand by the hilt. Then he bent down and plunged the knife into Dane's thigh and yanked downwards, carving a jagged line and severing the main artery in his leg.

Dane's face went white as snow and he collapsed back against the side of the log cabin.

Arterial blood poured from his leg.

He was dead. He just didn't know it yet.

103

Alexis entered the empty church with her gun up and cleared every potential hiding space in the nave and the transept before bounding over the altar.

She threw the sacristy door open, ran down the hallway, and burst into the room.

Her heart hammered at the sight. She almost fired out of impulse.

Then she realised all wasn't what it seemed.

Brandon had Addison's gun. He was no longer restrained, but he wasn't jumpy or antagonistic. He sat in the desk chair, and when Alexis burst in he didn't aim the weapon at her. Alexis swept the room, fearing the worst, expecting to see the young girl facedown in a pool of her own blood.

But Addison was unharmed. She sat against the far wall with her knees tucked up to her chest and her eyes red with tears.

Alexis aimed her weapon at Brandon. 'Put it down.'

Brandon put it down immediately, and lifted his hands into the air.

Alexis said, 'What happened here?'

'I didn't like being tied up,' Brandon said. 'So I got free.'

'On your own?'

'Yes.'

Alexis turned to Addison. 'You let it happen?'

The girl looked up, her face sorrowful. 'Of course. He's my brother. I couldn't hurt him.'

Alexis said to Brandon, 'And when you got free, you took the gun off her?'

'She handed it to me,' Brandon said. 'I know how to use it.'

'But you didn't hurt her?'

'Of course not,' Brandon said, refusing to look away from Alexis. 'She's my sister.'

Alexis sighed.

Humans were complicated animals.

She said, 'And me? You didn't try to shoot me.'

'I probably would have missed,' Brandon admitted. 'I've only shot a gun a couple of times before. And … I'm tired.'

She could see that. His shoulders were slumped, his back bent like a hook. There were black bags under his eyes from lack of sleep. In comparison to the simplistic, straightforward existence of ordinary life in the commune, the previous twelve hours had been a whirlwind of emotion and stimulation. Brandon was committed to the cause, but it had worn on him all the same.

Brandon said, 'Are you going to kill me now?'

'No.'

'You should.'

'I was never going to kill you.'

Brandon looked at her with vacant eyes. 'Did you do what you said you were going to do?'

'It's being done,' Alexis said, 'as we speak.'

Brandon's gaze drifted to the desk.

She said, 'How does that make you feel?'

'This is an important movement,' he mumbled. 'We mean no harm. You shouldn't...'

He trailed off, recognising the hypocrisy of his own words.

Alexis said, 'Maeve sends you to kill people and you mean no harm?'

Brandon said, 'Which is why you should kill me. If you're here to do the right thing.'

He was starting to insinuate that he knew Mother Libertas and its founders were evil.

It was all the progress Alexis could ask for.

She said, 'Come on. Up. Both of you.'

Brandon slumped back in his chair. 'Why?'

'We're getting out of here. I don't like tight spaces. We'll go to the mess hall and wait there.'

'Isn't that risky?' Brandon said. 'They're still prowling the commune, looking for you.'

Alexis said, 'Not anymore.'

Brandon stiffened.

Alexis repeated herself. 'Up. Both of you.'

Addison worked her way to her foot like she was carrying an extra hundred pounds of weight.

Brandon followed suit.

Recalling what she'd found when she searched the office drawers, she retrieved a pair of binoculars from deep in one of the lower drawers and tucked them into the back of her jeans. Then she fetched the second Beretta off the desk, held the pistols akimbo, and led the brother and sister at gunpoint out of the sacristy. She wasn't sure why she was putting so much effort into ensuring their wellbeing.

That's a lie, she told herself. *You know why you're doing this.*

She couldn't save everyone in Mother Libertas from the downward spiral, but she could help two people.

That was a realistic goal, and purpose in life comes from setting and achieving realistic goals.

She led them out of the empty church and over to the mess hall. The same tight clusters of disciples were scattered across the commune, but they deliberately avoided eye contact with Alexis, pretending she wasn't there. Like they could deny the fact their world was coming down on their heads simply by closing their eyes and covering their ears.

Alexis swept the exterior corridors of the mess hall. The hallways were long and empty and lathered in shadow, devoid of human life. She guided Brandon and Addison to the side of the building that faced the farmhouse up the hill.

A small window stained with fingerprints was set into the exterior wall at head height.

She crossed to it and looked out, keeping the Berettas at shoulder height for precaution.

She saw two people's backs like tiny specks as they made their way up the trail to the farmhouse.

King and Violetta.

Awaiting them was a crowd of disciples.

Maeve must have summoned them to the house to protect her.

Brandon was also staring out the window. 'What's going on up there?'

Alexis said, 'We're about to find out.'

104

Dane looked pathetic sitting against the wall, staring through a haze of shock at his leg.

Slater threw the switchblade away and sat down beside him.

Dane said, 'I'm dead, right?'

Slater said, 'Yeah.'

'What if I put pressure on it?'

'Won't help you. I severed your femoral artery.'

'Will it give me some time?'

'Maybe. A couple of minutes more.'

Dane pressed down hard on the jagged gash in his quadricep. Blood oozed through his fingers in thick streams. There was so much of it. An impossible amount. It flowed down the sides of his thigh and coagulated in the dirt.

Dane said, 'It doesn't hurt.'

'You're in shock.'

'How long do I have?'

'Not long.'

'I want to talk.'

'Won't do you much good.'

Slater was done with it all. He didn't want to hear another word that came out of this scumbag's mouth, but for some reason he couldn't muster the determination to get the blade back out and cut Dane's throat. The man fascinated him in some strange way. Dane had achieved so much for the worst reasons.

And the sunrise was beautiful.

They could watch it together.

Dane said, 'Maeve is worse than I ever was.'

Slater scoffed. 'I thought you were a demigod. Why are you trying to find salvation now? You changing your mind about everything?'

Dane sat there for a beat, his face ghost white, his eyes unblinking. It took a long moment for his internal computer to process what Slater had said. Then he said, 'I'm not my wife. I know it's a lie.'

Slater said, 'I don't understand why you're even talking.'

Or how you're capable of talking, Slater thought. Dane was losing blood at a harrowing rate. His grip on reality was slipping as it drained out of him, but he still talked like he was perfectly lucid.

An odd thought struck Slater.

Is this the first time he's saying what he really thinks? Is this the first time he sees clearly? When he knows it's the end of the road.

Possessed by the urge to know, Slater said, 'Go on.'

Dane said, 'She believes her own delusions. She thinks she's a god.'

'Was she always this way?'

Dane smiled and shook his head. It was a ghastly sight. 'No. She was a small-town sweetheart when I met her. You know, the girl next door. I was fucked up back then. Still am. Psychopathic personality disorder. I … had a bad childhood.

I won't go into it. Anyway, I corrupted her. Changed her brain over the course of a few years, feeding her all sorts of sick ideas about the world and what the people in it deserve. This is all my fault. Because she listened to me...'

He trailed off, searching for the energy to continue. Slater didn't interrupt.

Dane let out a guttural sigh, which made him wince, then he composed himself. 'She ... uh ... she became a narcissist. She had empathy where I didn't, and she couldn't shed it easily, so I guess she turned all that empathy on herself. It finally clicked for her. She started thinking everyone besides her and I were subhuman. I was the reason for that, so I guess if there's a hell, I'm going there.'

Slater said, 'I'd put money on it.'

Dane said, 'All that empathy she started with made her a people pleaser. She was charismatic and extroverted. She could convince anyone of anything. I was paranoid and internal. I couldn't make small talk to save my life. So she started ... I guess you could call it brainwashing people ... to get her way in life, to create something for ourselves. I was like ... the director. I called the shots behind the scenes, guided her to the targets, to the easily exploitable. We came up with this thing together. But you know how it goes...'

Slater realised Dane wanted him to fill in the blanks. 'It caught momentum? Took on a life of its own?'

Dane shook his head. There was no colour left in his face. He had no energy to talk, but something was keeping his lips moving, something Slater couldn't comprehend.

Dane said, 'The movement never did anything on its own. *Maeve* caught momentum. She went from understanding it was all a ruse to believing the words that came out of her mouth. I mean, why wouldn't she? It was working too well. We hit the perfect storm of Maeve's charisma and my concoction of Bodhi. She—'

'Bodhi was yours?'

'Mostly. The benefit of being a psychotic paranoid is that when you put your mind to something and convince yourself it's important, it gets done. Nothing stands in your way. I absorbed every piece of scientific literature I could get my hands on and put a few chimeras together.'

'Chimeras?'

'Combination of compounds. I thought I'd stumbled upon the perfect dosage. It was—'

'Dextroamphetamine, MDMA, and Benzos.'

Dane paused, but nothing fazed him. Not now.

'Yeah,' he said, not bothering to spend what little time he had left asking how Slater knew. 'I had a few formulas for different dosages. I paid a buddy of mine from college who'd gone on to get his PhD and worked in a reputable lab. It was all my money at the time, but I knew to bet big on myself, and that was the amount I needed to corrupt him. He put them together, and we tried them together. The third iteration hit like nothing I'd ever experienced. Then I knew we had something unstoppable.'

'Did Maeve use it?' Slater said. 'Is that why she went off the deep end?'

'Never. Not once. She … got her high from manipulating people. She didn't need anything else. But she used it on everyone, and suddenly she had control of them all, and she became messianic. Which made her prone to losing her temper, but it never happened outwardly. Only in private, with me.'

Slater grimaced. 'Sounds like the perfect dichotomy.'

Dane nodded — or, at least, he tried. He lowered his

chin but it hung there, resting against his chest. He didn't have the cognisance to lift it back up.

'Yeah,' he mumbled at the ground. 'She was ... an ice queen in front of the disciples. But ... a monster behind closed doors. Everyone trusted her, worshipped her. I wasn't working with her anymore. I was serving her. I had no choice.'

'You could have walked away.'

Dane let out a grunt that sounded like an affirmation. 'And yet, no one ever walks away. I wonder why...'

Slater said, 'I wonder too.'

Dane said, 'Don't ... trust a word she says. That's if you want to make it out of here alive.'

'I don't think that'll be a problem,' Slater said. 'You gave me a mammoth dose of Bodhi and I never trusted *you*.'

Dane's face twisted. 'You know...'

He couldn't talk anymore. He sucked in air, trying to muster the energy.

Slater could see whatever came next would be his final words.

He said, 'What?'

Dane said, 'In all my years ... all the things I've experienced ... that was the greatest feat of willpower I've seen.'

Slater didn't respond.

Dane croaked, 'Whatever you do ... wherever you go ... don't stop doing this. You were ... born for it.'

Slater said, 'Wouldn't have to if people like you didn't exist.'

Dane used everything he had left to shrug. 'But we do.'

He settled against the cabin wall, his chin now crushed to his chest, and the life went from his eyes.

Slater got up and walked away.

105

The spectacle demonstrated exactly where Maeve had gone wrong.

King and Violetta walked across the fields, approaching the farm house. There were no defences. No one was bunkered down or barricaded in. The disciples of Mother Libertas milled around the wraparound porch, which was home to a single occupant.

Maeve Riordan wore her farm dress. She was perched on the top step above her followers. They were armed, but not well. Perhaps there was no armoury after all, no crates of weapons, just a single M4 carbine reserved for desperate measures. The disciples had instruments they'd fashioned themselves — spiked bats, clubs, two-by-fours, even a couple of pitchforks, like they weren't permitted to be subtle with the symbolism. They'd taken what they could from their quarters and come up with a janky homemade arsenal straight out of the nineteenth century.

Everyone saw King and Violetta coming.

King estimated there were more than thirty of them — he didn't have time to count them individually. He was focused on Maeve, watching her every move, scrutinising her behaviour.

There wasn't even a hint that she knew her husband was dead.

King realised she probably didn't care either way.

He paid careful attention to Maeve's hands.

They were empty.

That's when the full extent of her egotism became clear.

She undoubtedly had a gun inside the house, tucked in a drawer in her office or hidden in a safe in the kitchen. There wasn't a chance she worked here every afternoon without safety measures. But if she pulled it in full view of her cult, the gesture alone would spread discontent. She was a god, after all. Relying on man-made hardware would tarnish her image, make her seem vulnerable, make her…

…human.

King realised just as Dane was a slave to his wife, she was a slave to Mother Libertas. The unwritten rules she'd created and fed to her followers couldn't be disobeyed, not even by herself. If she wanted her disciples to act as her personal guard, she needed them to believe. And that meant taking the risk of standing in full view of the approaching enemy. It meant projecting the image of invulnerability. If she didn't, they wouldn't defend her so fanatically.

He could see on her face, even from a hundred feet away.

False confidence on the surface.

Crippling doubt underneath.

He stopped at the head of the dirt driveway and put a hand against Violetta's stomach, keeping her back, instinctively protecting her. The mob watched in cold silence. The sky behind the farmhouse was light now.

Maeve regarded them with derision.

Over the heads of her disciples, she shouted, 'Come to beg?'

King brandished the M4 and held it up in case anyone had accidentally missed the sight of it. 'Let's talk inside, Maeve.'

'You don't make the demands here.'

Violetta muttered, 'She's in too deep.'

'No shit.'

One of the disciples up front held a baseball bat above his head, mirroring King raising the carbine. He was wiry, neither skinny nor muscular. His straight brown hair fell in a bowl cut over his forehead and the tops of his ears. He couldn't have been older than twenty. King's stomach twisted in anger that he directed solely at Maeve, the woman who'd sold these people false hopes and dreams of a better life. The majority of them might never work their way back to the truth again.

They'd been sold lies so they could become pawns.

King looked over the heads of the crowd and shouted to Maeve, 'Let's be smart about this.'

'Be *quiet!*' she screamed back. Her voice was nails on a chalkboard. 'You come here spreading pestilence and discontent. You are devils in human form. Do you honestly think you can stop the cause? We have work to do, we have the soul of this planet to free, and you come to this temple asking to *talk?* You've caused enough misery in this commune. One chance. Walk away. I suggest you fucking *take* it.'

Right there, he knew he had her.

A couple of the disciples twitched as Maeve's words reached their ears, the use of "fuck" setting them on edge. Maeve had lost her cool hundreds of times in private, in the presence of Dane, but never before the disciples. Her words were empty now, devoid of the calm and confident rhetoric that had become a staple of her public speech.

She knew this confrontation had to go well for her, and that put pressure on her to perform.

She'd never dealt with stakes like this.

King tapped a finger on the trigger guard. 'We talk, or I shoot you.'

Something flashed on her face — only King and Violetta saw it. The crowd was facing away from the house, transfixed by their brainwashed rage.

But Maeve showed true fear for the first time in public.

It disappeared — she got a grip on her emotions fast — but that didn't hide the fact King and Violetta had seen it.

They'd worked her into a corner.

She had to pretend she was omnipotent if she wanted the protection of the masses.

'You can shoot!' she screeched, but her voice wavered in shrill staccato. 'But you won't kill. You won't even harm. And to get to me, you'll have to go through my children. All of them. We are all devotees to the cause, and the cause will live for the rest of time.'

King read between the lines.

What she was really saying was, '*If you want me dead you'll have to kill all these people between us. They'll protect me because I live in their heads. I control their every thought. Beneath my brainwashing they are innocent, and you know it, so you'll have to get the blood of thirty people on your hands if you want a hope of getting to me. I'm sure you can do it, but you won't. You're good people with morals. That won't cut it here.*'

He hated her.

He briefly looked at the faces of the crowd before him.

There would be no persuading them of anything.

They swelled with the energy of devotion. This

commune was their lives, and they'd sacrificed all chance of an ordinary existence to come out here, so even if some of them were questioning the motives of the Riordans', none of them would act on it. And the anonymity of the group gave them confidence. Here they were free to sin with impunity. They could beat King's brains in, and then Violetta's, and they could go the rest of their lives shirking their guilt because they were anonymous in the masses. When the blame is able to be spread between dozens of people, humans can commit shocking acts of depravity.

But King had a lifeline.

And no choice but to use it.

This house of cards was built on Maeve's performance as a god.

If that came crashing down…

King shrugged, looked dead in Maeve's eyes. 'If that's the way it has to go…'

A long moment of silence.

The disciples were practically foaming at the mouths.

Maeve spread her arms wide at the top of the stairs, letting her dress billow out. She opened her palms and spread her fingers, searching for power she was sure existed, channeling the energy of Mother Earth into her bones and brain.

Her eyes went wide and she screamed, '*Get them!*'

The disciples moved forward in a wave.

Slowly.

Methodically.

Maeve's eyes went wide, like they were all-seeing, all-knowing, all-powerful, and she lifted her arms to the sky and—

King raised the M4 over the heads of the disciples and shot her in the chest.

106

Two bullets smashed through her vital organs, but she didn't go down.

She rocked back on her heels, almost toppling, but she managed to right herself and stayed just lucid enough to look down at her chest and see the blood billowing from the entry wounds, spreading across the front of the farm dress, darkening the peach colour. Her mouth went agape. King knew she was deep in shock, feeling no pain, and she probably thought it was due to her invincibility.

She looked up at King and smiled. Her mouth twisted as she tried to speak, to lend power to her followers. She was about to let them know she couldn't be stopped.

Bullets are worthless against the power of—

Her body gave out and she crumbled, collapsing first at the waist.

She pitched forward, falling head-first.

Her shoulder hit the top step and her frame splayed as she tumbled down the short flight.

She came to rest in the dirt.

The front of her dress was soaked now, and her skin was white as a sheet. Her mouth flapped uselessly. She couldn't get the words out.

She rolled to her side and lay still.

The air seemed to thicken. The wave of disciples slowed. A couple of them looked over their shoulders, which started a chain reaction. The rest followed, their focus torn from the enemy. Some of them screamed. Most of them fell silent. One man at the very front turned back to King, his eyes bloodshot, his face ghoulish. He was red-haired and broad-chested, with a ruddy complexion and a squashed nose. He carried a bat spiked with barbed wire, and he still had every intention of using it.

King realised everything would come down to a spark.

If one of the disciples became a kamikaze, the rest would follow. It turned his stomach end over end. There was nothing he wanted more than to leave these people alone. They had their own crises to grapple with now, the horrific disillusionment of realising everything they'd been fed was a lie. They didn't have to pay with their lives.

Unless…

The red-haired, red-faced man screamed, '*She lives!*'

He charged at King.

King willed himself to raise the carbine again, but he couldn't. Something was different. This man was aiming all his dark rage at King, but King was frozen by the fact that he knew the anger was misplaced. In the past, he'd willingly taken the life of anyone who tried to take his own. Simple self-defence. But here it was so obvious the guy was brainwashed, so clear he wasn't in control of his own actions, that King couldn't bring himself to do it.

Even though one hit from that spiked bat would permanently maim or cripple him, and the follow-up shots would kill him.

Violetta said, 'I'll do it if you won't.'

By then it was too late.

The guy was on them.

He swung the bat, looking to take King's head off with the first swing.

King went from a statue to a berserker in a split second.

The bat swung through empty air that he no longer stood in, and then he was right beside the man. The guy only had time to tense up for the punch he knew was coming, but it didn't help him. King had already dropped the gun to free his hands, and he threw an elbow so fast it was barely visible to the human eye. It separated the guy from consciousness with a rare brutality. His head snapped sideways and ricocheted off his shoulder and he went down like he was dead.

He wasn't, but he might as well have been.

Cognitively, he might never be the same.

The price you pay.

King retrieved the M4, planted a foot on top of the guy's motionless form, and stared hard at the rest of the procession.

'You're human,' he said, filling the silence. 'You'll get what he got. Walk away.'

They didn't disperse.

But no one charged.

A couple of the followers sat down hard in the dirt, their morale crushed, their worlds turned upside-down. It seemed to kickstart the next chain reaction, in which the entire procession let their deepest emotions come to the surface. Most turned back to face Maeve's crumpled form, her dress now more crimson than peach. A couple whispered incantations under their breath, but the large majority stared in silence. A few outliers walked away into the twilight. They dropped their bats and clubs and didn't look back. They were either headed to other outbuildings, or they were simply walking with no destination, rendered useless by sensory overload. They might keep walking until they dropped of exhaustion or stumbled upon a town.

King didn't have the energy to stop them.

Violetta said, 'She's alive.'

'What?'

King looked through the crowd and saw Maeve's lips fluttering. It wasn't a miraculous reincarnation. She was on death's door. She had maybe a minute left.

Violetta said, 'I need to speak to her.'

King said, 'No.'

Violetta said, 'There's no threat. Look at them.'

The disciples were catatonic. Half of them were still standing, but eventually the ones still milling around the house would all sit in the dirt, reconsidering everything. King had no idea whether they'd double down on their beliefs or shirk them. He wasn't about to hang around to find out. He wasn't a counsellor. He was an operator.

Violetta walked forward and moved through the crowd.

No one stopped her.

King stayed where he was.

If Maeve had anything to say, he didn't need to hear it.

107

For the first time, Maeve looked human.

Probably because she was so vulnerable.

Violetta knelt down beside her. Maeve was curled into the foetal position, her face pressed to the pool of blood that had formed from the excess fluid running down her back. The exit wounds had bled far worse than the entry wounds.

Her eyes were half-open.

Violetta had no idea whether she'd get a response or not, but she said, 'Do you know what's happening to you?'

Maeve's eyes opened a millimetre further. She tried to focus unsuccessfully, but she seemed to sense the blurry blond hair kneeling over her and half smiled in recognition.

Violetta said, 'Did you hear me? You're going to die. Do you understand?'

She didn't know why she was saying anything. Maybe she wanted to see under the mask, and this would be her only opportunity. Would Maeve die delusional, or would she finally see the truth?

Maeve's voice was barely a whisper. She mumbled

something.

Violetta bent down. 'What?'

Maeve muttered, 'It doesn't matter.'

Silence.

Violetta said, 'It should matter. You thought you were invincible.'

'Oh, well. It's ... not about me.'

A rare statement for a destructive charismatic.

Violetta said, 'What's it about?'

'Bodhi,' Maeve whispered, her dying eyes now alive. 'It'll outlast all of this. Just watch. We're flesh and blood. It's everlasting.'

'It's a bundle of drugs.'

'Yes.'

'So you acknowledge it's not the key to enlightenment?'

'When ... did I say that?'

Violetta said, 'It's dex, MDMA, and benzos.'

Maeve's hazy gaze finally settled on Violetta, and she managed to focus for a single moment. 'You've seen what it *does*. You think it matters what it *is*?'

She let go, and died.

Violetta stayed crouched over the body for a long time, stewing over the words. It was hard to accept that Maeve was right. So long as someone had access to the compound and knew a smattering of persuasions, the dream of Mother Libertas was alive. The Riordans were the founders, but cults don't die with their creators.

Ideas live on.

She knew what she needed to do.

She couldn't change what Bodhi did, but she could change what those who took it understood about it.

She stood up and turned around.

Those who were left watched silently. They were harmless, anaesthetised by despair.

Violetta said, 'You were all taking Bodhi to reach enlightenment. What you never knew is what it really is. It's a mixture of three powerful chemicals. Dextroamphetamine, found in Dexedrine; MDMA, also known as molly or ecstasy; and benzodiazepines. That's why you felt the way you did. Just because it's not mystical doesn't make the feeling any less incredible, but I want you all to know exactly what it is they were doing to you. You were drugged without your consent or knowledge. If some of you have more of the stuff, there's nothing stopping you taking it. But understand the cognitive dissonance. Think about what it is and why you're dependent on it. There is no cause. There is no creed. The mantras were false and empty and only existed to keep you loyal to the Riordans. You were slaves.'

The disciples stared back. A handful understood. The rest had vacant expressions on their faces.

Violetta said, 'There's nothing more I can say. What you do now is entirely up to you. Hopefully at some point it hits you what happened here. If not...'

She didn't finish.

She walked back through them, and again no one stopped her. The animosity was gone, snuffed out with Maeve's life. Any followers that were still enraged were keeping it suppressed after seeing what King had done to the red haired man.

Violetta joined King on the other side of the crowd.

It wasn't much of a crowd anymore.

She counted eight people left standing. Maybe a dozen sitting down. The rest had dispersed.

King said, 'What do we do now?'

Violetta said, 'Nothing. We're done here.'

They walked away to find Slater.

108

Alexis heard the gunshots.

She stood up, lifted the binoculars to her eyes, and stared out the window.

Took in the scene.

When she lowered them, she found Brandon and Addison on their feet. The hallway was still empty, unpopulated. The remaining disciples were all over the commune — running, hiding, walking away. Some maybe mustering the courage to fight. But whatever resistance they could manage would be futile after what Alexis had seen.

Brandon said, 'What is it?'

Alexis aimed her Beretta at his chest.

Addison muttered, 'No. Please.'

Alexis lifted the aim to his head.

Addison screamed.

Alexis waited for the echo to fade, dissipating from a screech to a whisper as it bounced off the distant walls and the roof far over their heads.

In the following quiet, she said, 'I'm not going to kill you. But I need to make sure you don't try to kill me.'

Brandon said, 'Why?'

'Maeve is dead.'

His eyes burned. His tongue lolled in his mouth. His cheeks went bright red and his brow furrowed, like someone had flipped his entire world on its head. In the sacristy he'd been anaesthetised by fatigue, impartial to what came next, but now the foundations of his belief system were shattering.

Addison's frown turned to a relieved smile.

Alexis said, 'Do you understand, Brandon?'

'It's impossible,' he spat. 'She's—'

'She's a dumb bitch,' Addison said, finally letting out what had been trapped within for months. 'Don't you see that?'

Brandon wheeled, his face twisted in disgust at hearing blasphemy, and started for his sister.

Alexis said, 'You lay a finger on her and I'll blow your brains out.'

He stopped in his tracks.

He was angry, confused, destroyed ... but that didn't mean he wanted to die.

He turned back to Alexis, his bottom lip quivering. 'Who ... who killed her?'

'My friends.'

Brandon's eyes went wide. 'The woman! Violetta! The one with the baby. You know what this means? She's the chosen one. No one but her and her unborn child could kill our messiah. Don't you see? She can lead us into a new futu—'

'Brandon,' Alexis interrupted. 'Shut up.'

His face fell.

She could see him trying so hard to keep the dream alive, to keep the illusion believable.

If he twisted the facts hard enough, it could all make sense...

Alexis said, 'Nothing you were told is real. They enslaved you.'

Brandon scoffed, like she'd said something so ridiculous it couldn't be taken seriously. But behind the curtain, everything was unscrambling. Internally he was holding on for dear life. He turned to his sister and saw her staring up at him with something close to contempt.

That made him pause. 'Addison? You don't really believe this shit she's spewing, do you?'

Addison said, 'I knew it was all lies before we even killed Karlie.'

That's what broke him.

He'd been using Maeve's creed and mantras to justify all the terrible things he'd done. It was the only way he could stay sane — continuing to deny the truth so he didn't have to accept he'd dug himself a grave he could never climb out of. But here was his beloved sister, the person who meant the most to him out of anyone in the commune, accepting guilt for what she'd done, taking the blame off the conditioning of Mother Libertas and placing it squarely on her own shoulders.

Which must have felt horrible, but what's right often feels the worst.

Now Alexis could see Brandon's face quivering, but she needed Addison to keep going.

Alexis said, 'Are you saying what I think you're saying?'

She met Addison's eyes and a deep understanding passed between them. Addison got the message. If she wanted to bring her brother back, she had to be ruthless on herself. It was the only way to save him.

If she led by example.

Addison looked up at Brandon and said, 'It was always a cult. I beat that girl to death knowing full well none of it was real. I was too scared, too weak, to protest. That's what this place does to us. That's what it's doing to you, Brandon. But you know what would make me weaker? You know what would make me even more pathetic? If I pretended I believed it so I didn't have to feel shame about what I'd done.'

Brandon stood in thunderous silence.

Addison said, 'Don't be weak, Brandon. Don't be pathetic. You took care of me when our parents walked out. I don't even want to call them "parents" — they were adults who never wanted us. But you were strong then. You gave us a future and it took all of your willpower and then you had nothing left when this place got into your mind. It got into mine, too.'

He lowered his gaze and stared at the floor.

Too ashamed to look at his sister, let alone respond.

Addison said, 'Let it out, Brandon. Let this place out of your head. Come back.'

Brandon sat down on the bench, put his head in his hands and, for the first time since he'd joined the cult, he cried.

109

Slater reunited with Alexis, and together they went up to the farmhouse.

They left Brandon and Addison in the mess hall, locked in an endless embrace, going through every emotion together.

They met King and Violetta on the front porch of the farmhouse.

There were still a few disciples scattered across the hillside, but none of them were aware of their surroundings. They were grappling with existential dread, much like Slater's experience the previous night. But there was no Bodhi in their systems, just an overwhelming confusion at what they'd spent the last few months of their lives doing. What they'd believed. How deeply they'd become entrenched in Maeve's web.

They'd figure it out eventually.

Or not.

Slater knew some wouldn't. It would simply be too hard, and they'd return to civilisation rambling to themselves, lost to mental illness as the burden of facing their demons proved too much. There was nothing he could do for them.

He looked at King. 'What the hell do we do now? There's two hundred people here.'

'Where's Dane?' King said.

Slater shook his head.

King said, 'Then there's nothing left to do.'

'I—'

'What?' King said. 'What do you think we can do? Hold a service of our own in the church? Speak the truth to them? We're not prophets. We don't have all the answers. We just know lies when we see them.'

Slater said, 'Some of them will break.'

King said, 'I know. But you know why we can't stay. Our names...'

Slater understood.

Dredging their pasts up from the files wouldn't go unnoticed. Whoever had done it for Dane, he was deep in government black-ops. He'd trigger alerts. For all they knew, half the secret world would descend on Thunder Basin if they got a whiff that Jason King and Will Slater were out there.

King said, 'We can't leave them here without resources.'

Slater said, 'There's only one resource they need.'

He left the group, went into the farmhouse, and down to the basement. It used to be an intelligence centre. A technological workstation. Now it was nothing. Slater gazed out at rows of torched hardware, drenched in lighter fluid and set alight. Whatever information had existed in the cloud was no doubt wiped.

Maeve had known it was the end of the road.

All her plans, all her contacts, all those people out in the real world that she'd sunk her hooks into, fed Bodhi, brainwashed...

No evidence.

No proof.

Slater had to hope that the decapitated Mother Libertas wouldn't regrow its head. With the Riordans gone, the Bodhi would stop flowing, and at least half of the disciples here in the commune were already disillusioned. The movement was shattered.

But was it dead?

Only time would tell.

Slater found what he was looking for in a cabinet up the back of the basement. It was untouched by the dying flames. All around it, embers licked at melted computer towers. But when Slater opened the cabinet door he found two satellite phones intact, capable of contacting the outside world despite the lack of cell towers out here in Thunder Basin.

He took them back up the stairs and went out to the porch again.

The trio were still there.

Slater handed the sat phones to Alexis. 'Do you know what to do?'

She stared at them, then it clicked.

'Yes,' she said.

110

Alexis sat across from Brandon and Addison in the empty mess hall.

Brother and sister had arms around each other's shoulders.

They'd been through hell, and they still had a ways to go, but they'd soldier through it together.

Alexis said, 'The four of us who arrived here a couple of days ago ... we need to leave.'

Brandon said, 'Obviously.'

'In other circumstances we'd stay. We'd help out. We'd help coordinate. But my friends have past lives. Those past lives are ticking time bombs, and Maeve and Dane found out who they really were. Seems the Riordans had contacts in the government. On the off chance that some undesirable people swoop down on this place looking for us, we need to be elsewhere. Do you understand?'

Brandon said, 'You don't owe us anything.'

Alexis stared at him. 'Do you understand what Maeve did to you?'

'Yes,' he said.

It hurt him.

He didn't like saying it.

But he seemed to have made it a priority to tell the truth.

Alexis turned to Addison. 'And you've always known, haven't you?'

Addison said, 'Yes.'

Alexis placed the two sat phones on the table and paused for a beat. 'We're not going to be here, so whatever choice you two make, it has to be made on your own.'

They didn't respond.

Alexis said, 'You can use these phones to call the authorities. You can explain everything that happened. You might go to jail, but probably not for long. That's if you put the blame on the Riordans, which is where it damn well should be placed.'

Brandon stared with wide eyes.

Addison gulped.

Alexis said, 'Some of the people here aren't going to want that to happen. They'll protest it. They'll argue that you should pick up where Maeve and Dane left off, continue to grow Mother Libertas into a powerhouse, but it won't work. To be frank, none of you in this commune have the qualities that the Riordans possessed. You're not psychopaths, you're not narcissists, you're not sociopaths. You were lost and you listened to someone you shouldn't have. You let them sink their hooks in and allowed them to command you.'

Neither of them replied.

Alexis said, 'When you make it out of this mess and wind up back in a normal life, you're going to feel guilty. That's a good thing. You can't grow unless you feel pain. I'm not going to ask you any questions about it, but I take it something happened with a woman named Karlie, and it's going to tear you both up inside, because you're not evil. You might even think about killing yourselves.'

Addison was a statue.

Brandon's brow was furrowed, like he didn't want to believe it but knew it was true.

Alexis stayed quiet.

Finally Addison said, 'Are you going to tell us not to?'

Alexis stood up. 'No. It sounds like you beat an innocent woman to death. If I were you, I'd think about suicide. I might even do it. But if you make it out the other side, and there's no guarantee you will ... then make up for it with the rest of your lives. Act charitably. Help other people. Try to repent for what you did.'

Again, Brandon fell back on the question he couldn't get his head around. 'Why don't you just kill us? You know we're murderers.'

'Because it's too grey,' Alexis said. 'It's a mess morally. How much influence did Maeve have on your actions? How much of it was you, and how much of it was her? I can't answer those questions, and I'll never know the answers, so I'm not the one to pass judgment. That falls on your own shoulders.'

They bowed their heads.

Alexis said, 'Ask yourself those questions. Then do the right thing, and use those phones for the right reasons.'

Brandon lifted his head and stared Alexis in the eyes even though it made him intensely uncomfortable. 'I will. I promise.'

Alexis shuddered.

She wasn't sure why.

Then it hit her.

He'll do anything I say now.

If she stayed, she could be Maeve.

She could wield power over the gullible.

It made her stomach churn.

She nodded farewell to both of them and said, 'Underneath all this, you two are strong. And you know it.'

They nodded back.

She left them to an uncertain future.

It was all she could do for them.

111

King sat drumming his calloused fingers on the sun-baked wheel of the pickup truck.

It was the same vehicle Maeve had used to bring them out here. It was in good enough condition to get them back to Gillette, and from there they could make their way back to Vegas before the government got wind of their presence in Wyoming.

Alexis and Violetta slipped silently into the rear seats.

Violetta said, 'Creeps me out.'

King said, 'What does?'

'Them.'

King looked past them in the rear view mirror, out the back windshield of the pickup. He saw perhaps a dozen disciples milling around the end of the trail, staring vacantly at the truck, arms by their sides. Like walking zombies. They didn't know what to do or where to go. Then again, they'd never known.

That's what made them perfect victims in the first place.

King said, 'They'll figure it out.'

'I don't think so,' Violetta said. 'I don't think they'll reintegrate well with society.'

'There's millions of people who aren't integrated,' King said. 'That's how the world works. This commune's just a tiny speck in comparison to the real problem.'

'The world's better off without the Riordans,' Alexis said.

King nodded.

In a world of grey, that much was black and white.

He met her gaze in the rear view mirror. 'Did you talk to those kids? What were their names?'

'Brandon and Addison,' Alexis said. 'They'll do the right thing. They saw the error of their ways.'

'You sure?'

Alexis looked him dead in the eyes. 'Absolutely.'

King breathed out, satisfied.

Slater got in the passenger seat. He'd been sweeping the farmhouse for important evidence, but when he slipped into the truck King saw he was empty-handed.

Slater exhaled in opposite fashion to King, clearly dissatisfied. 'They were thorough. There's nothing left.'

King said, 'It doesn't matter. They're dead.'

Slater said, 'Do you think they told anyone about our identities? Will the disciples speak to the authorities?'

'It doesn't matter,' King repeated. 'By then we'll be back in Vegas.'

'I don't like this.'

'What?'

'Leaving them here. What if they do exactly what we think they might do? What if they double down on their beliefs?'

Alexis said, 'Brandon and Addison are the ones with the phones. And they're not doubling down on anything.'

'How can you be sure?'

She said, 'I just know.'

King said, 'If none of this hits the news cycle, we'll know. Cults are good for headlines. It'll spread through the media like wildfire.'

'And if it doesn't?' Slater said.

'Then we come back and deal with whoever took over.'

It settled Slater, and he rested back in the passenger seat and closed his eyes momentarily, decompressing from the madness.

King didn't take his eyes off Alexis.

She stared back.

He could tell that she knew, deep down, that Brandon and Addison would try to fix the wrongs they'd committed.

She'd convinced them beyond doubt, and she was aware of it.

'Congratulations,' he said.

She cocked her head to the side. 'For what?'

'You proved you're no less capable than any of us.' He paused. 'You're an operative now.'

She let the words sink in, and then she smiled.

She said, 'Wouldn't want to be anything else.'

Violetta gripped her knee and gave it a reassuring squeeze.

Slater clamped his hand down on King's shoulder and did the same.

Over and over and over again, they went into hell and made it out.

Together.

King drove away from the commune.

EPILOGUE

Connor had never felt more alone.

The windowless room that was his office had always accentuated the isolation and loneliness of the job, but he'd never taken notice of it until now. A natural introvert, he'd never needed human interaction to thrive. He found satisfaction in the minutiae of his job — compiling intelligence, sifting through interceptions, summarising the important points and passing them up the chain of command.

It suited his personality.

He'd taken the Myers Briggs test nearly a decade ago and it had labelled him an INTJ — Introverted, Intuitive, Thinking, and Judging. Before the test he'd considered it bullshit pseudoscience, but he'd never been described so accurately. He'd always been quiet and bookish, the architect of his own mind, and that left little time for the frivolous gossip that plagued ordinary work environments. So he'd bounced between government admin jobs, making no friends but tearing through work like a man possessed, and five years ago he'd caught the attention of a certain division of the government that operated under the radar, just like him.

They were similar in that regard.

His employers didn't waste time getting choked by the systemic logjam of bureaucracy, and he didn't waste time getting choked by the frivolities of unnecessary human interaction. They offered him a job doing the same thing he was already doing but focused instead on the world of black operations and espionage. It came with quadruple pay. He'd accepted the same day, tucked himself away in this one-man office without complaint, and spent the last five years curating intelligence for the division that kept America at the top of the food chain while still being able to pretend they were a transparent democracy.

But sooner or later, everyone needs an outlet. He had no friends. How could he get close to people his own age? They busied themselves with climbing the rungs of law firms or tech start-ups and spent their free time bar crawling. He couldn't think of anything more alien. He wanted to discuss big ideas, the overarching principles of the country he lived in, the morality of the messy things that went on behind closed doors.

Then he'd found an ear ... or, rather, it had found him.

A whisper from the grasslands of Wyoming had caught him, and he'd listened.

Now he had someone to whisper back to.

He tried Dane's number again. It was three days since the man had contacted him, and Connor hadn't gone that long without hearing his voice in months. He had the sense to call from his personal phone. Six months of devotion to Mother Libertas, six months of unimaginable rewards, and no one in the building had a clue. It was almost too easy.

Now it was horrifying.

The line rang, and rang, and rang.

It went to voicemail.

Dane's quiet, soothing voice said, 'It's me. Leave a message.'

Connor never had.

Now he did.

'Hey,' he said. 'I have more information on King and Slater. I did a deep dive into their files. There's things we might have overlooked. Call me immediately. It's urgent.'

He'd never lied to Dane before.

There's a first time for everything.

But he longed desperately for the attention, for a co-conspirator, for anything…

Anything to make him needed.

He'd already given the Riordans everything he had on the two black-ops legends. It had put him in an awkward position — he recognised Mother Libertas were in danger with King and Slater in their midst, but he couldn't alert his employers without putting a spotlight on parts of rural Wyoming that absolutely needed to stay dark. The movement was still in its infancy, and the resources he'd have to use to wipe out the ex-operatives for good would also end up destroying Mother Libertas, too.

For the first time ever, he tried Maeve.

In the cold silence of his office, the mobile at his ear buzzed its outgoing call tone.

He didn't expect her to pick up. He was nothing compared to her, and the reincarnation of Gaia had bigger things to worry about than a lowly intelligence analyst. But he'd given them so much, helped protect them, crushed any news of their growing presence in the mainstream media…

The least they could do—

A thought hit him like an electric shock.

He couldn't believe he hadn't considered it, but devotion had blinded him to the very real possibility that Mother Libertas had been compromised. He'd read King and Slater's rap sheets, and they were something to behold, but was there a chance...?

He pulled up a customised newsfeed on his phone of articles relating to a specific section of Wyoming he'd book-ended in case of disaster.

Empty.

He waited in a trance, a dark premonition stewing in his mind.

He could have been sitting there for hours.

A light knock came at the door.

He lifted his eyes off the phone screen and jolted. Devin Nelson, the President's right-hand-man on all discreet matters, hovered in the open doorway. He was Connor's direct superior and one of the most powerful men in the country.

'You look like you've seen a ghost,' Nelson said. 'What's going on?'

'Nothing, sir,' Connor said. 'Just ... you know ... think I'm stressed. I'll get over it.'

Nelson's beady eyes bored into him. They'd already said more to each other than they had in the last week. They knew their roles, and their system was as efficient as it was opaque.

Nelson said, 'Let's go for a beer tonight.'

Connor couldn't hide his surprise. 'What?'

'Watch your tone, kid.'

'Sorry, sir. It's just—'

'I know,' Nelson interrupted. 'You didn't think I existed outside of work. You need to decompress. I can see it in your eyes. I'll have you out of here if you don't comply. Goat

Rapids Tavern across the street in two hours. I know a kid who needs a beer when I see it.'

He left abruptly, probably to take care of tasks that were critical to the interests of the nation.

Connor knew he must have looked near-suicidal if Mr. Nelson had reacted like that.

Shaken up, he lowered his eyes back to his phone.

An article hovered there.

He only had to read its headline.

MASSACRE IN THUNDER BASIN AFTER CULT IMPLOSION: SIX DEAD, OVER A DOZEN WOUNDED.

If Nelson's proposition had shaken him, this broke him to the core.

He didn't open the article; he didn't have to.

They were dead. The Riordans were gone. Mother Libertas was crippled, perhaps forever. Despair washed over Connor, rounding his shoulders, putting a thousand-pound weight on his windpipe, threatening to spiral him into a total meltdown. He tried to breathe, but he couldn't. The walls of the office closed in, and icy detachment gave him a dizzying out-of-body experience.

Then his inner architect took over.

Crafting grandiose plans, hardening his resolve, deepening his devotion.

You are responsible for the cause, a voice boomed.

He wasn't sure if he was talking to himself, or if Gaia was speaking through him.

You are tasked with taking this to the next level.

Not Dane, not Maeve.

You.

He got up, went to the bathroom, and splashed his face with water.

When he met his reflection's gaze in the mirror, he noticed his eyes were alive with determination.

∼

CONNOR STEPPED into Goat Rapids Tavern at precisely nine p.m.

Nelson was already in a corner booth, draped in shadow, like a physical representation of his role in this country. Earlier that day Connor might have been intensely uncomfortable with the prospect of social interaction with his employer, but now he knew every word that came out of his mouth had a purpose. However, if he came in with unusual confidence Nelson would suspect something, so he reverted to the façade of shy introspection.

He walked up to the booth and sat down across from the man.

Nelson pushed a cold pint across the table. 'Drink, boy.'

Connor sipped at the frothy head. 'This is odd, sir.'

'I know,' Nelson said. 'But for once in my life I have a free evening, and you need to get your head out of the cave you've been swimming around in.'

'Sir?'

'What we do,' Nelson said, 'breaks people. Not physically, but there's an invisible toll to all the secrecy. You can't talk to anyone about what you really do. So tonight we're going to do our best to pretend we're normal people. We're going to drink, and you're going to talk to me about your life. You don't have to mean any of it, but it'll be cathartic. Trust me. I've been in this game longer than you've been alive.'

Connor shrugged. 'I think you might be right.'

'I know I'm right, boy. Now drink.'

They drank.

One pint led to two, which led to three, and before they knew it they were mentally lubricated enough to disperse with their reluctance to open up. More beers followed and Connor found himself sharing a list of insecurities he'd never written down, let alone vocalised. It made sense that he'd never discussed them with anyone, because he had no one in his life to talk to besides Dane and Maeve. He started to realise the deep flaws in his soul might have been the reason he turned to Mother Libertas in the first place, but another pint washed away those thoughts. If he went there, he might shatter the only belief system he had left.

So he did what most people do when they're faced with opposing beliefs.

He doubled down.

'—and that's why you need nights like these,' Nelson was saying, more talkative than Connor had ever seen him. 'To cut through the bullshit. We're humans, man. We're social creatures. Gotta listen to your animal impulses every now and then. You want some action? I know a place. Top-shelf product.'

Connor smiled a sinister smile. 'I had a different vice in mind.'

Nelson raised an eyebrow, tantalised. 'Oh?'

'I ordered something off the dark web,' Connor said. 'I'd never tell you that, but I'm feeling *good* tonight. I was going to go home and take it on my own, but, damn, it'd be fun with a friend. You want to partake?'

Nelson only needed a moment's consideration, and Connor now understood his serious façade in the workplace was only masking a degenerate at heart.

'Hell yeah,' his boss said.

Connor's place was nothing to scoff at.

It was only a small apartment, but he didn't need much space, and he'd live in a closet if the location was good. The two-bed-one-bath dwelling rested on the top floor of a luxury complex in Berkley, next to Glover Archbold Park. The little balcony overlooked all of downtown D.C.

You could see the White House from his living room.

Nelson was a couple of pints over his limit.

He staggered through the front door, and Connor could see the indecision behind his eyes. He was one of the most powerful men in Washington, and he'd thought a few beers with an underling would be good for his employee's mental health, but now he was about to do something illegal with someone he didn't completely trust. Connor loved the irony.

Everything they did was illegal.

And alcohol is universal in its ability to silence the concern of short-term consequences.

So Nelson let the indecision fall away as he said, 'Fuck it, let's do this. What have you got?'

Connor went to the small kitchen, quickly took a handwritten sheet of the Mother Libertas creed off the fridge, and swept the piece of paper behind the coffee machine. Then he opened the cutlery draw and withdrew two tiny vials of cloudy golden liquid.

He held them up and grinned.

Nelson shrugged off his jacket and laid it over the back of the nearest armchair. 'What is it?'

'Nothing too crazy,' Connor said. 'Just a few uppers. Trust me, it's good. And remember what you said earlier. It's important to decompress.'

Through the blur of inebriation, Nelson thought to look at his watch. 'I have a debrief with the President early in the morning.'

'It wears off after a few hours. You'll be right as rain by then. Better than if you kept drinking, as a matter of fact.'

'That *is* a fact,' Nelson said. 'Most drugs are better for you. If only our population didn't need controlling. Then everyone could have a blast without worrying about a ten-year prison stretch.'

Connor said, 'You don't keep people enslaved by showing them the light.'

Nelson's eyes twinkled. 'You know, we have more in common than I thought.'

Connor handed him a vial.

Nelson said, 'What do I do?'

'Put it on your tongue.'

Connor surreptitiously took a half-dose, and watched as Nelson downed the full hit of Bodhi.

Thirty minutes passed — they cracked open another beer each from Connor's fridge, rambled about life, went out on the balcony and overlooked the city.

Nelson said something, but trailed off mid-sentence, his voice lowering in tone with each syllable.

He got a faraway look in his eyes.

Colour flushed his cheeks.

Connor kept his voice meditative and atonic as he started to speak. 'Listen to me, Nelson. You are capable of so much more than you think. This world is a game, a collection of synapses and cells. It's there for the taking. Don't you see? Mother runs through everything. She runs through the water, the trees, the buildings, the people. Look out on this city. Look out on this world. Do you see what is possible if you harness her power?'

'W-what?' Nelson mumbled, but something was firing behind his eyes.

The come-up of all come-ups.

Connor didn't change his tone. 'You can feel it awakening within you. That power in the pit of your stomach, working its way up to your chest, your neck, your face. That is Mother. Feel every cell in your body firing. Feel yourself becoming one with reality. And understand, in your heart, that she has a purpose for you. She is here, deep within you, and she will enlighten you. She will enlighten everyone who wishes to be set free.'

Somewhere in the avalanche of words — more words than he could remember ever saying at once — Connor suddenly understood. How easy it was to manipulate, how readily you could bend people to your will if you stripped them of all their defences. He saw with startling clarity what Maeve had been doing all along.

And now she's gone.

So why can't you do it?

Nelson swayed in place, transfixed on the skyline.

Connor reached out and gripped the back of his neck with a spindly hand. Turned his employer around so they were face to face.

Connor looked deep into his eyes.

'Do you see the light, my brother?' Connor said. 'Do you pledge yourself to the cause?'

'Cause...?' Nelson murmured.

His eyes blazed.

Then the full force of Bodhi hit him.

His head lolled back, his face awash in ecstasy.

Connor raised his voice for the first time. 'Do you see?'

Nelson smiled, brilliant and wide.

He said, 'Oh. Wow.'

'Do you see?'

'I see.'

Connor said, 'If we are to spread the cause, there are

things you must do. Your meeting tomorrow. You'll need to show the President the light. Will you do it? Will you serve Mother?'

Mr. Nelson, a lanky stooped intelligence asset with more smarts than anyone in D.C., was a helpless slave to the miracle compound in his system.

His pupils swollen, he said, 'I'll do anything.'

Connor thought, *Gaia lives.*

KING AND SLATER WILL RETURN...

Visit amazon.com/author/mattrogers23 and press **"Follow"** to be automatically notified of my future releases.

If you enjoyed the hard-hitting adventure, make sure to leave a review! Your feedback means everything to me, and encourages me to deliver more books as soon as I can.

And don't forget to follow me on Facebook for regular updates, cover reveals, giveaways, and more!
https://www.facebook.com/mattrogersbooks

Stay tuned.

BOOKS BY MATT ROGERS

THE JASON KING SERIES

Isolated (Book 1)

Imprisoned (Book 2)

Reloaded (Book 3)

Betrayed (Book 4)

Corrupted (Book 5)

Hunted (Book 6)

THE JASON KING FILES

Cartel (Book 1)

Warrior (Book 2)

Savages (Book 3)

THE WILL SLATER SERIES

Wolf (Book 1)

Lion (Book 2)

Bear (Book 3)

Lynx (Book 4)

Bull (Book 5)

Hawk (Book 6)

THE KING & SLATER SERIES

Weapons (Book 1)

Contracts (Book 2)

Ciphers (Book 3)

Outlaws (Book 4)

Ghosts (Book 5)

Sharks (Book 6)

Messiahs (Book 7)

LYNX SHORTS

Blood Money (Book 1)

BLACK FORCE SHORTS

The Victor (Book 1)

The Chimera (Book 2)

The Tribe (Book 3)

The Hidden (Book 4)

The Coast (Book 5)

The Storm (Book 6)

The Wicked (Book 7)

The King (Book 8)

The Joker (Book 9)

The Ruins (Book 10)

Join the Reader's Group and get a free 200-page book by Matt Rogers!

Sign up for a free copy of '**BLOOD MONEY**'.

Meet Ruby Nazarian, a government operative for a clandestine initiative known only as Lynx. She's in Monaco to infiltrate the entourage of Aaron Wayne, a real estate tycoon on the precipice of dipping his hands into blood money. She charms her way aboard the magnate's superyacht, but everyone seems suspicious of her, and as the party ebbs onward she prepares for war…

Maybe she's paranoid.

Maybe not.

Just click here.

ABOUT THE AUTHOR

Matt Rogers grew up in Melbourne, Australia as a voracious reader, relentlessly devouring thrillers and mysteries in his spare time. Now, he writes full-time. His novels are action-packed and fast-paced. Dive into the Jason King Series to get started with his collection.

Visit his website:

www.mattrogersbooks.com

Visit his Amazon page:

amazon.com/author/mattrogers23

Printed in Great Britain
by Amazon